I0739566

Cashmere

TEMPLE WEST

AN IN MEDIAS RES BOOK

CASHMERE. Copyright © Temple West 2017. All rights reserved. Printed by IngramSpark.

In Medias Res books may be purchased for business or promotional use. Go to www.ByTempleWest.com and use the contact form to request additional information.

West, Temple.
Cashmere / Temple West.

Summary: Searching for Lucian, Caitlin and Adrian must form new alliances and trust strange magic to stay one step ahead of the Council and Adrian's father, all the while investigating whether or not Caitlin is more than what she seems — and if she is, what they're going to do about it.

ISBN 978-0-9983415-0-7 (paperback) — ISBN 978-0-9983415-1-4 (e-book)
[1. Love — Fiction. 2. Vampires — Fiction. 3. Demonology — Fiction. 4. Supernatural — Fiction. 5. Bodyguards — Fiction. 6. Orphans — Fiction.]

Book design by Temple West. Photo by Matthew Simmons.

First edition: 2017

10 9 8 7 6 5 4 3 2 1

www.bytemplewest.com

Dedicated to Kate Beckinsale. Thank you for *Underworld*. Also, your hair is amazing. Please teach me your ways.

CONTENTS

PROLOGUE

So many things could have gone wrong. If my parents hadn't died, I wouldn't have moved to Stony Creek. If I hadn't been angry at Rachel, I wouldn't have been out in the woods. I wouldn't have gotten caught in the storm. I wouldn't have become involved with Adrian or Lucian or their father. Without them, I wouldn't have found out who I was. I wouldn't have known what I could do.

And that would have changed everything.

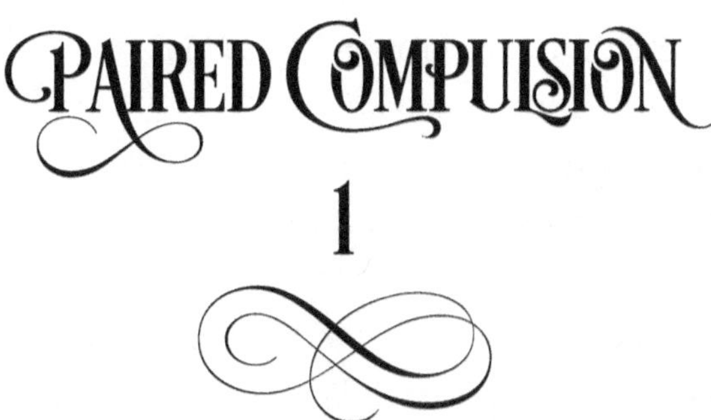

Tommie was staring right at me.

He was alive, no gaping wound in his neck from where I'd stabbed him, no bubbling flesh from Adrian burning him. Across the clearing, another version of me sat hunched over Adrian's lifeless body, sobbing silently in the bloody snow. There was no sound in this place, no heat or cold, no smell. While Other Me tried to revive Adrian, Tommie continued to stare at me, the real me, with a puzzled look on his face.

I advanced carefully on him, my feet making no dent in the unblemished snow. He tilted his head slightly, watching me approach. Waiting.

"Why are you here?" I asked. I knew how this went by now, but I always asked. My voice echoed slowly, like I was in a cathedral.

He blinked, and looked over at Other Me, frowning.

"I don't want you here anymore," I told him.

Immediately, he disappeared.

I turned in circles, scanning the edge of the forest to see if he'd simply jumped to a new location, but as usual he appeared to be totally gone.

I looked back over at Other Me. She'd given up and was lying on Adrian's ice-cold chest, asleep. I didn't really want to see that again, either.

No sooner had I thought this than they, too, slipped away.

I came awake slowly, sunlight filtering through the wooden slats of my blinds, casting prison bar shadows across my room. My phone buzzed on my dresser. It was Adrian.

Same dream?

I texted him the same thing I texted him every morning: *Same dream.*

Adrian's eyes flared into silver, the molten irises swirling slowly around his pupils. "In five seconds, walk toward me," he commanded.

He walked off twenty feet and stopped, turning to face me. Five seconds went by.

My leg twitched. My toes curled in my boots. My heart raced.

But I stayed in place.

"That's good," Adrian called from the opposite side of the parking lot a full minute later. "You're improving."

We walked toward each other as the first of the teachers began to pull up to the school. They were used to seeing us out here by now, earlier than them. They always looked at us like we were crazy, but they were used to us.

"It's not good enough," I told him, massaging my temples, shaking off the remnants of his compulsion. "I can only resist when I know you're about to do it, and only barely. If a bird so much as chirps, it breaks my concentration."

"It's going to take time."

I snorted. "That's exactly what you said about algebra and I'm still getting a D."

He wrapped his arms around my waist and smiled. "Yeah, but you're slightly less motivated when it comes to algebra. And you are improving. I'm not just saying that because I think you're hot."

I snorted again. Adrian kissed the top of my head and let me go, but I grabbed his jacket. "Whoa there, fella, my face would like some of that."

He grinned, wrapped me back up in his arms, and planted an intentionally sloppy kiss halfway on my mouth and half on my chin.

"Gross."

I was about to pull him in for a real kiss when I saw a familiar truck pull into the parking lot—as far away from us as possible. Seeing who it was, Adrian pulled away from me respectfully, though he wound his fingers through mine.

It had been three months since the fight with Tommie, since the night Lucian disappeared. I'd gone back to school the following Monday to find that Trish was no longer speaking to me. Why, exactly, I wasn't sure, because she hadn't said more than two words to me since, but I was pretty sure it had to do with Adrian. I wouldn't have pegged her for being a Silent Treatment type, but it turned out she was a pro.

Trish didn't even glance at us as she made her way to Mr. Warren's class.

Adrian squeezed my hand. I smiled up at him halfheartedly.

"It'll get better," he promised.

I wasn't so sure. Adrian didn't know girls. Girls could be mad for a lifetime. And I had no idea how to talk to Trish. I had no idea how to make things right because I couldn't tell her the truth.

"Maybe," I said, more to change the subject than anything else. "We going to your place today?"

"Yeah. Told Dominic I'm helping you study for a test."

"Sneaky."

He kissed my cheek tenderly, scanned the parking lot—something he'd taken to doing whenever he left me alone—and headed off to class.

At lunch, Stephanie braved my little outcast half of the picnic table and set her lunch bag next to mine. Trish wasn't exactly forbidding the other girls to talk to me, but she had always been the head of our group and they followed her lead. Meghan had instantly sided with Trish, even though she didn't really know why we were fighting. Laura didn't care and Jenny had taken to eating by herself, uncomfortable with the tension that had sprung up between all of us. Stephanie was the only one who felt bad enough for me to risk Trish's displeasure.

I wasn't exactly the most popular person with the other grades, either, as least as far as the girls were concerned. It had somehow gotten around school that I had been the one to break up with Adrian after Winter Formal, an offense that was to be held against me for the foreseeable future. The more unforgivable crime, however, was getting back together with him a week later.

"You excited for summer?" Stephanie asked.

I glanced across the table at Trish, feeling that slimy adrenaline coiling restlessly in my stomach. "Yeah. It'll be nice to get away from the whispers for a while. Are you guys still going shopping this weekend?"

She blushed. "Yeah. But I could go again with you, if you want?"

I waved my granola bar at her. "I'm making my dress anyway. It's all right."

She looked relieved.

"Y'know, I think…" Stephanie glanced around, then leaned in close. "I think Trish really misses you. I hope you guys can make up soon."

I smiled tightly at her. "I hope so, too."

I glanced at Trish, only to accidentally catch her eye as she turned to talk to Laura. She didn't glare at me, didn't even frown, just met my gaze for a moment, then moved on with her conversation as if I wasn't even there.

"Got anything?" Adrian called from twenty feet below me.

"Lotta stuff in dead languages," I called back, my harness starting to bite into my hips from perching in one position for so long. I had both bare feet planted on the bookshelf ledge while I leaned back, pulling out leather-bound tomes one by one to see if they were in English, and therefore readable.

We were in the de la Mara's massive library, cinched into the free-rolling magnetic harnesses, searching for answers. We had an excuse prepared: Adrian was demonstrating the theoretical role of tachyon particles for my final physics presentation. So far, Mariana and Dominic had pretty much left us alone, though, so we hadn't had to test the alibi.

"I should really teach you Latin sometime," Adrian muttered to himself, eyes rapidly scanning the massive leather-bound book he was holding.

"Yeah, in all that spare time we have," I muttered back. "I'll just cover the one-point-eight-million *English* books in this stupid library, how about that?"

He glanced up at me, saw the sour look on my face, then hopped up the shelves, the lines of the harness receding every time he climbed higher. He came to a stop next to me, waiting quietly, knowing I'd eventually spit out what was wrong. I stubbornly stared at the book I was holding, then gave up.

"It's been *three months*." I shook my head, frustrated, and slammed the book back in its place on the shelf. "We've been looking for three months. School will be over soon, and we don't know if the Council will let you stay as my bodyguard. We don't know if I'll be allowed to come here anymore. This is the only way I can help, and I don't have enough time. I can't read Latin, I can't read French, I can't read German or Slavic or even freaking *Spanish*. I'm just pulling out books for you to check. And the ones I can read I don't understand. You've got thousands of years of history I have no context for. Names and dates and places and vampires I've never heard of, all referenced like it's common knowledge. I'm not picking it up, I'm not catching on, I'm not *helping*. And he's still out there, somewhere. And it's my fault."

Adrian grabbed my harness cables, turning me toward him. "We've been over this, Cait."

"Just because you say something doesn't mean I agree with it," I muttered. I was staring at the shelf, avoiding eye contact.

He let out a long breath and rubbed his forehead. "Believe me, I know it's tempting," he admitted. "It makes it seem like you're doing something just by feeling guilty. But you're hurting Lucian when you blame yourself. He's waiting for us to find him. So we have to find him. That's it."

He looked at me until I finally looked back at him. He was right, damn it. I nodded at him, slumping in my harness. He pulled me into a hug and I buried my face in the crook of his neck, his hair tickling my cheek. I was tired, angry, holding too many secrets from too many people. Adrian and I had become friends a long time ago, but since Lucian had disappeared, we'd become partners, too. The Council had sent a War Council the day after our fight with Tommie. After interrogating me and Adrian and searching the grounds for the next three days, they'd been downgraded to a Praetorian Guard, as both Lucian and his father seemed to have completely disappeared from the area and the threat was no longer as severe. They'd been gone almost as long as Lucian was, following leads about where they thought he might be.

At least, that's what Mariana told us. For all we knew, they were in Cancun drinking Mai Tais and getting beach-side massages.

Adrian had been reinstated as my day-time bodyguard, but since my nightmares had stopped, he no longer came over to the house to sleep.

Which was a huge bummer.

Life had, in a weird way, returned almost to normal. Except for the fact that Lucian was missing.

We'd long ago assumed that we were the only ones looking for Adrian's brother. Even Julian had gone back to his regular life in New York, seemingly unconcerned with Lucian's disappearance.

So every day we could manage it, Adrian and I came here to the library to look for clues. He searched for archaic references to why he'd been able to melt the flesh off his father's body, and I searched for references to demons, trying to get some clue as to why he would attack *me*, but take Lucian. Why he waited so long, only to fail at getting me pregnant. Why he told us the Council wanted me dead. We had pieces from what felt like different puzzles, and none of them seemed to fit together. After three months, it was starting to feel pointless.

I pulled out of the hug and wiped at my eyes. "I'm sorry," I murmured. "I'm just tired."

Adrian kissed my forehead tenderly. "I am, too," he admitted. "But—"

Just then, we heard the sound of the far doors opening. Though well-oiled, they were massive enough that they couldn't help but make a distinctive sound every time they opened, even from the opposite side of the enormous room.

Adrian and I glanced at each other, then pulled apart and rappelled to the floor just as Dominic walked in with none other than Farrar.

My heart just about stopped in my chest.

"Ah, Caitlin," Dominic said, his sandy-blonde hair perfect as always. He was wearing khakis and a sweater and loafers, like some Calvin Klein version of a young, trendy dad. "You remember Farrar?"

I almost snorted. Of course I remembered. He'd interrogated me for almost five straight hours back in February. What he was doing here now, though, I had no idea.

He glanced at our harnesses. "Are we interrupting?"

"We were almost finished," Adrian said smoothly.

Farrar was frowning ever so slightly and it made me nervous. "Our final projects are to study and analyze theoretical physics from science fiction. I'm a, uh, visual learner," I added, trying to keep my heart from racing. Farrar was a big dude. Tall, barrel-chested, with dark eyes, shoulder-length black hair, and an old-school aura of nobility. He had a slight accent I couldn't place, and every time I saw him, the hair on the back of my neck went up.

He glanced between us again, then seemed to accept our explanation.

"You're back," Adrian said, trying to hide his tension. "Does that mean you've found something?"

"Not as such," Farrar murmured. "But I was hoping to speak to Caitlin. If you would?"

Adrian went very still. I glanced between him, Dominic, and Farrar. After a moment, he relaxed, then smiled, unclipping the carabiners from the overhead cables. "Of course," Adrian said politely. He nodded at me. "Caitlin."

He walked off as if he couldn't care less about whatever Farrar was about to ask me.

"Thank you, Dominic," Farrar said, clearly dismissing the other vampire.

"I'll assign everyone rooms," Dominic replied. "Mariana wanted me to inform you that dinner is at six."

They both nodded at each other, and Dominic left.

"The others?" I asked.

"The entire Guard has returned," Farrar explained. "Please, have a seat." He gestured at the nearby trio of plush, white couches facing the enormous twelve-foot fireplace.

I sat, cautiously.

"How have you been feeling?" he asked, seating himself opposite me.

I frowned, not knowing where he was going with this. "Exams are coming up; I've been a little stressed out."

"And your nightmares?"

I froze. How much to say?

"They, uh, pretty much went away. I have bad dreams now and again, but nothing like they were before."

That was the understatement of the century.

His face remained blank, unreadable. "And nothing unusual has happened since we last spoke?"

"One of the horses got sick, but it's better now. Meghan's dad got a DUI. That's all I can think of. Small town, not much happens here."

I knew that's not what he was asking, but truth be told, nothing unusual had happened on the supernatural front either.

He nodded, as if expecting my answer. "And Lucian has not attempted to contact you?"

The surprise on my face was genuine. "No. But I assume that you think he's still alive?"

Some small emotion passed over his face briefly but it was gone before I could tell what it was. "It seems probable," he said softly. "We'll be having a meeting tomorrow with the full Guard. I would appreciate it if you could be here."

"Of course," I replied. "Anything to help."

He looked at me another long moment, then stood. "I will let you get back to your project."

I nodded an awkward thanks, then made my way out of the library and into the kitchen, passing by an office where the rest of the Praetorian Guard seemed to be loading in bags and suitcases.

When I got to the kitchen, someone grabbed my arm and I yelped.

"It's just me," Julian said, looking irritated.

"*Vampire—*" I hissed, pointing at him. "*Human,*" I said, gesturing at myself. "Gotta make more noise, man. You're gonna give me a heart attack. And when did you get back?"

"Farrar pulled me from New York when the Praetorians got called back. I came in with them. Where's Adrian?"

"I don't know. We were in the library studying when Farrar asked to speak to me alone."

Julian stopped dead and grabbed my shoulders, peering into my eyes frantically.

"What?" I asked, weirded out.

But he didn't elaborate. Finally, he pulled back. "Come on, we don't have much time."

He whipped out his phone and sent off a text, pulling me into the white marble foyer. A moment later, Adrian appeared on the third story landing and descended, meeting us. "What's going on?"

"You know that *option* I told you about?" Julian asked, face tight.

Adrian nodded. "I told you I wasn't doing it."

Julian grabbed my coat and helmet from the hall rack. "You need to strongly reconsider."

He shoved the coat and helmet at me, looking at Adrian the whole time. "And I mean *now*."

They held eye contact for another moment before Adrian nodded. Julian glanced at me, then walked back down the hall into the kitchen.

"What was that all about?"

"Let's get you home," Adrian said, dodging my question.

With a house full of well-hearing vampires, I knew better than to question him further. I zipped up the coat and followed him out to the Harley.

Instead of turning left to go the mile or so back to the ranch, he turned right, zipping up the mountain. We came to the scenic pull-off area on the side of the mountain, the same place he'd taken me my first week in Stony Creek, before I knew about vampires and demons and portals to hell.

He stopped, killing the engine, and we got off and walked to the guard rail. After a moment, he sat, and I followed him.

But he didn't say anything.

I touched his knee gently. "You want to tell me what's going on?"

"Not really." He frowned, and kicked at a rock. "I was just hoping it wouldn't come to this."

"Does it have something to do with the Guard coming back?"

Adrian nodded. "What did Farrar ask you?"

I shrugged. "If I was having nightmares still. If anything unusual was happening. I told him no."

He thought about that for a long moment, then turned to me. "What do you remember about when Farrar was here last time?"

I blinked, thinking. "He asked a lot of questions. He was scary, but polite. I was tired. I don't remember everything."

Adrian nodded, staring off into space past my shoulder. "Julian is old friends with Kalare; she's in the Guard. You met her briefly, the one with the short hair, wears a lot of leather. She told him that Farrar had been given sanction to compel you to answer his questions truthfully back in February when they were here."

I felt all the blood drain out of my face.

"She also told Julian that Farrar chose not to. That he didn't deem it enough of an emergency. That he thought you were being candid and there was no point going to those lengths. Apparently he's pretty old-school about not abusing his powers."

Adrian let out a slow breath, looking down at our knees. "Julian also told me about the consequences of the Council finding out how I feel about you. You're allowed to love me; they can't forbid that because you're not one of us. But I can't love you. Since vampires can't compel other vampires, as long as I act my part, as long as I'm careful, they'll never know how I feel. But if they compel you…"

If they compelled me, I would have no choice but to tell them how Adrian really felt.

"It's worse than that, though. They could find out what actually happened with my father."

We'd straight-out lied to Farrar about what Adrian had done. The wind-tunnel, the eye-light, the flesh-melting, the whole damn fight, practically.

We'd also lied about what Tommie had said. That I was more than what I seemed, and the Council wanted me dead because of it.

"Is that why they're back?" I asked finally. "They're going to compel me to tell them the truth?"

Adrian shook his head. "I don't know. I didn't even know they were coming, Mariana didn't tell me. Julian texted me, but I left my phone in my room when we got back to the house. I didn't see it in time."

"What did he mean when he said there was another option?"

Adrian ran his fingers through his hair, looking frustrated. "After our first interrogation, after he found out Farrar had been given permission to compel you, Julian told me about a way for us to avoid similar situations in the future."

I frowned. "This sounds like good news. Why do you look like someone just died?"

He leaned back, gesturing wildly. "Because it's not an option. It's not…it's not good. I told him no for a reason. That's why we started practicing, trying to get you to resist compulsion naturally. But we may be out of time. We *are* out of time."

I put my hands on both his knees and caught his gaze. "Just tell me."

His eyes sparked into their luminous silver. Which meant he was worried. Which meant I should be worried.

"With our kind," he said finally, "everything is held in balance. For every advantage, there seems to be a disadvantage. The same goes with compulsion. There is a way to keep anyone from ever compelling you again. Anyone but me."

I waited impatiently for him to continue as he thought about how to say whatever it was that he needed to say. Back on my birthday, when he'd told me about vampires and demons, he'd had just as much trouble putting all of this supernatural stuff into words. I wasn't sure if it was because it made him uncomfortable, or because he thought it would weird *me* out. After nine months of being involved with Adrian and his family, I was way past thinking this crap was unusual.

He tucked his hair behind his ear absently and met my gaze. "It's called paired compulsion. I honestly don't know all the details, it has something to do with pheromones and endorphins and bonding receptors, but it's a permanent sort of compulsion. If I pair with you, *no one else* will be able to compel you, not vampires or demons. But I won't be able to compel anyone else. That's the trade-off. Not many of us do it because there's rarely a good enough reason to give up our compulsory abilities just so we can claim a single individual. The link is permanent and irreversible until the human dies."

I stared at him. "I…honestly don't know how I feel about that."

He'd compelled me twice before, both times to save my life. Well, technically he'd been compelling me every morning in the school parking lot to get me to practice *resisting* compulsion, but he only told me to walk toward him. I'd finally gotten to the point where I could ignore his command if I was far enough away, but it gave me one hell of a headache. Resisting a command that I *wanted* to do was extremely difficult, which is why he'd chosen it for practice. Just to show me the limits of the magic, he'd once compelled me to turn into a rabbit. Of course, I couldn't. Even under compulsion, I didn't even try. Apparently you couldn't compel someone to do something they were not physically or mentally able to do.

"I know this is a lot to digest," he continued, "but we need to decide. We won't be alone again before we see Farrar tomorrow. If we're going to do this, it has to be now. I mean literally *now*, before I take you home."

My hands clenched around his knuckles painfully. My instinct was to pull away, to be angry that he hadn't given me enough time to decide. But I'd made him promise me that he wouldn't pull away, that he wouldn't deal with things that affected both of us on his own, that he would tell me how he was feeling. It was only fair I do the same.

"Why didn't you tell me this before?" I said finally. "Let me choose for myself?"

"Because I wasn't willing to do it. I didn't want to have that kind of control over you. And I didn't know what might come up in the future, if I might need to compel someone else in order to protect you. It wasn't worth it."

I frowned. "You should have told me. That should have been our decision."

His jaw was tight, but he nodded. "I'm sorry," he admitted. "I didn't want to burden you with anything else."

I was angry, but I tried to keep it out of my voice. "When it comes to this stuff, it has to be *our* burden, together. Our plan. Our choice. I have to be able to trust you or this is all going to fall apart. You know that, right?"

He nodded again, looking down at the ground.

I touched his cheek gently. "I'm not mad. But you have to promise me you won't keep things from me because you think I can't handle it. I can."

He leaned into my hand. "I know. I know you can. I just forget sometimes."

I smiled and he looked relieved.

"Before we make a decision, why in the world did Julian tell you all this?"

Adrian shook his head. "I honestly don't know. Why didn't he tell Mariana about us? Why hasn't he told the Council?"

"I don't like this. I don't trust him."

"I don't, either," Adrian admitted. "But I'm not sure what choice we have. Between the Council, the Praetorian Guard, and Julian, I have to admit that I trust Julian most."

He had a point there.

"If we do this," I said slowly, "you can compel me. To do anything."

"Yes," he answered, honestly. "But to be fair, I can *already* compel you to do anything. This just eliminates anyone else having potential control over you."

I let out a short, angry breath. "Y'know I can handle the swirly eyes and the teeth and the blood and the immortality and portals to hell, but compulsion makes my skin crawl. Even if it's just you, it's…" I trailed off, shaking my head. I hated it. He knew that.

He looked at me a long moment before sliding off the guardrail and going to one knee. For a split second, it looked as though he was about to propose. Holding my hands, he looked me straight in the eye. "I swear to you, Caitlin Marie Holte, I will never compel you again as long as I live."

I searched his eyes, his face. "You really think this is the best option?"

He nodded. "I didn't before, but I do now. This is the best way for us to protect each other. And it's not all bad. Julian says they call it 'the sacred bond.' Although that may just be him bullshitting me. Of course it can be abused, but from what he says, most vampires who have done it have expressed a deep connection to the human they're paired with. It becomes more about synchronicity than mere compulsion. I affect you, but you also affect me."

I smiled a little. "That does sound slightly less terrible."

He smiled back, waiting patiently for my verdict.

I let out a deep breath. "Our decision, right? Yours and mine?"

He nodded.

"Then let's vote. I vote yes."

He looked relieved. "I also vote yes."

"Then let's get synchronous." I frowned. "That didn't sound as dirty as I wanted."

He laughed, then shrugged out of his motorcycle jacket and slipped it around my shoulders over my coat. I looked at him funny.

"Thanks, but I'm actually pretty warm."

"You're about to get very, very cold."

"Ah."

"Are you ready?"

"No. But go ahead."

"I love you."

"I know."

He smiled at the *Star Wars* reference and kissed me, letting it linger, letting it turn serious. Just as I was about to suggest we postpone the whole compulsion thing until after we'd made out, he pulled back, shaking his head apologetically.

"Suppose we don't have time for that," he muttered.

I kissed him again, lightly. "I think you owe me a date after this."

He grinned, brushed my knuckles with a kiss, and put his hands on either side of my face, leaning in. Once again, his eyes flared from gray to molten, liquid silver. Since this was compulsion, not just a scan, or whatever they called it, his irises morphed, swirling slowly.

He murmured words, lyrical and soothing, in whatever language it was that vampires used to compel people. Not English—not anything I recognized. Maybe not even really words at all. Maybe it was more of a song, power manifesting as sound.

And then suddenly, it was cold. It was unbearably, soul-shatteringly cold. My lungs froze, unable to contract. My blood felt sluggish in my veins. There was a ringing in my ears, a sudden, sharp scent of pine trees. The light was all at once so bright I thought my skull would split open.

A headache began to form right between my eyes; a scalpel pushing its way through the back of my head. A full minute later, he blinked, and I blinked, and it was over.

He brushed the tears away from my cheeks, searching my face, looking worried. "How do you feel?"

I closed my eyes and pressed them into the heels of my hands, the daylight still too bright to handle. "Like you drove an icicle through my skull," I grumbled. I felt dizzy, sick to my stomach, and extraordinarily sensitive to the cool air, but he didn't need to know that. "Otherwise fine. Is it done?"

"It's done."

After a long moment my stomach settled and I opened my eyes. "Whoa."

"What?"

"I can feel you."

Adrian blinked, then frowned. "What do you mean?"

"Like, like, I can *feel* you. Sitting there." I closed my eyes. It was still there. "I don't know how to explain it."

"Does it feel bad? Are you in pain?"

"No," I said, frowning. "It's… it's like when you walk into a dark room but you know someone's there. Except in this case it's not a creepy feeling, just a sort of…awareness. Wait, go hide behind a tree or something."

He looked at me funny, but when I closed my eyes, I could feel him move off. Covering my eyes just to prove to Adrian I couldn't see him, I pointed at him with my right hand, following his progress. Eventually I could feel him moving back to me.

"How did you do that?" he asked, sitting down.

"No idea," I replied, opening my eyes. "You were like a magnet."

"That sounds like emotional sonar, like what we do when we're monitoring you from the mansion."

"Can the paired compulsion manifest like that? I'm the human one."

"Maybe when you're in love with the human you're paired with, it really is a sacred bond."

He hadn't meant it as a romantic statement. Heck, he wasn't even looking at me, just staring off into space, eyebrows furrowed in thought. But hearing him say it out loud, that he loved me…

I would never get tired of that.

The feeling of Adrian's presence slowly faded. I had him test the awareness again. He walked off and I tried to point at him with my hand while my eyes were closed. When I opened them, he was literally the opposite direction of where I was pointing.

"Huh," I said. "Maybe it was just a one-time thing."

"Maybe," he agreed. "But let's not count it out just yet."

SPIRIT WEEK

2

This time, Tommie was watching Other Me stab him in the neck. The moment played on a loop, like he was a football coach reviewing game footage.

He glanced over at me as I floated into the dream. "Interesting choice."

"What?"

I banished him easily last time, I could risk a little conversation.

"Stabbing me," he replied casually. "Interesting choice."

I shrugged. "Carpe demon and all."

Other Me reached into her hair, pulling out the pencil that was holding her bun in place. She didn't hesitate at all before plunging the flimsy weapon into Other Tommie's neck once, twice, three times. Blood spurted from the wounds in gory red fountains before the memory jumped back to the beginning and played again.

"Why did you stab me?" he asked again.

"You were trying to kill us," I replied. "Seemed an appropriate response at the time."

"No—" he turned to look at me fully. "Why did you *stab* me?"

I had no idea what he was getting at. "Because there was nothing else I could do."

Tommie frowned, as though I wasn't getting something. "You don't know yet."

"You said that before," I said, watching Other Me out of the corner of my eye. She looked savage, panicked, a little insane. "That I don't know what I am. So tell me—what am I?"

Tommie nodded at Other Me. "An interesting choice."

I frowned, irritated, and waved my hand at him. "Begone, or whatever."

Instantly, he vanished.

"What happens if someone tries to compel me and then I don't do what they try to compel me to do?"

Adrian had just parked on the side of the de la Mara's massive, multi-car garage. I handed him my helmet as he swung off the bike.

"Julian suggested we tell them I performed the paired compulsion during the attack, to keep my father from compelling you further. It would have been reasonable for a young, inexperienced vampire such as myself to resort to that measure given my enthusiasm for proving myself and my understanding that my compulsory abilities would pale in comparison to a demon. It would be considered unorthodox, and perhaps stupidly brave, but not treasonous, given the circumstances."

We both headed for the front door. "That sounds convincing. But won't they be suspicious that we didn't mention that little detail when they interrogated us the first time?"

"If questioned, I would act embarrassed that I had to resort to that method to protect you. Hence not mentioning it to our ruling Council."

He punched in the security code on the keypad, pushed open the front door, and let me inside. I got about two steps before something stopped me dead in my tracks.

"Is he—is that?" I stuttered, staring at a small pair of shoes by the front door. I looked up wildly. "Lucian?"

Adrian turned white. Mariana strolled in from the direction of the kitchen and saw us staring at Lucian's shoes. "He's not here," she said in that infuriatingly demure voice of hers. "Farrar was going over some of his belongings to see if he picked up anything."

Adrian looked like he'd gotten the wind knocked out of him but tried to hide it.

Mariana nodded coolly at me before ascending the winding, grand marble staircase.

I put my hand on Adrian's arm—partly to steady myself and partly to offer comfort.

"I'm…gonna…" Adrian trailed off. He cleared his throat, then nodded toward the second floor. I smiled at him tightly while he trudged up the stairs after Mariana.

While Adrian went to put away his backpack (and, I suspect, to check Lucian's room as if he might magically appear there, as I'd caught him doing several times before), I headed for the kitchen with the cookies Rachel had insisted on baking for Adrian and his family. She sent me over at least once a with a week with some sort of food tray. I didn't have the heart to tell her that Mariana was a 150-year-old chef and probably just threw her food down the garbage disposal.

Caught up in thoughts of Lucian, I was halfway down the hall before I heard low voices. I stopped, hesitating. I didn't really want to re-introduce myself to the Praetorian Guard without Adrian literally at my side. I was turning around when I heard Julian ask, "Is that swing still there?"

Someone—a woman—snorted. "Yep. I remember when you jumped off and broke your arm and had to stay inside while it healed."

I could hear the smile in Julian's voice. "You visited me every day."

"Only so I could pick up some of those nice French swear words."

"*J'ai eu le plaisir de vous enseigner,*" he said softly.

The woman—Kalare? Had to be, didn't sound like Sabine or Mariana—laughed, and replied, "*Conneries!*"

"*Non, non!*" he protested. "*Je le jure, vous avez été un très bon élève.*"

"I don't believe you," she replied, voice light and teasing.

I didn't know Kalare very well, or Julian really, when it came down to it, but it suddenly dawned on me that they were flirting. Granted, I could only understand the English half of the conversation, but there was no mistaking tone. Two vampires, in a kitchen, flirting. The novelty of it kept me rooted in place.

"Would I lie to you?" Julian asked, his accent thick now that he'd been speaking in French. Normally, he sounded like any other American. I kept having to remind myself that he and Adrian had spent a large portion of their childhoods in Europe before moving here. I also had to remind myself that Julian was thirty-five, not twenty, like he looked.

"*Qu'est-ce que c'est?*" a new voice asked.

That must be Sabine. I tucked myself further against the wall. If they were paying attention, they could probably sense that I was standing just down the hall. The one brilliant thing I'd recently realized, however, is that just like humans, they weren't paying attention 100% of the time.

"You are speaking my language and did not invite me?" Sabine asked them.

"*Un millier d'excuses*, Sabine," Julian said quickly as I heard the sound of a stool scraping back against the floor.

"*Pas besoin d'excuses,*" she said in a deceptively demure voice. "Kalare, I did not know you spoke French?"

"I don't, really," I heard Kalare reply, the tone of her voice shifting from low and teasing to brusque and professional. "Only a few phrases I picked up when Julian and the Laroches toured America to drop off Adrian with Mariana and Dominic."

"Well, he was always a better teacher than he was a student," Sabine replied cryptically. There was a moment of silence and then, "Julian, we should prepare. We're leaving soon." I heard her footsteps retreat back into the library. A moment later, I heard a stool being scraped back and what I assumed was Julian following her out, based on the heavy sound of his shoes against the hardwood floor.

I peeled away from the wall and walked cautiously toward the kitchen. When I cleared the doorway, I saw Kalare sitting at the island, staring vacantly at the marble countertop while a mug of tea steamed in her hand, forgotten. She looked up sharply as I entered. "Oh, Caitlin. How are you?"

I laid the bag of cookies on the counter and took a seat across from her. "Good." She and I had never spoken one-on-one, and I wasn't sure how dangerous she was. "How are you?"

She smiled, but it wasn't a particularly happy smile. "I am remembering why I live alone."

I tried to think of something to say and only came up with, "Want a cookie?"

She smiled again, and this time it looked real. "Why not?"

I passed her a cookie on a napkin and poured myself a glass of milk from the fridge.

"You bake these?" she asked.

I shook my head. "My aunt, along with everyone in Stony Creek, seems to think that the best way to deal with a crisis is to cook. Even if the crisis is three months old."

"Food is the number one comforter," she agreed. "Next to a good bottle of whiskey." She blinked, realizing she was talking to a seventeen-year-old. "Not that you should try that."

I smiled and dug into a cookie. So far so good—at least she wasn't trying to glare me to death like Sabine or silence me into submission like Mariana. Even physically she seemed more approachable than the other Praetorians, with purple-tipped dark hair, bright red lipstick, and a black leather vest over a loose grey tank top and black skinny jeans. More fun punk rocker than aloof immortal warrior-slash-dispenser-of-Council-justice.

"If you don't mind me asking, are you from Jersey?"

Her accent was light, not ridiculous like you saw in movies sometimes, but it was there.

She looked up at me with a wry smile. "Born and bred. I'm the only one here who hasn't spent much time outside the ol' U.S. of A."

"Why is that?"

She shrugged. "I was placed in a Trenton orphanage when I was born. The Council didn't know I existed until I was almost a year old. Bonded with some nuns, got attached to the place."

I thought through the logistics of being an infant vampire in a human world. "How did you deal with, y'know, blood? You weren't born with little fangs, were you?"

She laughed and took a sip of tea. "Nope, no fangs. Baby vampires aren't very dangerous, so even if I tried to gum someone to death, I didn't do much damage. Nobody could figure out what was wrong with me, so I spent most of my first year of life in the hospital getting blood transfusions. It kept me alive until the Council found me."

"Wow. When was that?"

She cocked an eyebrow. "It's generally not polite to ask someone older than you their age."

"Oh," I said blushing, "I'm sorry. You just look so young, I forget—"

She cut me off with a smile. "I don't normally get to discuss my life with humans, so it's funny to hear you ask so many questions. I was born in 1964."

If I knew how to whistle, I would, in disbelief. Kalare looked like a college student.

She smiled at me pleasantly, watching the various reactions flit across my face as she took a bite out of her chocolate chip cookie.

"You do take it all in stride rather well," she put in after a moment.

I took a bite of my own cookie and grunted. "You've seen one vampire, you've seen 'em all."

Adrian walked in then, running a hand through his dark, wavy hair, and the sight of him hit me low in my stomach. He caught my eye and smiled, and I had to bury the rest of the cookie in my mouth to hide the big, splotchy blush that had taken over my face. This was one of those more-than-occasional urges I had to drag him into the nearest closet and lock the door. He'd been in a good mood all day, and I wondered if it was because they were actually going to start doing something to find Lucian.

Kalare glanced at me, then at Adrian, but said nothing. Damn it, I needed to work on my emotional blocks. I wasn't forbidden from being attracted to Adrian but it complicated the hell out of things. Adrian had started to teach me how to imagine my emotions as an origami bird (or an origami anything, really). If I could fold it up, change its shape, I could hide it. It was an abstract concept and hard to pull off but with the Guard back, keeping my emotions in check was suddenly vital.

"Mariana told me the meeting was scheduled," Adrian said, turning to the older vampire. "Is it time?"

She peeked over her shoulder down the hall. Farrar was coming our way. "Seems so."

The leader of the Guard came to a stop at the door and inclined his head at me ever so slightly. "Caitlin, Adrian, please join us."

Farrar frightened me, in a way, partially because of his sheer, intimidating size, but also because I couldn't figure out his angle, whether he was nothing more than an agent for the Council's as-yet-to-be-determined-agenda, or if he was truly trying to find Lucian and bring him home. He'd been completely emotionless when he'd interrogated me and Adrian back at the end of February. It didn't help that I was at a severe disadvantage being human and unable to read emotions, body temperature, or heart rate.

I followed as they made their way to the back wall of the library. It was a meeting of the entire Praetorian Guard—Farrar, Vincent, Javan, Sabine, and Kalare—with Adrian's family, minus, of course, Lucian.

Vincent was tall, muscled, with red-blonde hair and pale green eyes. Javan was almost as tall but leaner, with short, dark hair. He looked Hispanic—or maybe even older, Mayan or Aztecan. I had no idea how many centuries he'd lived or where exactly he was from.

Kalare was currently the only one who'd dared smile at me. Of the group, she and Sabine were the only two who looked younger than 30, the age at which vampires stopped maturing physically. But Sabine was her polar opposite: petite, with incredibly long, naturally platinum-blonde hair and eyes so lightly blue they looked almost white.

Farrar took a stand in front of the massive fireplace, speaking quietly.

"Our attempts to locate Lucian have been unsuccessful," he

began without preamble. "We have returned because the Council has determined that the best course of action is to re-investigate the source of the gateway and Lucian's last known location. We will be making our way to hell in one hour. Kalare—" he turned his head to look at her. "You will act as guardian. Mariana, Dominic, please assist as necessary."

They nodded while I glanced at Kalare, unsure whether this was a punishment or an honor. She only nodded briefly, face set in that perfect vampiric neutral.

Farrar glanced around the group, eyes lingering for half a moment longer on me and Adrian. "Julian, you have been officially assigned to the Praetorian Guard, effective immediately, and will be accompanying us." Julian's eyebrows went up a little at that, but he said nothing. I glanced at Adrian, Mariana, and Dominic. They looked equally surprised, but also said nothing. "Sabine, Julian, coordinate with Vincent and Javan about preparations. Are there any questions?"

"Why am I not assigned as well?" Adrian asked.

I looked at him, surprised. He was usually so silent during these types of meetings that I forgot he was there. I was even more surprised to see him actually *frowning* at Farrar. Damn, he was really upset.

"You are not required," Farrar replied vaguely.

"I'm of age," Adrian countered. "And he's my brother, too. I should go."

"Adrian—" Mariana warned, but he cut her off with a sharp look.

"No. I have a right to know why I haven't been assigned to this excursion. If Julian has been promoted, there's no reason I shouldn't be."

Farrar's gaze didn't change so much as…harden. "It is a Council decision. You are required to remain in your current position as Caitlin's daytime bodyguard. You will serve in this role until the Council deems it no longer necessary. Am I understood?"

Adrian's frown almost slipped into a glare, but after a long moment he nodded.

Farrar looked around, daring anyone else to voice a complaint. When no one did, he said, "Dismissed."

I stood along with everyone else, but Farrar called out to me. "Caitlin—a moment."

I slowly walked over to him by the fireplace, determined not to seek out Adrian's eyes.

Farrar waited for everyone to leave. Adrian lingered for a moment at the edge of the bookcase, but one look from the Praetorian leader made it clear he was not welcome to stay.

Finally, Farrar turned to me, hands clasped lightly behind his back. "I am told you had a certain affection for Lucian."

I shrugged, trying to keep my heart from racing, trying to adopt the blank look of the vampires. "He was a sweet kid. Weird kid, too, but we got along."

It was a hard line to balance. They could feel my emotions, I couldn't lie on that front. But I could downplay it.

"Is there anything I can do to help?" I asked, because hey, it couldn't hurt. At worst, it would look like I was ingratiating myself to Farrar. At best, they'd actually give me something to do.

Farrar shook his head, no overt threat in his posture or tone. "Not at this time. If, however, Lucian contacts you, slim though that chance may be, I would appreciate it if you let me know as soon as possible."

I nodded, then frowned. "Aren't you going on the…trip? Thing?"

He nodded. "Inform Kalare if he contacts you while I am gone."

"Do you think he will? Try and contact us, I mean?" It was hard to keep the hope out of my voice.

Farrar inclined his head slightly, thinking. "Lucian was not raised as we were. We do not know what he might do."

Something about the way he'd phrased his response set my hackles on end.

He searched my face for a moment, as though he was looking for something. But all he said was, "On behalf of the Council, we appreciate your continued participation in this investigation. Inform Kalare if you have any concerns."

I nodded, then waited, unsure if I was dismissed or not.

A faintly amused look crossed over his face. "You may go."

I left as fast as possible.

Adrian met me at the door to the kitchen, guiding me away from Vincent and Julian who were chatting by the fridge, and up to my studio on the third floor, closing the door softly behind us.

I pulled out my phone and typed *Are we alone?* and showed the screen to Adrian, unwilling to actually text him the question. He'd warned me almost three months ago about putting anything incriminating in writing, especially anything that hinted that we were in league or keeping secrets from the Council.

Like the fact that we'd sort of fallen in love against their permission.

He took my phone, erased my question, and typed back *Be careful with wording.* After a moment he typed, *Did Farrar question you?*

I typed back, *Yes. Asked me to let him know if Lucian contacted me. I assured him I would.*

Adrian looked a little gray. I typed again, *Should I be concerned?*

Out loud, Adrian replied, "I don't know."

I nodded and put away my phone. "So, hell, huh?" That seemed like a safe question—or at least one I'd be naturally curious about as a human. I pulled my Prom dress off the mannequin and set it on the cutting board. I wasn't planning on working on it right that moment, but I wanted to have a visible excuse for why Adrian and I were talking alone in my studio.

Adrian paced. "I think this is good. They wouldn't waste a trip if they didn't think he might be there. It's not a convenient process."

"But they didn't see a portal open up again. Why go now?"

He shrugged. "My father could have opened a gateway somewhere else, even somewhere underground where we wouldn't have noticed. We monitor global satellite feeds to observe portal phenomena but the geothermal agitation can be hidden by other weather events."

"Were you really mad at Farrar, or were you just trying to make it look like you were more focused on Lucian than on…other things?"

His shoulders tensed. "Both."

I sat on the padded work bench next to my sewing machine. I was about to reply but Adrian held up a hand, tilting his head as if listening to something down the hall that I couldn't hear. He flashed a warning glance at me, then stood, slipping into his vampire camouflage: pure indifference. I stood, too, pretending to rip out a stitch on the hem of the dress.

A moment later, Sabine opened the door to my studio without knocking, glancing at both of us with thinly veiled…something. Something not nice. Disgust?

"Farrar says to take your human home. It's time."

I stiffened, feeling a flush of rage creep over my skin.

"Yeah, hi," I said, turning toward her and waving my giant fabric scissors in mock greeting. "I'm not Adrian's human. I'm not anybody's human. My name is Caitlin, and you can call me Caitlin. 'Kay?"

I smiled brightly and, without waiting to see her reply, turned back to the dress, grabbing my seam ripper to tear out a row of stitches that didn't actually need to be torn out. I just needed to give my hands something to do.

Let Sabine feel my anger. I was tired of being talked down to by these arrogant, beautiful, scary, immortal bastards.

After a moment, the door closed and I heard her footsteps disappear down the hall. I set the seam ripper down and sat heavily on the stool.

Adrian looked impressed.

He got out his phone and typed something, then showed me the screen: *Don't slap me, but you're kind of hot when you're angry.*

I snort-laughed, erased his message, and typed back: *Don't compliment me when we're surrounded by vampires who can feel when I want to kiss you.*

His mouth twitched in a smile, his eyes sparking into silver.

We thought about it for a long moment, weighing the pros and cons silently as we stared at each other.

Then Adrian shook his head, typing: *Tomorrow, lunch, supply closet.*

I bit my lip, smiling, and typed back: *So romantic. Wear something sexy.*

He grabbed the phone and typed back: *Everything I own is sexy.*

I laughed out loud at that, clapping a hand over my mouth at the last second so the sound wouldn't carry.

He grinned at me, waggled his eyebrows, and erased the message, slipping the phone back in his pocket.

"Come on," he said out loud, "I gotta take you home before you have nothing left to wear to Prom."

Spirit Week happened about a month before the end of school every year. Sort of a post-Spring-Break, pre-summer-vacation tactic to get the restless kids interested in going to class. Monday was Decades

Day (the 50s), Tuesday was Pajama Day (literally everyone in the school participated, including Mr. Warren and Principal Daniels), Wednesday was Disney Day (which was mostly people wearing Lion King t-shirts and branded sweatpants because two days in a row of sweatpants was not an opportunity anyone was going to pass up), Thursday was Tie-Dye (they actually had a tie-dye station for us at school on Wednesday afternoon so we could come to school Thursday with our new, groovy shirts), and Friday was Movie Madness.

True to his word, Adrian wore something sexy.

He'd picked out our costumes months ago: he went as Harry Potter, I went as Hermione Granger. He even came over to my place early so Rachel could put a fake lightning-bolt scar on his forehead with make up, which she thought was adorable and Joe thought was…odd.

Adrian already owned the official Harry Potter glasses, wand, scarf, sweater, and Invisibility Cloak and had gone to the trouble of buying me a matching outfit. I even crimped my hair and used a ton of hairspray to make it all poofy and wild, like Hermione's. Adrian blasted the Harry Potter soundtrack from his phone as we pulled up to school on the Harley, cloaks flying. He adjusted his round-frame glasses and pretended to walk in slow motion through the parking lot while I carried an overly-large stack of books and a wand with an LED light. *Lumos*, beyotch.

We'd committed to speaking in British accents all day, which Adrian was better at because he'd actually been to England several times. It was so infectious that people who came as non-British characters found themselves speaking in awful half-accents.

At lunch, I snuck into the gym and knocked politely on the storage closet.

It opened, and Adrian stood there wearing only his scarf, pants, and Harry Potter glasses.

I laughed so hard I almost got us caught.

He pulled me into the closet, stuck a broom through the handle (whispering *Nimbus 3000*), and swept me into his arms. He kissed me, backing me up into a row of gym mats, which upended a basket of dodgeballs. They rained down around us as we enthusiastically made out.

"You know this isn't canon," I said breathlessly, pulling back.

He blinked. "What?"

"You're Harry, I'm Hermione. Ron ends up with Hermione, not Harry. We're breaking canon."

His eyes melted into silver as a grin took over his face. "You know I can't resist when you talk nerdy to me."

It was a good thing that both Harry and Hermione were described as having somewhat unruly hair, because by the time the bell rang, we were both very disheveled.

I pretended to be mad when he put his Gryffindor sweater back on and he pretended to be mad that I'd never taken mine off. We got distracted once again and were almost late for the school assembly that was happening right outside the door, barely slipping in with the last of the crowd, though I'm pretty sure Stephanie and Jenny saw us leaving the supply closet because they both gave us a big smile and a thumbs-up.

Principal Daniels got up to the mic in the center of the gym floor and told us all to pipe down, then handed out several prizes for the most inventive costumes.

"First place goes to Caitlin Holte and Adrian de la Mara for Hermione Granger and Harry Potter. Come get your very exciting D.A.R.E. stickers as a reward."

Adrian grabbed my hand and marched up to the mic, wand pointed straight at the sky. The whole gymnasium cheered. I turned red, but finally I thrust my wand skyward, too. We weren't supposed to give speeches, but Adrian nudged Principal Daniels out of the way and said, "Thank you, thank you, fellow mortals. We'd like to dedicate this win to the poor Muggles of the world who will never be as awesome as we wizards. Go Gryffindor!"

The crowd of students shouted back, "Go Gryffindor!" and "Hogwarts forever!" and cheered us as we marched back into the stands.

Though we won, Tim gave us a run for our money when he showed up to first period in a loose button-up shirt, tighty-whities, and socks—and nothing else. Principal Daniels almost looked sad that he had to tell Tim to change into something more appropriate. He did a spot-on *Risky Business*.

Seeing me and Adrian do something so nerdy together thawed some of the ice at school with the random girls who hated me. It wasn't a secret anymore that I wanted to be a fashion designer, and I think some people had used that as an excuse to think of me as a snob. Clutching fake wands and chasing Adrian around the picnic tables had finally changed some people's minds. Rolling my eyes and saying, "Levi*osa*, not levio*sa*," to Adrian during break while pretending to levitate a baby carrot had also won some grudging respect.

On our way back to the Harley after school, I waved at Ben as he walked next to Trish. He waved back, smiling, even if Trish didn't. They'd come dressed as some sort of spandex-ed, bedazzled wrestlers I wasn't familiar with. Trish, of course, completely ignored me.

Besides my best friend being mad at me, school had become a not terrible thing. In fact, in a way, it was the part of my life I liked most: it was repetitive, structured, and predictable. But most importantly, it allowed me to kiss Adrian without anyone being the wiser.

CLIFFHANGER

3

"Shit, shit, shit, shit, shit, shit, shit," I muttered, dashing from Adrian's truck through the rain. We still drove the truck when the weather was bad.

"Uh, bye?" Adrian called to me.

I whirled, waving at him, but we were super late because we'd pulled off onto a side-road halfway here to make out and I didn't have that many tardies left. "Bye, babe!"

He smiled at me in a way that clearly said I was a huge dork and headed into class.

I whirled back around, tripped over one of those stupid yellow concrete parking lot bumper things, and went flying onto the sidewalk, messenger bag flopping open as it skidded away from me. Luckily, Adrian was already gone and didn't witness my fall. I felt clumsy enough around him as it was. I *wasn't* actually that clumsy. I was averagely clumsy. But when you're constantly around beings whose resting hear rate is ten beats a minute, you can feel a little twitchy.

Speaking of — "*Shit.*"

My designs were all over the place, getting rained on.

I started grabbing at the papers like a mad woman, my overly large and floppy hood getting in the way. A moment later, a hand reached under my hood, holding a stack of designs. I looked up.

It was Trish.

We stared at each for a moment before she cleared her throat.

"What are those for?" she asked, nodding at the papers.

"What? Oh, just some ideas." And because that was not a full explanation, and she was waiting patiently for me to continue, I babbled, "I'm applying for a design internship this summer in New York."

"Oh," she said, looking surprised. "That's…great, actually."

I risked a small smile. This was the most she'd said to me in months. "Yeah, Adrian kind of set it up for me."

The almost-friendly look on Trish's face instantly disappeared. "We're late."

"Trish—"

She reached for the door as the bell rang, crossing the threshold just before it stopped buzzing.

I stood out in the rain like an idiot. Through the door, Mr. Warren frowned at me. "You're tardy, Ms. Holte."

"Yeah, yeah," I muttered, stuffing the designs in my messenger bag. "What else is new?"

The Guard had been in hell a week.

I'd go over to the mansion almost every day to spend time with Adrian, do homework, make halting progress on my Prom dress, and hack away at designs for my summer internship application. I was originally supposed to apply for next summer, after my senior year, but a month away from the craziness—and a house full of irritable vampires—sounded extraordinarily appealing. Now that the Praetorian Guard was back at the mansion, Adrian and I couldn't search the library anymore. There was too great a chance they'd catch us and figure out what we were up to. But because everyone but Mariana, Dominic, and Kalare was asleep—or rather, in hell—we snuck into the library to do more reconnaissance. I stuck to the lower bookshelves where the frustratingly non-informative books were. If we wanted to check higher shelves, Adrian did it when I wasn't there, so as not to draw attention to ourselves in case Kalare or Mariana found us poking around. So far, I'd come across absolutely nothing that would help us, though I did find an interesting book on Council laws from the fourteenth century. It was out of date and hand-written in what I thought was Middle English, so I could barely make it out, but what I could understand was fascinating. I could only risk spending about an hour a day in the library, however. After that, I always went to my studio to work on my Prom dress. Partly to keep up appearances, and partly because I actually needed to finish the dang thing.

Walking down the hall toward my workshop on the third floor, I had to pass the dungeon (as I called it) where the Praetorians' bodies were being stored while they were in hell. Apparently, since hell wasn't really a physical dimension, only their minds or souls or whatever went along for the ride while their bodies remained behind. Adrian had described it briefly to me, but even he didn't have a complete picture of what was involved, having never done it himself.

The door to the room was ajar, so I popped my head in to get a peek, curious about what sleeping vampires looked like. Did they snore? Did they dream of chasing down humans like dogs dreamed about chasing rabbits?

I cracked open the door a few inches further, unable to make them out from the sliver of light from the hall. But in the darkness, something moved.

I let out a little shriek at the same instant the figure whirled and pulled a gun on me. We both froze. Then the figure tilted its head to the side. "Caitlin?"

I stopped shrieking and peered closer. "Kalare?"

"Good god, girl, try knocking next time," she muttered, sliding the handgun into a holster on the back of her jeans.

"Sorry," I replied, heart still racing with adrenaline, "I didn't think anyone was in here. With a gun. Don't you guys have fangs?"

Kalare scrubbed a hand over her face and muttered, "It's not always convenient to chew someone to death."

"What're you doing?" I asked, not daring to step any closer than the doorway.

A flicker of light bloomed in the dark room. "I'm doing my friggin' job," she replied around the end of a cigarette, strangely defensive.

"You smoke?" I asked, more in surprise than anything else.

"Can't die, might as well," she said. "'Sides, I'm from Jersey," she finished, as if that explained it.

I stared as she pulled slow drags from the cigarette. "Are you okay?"

She blew out an impatient stream of smoke and turned to look at me. "Yeah," she said, scrubbing her free hand through her short hair, making it stick up in odd places. "Yeah, just worried. You're not the only one who's new to all this."

I'd never really thought about it that way. "Do you…need anything?"

She smiled tiredly and shook the pack of cigarettes. "Let me finish these and I'll be good."

I smiled and said, "Okay," and shrugged back out the door, closing it behind me.

I was halfway down the hall before it registered that Kalare had been kneeling next to Julian.

"Sweetheart, do you think Adrian's parents are throwing him a graduation party?"

"Aunt and uncle," I automatically corrected her, tossing a paper airplane into the fireplace. The edges curled back, smoking, revealing the ugliest design I'd ever done. A stack of similar planes sat next to me, waiting to be burned.

"Honey, don't ruin those, they're good!" my aunt said, scooping up the papers.

"They're not good enough for the application."

"You've got hundreds of designs in those journals of yours, why don't you use some of those?" she asked, smoothing the paper back into a mostly flat shape. "And these *are* good."

I sighed. "They're not bad because they're *bad*, they're bad because I went onto Myriad's website and saw their latest collection and then panicked and basically plagiarized their entire line because I thought that might give me a better shot at being accepted. And then I realized that was a terrible idea and that I honestly don't like their aesthetic and if they don't like my style and I don't like theirs, I probably won't like their internship anyway. Hence the paper airplane fireplace kamikaze situation."

I heard a door open upstairs. "We burning Caitlin's designs now? I want in."

Rachel shot a stern look up at her daughter, who was draped over the balcony, grinning. Norah had grown two inches over the past few months and was now as tall as me, which was super not cool.

"Be nice," my aunt warned. "This is a big deal for Caitlin."

I snorted involuntarily. "It doesn't even matter. Unless I get their big package scholarship, I can't afford to go. And the chances of getting that spot are one in…uh, a lot."

I stole a plane back from Rachel and launched it into the fire.

Rachel grabbed my shoulders and swiveled me toward her, looking serious. "It matters, Caitlin. You have a gift. You have an *opportunity*. You may not understand this now, but that combination is rare. No one else is going to care about this for you and no one is going to hand it to you. If you want this, go for it. Take it seriously. I know it's cool nowadays not to care about anything, but honestly that's just…well, it's stupid. If you don't get their scholarship, we'll help figure out a way for you to go. You'll have to work for it, but we'll help."

I stared at Rachel, equal parts uncomfortable and grateful. "Well, yeah, okay. I want it. I do." I looked down at the floor. "It's just hard to want something you don't think you're going to be able to keep."

I meant the internship. I meant that whole future, that career, my dreams.

But I also meant Adrian. Hell, I even meant Lucian.

She patted my knee. "I know. But some things are worth fighting for." She looked up at Norah. "For both of you girls. I want you to know that we believe in you. Not because you're our daughters—" She froze, and blushed, glancing at me. "Well, daughter and niece. I mean…oh, you know what I mean. But because if you work hard—if you work really, really hard, if you take yourselves seriously—there's no reason you can't achieve everything you set yourself to. And no matter what you do, whether you win nationals, Norah, or become a famous designer, Caitlin, if you can take pride in yourself and in your work, then you will have a full and beautiful life."

I was stuck staring at the carpet, trying not to cry. Sometimes Rachel was the cheesiest person in the world, and sometimes she just slipped in past my defenses and made me feel like I was actually a part of her family.

I glanced up at Norah to find her looking as conflicted as I felt. "Thanks for the speech, Mom. Oprah would be proud." She gave Rachel an exaggerated thumbs up.

Rachel rolled her eyes, but smiled. "Now, about Adrian's gradua—" She interrupted herself with a sneeze. She bent her face to her elbow, hiding the next sneeze in the crook of her arm.

"Bless you," I said automatically.

She made her way into the kitchen, sneezing the whole way. "Anyway, Caitlin, think about a party for Adrian. We'd love to celebrate with him and his family."

"Okay," I called back to her, then quickly stole the rest of my designs and folded them back into paper airplanes.

Kalare sat in the crypt, chain smoking. I soon figured out that chain-smoking meant she was worried. Regular smoking meant she was, well, Kalare. I'd also started coming up with a variety of fun names for the room where the Praetorians were sleeping. Top choices so far were The Lounge, The Morgue, and The Sauna, mostly because they kept it super warm in there and Kalare's cigarette smoke made it look like it was steamy.

They'd been in their comatose state for two solid weeks without so much as a twitch of movement. Two weeks was pushing it—if they didn't come back soon, their organs would eventually shut down, not from lack of blood, but lack of food. Vampires ate three times more than normal people-people.

When I asked if we couldn't open a window or two to let in some light, she said they had to keep it dark, because without more blood getting into their system, their skin was incredibly sensitive and could burn—not in the flame sense, but in the spent-too-many-hours-at-the-beach sense. While comatose, they couldn't heal themselves half as quickly as normal, either.

So she crouched in the dark, mostly by herself, until I started to get concerned. Mariana and Dominic, of course, kept to themselves and didn't seem all that worried. They switched rotations with Kalare every now and again to give her a break, but it seemed like she was the one mainly in charge of keeping watch. For an hour or so every time I came over, I'd sit with her and play card games or talk or read cheesy romance novels by the light of a few shielded lamps, just to make sure she didn't go insane sitting there by herself with the bodies. Adrian used the time to scour the library.

"Why sevens again?" I asked as she slapped her hand down on a stack of cards and added them to her deck.

"House rules," she muttered around the end of a cigarette. She flipped a jack over and set it down in the space between us. I laid down a five and she took the hand again, and laid down a nine. I came up with a queen and then hers ended up being a queen, so I slapped the double before she could. I suspected that she intentionally slowed herself on occasion, and didn't slap half as hard as she was capable of—otherwise I'd lose every time and the bones in my hand would, y'know, shatter.

Kalare looked up and to the side suddenly—a movement I had finally gotten used to—and stood. She somehow knew exactly when an hour had passed, and went to check the pulse and vitals of the vampires, starting, as always, with Julian.

They were laying on thin mats on the floor, grouped in a circle like spokes on a wheel. I could see their chests rise and fall with each breath but they were otherwise so still they looked dead. I'd spent time circling them, just looking at their faces, trying to pick out anything that would tell me they were vampires, but in sleep they looked perfectly human. Vincent even let out a little fart once.

"Still alive?" I asked as she checked Julian's pulse.

"More or less," she muttered, moving on to Sabine.

"I'll probably beat them to the grave with all this secondhand smoke."

"I switched to herbal when you started hanging out here."

"Really? And, wait, herbal or *herbal*?"

"The non-fun kind," she said dryly. "No hotboxing for my little teenage sidekick. For all I know this is just oregano and parsley."

I snorted a laugh. "You didn't have to actually switch, though, I was just kidding."

She blew a perfect smoke ring that landed on Sabine's perfect face before dissolving. "Rule number one: *operor non vulnero humanus*. Do no harm to humans. I am duty-bound not to give you cancer," she said, and returned to our card game with a wry smile.

My throat suddenly tightened. "Considering that's what my mom died of, I appreciate it." She glanced at me and it got quiet for a long time. She flipped a seven over and slapped it, stealing the hand. I cleared my throat. "Where'd you learn card games?" I asked, breaking the awkward silence I'd created. She gave me a funny look and I blushed, feeling rude. "Sorry, I mean, none of the others seem to know how to play games or sports or anything."

She stubbed out her cigarette and lit a new one. "We are what you'd call a dignified race. That's code for 'egocentric pains in the ass.' " She smiled around the cigarette. "Which brings us to rule number two: *subsisto ex humanus res*. Stand out of human occurrence. Or as I like to call it: stay out of the damn way." We flipped cards back and forth as she talked. "When a vampire does deign to dabble in the affairs of humans, it is only to find the intellectual merit in their activities. They play games—Pente, chess, even various forms of poker since in the end it's about mathematics and statistics and probabilities. But the day a vampire sets foot on a Twister mat is the day the sweet Lord is comin' back."

I only had two cards left in my hand, and neither of them were worth anything. Kalare quickly won, settling back with a small, satisfied smile.

"But," I prompted as she shuffled the deck, "*you* do. I can very easily picture you on a Twister mat, tequila bottle and cigarette in hand, kicking Twister ass."

The smile stayed on her lips, but it turned bitter. "A Trenton-bred vampire isn't something the Council likes to brag about. Can't exactly play Twister with the humans, if you know what I mean—" she waggled her eyebrows to let me know she meant the *other* kind of Twister, "—and it took me a painfully long time to realize that my kind just don't like to have fun. I didn't fit in with them, but it was both illegal and inadvisable to get attached to the wee humans." She glanced at me. "No offense."

I dealt the cards. "Why is that?"

She shrugged casually. "They die."

I snuck a glance at her while arranging my hand. "That why you guys only marry among yourselves?"

"Yep," she replied, scooping up her cards. "So you'd best forget about Adrian as soon as this all blows over. As your friend, I'm telling you it's not gonna happen."

I paused with a card mid-flip, my heart lodged somewhere in my throat. "What makes you think I like him?" I asked, laying the card down carefully.

"Sweetheart, every vampire in this house knows how you feel about him," she said, eying me from behind her lazy cloud of smoke. "It's understandable, given the circumstances. He's attractive, similar in age, and he's been protecting you. That white knight vibe is hard to resist. I know you're a smart girl, I can see that, so I'm going to assume you know that this can't go on forever. Culture and law aside, you're gonna die and he's not, it's pretty black and white on that count. I only bring it up because in case you were tempted to think you were the exception to the rule, just know that I've seen this happen before, and it doesn't end well."

I swallowed thickly, terrified that she'd seen right through me. "What do you mean?"

She sucked in a long drag from the cigarette, closing her eyes as she let it out again, her shoulders slumping a little as she did.

"All right. If I tell you this, you gotta swear not to mention it ever to anyone. Not because it's a rule, but because it's still a very tender topic among present company," she said, nodding her head in the direction of the sleeping vampires. "Though God knows it's been long enough that it shouldn't be."

I nodded.

She scrubbed her hands over her face and through her hair, making it stick up funny, which actually, in a way, made her look more awesome.

"Okay, no one likes me anyway. See Sabine there?"

I looked over at the white-blonde hair fanning out perfectly beneath the pale face of the vampire.

"She was born in 1901. Grew up in France, got placed with Farrar and his wife." Kalare gazed at the sleeping woman somberly. "When she was seventeen she fell in love with a human; Tristan. Wanted to marry him. The Council said no while Tristan was sent off to fight World War I. Died horribly, mustard gas and a bullet to the head. Insult on injury if you ask me. Anyway, Sabine there has spent the intervening years hating everyone—the Council, for denying her permission to love a human, Farrar for being the one to bear the news, humans for being so fragile to begin with—and you." Kalare looked at me and I couldn't read her expression. "She hates you because you are, however temporarily, not only allowed but encouraged to have the one thing she was denied."

There was a moment of silence that I couldn't find the words to fill. Kalare leaned forward, smiling darkly. "But wait, the misery spreads further. Julian also grew up with Farrar, and Sabine was still in their house all those years later. Julian—though he'd never admit it—fell in love with her. But she was and is still in love with Tristan. She rejected Julian, and Julian rejected everyone else."

She sat back again, out of the light from the lamp, enveloped in the cloud of smoke.

"You love him," I murmured, not really meaning to say it out loud.

She didn't reply for a long time as her cigarette swirled little tendrils of smoke up toward the ceiling.

"Yeah, well," she muttered finally, "seems like everybody wants what they can't have."

Someone sighed heavily, and it took me a moment to realize it wasn't Kalare. She and I both turned at the same time. On the floor closest to Kalare's chair, Julian stirred on his mat. His eyes slowly opened, although he looked groggy and disoriented.

Kalare dropped her cards and rushed to kneel by him, checking his pulse. I heard a few more sighs from around the room as the other vampires began to awaken. Julian closed his eyes, mumbled Kalare's name, and leaned his face into her arm.

And then he bit her.

She didn't scream or jerk away, just let him drink. Which didn't make sense. Vampires couldn't feed off other vampires. She looked over her shoulder at me, her face white, terrified.

"Caitlin, leave—*now*."

"What?"

She glanced at me like I was the stupidest person she'd ever met. "They're *hungry*, you idiot."

The circle of vampires woke, sitting up groggily as they sniffed the air.

And then they opened their eyes.

And then every single one of them looked directly at me.

It took my brain way, way too long to process what my body was already begging me to do.

I ran, slamming the door closed behind me. I stumbled down the three flights of stairs, screaming for Adrian.

He ran into the foyer, catching me as I tripped on the last step.

I was trembling so badly I could barely speak. Finally, I spit out, "*They're awake.*"

For half a second, he just stood there. Then he grabbed my arm and dragged me outside, slamming the front door behind us, punching in the code to lock it digitally. We climbed on the Harley, waiting impatiently for the massive wrought-iron gate to swing open as a dozen hands scrabbled against the front door behind us, trying to open it.

As soon as the gate creaked open he wrenched the bike into gear and pealed out of the drive and down the road, not toward my aunt and uncle's ranch, but higher up into the mountains where no one lived, where no one could get hurt. Just as we hit the road, I heard the front door groan, splintering. Then feet running on pavement.

Without a helmet, my hair whipped in the wind, stinging my eyes, so I kept my face glued to Adrian's shoulder. Over the angry hum of the motorcycle, I couldn't hear a thing. I had no idea if they were following us.

We drove for several miles until the road ended, turning into a winding gravel trail that ended in weeds and waist-high bushes, rocks pinging off the underbelly of the bike. If Dominic didn't restore classic cars for a living—and if bloodthirsty warrior vampires weren't chasing us—I'd have been worried about the bike getting damaged. Weird thoughts cross your mind in moments of panic.

Adrian stopped when the path ended. He swerved the bike into a sudden stop and pulled me off the Harley and into the dense trees, slowing himself just enough for me to keep up. My lungs and legs were soon burning from the exertion as I followed him blindly. Behind us, I could hear feet running, cracking twigs and branches, snarling. How had they caught up to us so fast? Without warning, Adrian suddenly grabbed me and spun me around, my legs flying out over empty space.

Great—we were at a cliff. Why did we have to live on a freaking *mountain*?

Adrian pulled a pocket knife out of his jeans—the kind that's a multi-tool with nail files and screwdrivers—opened the blade, and slapped the handle in my palm.

"Anyone gets too close, use it," he commanded, pausing long enough for me to nod. And then they were on us.

Julian went straight for his brother—actually, he probably went straight for *me*, the human chock full of delicious blood, but Adrian pivoted, taking the hit. They both exploded backward with momentum, struggled for a moment on the edge of the cliff, then went down in a graceful fall, straight over the edge. My heart stopped for two whole seconds until I heard them hit a ledge.

Sabine appeared out of the trees, advancing slowly, like some sort of jungle cat, a look in her eyes that was far from human. Her irises glowed a strange ice blue. I adjusted my grip on the knife, knowing if it came down to me needing to use it, it would be way too late. Farrar stepped out of the trees as well, his dark eyes glowing faintly purple, almost like a black light. The branches of the trees brushed his shoulders as he stepped into the tiny clearing.

Shit.

Below, I could hear curses from Adrian and a strange, growling noise that I'd never heard a human *or* vampire make before—and then there was silence.

Double shit.

I felt dizzy, suddenly, my vision blurry, my breath short. It was a really, really inconvenient time for a panic attack.

I turned my attention back to Sabine, sparing a quick glance at Farrar. I was surprised to see him staring not at me, but at her.

"Sabine," he warned, an edge to his voice.

"She does not deserve to live," she hissed, voice raspy and thin through her elongated teeth.

Whoa.

I'd never actually seen one of them with fangs out before, even though Adrian had taken blood from me. They weren't too much longer than regular incisors, but they tapered off to needle-thin points of bone.

"That is not for you to decide," he said, voice so low it was almost a growl. He seemed to be speaking and acting normally—maybe I didn't have to worry about him attacking me.

Sabine kept inching closer to me, but her gaze flicked to Farrar. "No—that's your choice, isn't it?"

His expression was neutral. "I will not let you hurt the girl." It wasn't a threat, just a fact. Behind Farrar, Vincent ran up, eyes glowing green, followed by Javan, eyes a molten amber. They came to an abrupt halt at the edge of the trees, staring at me hungrily like monsters from a fairy tale.

Something large landed at my feet with a sudden, dull *thud*. I glanced down.

It was Julian.

Sabine was momentarily distracted as Adrian climbed back over the cliff, bleeding from half a dozen wounds, one of which was a foot long and an inch deep running down his back. The fresh blood caught Sabine's attention. Julian caught Farrar's attention. Adrian's swirling silver eyes caught my attention. Why was he in compulsion mode?

"Is Julian alive?" Farrar asked.

Adrian nodded. "He is not conscious."

Farrar and I looked at him strangely. Julian was a limp, immobile heap at my feet.

Adrian's face was strained, streaked with sweat, dirt, and blood. "I don't know what happened. He just collapsed."

Sabine advanced another foot in my direction, her gaze flicking between the open wounds on Adrian's body and the pulse in my neck.

"Can you stand?" Farrar asked Adrian, his gaze traveling to Sabine.

Adrian shook his head weakly, his eyes going dim. "Too tired."

He collapsed to his knees, trembling. Instantly, Sabine pounced, heading straight for me. I reflexively threw the knife and it, even more surprisingly, buried itself in her thigh, tripping her. Farrar threw himself on her, crushing her face-down into the dirt, pinning her arms behind her back.

"Where's the blood?" Adrian's voice was strained with exhaustion.

"On its way," Farrar replied, his voice gritty and low. Vincent and Javan had inched closer, their gaze flickering between me and Farrar.

"Why aren't you attacking me?" I asked Farrar in a moment of sheer stupidity.

His blazing eyes flicked to me. "If you continue to bring attention to yourself, we soon will be."

I immediately shut up. Vincent shook his head, as if trying to wake up, red hair trembling as he instead closed his eyes. He sank to his knees, followed by Javan. They clasped arms, heads bowed, almost like they were praying, but their muscles were so tense their entire bodies shook. Maybe if they couldn't see me, they wouldn't hurt me.

A few moments later, I heard the tell-tale whispers of feet running through the woods, and then Kalare was there, bag slung over her shoulder, a purple bruise swelling on her wrist around half a dozen puncture marks. Her whole hand was stained red with blood. She came to a stop when she saw Julian lying on the ground, and I saw the fear in her eyes.

"Is he—"

"*Kalare*," Farrar growled, his voice beginning to show signs of strain.

She snapped out of it, knelt, and withdrew a plastic IV bag from the satchel, passing the first to Farrar, who freed one of his hands to rip it open and drink. His eyes slowly stopped glowing. Kalare tossed bags to Vincent and Javan, but since their eyes were closed, she actually hit them in the side of the head. They slowly opened their eyes, grabbed the bags from the ground, and drank.

Kalare knelt to force-feed another bag to Sabine who was still struggling against Farrar, glaring at me hungrily with her molten ice-blue eyes. Adrian had once told me that when a fresh source of food is nearby, it's hard to get excited about bagged blood. Apparently it was even worse when you had a personal grudge against the food.

Leaving Farrar to deal with Sabine, Kalare scooted over to Julian.

"Is he dead?" she whispered.

Adrian shook his head, his eyes no longer swirling. "Get ready to hold him," he murmured, and a look of concentration stole over his face. "I'll see if I can wake him up, but I don't want him to attack Caitlin."

Kalare held an open bag in her teeth and pinned Julian down with her arms and legs. Adrian bent over his brother, his face contorted, and seemed to whisper something in Julian's ear. A wave of dizziness hit me, and my vision went blurry again. I'd mostly stood in one place jacked up on adrenaline, but hadn't done anything with it except fling a knife at Sabine. After a few moments, my vision cleared and I saw Julian's muscles relax. Finally, he stirred. When he opened his eyes, Kalare let out a deep breath, then let go of his arm to tilt the blood bag to his lips. He sat up while Kalare knelt over him—the posture appearing to be protective, both of Julian and of everyone else. He ignored me mostly and drank until the bag was empty.

Looks like I wasn't going to be lunch after all.

Farrar's phone rang. He listened, then nodded. "Good. We're stabilized. Send the truck."

Satisfied that I wasn't going to be mauled by anyone, I knelt by Adrian, whose eyes were glassy and unfocused, and brushed the rocks and dirt away from his open wounds the best I could. He turned to me and smiled. Almost immediately the smile vanished and he grimaced, leaning against me heavily.

"Adrian?"

He didn't answer, just slumped over onto my shoulder. He easily weighed a hundred pounds more than me, so I crumbled, his chest pinning me to the ground as everyone turned to stare. For a frenzied half a second, I thought he was dead. But after a moment I could feel his heart beating, though it was slower than normal, which was saying something, since it only beat once every six seconds or so.

"He's alive," I muttered, unable to get anything else out with Adrian crushing the oxygen out of my lungs.

"His injuries are not that extensive," Farrar remarked.

"Could someone get him off me?" I asked, gasping. Kalare leaned forward and easily picked him up, propping him against a boulder to keep the dirt out of his cuts.

Far away, I could hear tires drawing closer on the dirt road. Farrar bent to pick up Adrian as easily as he might a small child. Vincent picked up Sabine in his arms while Javan grabbed the knife buried in her thigh and yanked it out. He wiped the blood on his jeans before folding up the blade and handing it politely back to me. We followed Julian through the forest back to the truck where Mariana and Dominic were waiting. Farrar laid Adrian in the back and climbed in behind him. They all seemed calmer now, though still a little wild-looking around the eyes.

"I'll take the bike back," Kalare offered.

"Go with her, Julian," Farrar ordered.

Julian nodded and climbed stiffly on the Harley behind Kalare, leaning heavily on her. The truck pulled away, and I spent the return trip holding Adrian's head in my lap so he wouldn't jerk around on the potholed back road. Although I didn't look up, I could feel Sabine's pale, unfriendly eyes on me. At least she had a reason to be mad at me now. I had definitely stabbed her. It was funny. My second time stabbing someone and I didn't feel the least bit bad about it. Probably helped my conscience that she'd been trying to kill me. And that she'd be perfectly healed within a few hours.

It wasn't until we were almost back to the house that I realized I hadn't seen Lucian.

4

The door was raked with claw marks, deep gouges staining the old, dark wood. The latch was splintered, ripped from the door.

I knew vampires were strong, I'd seen it from Adrian firsthand, but this scared the hell out of me. The door was thick enough to stop bullets and they'd casually torn it apart.

Dominic and Mariana had Adrian by the arms and legs, carrying him across that startlingly white marble foyer, his wounds still dripping blood. Without thinking, I moved to follow them up the stairs, but a hand clenched down on my wrist, stopping me.

It was Kalare. She immediately let go, but shook her head at me softly in warning.

Sabine limped past us, eying me—with suspicion or hunger or hatred, I couldn't tell, and headed for the kitchen, not even sparing Adrian a glance.

My heart hammered as they carried his unconscious body up the stairs. His cuts were still bleeding, which wasn't normal. Based on his rate of healing from our battle with his father, a couple of cuts like that should already be closing up. The fact that they weren't was freaking me out. I tried to get myself under control because every damn vampire in the house could hear my heart beating, but Adrian was hurt and it killed me not to be by his side.

Farrar came in a moment later with Julian, who looked puzzled and tired. They had been speaking quietly, but stopped when they saw me. Julian glanced at Farrar, then headed up the grand staircase to the third floor, where Adrian's room was.

In the sudden quiet, Farrar turned to me. "My apologies for that… unpleasantness."

I opened my mouth, but Kalare interrupted. "Don't apologize to her, apologize to *me*. Where was my warning, Farrar? And what the hell happened with Julian?"

Farrar's eyes narrowed marginally. "I know you were raised more casually than the rest of us, but do not question me like that again in front of our guest."

Kalare fumed, but cut her gaze down to the floor in deference.

Farrar turned to me. "Caitlin, did Lucian contact you?"

"No," I said truthfully, trembling from adrenaline and fear—Farrar hadn't raised his voice but even without vampire powers he was big enough to crush me like a bug. "I would have told Kalare. He didn't come back with you, did he?"

"No," he confirmed. "He did no—"

He was cut off by an agonizing cry from the floor above us—Adrian.

I immediately took a step toward the stairs but once again found Kalare's hand on my arm, the motion hidden behind her back as she swiveled in front of me.

"We can't just leave our *guest* standing here," she said pointedly.

Kalare's hand was a vise on my wrist. I knew she was covering for me, I knew I had to pretend like I didn't care, but every cell in my body was telling me to go take care of Adrian.

After an agonized moment, I relaxed, and Kalare let go of my arm.

Dang, that was going to bruise tomorrow.

Farrar glanced up the stairs, then back at me. He reached past Kalare and put a hand gently on my shoulder, looking me straight in the eyes. "Caitlin, Kalare is going to take you home. You're not going to discuss this with anyone. You're going to remember that something strange happened, but that everything is fine."

He blinked, and it took me a second to realize he'd just compelled me.

Or at least, he'd tried to. His eyes were so dark I hadn't even noticed them swirling into vampire mode.

And it hadn't worked.

Adrian's paired compulsion really *had* blocked another vampire from compelling me.

Scrambling to play along, I blinked as well, and nodded. Wait, shoot, was I supposed to play along? My brain was so flooded with adrenaline I couldn't remember what we'd agreed to.

Also, I wasn't totally sure how this worked—when Adrian had compelled me the first time, it was to tell me to forget everything—so I did, instantly. The second time he'd compelled me to kiss him, which I'd also done instantly.

This was a less direct command. Farrar was telling me how to feel, not what to do, so I wasn't sure what reaction they were looking for. Should I say, "Yes, Vampire Master" and bow?

Before I could do anything else, however, he relaxed, apparently satisfied with my simple nod, so I turned to Kalare obediently, trying to keep a blank look on my face. Her eyes narrowed a fraction of an inch, but she stuffed me into my coat and dragged me out the door, grabbing Adrian's truck keys from the rack on the wall.

She practically threw me in the truck and shot down the drive and through the still-open gate. As soon as we were out of sight of the mansion, she slammed on the brakes, pulling to the side of the road. She threw the truck in park and grabbed the front of my jacket.

Terrified, I searched her eyes as she searched mine.

After a long moment, she tossed me back to my half of the bench seat.

"He fucking paired you, didn't he?"

Trembling, I didn't answer.

"Fuck," she repeated, running her hands through her hair. "That idiot is going to get both of you killed." She threw the truck in gear and kept driving. "What was he going to tell Farrar when he found out?"

I didn't move.

Kalare glanced at me and rolled her eyes. "I am the least of your problems right now. What were you going to tell him?"

"That Adrian did it during the fight with his father," I whispered. "That he didn't have a choice."

Kalare's eyes raced back and forth, considering.

"Is it true?" she asked after a long moment. Then she shook her head and held up her hand. "Never mind, I don't want to know. We'll say it's true. Shit. You shouldn't have played along." She chewed her lip, deep in thought. "Though maybe you can play it off like you were just being respectful or something. Following his order by choice."

She sank back in the seat, looking frazzled. "The next time someone compels you, *do not play along.* They'll realize it sooner or later, and the longer you pretend to be compelled, the more they'll be pissed when they realize you were faking the whole time. God, your boyfriend is an idiot."

Adrian was injured, possibly dying. It was stupid, but I suddenly felt the need to defend him. "I can't trust you," I told her, sitting up. "Any of you. But I trust him. It was the best way to keep me safe from all of you."

Kalare snorted. "Well that's some grade-A romantic bullshit."

She pulled onto the long driveway to the ranch and slowed down, driving more carefully now that we were closer to regular humans—a.k.a. my family. I could see Rachel peer out at us curiously from the kitchen window.

Kalare turned to me after parking. "Caitlin, I like you. But I am dead fucking serious when I say you need to cut this shit out with Adrian. *Now*. They will find out. They will hurt you. And they will take Adrian away from you."

"Why?" I pleaded hoarsely, suddenly on the verge of tears. "Why do they even care?"

She stared at me hard. "Because love is chaos. *Humans* are chaos. They're messy and temporary and inconvenient and I don't know why they care, but they care. You think Tristan died randomly in that war? Sabine's not mad because he was a soldier and soldiers die, she's mad because he was a human and he was *executed*. She was warned and she didn't listen, and Tristan died for it. Don't be Adrian's example. Don't be the reason he has to learn that lesson the hard way."

Her phone started buzzing, but she ignored it. I stared at her for a long moment, unable to speak.

"Get out," she said finally. "I have to get back or they'll wonder what took so long."

I un-clicked my seatbelt mechanically and opened the door. Then I turned back to her. "Please just tell me if he's okay."

Kalare glared at me like I was an idiot. "You're an idiot," she said, and pulled away, the sudden acceleration slamming the door closed.

As the truck rumbled viciously down the drive, the front door opened behind me. I quickly wiped the tears away.

"That was Adrian's truck, right?" Rachel asked, walking up to me. "Who was that?"

"Adrian's…cousin," I replied lamely, my sluggish brain refusing to come up with a speedy lie. "He's got a lot of family in town for graduation."

"Oh," Rachel replied, sounding like she didn't totally believe me, but she wasn't sure why. "Is everything okay? You look upset."

I choked back a fresh wave of tears. Sometimes I desperately wanted to tell someone what was going on. "Just family drama," I half-lied. "It'll blow over."

She didn't look convinced, but she was too polite to say so. Then her eyes widened. "Is that…is that blood?"

I looked down at the knees of my jeans. Adrian had been leaning against me in the truck, his back torn to shreds. I hadn't even noticed that he'd gotten blood on me.

"Uh, yeah," I said, stalling. "Lotta testosterone in the house. Adrian and Julian were wrestling and it got a little out of hand. I was helping clean up."

Rachel looked at me, alarmed.

"Just roughhousing, sharp corner on the coffee table. They're fine."

"Well, put some pre-spot on that and put it straight in the washer, you don't want it to stain."

I nodded, suddenly worn out. She saw the look on my face and looked like she was about to pry further. Instead, she wrapped her arm around my shoulders. "Let's go inside. You want to make cookies?"

I nodded again and leaned into her hug. She froze for a moment, as if surprised, then gave me a squeeze and led me into the house.

IVY LEAGUE BOYFRIEND

5

Adrian was dying, and it was my fault.

He lay frozen on the ground, chest riddled with holes, blood frozen in flaky crusts, the snow around him puddled black in the moonlight.

"No," I whispered in tandem with Other Me. She was bent over his chest, however, while I was off about twenty feet back, like usual.

"He should have died, you know."

Beside me, Tommie was observing the scene casually, arms clasped behind his back. "Even for a vampire, he should have died. Remember all that science he explained to you?"

"He's a vampire," I muttered at him. "He defies physics."

"No," Tommie corrected sternly. "He doesn't."

He walked over to Adrian's body, leaving no imprints in the snow, because he was not a part of this memory. "Look at that," he said, bending over Adrian's torn-up chest. "Like ground meat."

"What's your point?" I asked, on the verge of banishing him.

Tommie sighed as though disappointed.

Suddenly, the dream shifted, jumping backward in time. Before us, Other Tommie stood holding Other Me by the arms.

"Then tell me why they haven't told you who she is," he said. "Tell me why she wasn't better guarded."

Adrian, a few feet off from us, didn't respond.

"Tell me," Tommie murmured, "why they assigned a *boy* to guard this girl's life."

The memory paused, the other versions of us frozen perfectly.

The real Tommie looked at me, waiting. As if asking the question all over again.

Why?

Why?

I woke suddenly to the chime of my phone. I scrambled for it, hoping it was a text from Adrian, but it was just my alarm. I was sleeping through the nights now, but always awoke disoriented, often confused about where I was or even what day it was. There were always a few wild seconds of panic until I remembered.

I was about to text Adrian, just to let him know, as I did every morning, that I'd had the same dream, but Kalare's warning yesterday came back to me loud and clear: Adrian and I were idiots. We were sloppy. We were naive.

We were going to get caught.

I set my phone down.

At breakfast, Norah got grossed out when Rachel sneezed all over the scrambled eggs. Joe reminded me to ask Adrian to ask his aunt and uncle about a graduation party. Rachel reminded me to finish my essay for history. I barely heard them, consumed with thoughts of Adrian lying unconscious in the back of the truck.

I was rinsing my plate when I heard the sound of tires on the gravel drive. I grabbed my backpack and ran out the door. Adrian was just getting out of the truck when he saw me. He smiled and I ran into his arms, throwing him back against the door of the truck.

"You're okay," I whispered, pressing my face into his collarbone.

He hugged me tightly, resting his cheek on top of my head. But all too soon soon he let go. Taking a step away from me, he waved at Rachel, who was peering at us through the kitchen window.

He wasn't saying anything, which made me nervous. I went around the truck and crawled onto the passenger seat. He pulled down the driveway and onto the main road, still saying nothing.

I got out my phone and typed, *Can we talk?* and showed him the screen.

He shook his head.

I erased the message, put the phone back in my messenger bag, and sat very intentionally on my half of the bench seat.

But I couldn't help but glance over at him every few minutes. He seemed quiet, the corners of his eyes a little tight, though from stress or exhaustion I couldn't tell. He hadn't shaved this morning, which was unusual.

I couldn't stand the silence.

"Have you heard back from Harvard yet?" I asked, trying to sound casual.

He'd applied to every Ivy League school in the country. Vampire or not, he was crazy smart. But he hadn't mentioned them once since he let slip that he'd applied.

Adrian cleared his throat. "Yes."

He didn't elaborate.

If he went away to college, I'd be insanely proud of him.

But it would also kill me.

I mean literally, not having him there to help me navigate this whole Praetorian Guard fiasco might actually end in my being dead. There were too many moving parts, too many hidden motives for me to understand what was going on without an inside man helping me through.

And I would miss him like crazy.

"So," I prompted. "Your brain big enough for the big leagues?"

He smiled lightly, but kept his eyes on the road. "Apparently."

Shit. He was leaving me. He was going to go away and get smarter, and I was going to stay here and probably get killed.

"So I guess I can help you pick out dorm stuff. Don't worry, we'll get all pink accessories, sparkly and covered in rhinestones, just like you like. Wait, does Harvard have dorms?"

I was babbling, and trembling, and Adrian reached slowly across the seat and took my hand. I squeezed it until my knuckles turned white.

"I'm not going," he said finally. "Not this year anyway."

He pulled into the school parking lot. We were a little early and only a few students were milling around, waiting for school to start. We got out, and Adrian meandered toward the covered picnic tables. We sat for a long moment in silence.

I glanced at Adrian. His eyes were unfocused, and he seemed to be concentrating.

Or listening.

Finally, he relaxed.

"Are we good?" I whispered.

He rolled his shoulders and slung his arm around me. "Yes," he said finally. "Had to double check there."

"Why couldn't we talk in the truck?"

"I have reason to believe that Farrar has been ordered to spy on us. The truck might be bugged."

Well, shit.

Had they seen us making out in the truck? What about the dozens of treasonous conversations we'd had on the way to school?

"I believe that's a recent order," he reassured me. "We just have to be more careful from now on."

"Are there enough people here for me to hug you?"

He glanced around. Two more cars had just pulled into the parking lot.

"Yes."

I immediately put my arms around his waist and squeezed myself as close to him as I could. We'd established a rule, after the battle with Tommie, that we had to assume a vampire was watching us at all times. We'd gotten lax about it lately, but with this most recent brush with death and Kalare chewing me out, we were both more paranoid.

"The Council wanted me to go to college," Adrian continued, even though I was about to ditch that conversation and ask him about what the hell had happened the day before with, well, hell, and the clearing and Julian and everything. "Something about keeping up appearances. I told them that as long as Lucian was missing, I was staying. That it was in my character as a human in this community to remain here and continue the search for my brother. They didn't overtly ask if I was staying because of you but it was…hinted at. I acted indignant."

"I want you to go, but I'm glad you're staying," I admitted. "But we can talk about that later. Are you okay? Farrar shuttled me out of there as soon as we got back. I heard you screaming."

He tightened his hug. "I honestly don't remember that part. I remember climbing back up the cliff and seeing that you were all right, and then…that's it. Next thing I knew it was midnight and I was back home."

"You were bleeding everywhere. You scared the shit out of me."

"You scared the shit out of *me*."

"You're the one that had big-ass cuts all down your back! I didn't get so much as a scratch."

He winced. "When I went over the cliff, I thought for sure Sabine had gotten you. I've never seen one of us that starved before. I couldn't fight them all, not alone."

I stared out at the parking lot. "Farrar stopped Sabine—barely. Vincent and Javan held themselves back but wouldn't have resisted for long. Kalare's really the one that saved us both."

"Remind me to send her a gift basket."

That was good. If Adrian was joking, that meant things weren't completely bad.

"What happened when you woke up?" I asked.

He stared vacantly out at the parking lot, dark circles under his eyes. "I told them my version of events. My wounds finally closed up. Julian couldn't decide if he was pissed at me or not."

"What happened with that?" I asked, looking up at him. "Did you hit Julian with a rock or something? How did he pass out?"

Adrian snorted. "Wish I'd hit him with a rock; that would have been more satisfying. No, I…I don't know. I just knew that I needed him to stop, and suddenly, he stopped." He shook his head, then kissed my temple and left his nose resting against my cheek. "What I did to Julian, what I did to my father—I've never heard of either of those things happening before. The Council is already suspicious about me taking on a demon; I couldn't risk letting them know what happened yesterday. But…" he glanced down at me. "I asked Julian what he'd experienced on his end. Problem is, he was so bloodthirsty he can't really remember it. Says the whole thing felt like a dream. As of now, they're blaming his black-out on it being his first trip to hell, not on anything to do with me."

"But it *was* you?"

Adrian nodded. "I just don't know what I did. Or how."

"Well, you saved him, and me," I pointed out. "That doesn't seem like a bad thing."

"True."

Across the parking lot, a young boy with sandy blonde hair got out of a minivan to hug his older brother goodbye. It wasn't Lucian, but it looked vaguely enough like him from a distance that I'd almost run toward that kid several times before when their mom dropped them off for school. I snuggled further into Adrian, resting my head on his shoulder, dreading the answer to my next question.

"They didn't find him, did they?"

Adrian shook his head. "No. They didn't tell me much, but even Farrar seemed spooked by the trip. And the fact that they didn't give Kalare the proper signals that they were coming back....you shouldn't have been anywhere near them when they woke up. They could have killed you, and that was their fault, not ours. As for the rest, I can't get a straight answer out of anyone, and I can't act too curious, especially around Farrar."

"So what does that mean?"

"It means we lie low," he murmured. "Keep our heads down. Farrar reported back to the Council. I wasn't sure if they were going to let me go to school today or talk to you. It was Kalare who convinced Farrar that we needed to keep everything as normal as possible until they got more information."

My heart raced at the mention of her. I'd forgotten to tell him that part. "Adrian—Kalare knows about us."

He froze. A long moment passed. "That's not good," he said finally.

"She knows we're paired, too. Farrar tried to compel me yesterday and she just put it together on her own. Said we were stupid and reckless and going to get ourselves killed."

Adrian rubbed his forehead against mine, letting out a long breath. "She's probably right." A half beat later he pulled back and looked at me, face paling. "Did you say Farrar tried to compel you?"

"Er, yeah. Told me to go home and not talk to anyone about what happened. I kind of played along, but Kalare caught on. She's covering for us for now, but I honestly don't know why. She also told me not to play along next time someone tried to compel me. Because apparently there's going to be a next time."

Adrian opened his mouth, then closed it, then rested his chin on his fist, thinking. "Kalare might be sympathetic toward our…situation. She has access to levels of information I can only dream about. If she feels protective toward you we should try and exploit that."

I made a face at him. "Or not. Because we're not actually spies, here. Or terrible people."

He blinked at me, then nodded, slowly blushing. "Sometimes I forget that you're not one of us. Mariana wouldn't bat an eye at fostering a false relationship to further the Council's agenda. I'm…glad, that you wouldn't want to do that. And I'm sorry for suggesting it. I've been spending too much time around my family."

More cars were pulling into the parking lot. I saw Trish's truck, and my good mood vanished.

"Speaking of damaged relationships," I muttered.

He glanced around and saw Trish's truck. "Ah."

I leaned into his arm. "I miss Trish."

"Have you tried talking to her again?"

"Sort of," I muttered. "She helped me up after I tripped the other day. As soon as I mentioned you, she split."

Adrian winced. "I'm sorry."

It was my turn to wince. "That wasn't what—it wasn't your fault. I mean, yes, it is, but only because she thinks you're an ass. Because of the dance, and…stuff." I winced again. I wasn't good at this. I turned and looked him in the face. "She doesn't know anything. That's the problem," I said, watching her disappear into Mr. Warren's room. "She doesn't know anything."

Adrian tensed. "We've isolated you," he muttered. "*I've* isolated you."

I opened my mouth, then closed it. The bell rang. I stood up and pulled Adrian to his feet.

"We're doing the best we can. Like you said, we just have to keep moving forward."

He smiled weakly and put his arm through mine as we headed toward our classrooms.

"What I'm trying to say," I continued, "is that I love you. And I'm going to make Trish love you again, too, even if it kills me."

We stopped in front of Mr. Warren's room. Adrian reached down and kissed me tenderly on my cheek. "So stubborn," he murmured.

I pecked him on the nose and smiled, then headed inside.

Trish glanced at me as I came in but otherwise ignored me.

"All right, everyone," said Mr. Warren, standing at the front of the room. "Your final essays are due Wednesday, Thursday we're presenting in small groups, and Friday I'm bringing popcorn and we're going to have a party because I don't feel like grading any more papers."

A cheer went up around the room. Mr. Warren was pretty much everyone's favorite teacher.

After school, I caught up to Trish as she was fishing her keys out of her backpack. Maybe Adrian was right. Maybe I just needed to be direct.

"Hey," I said as I stopped next to her truck, overly cheerful.

She glanced at me, found her keys, and opened the door. "Hey."

"Look, Trish, I miss you," I blurted out. She raised an eyebrow at me. Yeah, not so smooth with the direct communication thing. "I mean, I know why you're mad, and I get it, but I want to be friends again."

She threw her backpack in the passenger seat. "You still dating Adrian?"

I frowned at her. "Yeah."

She turned back to me. "Then no can do."

Damn it, she wasn't going to make this easy. "I know you think Adrian hurt me, but we worked through it. You don't have to be mad at him for me anymore."

She gave me a look of pure disbelief and slammed the door shut. "You think I won't talk to you because I'm mad at *Adrian*? I'm mad at *you*, Cait. You used me. You used me to spend time with him, to cover up *sleeping* with him. And then you lied to me about it. You made me lie to your aunt and uncle about it."

I took a step forward to interrupt, to explain—but I couldn't.

Because I had used her. The sleeping part wasn't true, but the lying part was.

Well, the sleeping part, too, but that was literally *sleeping*, and it was only so that Adrian could prevent my nightmares from happening. Those encounters had been about as far from sexy as it was possible to be. She didn't know that, though.

Trish let out a frustrated breath. "Look, I'm not trying to punish you or anything, and you're free to hang out with the rest of the girls. But your relationship with Adrian is the definition of dysfunctional, and I'm not going to be a part of it."

This was so not how I wanted this conversation to go. "I wish I could explain to you why that's not true," I told her. Or at least why it was mostly not true.

"Yeah," she sad, opening the door. "Me, too."

She started to get in and I put my hand on the door. "Trish, just wait! Just—please. My aunt and uncle are throwing Adrian a surprise graduation party next Saturday. I'm inviting everyone from our class and Adrian's. I'd love to have you there. His aunt and uncle are even showing up. You can ogle them and make up funny backstories. You love making up funny backstories."

I could see her forming a polite decline, so I closed the door and pressed my nose against the glass. "Just think about it, okay?" I said mutedly, fogging up the glass.

Her mouth twitched, fighting a smile.

"See you at Prom!" I gave her a ridiculous grin and a thumbs up and ran away, limbs flailing dramatically. I didn't dare glance back to see if she thought it was funny.

I needed Trish back. I was willing to make a complete idiot of myself in order to do so.

The one thing I couldn't do was tell her the truth.

PROM-A-LONG-A-DING-DONG

6

hey were hoping you would fail," Other Tommie said bluntly. "They were hoping I would kill her—*because they know what she is.*"

"You're lying."

"Adrian," Other Tommie said sadly, "you were intended to let her die."

The moment froze and Tommie materialized next to me. "I was a bit over-dramatic there. Too much?"

It was weird that I was becoming used to these little dream conversations with an imaginary version of my stalker and would-be murderer.

"A tad," I confirmed. "But it was an intense moment, with you trying to rip my arms off and all."

"Good points, though," he countered. "You were intended to die."

"By the Council?"

He didn't reply.

"Why do you answer some questions, but not others?" I asked, irritated with him as usual.

He rolled his eyes. "Why do you think?"

I stared at him blankly.

He frowned. "You're really slow sometimes."

I frowned at him harder, more in thought than frustration. "There are some things you can't say, aren't there?"

He nodded.

"But why? Why some things and not others?"

He sighed, then very pointedly tapped his own temple. I had no idea what he meant.

And then it clicked.

"You only know what I know," I said finally. "Because you're in my head."

"Bingo."

I stared at Tommie. "This is weird. I'm basically talking to myself."

"Correct."

"All right," I said. "There's obviously something you're trying to get me to understand, but for whatever reason you can't just come out and say it."

He nodded.

"Except for these little instant replays and color commentary based on information pulled from memories of this actual event?"

He nodded again.

"Okay. Weird, but okay." I walked closer to the frozen images of Adrian, Other Me, and Other Tommie. With a thought, the moment played again.

"They were hoping I would kill her," Other Tommie said, "*because they know what she is.*"

With another thought, the moment froze. I turned to regular

Tommie.

"You seem to think I'm special. Am I?"

Tommie stared at me, saying nothing. Guess my subconscious hadn't made up its mind about that one.

"Fine, then," I told him. "Show me what you can."

Tommie grinned at me, as if pleased that I was finally catching on. The memory glitched, leaping backward in time.

Other Tommie was still holding me, keeping me from Adrian.

"Then tell me why they haven't told you who she is," he demanded. "Tell me why she wasn't better guarded."

A legitimate question, asked by the man the Council had repeatedly told me was my enemy.

And he was. He was definitely a bad guy.

But who said there could only be one bad guy?

Somehow Prom had been moved to the back burner of my life.

Adrian was a senior, graduating in a week, and this would be our last high school dance, so it really should have been more important, but between the little skirmish at the cliff where half the vampires tried to snack on me, finishing up my internship application, writing essays, studying for exams, searching the library for information about Lucian and Tommie, and worrying about Trish, Prom was upon me before I was properly prepared. I was up until midnight at Adrian's finishing my dress, which Rachel hadn't been too happy about, but I'd called her ahead of time to let her know I'd be home late. Joe, as usual, had been waiting up for me in the living room to make sure I got home safe, and probably to make sure that Adrian didn't sneak in again. To be fair, if Norah had a boyfriend, I'm pretty sure he'd do the same thing with her.

He was such a dad.

But I was kind of okay with that.

I slept in almost until noon, snoozing right through half a dozen texts from Adrian (what time should he pick me up?), Stephanie (should she do her hair up or down?) and Jenny (was it embarrassing to wear the same dress to Prom that she wore to Winter Formal?). I told Adrian to pick me up at six, told Stephanie that I loved her hair in a loose, curly bun, and told Jenny that if she wanted I could chop off the bottom of her gown and make it knee-length so that it looked different.

That's how I found myself sewing, talking on the phone, and kneeling on the floor of my bedroom in my sweatpants biting a row of pins between my teeth with only an hour to go before the most important dance of my life.

"Steph, I thin' ih loofs grea'!"

I made Jenny turn, pinning another section of her hem.

"But are you sure?" Steph asked, her voice high and tinny over the video-chat. "The pearl clips might be too winter-y."

I spat the rest of the pins onto my magnetic pin cushion. "You're wearing lace; pearls are perfect. I think the rhinestone ones would actually clash."

Stephanie sighed. "Oh, you're right. I hate this. But I love it. But I hate it. Thanks, Cait!"

I laughed and said goodbye, setting down my phone.

Then I stared angrily at Jenny's skirt. "Do you want the good news, or the bad news?"

Jenny paled, which was quite a feat given her complexion. "There's bad news?"

I sat back on the floor heavily. "Yes. The bad news is I forgot how heavy this fabric was, and if I try and hem it by hand, which I was planning on doing because I don't have time to go to Adrian's to use my sewing machine, it will look lumpy and bad."

Jenny looked crestfallen.

"The good news, however, is that I can still change the look of your dress without chopping any of it off."

She perked up. "How?"

I stood up, groaning—my right leg had fallen asleep from sitting on it too long—and limped over to my steamer chest. "I happen to have a roll of elastic and some extra chiffon in here from a project I never finished. I can whip you up an overlay skirt so it looks like your dress is two pieces."

I pulled out the fabric and showed it to her. It was a pre-hemmed, pre-creased dark blue, just a few shades lighter than her actual dress. It would add texture and movement and it would take about ten minutes to make.

"Can you really do that in time?" she asked.

I nodded. "It won't be the most sturdy thing in the world but I can hide the seams well enough for one night."

She smiled at me and I took that as confirmation. I limped over to her, pins and needles creeping up my leg, and measured her waist. "All right, you're all set. You can go do your hair and make up in the bathroom if you want while I finish this up."

She blinked at me. "Um…I…I didn't bring anything." She blushed vividly. "Trish helped me with all that for Winter Formal. And since you guys haven't been talking much lately, I didn't feel comfortable… well, I—I didn't want to bother her."

I mentally smacked myself. Of course Jenny was caught in the middle of our fight. "Just a sec." I walked out to the balcony and called over the railing. "Rachel? Can you help me for a minute?"

She came up the stairs with a basket of laundry. "You ready for me to do your hair?"

"Actually, could you do Jenny's? And maybe help her with her, y'know, face and stuff?"

Rachel peered over my shoulder at Jenny, who was still blushing furiously in the middle of my room. My aunt smiled at her warmly. "Of course! Come here and we'll get you ready."

Jenny followed my aunt into the bathroom. I could hear Rachel start to ask her what styles she liked and soon they were laughing and chatting like old friends. Rachel had a way of making people feel welcome, even against their will. I knew that firsthand.

With less than an hour to go, I stitched like mad, hiding the seam on the inside of the elastic. Fifteen minutes later I was done but Jenny wasn't, so I went ahead and put on my dress. Or rather, skirt and crop top. Spring had finally reared its humid head, and since Prom was outside, I'd decided to go for a more comfortable look. The waist-high skirt was made out of a stiff red silk that went just past my knees. The top was a black, hand-embroidered cap-sleeve crop top. Showed a hint of midriff, but was altogether far less scandalous than my Winter Formal dress and a heckuva lot easier to walk in. I threw my hair in an intentionally messy fishtail braid, added a couple geometric leather hairpins that I'd fashioned out of an old, lone glove that Rachel was going to toss out, and scurried into the bathroom with Jenny's overskirt. Rachel was just putting the finishing touches on Jenny, and like at Winter Formal, I had to stop and stare.

Jenny was tall, had nearly platinum blonde hair down to her waist, and had pale but remarkably unblemished skin. Without makeup— and in the well-worn baggy sweaters she favored—she looked pretty, but average, like the rest of us.

With her hair done and make up on, she was a freaking goddess.

Blinking, I handed her the skirt, which Rachel helped her shimmy into. It rested perfectly at her waist, giving the floor-length dress a whole new look.

"Dang," I said, admiring the ensemble. "Jenny, for real, you need to be in Vogue or something. Luke is going to faint."

She blushed again. "I'm not going with Luke."

"Oh!" I said, instantly embarrassed. "I'm so sorry for assuming; it's totally awesome if you go by yourself!"

"No," she said, blushing harder. "Um, Mark is actually my date? He came up early from Boston to…to go with me."

I stared at her for a moment.

"Dude!" I sputtered finally, shocked. "That's awesome! Way to scoop up a college boy!"

Rachel looked a little concerned, but Jenny wasn't her kid, so she didn't say anything. "Caitlin, Adrian is going to be here in fifteen minutes. You want me to do your make up?"

"Ah!" I said, looking up at the little bathroom wall clock. "Shoot, yes, please!"

Jenny stood up, smoothing out her dress. "Thank you so much for helping me, Caitlin, and thank you, Mrs. Master. I feel so pretty." She blushed, looking down at the floor. Rather impulsively, I leaned in and hugged her. Rachel even gave her a little squeeze.

I walked her to the front door and promised to sit at her table when we both got there, and then I ran back upstairs.

"All right, what kind of make up are we doing tonight?" Rachel sneezed a bit, hiding it in the crook of her arm.

"You still have that cold?" I asked.

She grimaced. "Won't seem to go away. I always get sick this time of year—changing weather, new allergens." She waved her hand as if to encompass all the other things that could cause one to have a cold. "All right," she said, sniffing a little. "We going smoky eye or what?"

"Yeah, I think so," I said, biting my lip. "But not too dark. Actually,

Rachel? Can you…teach me? So I can do it myself next time?" I realized that might sound rude. "Not because I don't want your help; I just never learned from Mom and I'd like to know how."

Rachel's eyes welled up, though from her allergies or from the mention of my mom I wasn't sure.

"Of course honey," she said. "All right, let's start with brushes. When's your birthday? I should really buy you a nice set."

True to his word, Adrian picked me up exactly at six, driving up in the Aston Martin. It was pretentious and terrible and I absolutely loved it. He'd worn a dove grey Armani suit, no tie, and the top buttons of his shirt undone, which was rather cheeky for him, but it was finally getting warm outside so maybe he was just hot.

I pinned his boutonniere to his coat slightly more successfully than I had at Winter Formal, and he slipped on my wrist corsage. It was made out of tiny pale green and blue succulents and mustard yellow craspedia (they were so unusual looking that I went and looked them up later—I'm not normally this savvy on botany). Against the red and black of my outfit, the corsage looked stunning.

Rachel took a million pictures, then Joe took pictures while Rachel posed with us, then Norah took pictures while Rachel and Joe posed with us, then Adrian took pictures while Norah, Rachel, and Joe posed with me. Norah had her tongue sticking out in every one, which was pretty much par for the course.

Finally, Adrian walked me out to the car and we were on our way.

Winter Formal was held in the school gym because there was no other building in town big enough to hold a dance. By spring, however, Stony Creek softened, blooming with wildflowers. The town square had a pavilion where most of the locals got married, attended funerals, set up craft fairs, and went, most importantly, to the local high school Prom.

As soon as we parked I could see that the pavilion had been decorated with strings of soft white lights. The trellises were overgrown with thick, green ivy. Tea light candles littered the dozen or so round tables that had been covered with white tablecloths.

Trish was already there with Ben, seated at the center-most table, which was going to make sitting away from them difficult. Maybe it was an invitation to join?

Ah, nope. There came Laura and Meghan with their dates, claiming the remaining seats. Ben caught sight of us and waved, but a harsh look from Trish had him sheepishly lowering his arm.

I spotted Stephanie just sitting down at a nearby table with Tim. I dragged Adrian over quickly so we could claim the seats next to them.

"Steph, you look gorgeous!" I said, giving her a hug.

She did—the pearl hair clips complemented her red hair beautifully, and the ivory, knee-length dress was a vision.

"Thanks!" she beamed. "It was actually my mom's Prom dress. She found it in the attic a few weeks ago, and it fit me perfectly. Can you believe that?"

Tim was wearing a powder-blue tux from the '80s, complete with a ruffly white pirate-esque shirt. It fit him well, but looked absolutely ridiculous. "My Dad's wedding tux," he explained. "When Stephanie said she was wearing her mom's Prom dress, I went digging in my attic and found this. Couldn't resist."

"It's certainly bold," Adrian said, trying to not to smile.

A few minutes later Jenny joined us, arm-in-arm with a very amused-looking Mark.

"Hey, everyone," she said, already blushing. "This is Mark. He's my date. And Trish's brother."

Everyone knew that already. It was a very small town.

"Hey, guys," he said, waving. He was wearing khakis and an old collared shirt with the sleeves rolled up to his elbows. His hair was up in a man bun. Jenny started to sit, but Mark stopped her so he could pull her chair out. She sat down, blushing harder than ever.

I glanced over at Trish. She was frowning deeply at Mark.

At least I wasn't the only one she was mad at.

Back at our table, there was a moment of strained silence as no one quite knew what to say. Then Mark laughed. "Not gonna lie, it's a little weird being back."

Jenny's smile slipped. She was the reason he was in town. He seemed to notice, however, and put his arm around the back of her chair, clearly indicating that he was there for *her*. "But I forgot how nice spring is here. Boston's already muggy, and I can't afford air conditioning."

Tim asked him about Boston and what the art program was like, and soon the tension eased. I caught Mark moving his arm from the back of Jenny's chair to her shoulder, holding on lightly, as if afraid she might break, or run.

She practically glowed.

Jenny was one of the quietest people I knew, but Mark somehow drew her out. Whenever he was asked a question, he turned it into a question for her. She was shy at first, as she always was, but within a matter of minutes she'd warmed up, almost like she'd forgotten that she normally only said a few words a day to other people. Before I knew it, the whole table was laughing. Tim had his arm around Steph, Adrian had drawn my hand onto his knee and had threaded his fingers through mine, and Jenny couldn't stop smiling and sneaking adoring glances at Mark. Rather than being condescending or acting like he was some college big-shot, Mark spoke with us like we were old friends.

And so did Adrian. Unlike Winter Formal, where he'd practically ignored everyone the entire night, he was now engaged in the conversation, trading jokes and insults as if he'd been doing it his entire life. He'd known all these people longer than I had—by years, actually—but he'd never *really* interacted with them until I came along. He was an avid rule-follower, and he'd taken the Council's mandate against friendships with humans very seriously. But he'd also been mandated to protect me by pretending to be in a relationship with me. By accident, I'd become his reason for interacting with people he should have been friends with all along. He'd even told me, to my face, back at Christmas up at the cabin, that I was his excuse for being the kind of person he'd always wanted to be. The situation that caused all this might have been awful, but not all the consequences were bad. He'd helped me through the darkest days of my mom's death. I'd helped him find his place in the human world. And tonight, it felt like we were finally ourselves.

Just as the sun set, Tim stood. "That's my cue," he said, pointing at the sky. He had Stephanie peck him on the cheek for good luck. Doing loud vocal exercises, he walked to the stage at the front of the pavilion.

"If I could have your attention for a few minutes, please, please," he said, mouth practically enveloping the microphone, "it is now time to announce the senior prophecies. Principal Daniels, if you would do the honors?"

An amused-looking Principal Daniels handed Tim a sealed envelope.

Tim opened it with a flourish and pulled out a sheet of paper, then put on a ridiculous pair of tortoise shell glasses. "We shall begin in alphabetical order," he said, adopting a hammy British accent. He cleared his throat dramatically and adjusted the glasses. "Luke Avery: you are most likely to become a fighter pilot, then the youngest president in the history of the United States, before saving the earth from an alien invasion."

Someone from the crowd yelled, "Ripoff!" while another person yelled, "*Independence Day!*"

"Hey, you guys wrote these, not me," Tim shouted back, hand cupped over the mic. "All right, all right. Jessica Barnes: you are most likely to join the Peace Corps and solve world hunger. Oh, well, that's boring."

Again, people laughed and cheered, and the senior girl blushed.

"Adrian de la Mara: you are most likely to cure cancer, write a fifty-eight-volume encyclopedia of the world, beat Stephen Hawking in a thumb war, and win the male and female versions of America's Next Top Model—all before breakfast the day after graduation."

Now people really cheered. I couldn't help but grin, too. Adrian was shaking his head, but I saw a smile. Tim finished up the rest of the prophecies, all about seniors I didn't know as well.

"And finally, we come to your Prom King and Queen!" Everyone began to cheer, but Tim cut them off, tossing the senior prophecies to the ground. "But due to changes in the administration's policy, we are no longer crowning kings and queens. Political correctness, I know, booooo. But you all know who the winners would have been—that's right, this sexy fella right here," he said, pointing to himself, "and my beautiful date, Stephanie Campbell!"

Our table hooted and hollered and Stephanie turned almost as bright red as her hair.

"Ope—I can see Principal Daniels coming to expel me, so before I get kicked out of school, let me announce that the dancing will now begin!"

He was swatted offstage playfully by Principal Daniels. Tim jogged over to our table, grinning, and we all congratulated him on his announcing skills. Mark suggested that he should try his hand at stand-up comedy, and Tim looked intrigued. He pulled Stephanie to her feet and started talking excitedly about what his first routine could be.

"You want to dance?" Adrian asked, smiling so softly it made my heart ache. Unlike the disastrous Winter Formal, it seemed as though he was genuinely here, fully invested in the moment, in the dance, lame and human as it was.

"Actually, yeah," I said, standing. "Gotta give this new skirt a whirl."

I led him out onto the dance floor. A horrifying pop song was playing, something so sugary and stupid I would normally have cringed and covered my ears.

But tonight was Prom.

And I was going to Prom as hard as I could.

I threw my hands up in the air and danced the crap out of it.

Adrian stared at me for a moment like he didn't know who I was. But soon we were surrounded in a crush of bodies, everyone seeming to catch on to the infectious, goofy spirit of it all. I danced around Adrian in circles, doing a half hokey-pokey, half jitterbug, with a little bit of twerk thrown in for good measure. A grin twitched at the corner of Adrian's mouth. I waggled my eyebrows at him, mouthing the words to the song. Finally, he burst out laughing.

"All right, you got me. How do the young folk do this nowadays?"

"Put your hands on your hips," I said, very seriously, "and kind of stick your butt out." He did as he was told. "And then put your finger up and waggle it around like nuh-uh, nobody can touch this butt. And then you move back and forth and throw in a few enthusiastic pelvic thrusts," I said, demonstrating, "and that's pretty much it."

He turned red. "Way to start me out with the beginner moves. I think I need to work my way up to the pelvic thrusts."

I laughed, he laughed, and we danced. After a few minutes, he was hot enough that he took his coat off and slung it back on his chair at the table. But when he came back, he was looking at me very seriously, unbuttoning the cuffs of his sleeves. And then he rolled them up.

He rolled up the sleeves of his *Armani* dress shirt.

"Oh damn," I said, looking at him gleefully. "Does this mean you're ready to bring it?"

Adrian nodded.

"I knew this day would come," I breathed. "It was foretold in the ancient prophecies."

Adrian reached up and unbuttoned two more buttons on his shirt until it was undone almost to his waist. Now it was my turn to blush. He was seriously committing.

The next song came on. It was *Footloose.*

"You ready for this?" he asked.

I nodded my head, then shook my head, then nodded my head.

As soon as the first verse came on, Adrian was lip-syncing.

Then he was going up to people and lip-syncing *with* them. He even stole the wireless mic from the stand at the edge of the stage and used it as a prop.

And then it got to the chorus.

And then he did the Kevin Bacon dance.

My straight-laced, Ivy League, Latin-speaking, European-raised vampire boyfriend was doing the Kevin Bacon dance.

There was a single moment of shock throughout the entire crowd—

—and then all hell broke loose.

He whirled over to me and dipped me almost to the floor, giving me a kiss that was half wild and completely comedic. A shout of cheers went up from everyone else, and it wasn't long before we'd somehow agreed, without speaking, to form ourselves into lines to do our best renditions of the Prom dance from the actual movie.

It was the stupidest thing I'd ever done.

It was the most fun I'd ever had.

It was absolutely perfect.

When the song ended, even the teachers cheered and clapped.

Adrian was sweaty, grinning down at me. As he wrapped me up in his arms, laughing, hugging me for the pure joy it, I couldn't help but feel proud. He was here. He was happy. He was really, genuinely, dazzlingly happy. It was startling and perfect. I thought I'd already fallen for him as hard as I could, but it was that moment that made me realize how much more there was. To him, to us, to life. A slow song came on, and he pulled me close, arms wrapped around my shoulders. I hid my face in the curve of his neck.

"That was amazing," I whispered so only he could hear. "I love you."

He pressed a tender kiss to my cheek. "I love you, too."

A wave of serenity washed over me. It felt like when Adrian had to spend the nights in my room on my tiny twin bed, to block the night-mares. I felt at ease. I felt safe.

I felt home.

We danced for hours to everything that came on: Top 40 hits, old Journey songs, classic rock, even jazz standards and an odd Christmas tune that had gotten mixed in with the playlist. We danced every style we could think of, from incorrect but spirited waltzes to the Nae-Nae. Even Jenny danced, though mostly on the fringe, and mostly swaying back and forth to the slower stuff. Mark was adorable with her. Trish threw me a brief smile in the middle of her favorite song, though she stayed in her circle with Meghan and Laura and Ben while I danced with Stephanie and Adrian and Tim.

We danced until we were sweaty and gross and the chaperones and teachers told us they were tired and wanted to go to bed, which meant we had to leave. It was the most fun I'd had in months, the lightest I'd felt since well before my mom died.

And it wasn't until we'd said our goodbyes and were heading toward the car that I realized the whole Praetorian Guard had shown up to watch.

MATCHMAKER

7

They were waiting just past the Aston Martin in the shadows beyond the lights of the parking lot. Nobody looked happy, not even Kalare.

"What's going on?" Adrian asked, tense.

"The Council asked us to provide extra security," Farrar said in that unreadably neutral voice of his.

"Was there a threat?" Adrian asked, his voice on the edge of sounding angry.

Julian pushed off from the Escalade he'd been leaning against. "Lucian's alive."

My heart surged in my chest. Beside me, Adrian went very still. "How do you know?"

Julian snorted. "He called the house."

"He—what?"

"He called the house," Farrar repeated. "And asked to speak to

Caitlin."

Everyone's eyes flicked to me.

"Before we could trace the call, the line went dead. It's safe to assume the demon still has him. We came here to make sure that you were safe, in case he was in the vicinity."

Or to make sure they could kill me and make it look like it was Adrian's dad.

"I didn't notice anything out of the ordinary," Adrian said slowly. "Did you, Caitlin?"

I shook my head.

"Except for your dancing," Julian muttered under his breath. I thought I saw Kalare kick him. Sabine eyed my Prom dress up and down, her face just shy of an outright sneer.

"Just as well," Farrar said. "Please be aware that we will be increasing security for the foreseeable future now that we know Lucian is alive, and still in this dimension. Adrian, you may take Caitlin home."

Adrian nodded curtly and turned, leading me back to the car. Through the window, I could see Kalare climb into a blacked-out Jeep. She turned the headlights on, but didn't pull away.

Looks like she was our escort home.

The others stood around the Escalade, speaking quietly. I pulled out my phone and typed, *We can't talk here, can we?*

He put a hand over my screen to block the light and shook his head.

I erased the message and hunched down into my seat, both elated and horrified.

Lucian had called.

Lucian had tried to call *me.*

Lucian was alive.

My internship application was due Monday, so tired as I was from Prom, I was spending all of Sunday at the mansion getting my portfolio ready. But not being able to talk about Lucian was killing me, so I'd had Rachel call Mariana to invite Adrian over for a late breakfast. Rachel was something of a secret weapon that I'd newly discovered—if she asked the de la Maras for something, they felt more obliged to say yes.

I'd tried not to scarf down the waffles and bacon she and Joe had made, impatient to have a few minutes to speak with Adrian alone. As soon as it was polite to leave, I told Joe and Rachel that we were going for a walk and hurried Adrian out the door and into the woods. We kept to the path until we got to the giant boulder where we'd technically first met back when I'd just moved here and The Storm had sparked the whole insanity with Adrian's family. We'd met again at this spot on my 17th birthday when he'd told me what he really was.

I climbed up the exposed roots of a neighboring tree trunk, loose dirt raining down onto my boots as I used the roots as a ladder. I wriggled impatiently onto the rock, looking around us in every direction. I didn't see anyone, but that didn't necessarily mean no one was there.

"We alone?" I whispered.

Adrian climbed up next to me and did a much slower, more careful rotation, listening.

"Birds and bugs, mostly. No vampires."

I sat down and took a deep breath. I didn't come out here often enough—it was quiet, the breeze rustling gently through the evergreens. It smelled like pine and summer.

Adrian sat next to me, holding my hand in his.

"So," I said, not knowing how to begin now that we were out here. "Lucian's alive."

Adrian looked grim, but a fierce smile crept over his face. "He's alive."

But the smile soon crumbled. He buried his face in his hands and for a long, confused moment I thought he was laughing. Then I realized he was trembling.

I scooted closer on the boulder and touched his arm lightly, not sure what was happening. He just sat there for an excruciatingly long five seconds, not acknowledging me. But then he turned slightly, resting his head on my shoulder. I wrapped my arms around him softly, and he buried his face in my hair, not crying, not making a sound, just shaking.

"I thought he was dead," Adrian whispered a minute later. "A part of me actually thought he was dead. We were searching the library, we were looking, but…" He trailed off, falling into silence.

I didn't have any siblings. My parents were both gone. But I had Rachel now, and Joe, and Norah. I didn't even like Norah all that much, but the thought of something happening to her, the thought of someone like Tommie kidnapping her, made me sick.

What was worse, in a way, is that it was Lucian. Lucian, who didn't understand so much about the world, Lucian who walked barefoot and crawled over furniture like a spider and hung upside down from library ceilings and looked half-dead except when he was laughing.

Lucian, who might simply have opened the door and walked away from all of us without a second thought.

"I know it's not fair," Adrian said slowly, pulling away from me, "but I'm jealous of you."

I blinked, perplexed. "Jealous?"

Adrian nodded, trying not to look bitter. "Lucian called you—not me."

I opened my mouth, then closed it. Then opened it and closed it again.

Adrian shot a quick smile at me. "I know. It's stupid. It's not your fault, and it's a miracle he called at all. He's alive, and I should be happy about that—and I am. But I was the one who took care of him. And he called *you*."

A dumb, stubborn part of me wanted to point out that I cared about Lucian, too, but I understood what he really meant: he'd loved Lucian when no one else in his family had. They had a bond I envied. I knew Adrian loved me, but he would literally go to hell and back for his brother.

"We'd been practicing, y'know, for graduation," Adrian said, staring down at the forest floor. "Holding mock ceremonies so he would know what was going on, how to act normal. I had to pester Mariana and Dominic about it for months before they agreed he could come. Too many humans, too much noise and excitement. We'd set up in the library and he would watch the imaginary graduates go by, and when he'd see me he would wave and jump up on his seat and clap. I finally got him to just sit still and smile as I walked by. He was so proud."

I felt my eyes burn with sudden tears. That would have been huge, for Lucian. To be around people. To be normal for one day.

"I'm going to kill him," Adrian said so calmly I almost didn't catch it. I looked up at him, startled.

"You—what?"

Adrian looked at me, eyes shimmering slightly in their molten silver. "I'm going to kill my father. He's hurt too many people. He killed my mother. He killed Mariana's mother and Julian's mother and Lucian's mother. He almost killed you. And now he's taken Lucian. So

I'm going to kill him."

Once again, I opened my mouth, then closed it. What does one say when one's vampire boyfriend vows to kill his demon father? Moral conundrums aside, *could* Adrian kill a demon? From what I understood, demons weren't kill-able, only banishable. But from the calm, blank look on Adrian's face, he didn't seem to be in the mood to discuss his plans.

I took his hand and brought his knuckles to my lips. "Adrian?" I said softly.

He turned to me slowly, and blinked, as if coming back from somewhere far away.

"Stay with me, okay?"

He blinked again, then nodded slowly. Shaking his head slightly, he let out a long breath, and smiled. "Always."

The de la Mara family connection may have gotten my name in the mix, but I actually had to work for my spot in the Myriad program. I needed designs for a full line (though I could pick any season I wanted), an artist statement, mood boards, brand name, rough logo, and photos of three complete outfits. My Winter Formal dress was serving as the evening wear sample so that shaved off a huge amount of time, but I still had to assemble a pair of jeans and a slouchy sweater. I was using pictures Stephanie had gotten of me the night before in my Prom outfit to serve as the day dress look, since it could lean casual or fancy. But that still left two outfits unphotographed.

It was time to bring in the big guns.

"Kalare?" I asked, peeking into her room. She'd taken over my former suite on the third floor, so she was literally across the hall from my sewing studio.

She was sprawled back on the bed, a cigarette dangling from her lips and a bottle of beer sweating onto the very expensive silk comforter.

"Yeah?" she asked, not looking up from her book. She was also wearing reading glasses.

"I have a question, but first, why are you wearing glasses?"

"That's already a question," she said, still not looking up from her book.

"Fine, then I have two questions."

She ripped a corner off the beer label and stuck it between the pages as a bookmark. "They're hipster frames, no prescription. Mariana's got the upper class covered so I figured I should represent the youth of America."

I couldn't help but grin at her. "You'll do perfectly."

She frowned at my grin. "I don't like the sound of that."

"Look, I have this application due tomorrow and I need your help."

She eyed me warily. "Doing what?"

I shot her an overly exasperated look. "Holding stuff, and stuff. Come on! Do you want me to live up to my potential or not?"

She snorted, but set the book down and scooted to the edge of the bed. "I'm not your mother, you doofus."

I grinned at her as she followed me into my studio.

"Take your biker death jacket off."

She glanced down at her leather jacket. "Biker death jacket?"

"It's all ripped and covered in spikes! You look like you belong in *The Lost Boys*."

"Keifer Sutherland was hot."

"Yeah, in the *'80s*."

"That was practically yesterday for me."

"Great! Jacket off."

While she frowned and slid the jacket off, I quickly texted Adrian: *Bring Julian to my studio.*

A moment later he texted back: *Why?*

Just do it, I typed. *It'll be funny.*

As soon as Kalare turned back to me I slid the phone in my pocket. She was down to her ripped skinny jeans, biker boots, and a white tank top. I half-expected her to be covered in tattoos, but her skin was completely free of ink. Maybe vampires couldn't get tattoos?

"All right," she muttered around the cigarette, "what hell have you in store for me today?"

"I actually need you to change into this," I said, handing her the dark green velvet dress that I'd made for Winter Formal.

She looked at the fabric as though it were Cindy Lou Who and she was the Grinch.

"Yeah, I don't really do dresses. Go get Sabine."

I stared pointedly at her. "Sabine literally wants to kill me. Help me, Kalare Whatever-Your-Last-Name-Is. You're my only hope."

"You weren't even born when that came out," she muttered.

"Dude, put the dress on. I just need to snap a picture for the application; it'll take thirty seconds."

"Why can't you put the dress on and I take the picture?"

"Are you a photographer?"

She feigned indignation. "I dabble."

I rolled my eyes. "I'm already featured in the other outfit. I can't be in both of them; that's like, narcissistic. I want them to take me seriously. Dress."

She glowered at me, but stuck the cigarette behind her ear and went behind the changing screen in the corner of the room.

"You owe me big time," she grumbled.

"Yeah, yeah."

There were the sounds of struggling and a string of inventive curses. "How the hellfire do you even get this *on*?"

"It literally just goes over your head."

Several more curses later, Kalare stepped around the edge of the screen at the exact moment the door to the studio opened. A very irritated Julian came into the room followed by a very confused Adrian.

Kalare and Julian stopped dead, staring at each other.

Then Kalare turned to me, glaring. "I'm going to kill you."

"Oh hush," I said, trying my best not to burst into giggles. The look on Julian's face was priceless. He was rooted in place, just staring at Kalare.

To be fair, it was a pretty freaking amazing dress—Adrian had had a similar reaction when I'd worn it.

The floor-length dark green velvet—which was barely floor length for Kalare, and was only floor-length for me when I was wearing very, very tall heels—had a hand-beaded halter neck and an open back—a completely open back. From the top of Kalare's neck to the top of her hips there was absolutely no material. It was somehow classy and risqué at the same time.

I was a genius.

Adrian looked at me like I was crazy. "You…needed us?"

"Julian, actually," I confirmed. Julian didn't even look at me, he was still busy staring at Kalare. With her dark, punk hair, bright red lipstick, and kickboxer's body, Kalare should have been at odds with the feminine gown, but instead she just looked like a sexy Bond girl, the kind with a thigh-holster and throwing knives.

"Adrian, you still have your Winter Formal suit, right?"

"Yeah," he said, finally seeing where I was going with this.

"Julian, if you'd be so kind as to put that on, we can get this done in less than five minutes."

He finally blinked, and glanced at me. "What?"

"The tux. Go put the tux on."

"I'm sorry," he said, glancing back and forth between me and Kalare. "I don't understand what's happening."

Still fuming, Kalare crossed her arms defensively over her chest, which actually only increased her cleavage. "Caitlin is a scheming son of a goatherder."

"Son of a goatherder?" I asked. "Maybe *daughter* of a goatherder, but not—"

"Why are you wearing a dress?" Julian asked Kalare rather bluntly. "You never wear…that."

Kalare blushed even more. "Our least favorite human has conned me into helping with her internship application."

"And now I'm conning you as well," I told Julian. "Adrian, if you please?"

Adrian grabbed Julian by the shoulders and wheeled him out of the room. "Come on, it's always faster when Caitlin gets her way."

As soon as they were gone, Kalare pounced.

"I am taking this off *now*."

She whirled and headed toward the changing screen. I grabbed hold of her arm, but kind of forgot she was a vampire. She just kept right on going. So I hugged her around the waist and ended up tripping her.

"No!" I said, clutching her ankles as she landed in a heap. "You will help me with my application if it kills us both! I need to get out of this hell hole for the summer! This *literal* hell hole! There was literally a hole leading to hell here just a few months ago!"

She sat up, glaring at me. "Is this really about the application, or are you playing Susie Matchmaker?"

I huffed a piece of hair out of my eyes, breathing hard—Kalare was strong. "Both."

I could see her about to protest so I cut her off. "But I legitimately need these photos for my application. One of them has to be staged with a second model and you two are both insanely attractive and look the same age."

That was a huge lie—the application said no such thing.

I was totally being Susie Matchmaker.

And making vampires blush was quickly becoming my new favorite sport.

"Besides," I continued, because she still didn't look convinced, "you guys have totally screwed up my life and I think I deserve to make you uncomfortable for five minutes. Call it poetic justice."

"Excuse me, I had *nothing* to do with screwing up your life. I came into the picture well after your life was screwed up. And that's not poetic—never mind, just, fine, let's get this over with. You've guilted me into feeling bad for you, you little punk."

I grinned. "Admit it. You like the dress."

She glowered at me. "It's…a dress."

She carefully arranged the hem around her bare feet.

I grinned, stood, and offered her my hand. She took it and almost wrenched my arm off, standing.

I was still rubbing my shoulder when Julian came back into the room.

Holy Coco Chanel.

Now, Adrian is attractive. He'd been attractive when he wore this very same charcoal-gray Armani suit to Winter Formal. But Julian was a paid, professional model. He literally oozed sexiness for a living. As far as I knew, oozing sexiness was actually one of his vampire powers.

Kalare's face twitched. She turned to me. "All right, you got us all gussied up, now what do you want us to do?"

I pulled out my phone and surveyed the room through the camera.

"Go stand by the window," I told them. Kalare shuffled over awkwardly while Julian strolled gracefully. Even highly uncomfortable he looked more self-assured than anyone I knew.

I peeked at them through the camera again, then headed for the light panel, winking at Adrian as I passed. Kalare stood woodenly, arms held straight at her sides. I dimmed the overhead lights until the room was dark, most of the light coming from the windows. Not only did it disguise the fact that we were in a sewing studio, it also made them look Gothic and moody and romantic as hell.

"Okay, I really want to show off the back of the dress, so Julian, stand by that giant curtain and face me, and Kalare, you stand and face him slightly off to the side."

Julian glanced at Adrian, then at me, then…smiled?

Wow, he actually smiled. It was an amused, patronizing sort of smile, but it was a smile.

Damn, I was good.

His hair was a golden, tousled mess and the suit fit him almost perfectly, though he'd left off the tie and had the white shirt unbuttoned almost halfway down his chest. Kalare stomped into place beside him and stared straight over his shoulder. I rolled my eyes.

"Please, Kalare, look more uncomfortable."

She turned and glared at me. "I said I'd cooperate, I didn't say I was good at this."

"Julian, would you work some magic, please?"

I half-expected him to complain or refuse, just to irritate me, which he was fond of doing, but instead he slipped his hand on Kalare's hip, pulling her closer. Her hand automatically came to rest on his chest— though to stop herself or to pull closer I couldn't tell.

I swooped in and shot them from a billion angles, afraid Kalare would bolt any second.

But she didn't.

Julian looked perfectly at ease, head tilted forward intimately. Kalare was frozen in place, but she was frozen rather beautifully. I wasn't even sure she was breathing. With her hand on his chest, her back was arched dramatically, which made the dress look stunning.

I really was a genius.

"Kalare, move your left foot back a little."

She moved her left foot back. I didn't really need her to move her foot, but I wanted her to feel like I was taking this seriously as a photographer.

Now I understood why Trish had encouraged me to go after Adrian last fall—this was *fun*.

"Perfect," I said after a few more shots. Adrian was off to the side trying not to burst out laughing. "Okay, I just need a shot of the front of the dress. Julian, any suggestions?"

He thought about it a moment, then turned Kalare in his arms, pulling her back against him. His hand was still on her hip, his other hand on her upper arm as he cradled his face in the curve of her neck.

I almost forgot to take the picture.

Adrian walked over and nudged me gently. I snapped a billion more pictures from a billion more angles, then cleared my throat. "Um, that was great, I think I got it."

Kalare blinked, then pulled away from Julian as if he were on fire.

He blinked as well, an unreadable expression passing over his face, before his usual smug smile crept back into place. He looked from Kalare to me. "Hope you got what you needed," he said lightly. He was at the door before he looked back at Kalare. "You look good, K."

He smiled genuinely for a moment, then left.

Adrian cleared his throat. "I'm going to, uh…get the suit hung up. Excuse me."

He nodded at Kalare and left, closing the door behind him.

I was giddy. I scrolled through the photos and practically danced over to Kalare. "Dude, you've got to see these, they're *amazing*—"

"You shouldn't have done that." I looked up to find Kalare glaring at me, eyes glistening, not in vampire mode, but in sadness. Like, she was *crying*.

"But—" I started, holding up the phone.

"No," she interrupted, wiping angry tears from her face, smearing her eyeliner. "That was cruel and you know it."

She looked down at herself as if the image she saw disgusted her. "I'm such an idiot. He was making fun of me. I'm older than him and he was making fun of me for having a fucking crush."

I blinked at her, still trying to process why she was upset. "He wasn't making fun of you."

"It doesn't matter," she said, starting to pull her jeans on under the dress. "I'll play along, pretend I thought it was a big joke like I always do. I'm getting fucking tired of it."

She walked behind the screen and a moment later tossed the dress over the top of it. She was pulling her tank top back on as she came around the screen. "Good luck with your application," she said blankly. "I hope you get in."

"Kalare—"

But she was gone, closing the door roughly behind her.

Maybe I wasn't a genius after all.

GRADUATION

8

"If you're my subconscious, and I punch you in the face, that would basically be like punching myself in the face, right?"

Tommie quirked his head at me. I was beginning to notice my own mannerisms in his behavior now. "More or less," he replied. That one sounded like Adrian, actually.

Which gave me an idea.

"Hey, can you appear as someone else? Other than Tommie?"

And because I was apparently thinking about Adrian, Tommie instantly transformed into Adrian. Now there was the dead Adrian laying in the snow at our feet, and the Subconscious Adrian Spirit Guide standing before me.

"Better?" he asked.

"Less confusing than having pleasant conversations with the demon asshat I would literally like to beat to death with a two-by-four."

Adrian nodded in a very Adrian-like way.

"Can you be anyone?" I asked, getting another idea. "Like, could you be Neil Armstrong?"

Adrian turned into a hazy, vaguely astronaut-y looking figure.

"I can appear as anyone you know," my subconscious said through a voice-box in the space suit. "Since you do not have a clear idea of what Neil Armstrong looks like, I cannot appear accurately as Neil Armstrong."

"Huh," I said, the hazy form of the astronaut giving me a headache. "All right, how about…"

Without my even having to say a command out loud, the astronaut transformed into my mother.

She smiled pleasantly at me, waiting, dressed not in the nurse's uniform of my previous nightmares, but in her usual tennis shoes and jeans and sweater. She looked healthy and large and alive, like she had before she got cancer.

Instantly, it was hard to breathe.

"Don't get upset, Caitlin," she said in the voice of my mother, "I'm not really your mom."

I waved my arm, and she disappeared, only to be replaced with Lucian.

He stood there, arms limp, eyes covered in those aviator goggles, sandy blond hair sticking out in odd directions.

I knelt so we could be at eye-level. "Lucian?"

He looked at me blankly.

"Lucian, do you know anything about where you are? Can you tell me anything? Do you know why you called me?"

He shook his head, back and forth and back and forth. It was a gesture that Lucian would definitely have made.

A part of me wanted to just sit there and look at him. It had been months, now, and I didn't have a singe photo of Adrian's brother, just my memories, and those, like the memories of my parents, were already beginning to fade.

But here, Lucian stood before me as clearly as if this was all real. But it wasn't. There were no smells here, and no horizon. The light never changed; the breeze never blew. It was a dream, but Lucian…

Here, Lucian was alive, and well. I almost wished I could bring Adrian here, so he could see his brother.

But it was too painful. God, I missed the little guy.

In the time it took to blink, Lucian had been replaced by Trish. I nodded politely at her. "That's better. What can you show me about what happened when they came back from hell and Adrian knocked Julian unconscious?"

From one moment to the next, the snowy night clearing scene from February was replaced by the afternoon forest of a week ago. Other Me stood clutching the utility knife, watching horrified as Julian tackled Adrian over the side of the cliff. Sabine was standing at the edge of the clearing looking feral and beautiful and terrifying. The moment was frozen.

Trish walked over to Other Me, looked at the knife I was clutching, and rolled her eyes. Then she walked over to Adrian, hanging out over open air, and examined his face. I joined her. She was looking at his eyes.

It was then that I realized something I hadn't noticed that day.

His eyes weren't their normal human gray *or* his vampire silver— they were white.

Completely and totally white.

"You got that?" Joe asked me as I balanced the massive leather saddle on my head, holding it steady on either side with my hands. It was Monday afternoon, the last week of school before vacation, and

Joe was in full prep mode for summer guests.

"Yep," I said, not entirely sure that I did. No reason for him to think I was more of a burden than I already was.

I followed him out to the stables, a place I rarely visited due to the smell and Norah's definite territorial vibes. She might have to share the house with me, but the barn was my cousin's sacred domain.

"Just put it there," my uncle said, gesturing at a hook that stood out from the wall. I set the saddle on it and almost collapsed. The thing weighed as much as I did.

Joe was carrying two saddles with ease, and set them on their own hooks. He'd been bringing them into the house at night to do minor repairs so he could spend time with me and Norah while we did homework in the living room.

"Thanks, Caitlin," he said, ruffling my hair like I was ten years old. Or a boy. Uncle Joe was funny sometimes, didn't know entirely what to do with me even though I'd been living with them for nine months.

"Need anything else?"

"Not if you've got schoolwork."

I shrugged. "A bit, but it won't take long. I was also gonna ask—do you guys need any help this summer?"

Most of the time, the ranch was dead. It was just me, Rachel, Norah, and Joe. Summer, however, was when the ranch made its money for the year. Joe often hired local help to manage the guests, which I knew they could barely afford.

"Don't you have that internship thing?" he asked, examining a few of the saddles he hadn't gotten to yet.

"Well, yeah, but it's super competitive; I probably won't even get in," I replied, realizing I was standing in a pile of dried horse poop. I wrinkled my nose and stepped around it.

Joe thought about it a moment, then shook his head. "Norah's been doing this so long now she might as well be running the place. I think we'll be okay."

"You sure?"

Did I really want to work on the ranch? No. I had too much going on, and I knew zilch about horses or about ranches or about guests. But I also knew how tight money was. And it's not like I was some foster kid that the state of New York paid Rachel and Joe to take care of. They'd inherited me pro bono.

Joe set down the saddle and turned to me. "Caitlin, when your aunt and I took you in, we wanted you to feel at home here. Which means that you don't have to work for us. If you want to help out, of course we'd love to have you, but you don't have to. Even Norah doesn't have to: she just loves it. You're allowed to be a kid. Hang out with your friends; enjoy the summer. Don't worry about us; we've been doing this a long time."

"Well, maybe I can help out a little? Baking stuff for the guests or something?"

"That would be great," he said, slinging an arm around my shoulder as we headed back to the house. "I'm sure everyone would love that."

I didn't know about that. Joe had never seen my baking.

I spent the rest of the day with Rachel in the kitchen while Norah and Joe did repairs outside. Rachel put on Harry Connick Jr., and we opened the windows and doors to let in the fresh air while the oven was on. Our goal: bake enough pastries for an entire week of visitors. Rachel could ride horses, she could handle the tractors and the machines on the ranch, but she was really more in charge of guest relations. It wasn't a bed and breakfast, so if people stayed for the summer, they stayed at the inn down in town, but Rachel provided at least one meal a day and snacks for up to twenty people for the duration of the summer. She was a hosting machine.

We made blueberry and raspberry scones with fresh, local berries. By the time we were done I had flour in my hair, under my nails, and somehow in the pockets of my jeans.

After dinner, Norah and I set up camp in the living room like we usually did. I'd borrowed *An Accord of Law* from the de la Mara library and covered it with that stretchy protector fabric, disguising it as a schoolbook. It was a book of vampire laws from the fourteenth century, hand-written in Middle English. I had to google every other word, and the handwriting was thick and cramped and difficult to make out, but I was determined to keep looking for answers, even if it was slow and tedious. It was fascinating to learn that they had an almost Communist-style political system. Everyone contributed to and pulled from a communal pool of resources and funds, but they were also subject to major personal restrictions and an extremely hierarchical authority structure. On turning eighteen (an age-limit that had changed over time), vampires were considered adults, and given a yearly stipend. Some vampires were tasked with playing in the human markets, investing in human companies, compelling human accountants, when necessary. It ensured the entire vampire community had a plentiful and constant money supply.

While all of that was interesting, it didn't help me when it came to Lucian.

It would have been easier to search through the Council database, but Adrian only had access to the non-restricted levels, even though he was of age. Mariana and Dominic had stocked the library with a mix of human literature and vampire records and research. The human stuff wasn't pertinent, and most of the vampire stuff was older than the last century, written in a variety of languages I couldn't read. Apparently the library served as a back-up site to the database, one of many physical reserves that the Council had placed all over the world. It was less the de la Mara's library and more the vampire community's as a whole. Sneaking a book out of there and disguising it as homework was definitely against the rules. But I was starting to care less and less about breaking them.

After two hours of reading, I had nodded off, my phone slipping out of my hand onto the floor. Norah fished it off the rug and handed it to me, but her eye got caught on the screen.

"Middle English translator?" she asked, blinking at me. "What class is that for?"

I sat up abruptly, taking the phone back. "English. Extra credit."

I said goodnight and headed upstairs, spooked by the fact that I'd fallen asleep with a vampire law book in front of my human family. I crawled in bed and forced myself to read more, eyes glazing over the weirdly-spelled words. Suddenly, a single phrase pushed through my fog:

"*The Severance of Familie lagh is unanimously up holden, 29 Decembre. 1507.*"

The Separation of Family law?

I'd never heard of that one before. Damn book didn't have a glossary or table of contents so I couldn't easily search for that phrase. I scanned the rest of the page for clues, but nothing stood out. If a law had been enacted before the newest volume of the law book had been printed (or, in many cases, copied by hand), they didn't describe the law in detail, only referenced it, assuming the reader would know what law the text was referencing. I, unfortunately, had not been brought up learning all this crap, so I was at a loss. The library also didn't have a newer edition of this particular book—I'd looked. I'd have to ask Adrian, but something told me he wouldn't know, either. Separation of family. The only family vampires had were their demon fathers and vampire brothers or sisters. Their human moms all died giving birth, and they couldn't have children themselves. As a hybrid breed, they were like mules: sterile. Adrian had originally lived with a different vampire couple in Greece, where he was born. He didn't move in with Mariana and Dominic until he was twelve, didn't even meet them until he came to the U.S. Maybe it had something to do with that, with siblings not living with each other. But that didn't make sense, either; he had eventually moved in with them. So had Julian and Lucian.

I set the book down, rubbing my eyes. I'd ask Adrian. He could snoop for me.

I burst out laughing, clapping a hand over my mouth at the last second to muffle the sound.

Adrian pulled back, frowning. "Am I amusing you?"

"You tickled me!" I protested.

I'd unbuttoned his shirt, more for the view than because we had time to do anything particularly fun. He'd been kissing my neck. We were in the gym supply closet under terrible fluorescent lights surrounded by B.O.-smelling dodgeballs and bins of unwashed towels.

It was perfect.

"Here I am trying to be romantic and you ruin it by being ridiculously ticklish," he said with a mock sigh. "Guess I should just cover up and get on with my day."

I slapped my hands on his bare chest. "No."

He grinned at me, then turned serious. "We've got four days left," he said, looking up and around at the supply closet, but meaning the whole campus. "Then we won't have an excuse anymore."

He was right. After this week, it was summer vacation for me and adulthood for him. The only reason we felt safe kissing at school was because if the Guard was watching—or rather, listening with their emotional sonar—they wouldn't be able to pick me out in particular. The school, small as it was, was densely populated with hormonal high schoolers. I was one among many.

As soon as it was summer, though, we wouldn't have a place to kiss. All our classmates scattered, some off to vacations, many to help out on family farms. I would be easily singled out by the Guard if I were in a certain…mood. Speaking of—

Adrian kissed me, sliding his hands up my spine, pressing me closer. I wrapped my arms around his waist and—

BZZZZZZ!

That was the one disadvantage of doing this at school.

I thunked my head against his chest, growling. "I swear they're shortening the lunch period."

"Mm."

I leaned back, frustrated, straightening my hair. "I'll leave first this time. And I forgot to mention I might have found something. Separation of Family law mean anything to you?"

He frowned, puzzled. "Never heard of it."

"Might be nothing, but it caught my eye. See what you can dig up?"

He nodded, buttoning his shirt. "I also have news. Farrar's sending Vincent and Javan to resume the search for Lucian."

"Just them?"

"He's splitting the Guard. I think it's a good sign. Vincent and Javan are much older, more experienced. He's sending them off to search while he stays here with Sabine and Kalare."

"Why wouldn't he go himself? They can't possibly think Lucian is still in the area."

"I'm almost certain he's been ordered to keep an eye on you. But his duty is to recover Lucian. He's splitting forces to accomplish both directives. Which means he's taking the search for Lucian seriously."

"It also means your father was right," I muttered. "The Council shouldn't have an interest in me, especially if Lucian and your father are gone. But they do. We have to find out why."

"I'm coming up against dead ends everywhere," he replied, buttoning the last button on his shirt. "We may need to consider riskier research methods."

"What, like hacking the Council database?"

He shook his head. "They'd track any attempts immediately. They're a lot tech-savvier than they used to be. No, I meant asking for help."

I frowned. "From who?" We had exactly zero allies.

He eyed me. "From my brother."

I frowned harder. "I thought we didn't trust him."

"We don't. But I'm not going to sit here any longer. We tried keeping a low profile. It's not working. I don't like it, but he may be our best resource. At the very least, he has a security clearance higher than mine."

"What if he says no? What if he turns us in?"

"He hasn't so far, and he could have. Look, he hates the Council almost as much as I do. He may be more helpful than you think."

"He could also be more dangerous than you think."

"If it were just about us, I wouldn't risk it. But we haven't made any progress. This would be for Lucian."

I thought about it, feeling ashamed that I'd only been thinking about myself. Finally, I nodded. "Do it."

The last week of school was a blur of exams, helping Joe and

Rachel prepare for the summer guests, planning a surprise graduation party for Adrian because I knew his family wouldn't, and struggling to translate the vampire law book. I hadn't come across another reference to the Separation of Family rule, and Adrian said Julian had never heard of it, which left us at square one. He'd also struck out on finding anything about his flesh-melting eye light abilities. The school year was ending, and we weren't any closer to the truth than we had been four months ago. My old anger threatened me more often, a seething rage that tugged at the edge of my days. I was frustrated. I was tense with the Guard constantly around. But Adrian was right when he'd said I couldn't focus on the guilt. We had to find Lucian. We had to keep trying. No one else cared about him as much as we did. So I went for walks when I got angry, or tried to mimic some martial arts kicks in my room based off YouTube tutorials. I sucked at them, but it drained some of my anxious energy.

I'd also sent Kalare a box of homemade cookies and a cartoon drawing that said, "I'm sorry for being dumb and inconsiderate," and she had, apparently, forgiven me. Unlike Trish, she didn't seem hellbent on holding a grudge.

Mr. Warren was true to his word: we spent the last day of class eating popcorn and snacks and just hanging out. He even came and joined us, sitting on top of one of the desks with his feet on the seat, sipping a cola and asking us about our summer plans and if anyone had started applying to college. It was actually kind of fun to just talk to him as a person and not as a teacher and have him seem genuinely interested in what we had to say, even though we were just his students.

My art final was a breeze, choir was a pass / fail, and algebra…well, I wasn't going to have to re-take the class—barely.

Friday evening, the last day of school, when the sun was molten on the horizon, my family drove back to Warren County High for graduation. Rachel and Joe immediately sat themselves next to Mariana and Dominic, though the rest of Adrian's "family" sat a row ahead. There were uncomfortable pleasantries, Rachel trying too hard to spark a conversation before the program finally began. The seniors walked between the two rows of white event chairs, caps and gowns pressed and clean. They sat up on the stage, shuffling restlessly as the principal and several teachers gave long-winded speeches. I caught Adrian's gaze and winked at him. He smiled and winked back.

"And now a speech from the valedictorian, Adrian de la Mara."

There was a wave of clapping and a few cheers. I saw Adrian stand in his black cap and gown and walk to the steps of the pavilion where the microphone was set up.

"Good afternoon," he said quietly, though his voice carried over the hushed audience. The warm light cast the whole event in gold while the breeze gently ruffled the trees. "First, I would like to thank each and every person here for their generosity and vigilance in the continued search for my brother, Lucian. It means a great deal to me and my family."

I glanced over at Mariana, Dominic, and Julian, then up a row at Farrar, Sabine, and Kalare. They all looked attentive, but blank. Well, actually, Sabine looked bored, Julian looked…I don't know, actually. Puzzled? There was something there I couldn't quite pin down. And Kalare just looked stiff and uncomfortable. The rest of them looked their usual, blank selves.

"We here today," Adrian began, "will head out into a world expecting our talent, our intelligence, and our perseverance. I can confidently say that we are ready for that world. My best wishes to my fellow seniors."

He stepped back from the mic and it took the crowd a moment to clap, caught off guard by the short speech. Norah, Rachel, and Joe sat to my left and whispered to themselves about it. I sat there, fuming. Adrian had written an incredible speech, timed at exactly five minutes. He'd been working on it for weeks, rehearsing in front of me while I sewed in the studio. Last night, Farrar told him the Council had written something for him instead. Something short and unmemorable. They wanted Adrian to leave as small a mark on this place as possible. And of course, he'd simply nodded and done it. I literally found his speech balled up in the trash can. In the grand scheme of things, in the grand scheme of Lucian being gone and my parents being dead and demons coming through portals from hell, it wasn't that big of a deal.

And yet it was.

That's what I kept coming back to. It was the everyday stuff that, in many ways, bothered me more than the big, catastrophic stuff. It was Adrian being told what he could wear and who he could speak to and what he could say. I found myself increasingly having to stuff my anger back down into the pit of my stomach every time something like this happened, throwing up my weak emotional blocks so Farrar and the Praetorians couldn't tell how pissed I was. They were crushing the joy out of Adrian one dumb, human experience at a time.

The principal got up and talked, but I didn't hear him. I just closed my eyes and let the sun hit my skin, let the air sift through my hair, let the rage inside me simmer. Lucian's birthday had passed. I had made him *Frankie, the Boy Part II*. But he was gone, so the book sat on the shelf in my room.

The principal started handing out diplomas. Pictures were snapped. Smiles were smiled. Hands were shaken. There was one final class photo and a round of applause and then people started standing and milling.

Joe and Rachel congratulated Mariana and Dominic on Adrian's valedictorianship. Joe expressed condolences over Lucian's disappearance. When Adrian finally walked back over to us, Rachel threw her arms around him and squeezed him tight in a hug.

"Congratulations, honey," she said, crushing his tall frame to her chest. "We're so proud of you."

Adrian's back was to the group of vampires, but I saw his face. There was a moment of total surprise. And then he closed his eyes and hugged my aunt back, looking for a brief moment like the vulnerable eighteen-year-old he was. By the time she let him go, his face had gone back to neutral. Joe clapped Adrian on the shoulder and shook his hand. They'd forgiven him for being in my room at Christmas. They'd accepted his place in my life. And because of that, they were here to support him as much as they supported me. It had taken me a long time to admit it, but Rachel and Joe were actually kind of incredible people.

And staring at Mariana and Dominic, at Julian, at Farrar and the Praetorian Guard, I realized that my family loved Adrian more than his own family did.

And that made me as angry as it made me sad.

Blinking back tears, I tried to look anywhere other than at Adrian. And it was then that I saw Trish staring at our group. Specifically at Farrar. There was a look on her face that worried me. It was her stubborn look. It was her buying-me-the-Green-Thing-behind-my-back look.

It was a look that meant she was about to start asking questions.

IT'S YOUR PARTY, BUT PLEASE DON'T EAT THE GUESTS

9

"What did Stephanie say?"

"That Tim was taking her on a real date."

"Yeah? Never thought he'd work up the guts to make it official."

"He has moved past his emo-punk Emerson days, it would seem."

It was sunny out, so we left our jackets and helmets on the Harley and headed for the front door of the ranch. I fished my keys out of my pocket, trying to keep my heart-rate down so Adrian wouldn't suspect anything.

The great thing about vampires was that they were like humans: they might have superior hearing and reflexes, but they also had to be *paying attention.*

Which Adrian was not.

I finally undid the deadbolt and swung the door in, pushing Adrian ahead of me.

"He say where they were—"

"*SURPRISE!*"

The whole room erupted in confetti and kazoos and people jumping out from behind furniture. In the blink of an eye, Adrian had me backed up against the wall, his arm out protectively, his eyes on the verge of turning silver.

Panicked, I whirled him toward me so no one could see his face. "Adrian! Babe, it's okay. It's a surprise party. For graduation."

He blinked at me, eyes slowly morphing back to gray while the guests stopped yelling, looking somewhat confused.

"Surprise party?" he asked finally.

I nodded. "For you." I looked significantly over his shoulder at the waiting guests.

He blushed, and released me, turning back to the room. "Sorry, everyone. Too much caffeine; I'm a little jumpy."

There were a few real chuckles and a few uncomfortable chuckles. He'd moved quickly. I'm sure someone had probably thought they'd seen his eyes do something funny. But they had also probably convinced themselves it was a trick of the light.

There was a giant banner hanging from the upstairs balcony that read "Congratulations, Adrian!" Rachel and I had baked a big-ass cake, there were snacks and balloons, and half my class and Adrian's had shown up. We already had summer guests, so Adrian was used to seeing a bunch of cars and trucks parked here. The surprise had gone totally according to plan.

I slipped my arm through his and whispered, "I got you good."

He leaned in and whispered, "You almost blew my cover."

"Ah, we're fine."

I grinned at him and pecked him on the cheek.

Mariana and Dominic were there. They had hidden behind the couch and popped up mechanically when everyone else did, but they did not shout any congratulatory statements at their nephew-slash-half-brother-slash-brother-in-law. We made the rounds, Adrian thanking everyone, slowly relaxing. Norah was still hiding upstairs in her room. This kind of thing bored her to tears.

I hadn't been so sure about inviting the Praetorian Guard, but Rachel had been insistent on wanting to invite *all* of Adrian's extended family. I hadn't even had to field that one; Rachel had called over to Mariana several times to arrange their surprise arrival. Julian and Sabine had been "hiding" in the kitchen behind the wall while Kalare and Farrar had hidden behind the curtains in the living room. She played the part well, lifting a glass in toast to Adrian when he came into the room, while Farrar kept a polite if neutral look on his face.

Luke, from Adrian's class, had spilled his drink all over the kitchen table so I shoved Adrian in the direction of my family and went to help clean up the mess. By the time I got back, Adrian was stuffed on the center cushion of the couch with Rachel on his left and Farrar on his right. Rachel was chatting up the ancient, high-ranking vampire like he was an old friend. Somehow sitting next to my petite human aunt, he didn't look scary, just comically large. Like Hagrid trying to drink tea with McGonagall.

Damn, Adrian was really rubbing off on me.

Sabine and Julian were standing languidly by the staircase surveying the party like gods of yore. He showed her something on his phone. A faint, barely-amused smile crossed her face before she returned to looking bored. Julian looked disappointed at her lackluster reaction.

Jenny and Jack were hovering near the food on the kitchen counter along with Stephanie and Tim. I was a little surprised to see that Mark was there, too, standing with his arm lightly around Jenny's waist. She hadn't exactly announced to the world if they were technically an item or not, even after they went to Prom together, but arm-around-waist certainly seemed like a couple thing.

Stephanie and Tim were definitely an item, finally. Apparently he had managed to convince the teachers to let him play one final song at the dance, after Adrian and I had left, and when it ended he kissed Stephanie full-on in front of everyone. He got a slap on the wrist for an "inappropriate display of affection at a school-run event" but he'd just shouted "Bangarang!" and the whole crowd had shouted it back. He and Stephanie had run out to the parking lot to a standing ovation. I was seriously sad that I'd missed it.

There were a few seniors from Adrian's class, and a few other random parents, but the one person I really wanted at the party hadn't shown up yet.

Trish was nowhere to be seen.

Before I could check my phone for the thousandth time to see if she'd texted me to ask for directions because she'd magically forgotten where I lived, Norah came bounding down the stairs in her riding gear.

"Who wants to see the horses?" she asked loudly, to the whole room.

Before Rachel could reprimand her daughter for distracting everyone from the purpose of the party (Adrian just sat there looking polite, of course), Stephanie perked up. "Ooh!" She turned to me, looking excited. "Caitlin, do you mind if I go?"

I glanced at Rachel, who nodded, so I smiled at Steph. "Of course not! I'm going to stay here and host, or at least pretend to host while my aunt hosts, but go ahead."

"Actually, I might look at them, too," Jenny said. "We just have farm horses at our place, not show horses. Do you think we could ride them?"

"My uncle will have to make that call but I don't see why not. Norah can show you everything you never wanted to know."

Jenny actually laughed at that and took Mark's hand. Dang, my baby was growing up so fast! I winked at Mark as he looked a little taken aback at Jenny's boldness, then let her lead him out the door after Stephanie and Tim and Norah. Jack stood for a moment in the kitchen, left behind, but then nodded at me awkwardly and wandered after them.

I turned to head back to Adrian only to find Sabine walking out the front door. Julian watched her leave, an unreadable expression on his face. I detoured and headed for the corner of the living room where Kalare was sitting in my uncle's wingback chair reading one of his paperback westerns with her hipster reading glasses.

"Hey," I said, nodding over at Julian. "What's going on there?"

Kalare glanced over the edge of the glasses at Adrian's brother. "He has been unsuccessfully trying to get in Sabine's pants for weeks now. Apparently she likes horses and humans better than him." She looked critically at me. "For such a matchmaker, you haven't been paying particularly close attention."

"Hey, you're the one that has a reason to be tracking that non-relationship like a hawk, not me." She frowned at me which made her look kind of owl-ish with the big glasses. "I mean, I'm not one to meddle, but have you tried, like, telling him how you feel?"

She snort-laughed, closing the book. "No."

"I hear it's a great way to communicate."

"Not my style," she said. "I prefer brooding silences built up over decades. Way sexier."

It was my turn to snort-laugh. "Remind me to never go to you for romantic advice."

"Speaking of romance, I can't…" she paused, looking at me curiously. "I can't feel anything from you right now. You're feeling things, right? You're not broken?" She poked my cheek as if to check. I slapped her hand away lightly.

"Not broken, thank you very much. There's a lot more humans around, maybe it's just muddling your senses."

She narrowed her eyes, cocking her head to the side as if weighing me. "Maybe. Or it could be Adrian is teaching you emotional blocks like the punishment glutton he is shaping up to be."

I sat, tight-lipped, which was answer enough.

"What are you two hiding?" she asked, turning serious. "Besides the obvious?"

My face turned red, against my will. "What? Nothing."

Damn, I would make a terrible spy.

"Cait," she said, setting the book down carefully. "I've said this before and I'll say it again: I like you. I think you're a fun kid, and I don't want to see you get hurt. So listen to me—really listen—when I say that keeping secrets from the Council is a bad idea."

"How can you say that?" I asked. "You don't dress like them or talk like them or act like them."

"I irritate them in superficial ways, but I don't break their laws. I don't mess around with humans and when they say jump, I say 'How high?' Why do you think I'm *here*?" Before I could answer she looked past my shoulder and stiffened. "Look, this is not the time or place to talk about this. Just use your brain. I'll have a talk with Adrian, see if I can't knock some sense into him. He's been giving you terrible advice."

Before I could respond she stood up and walked down the hall to the bathroom. The hair on the back of my neck began to rise and I looked quickly around. Mariana was watching me from across the room, but as soon as I met her gaze, she smiled politely and turned back to Dominic.

Kalare was trying to be my friend. Vampires weren't allowed to do that. Maybe I shouldn't flaunt my growing friendship with Kalare in front of people like Mariana and Farrar. I didn't want her to get into trouble. *I* didn't want to get into trouble.

Speaking of—

It took my brain a second to process that there was someone new standing at the door. Someone I'd been waiting all day for.

It was Trish.

Trish was freaking here.

I jumped up and met her and Ben halfway across the room.

"You came!" I said, stopping myself from hugging her just in time.

She nodded, standing woodenly next to Ben, who seemed far more relaxed. "We brought chips." She held the bag in her arms like a shield. Her gaze flicked to something over my shoulder, her expression turning curious. "Is that Julian?"

Hearing his name, Julian looked up at our group. He sauntered over and joined the circle.

"Not sure I've had the pleasure?" he said, holding out his hand.

Trish shook it, looking amused. "Trish. Fields. We've met."

They had?

Julian looked just as perplexed.

"Two Christmases ago we found you passed out in our cow pasture."

A look of realization crept onto Julian's face. "Ah, yes. That was a… rambunctious family get-together. Apparently I wandered away from the festivities."

"It was the darndest thing," Trish said, not taking her eyes off him. "Looked like you'd been out there for hours, no coat, fifteen degrees out. Didn't see your car or anything. We woke you up, and you just wandered back into the night."

"I like to hike," he said, as if that explained everything. His model-perfect smile was tight around the edges. Julian spent more time around humans than any other vampire except Adrian, but he hadn't spent much time around *my* humans.

Trish narrowed her eyes, obviously not buying that bullshit. To my surprise, she let it go.

"You must be proud of your brother," she continued. "Valedictorian."

Julian's smile tightened. "We're all very proud of him."

"Yes, all of you." She looked around, her eyes lingering on Farrar. "Who knew there were so many de la Maras?"

Julian's eyes narrowed. "A whole gaggle of cousins."

"And so crazy, how Caitlin and Adrian met. That storm—helluva thing. We're all so glad he was there to help her."

His smile tightened further. "As were we." He glanced at Ben, smiled, and looked over Trish's shoulder. "If you'll excuse me, I have to go save my brother from Caitlin's aunt; she's been talking his ear off for an hour."

He threw a sharp look at me, then left, hauling Adrian from the couch and walking out the front door.

Ben glanced at me, then at Trish. "I'm going to go get some food. Be right back." He kissed Trish on the cheek and abandoned us.

For a moment, I couldn't speak. She'd come, but she was being weird, even for her. I settled with a lame, "So, got any fun summer plans?"

For a moment, she looked disappointed, as if she'd hoped I'd say something else. "Yeah, whole family's going to England for a month to check out Oxford."

"Holy shit," I said more loudly than I'd intended. Rachel frowned at me from across the room. I blushed and turned back to Trish. "Wait, are you going there? For sure?"

"Not for sure, but it's looking more likely. Turning the college tour into an international family vacation."

"That's awesome! Although I'm sure Jenny will miss Mark."

An irritated look crossed Trish's face. "He's not going. He's studying abroad in Paris next semester, said he'd have all the time in the world to check out Europe then. He's staying behind so he can spend time with Jenny."

This obviously was a sore subject.

"Oh, well, that's…uh, yeah." I was an amazing conversationalist. "Look," I said, trying again, "thank you so much for coming. It means the world to me."

Trish looked around the room once more. Uncle Joe and Farrar seemed to be discussing hunting rifles. "Couldn't pass up an opportunity to see Adrian's family up close and personal. They're… different."

The hair on the back of my neck rose once more. Crap.

Trish was snooping.

"Lots of European family," I stalled. "They have some, uh…weird customs."

Double-crap, I was so bad at lying.

And Trish knew me too well.

Trish let out a frustrated breath and turned more fully to me. "You'll take care of yourself while I'm gone, won't you?" she asked, unexpectedly. "You'll stay safe?"

I frowned at her, not sure where she was going with this. "Well, I may be in New York at that internship, but if I am I'll try and be safe. Probably won't even leave the building; they tend to work people pretty hard at these internships."

"That's not—" Trish opened her mouth, then closed it, letting out a deep breath. "Look, let me be blunt. Adrian and his family weird me the hell out."

She glanced around, then nodded at the empty kitchen. I followed her in.

"I don't know what their deal is, but they worry me," she said when we were more or less alone. "*Adrian* worries me. I think…" She sighed again, looking uncomfortable, which was unusual. "I think they may be in some sort of cult."

I blinked. It was my turn to open my mouth and then close it, about to defend him and tell Trish that he was definitely, one-hundred-percent *not* in a cult.

But…

Well, in a way he kind of was. Super restrictive rules, kept tabs on their members, didn't have a ton of free will, had to obey a mysterious and powerful council.

Shit, Adrian was kind of in a cult.

But…not.

But sort of.

And as terrible as it sounded, it was better if Trish thought Adrian was in a cult than if she thought he was a vampire. The awful human half-truth was a better alternative to the unbelievable supernatural full-truth.

"I know," I whispered finally, looking around as though afraid someone might be listening. She whipped her face to look at me, surprised. "His family has a weird sort of religion thing. He's not comfortable with it."

"Then why the hell are you still with him?" she whispered fiercely at me, glancing at the living room full of vampires.

"It's not that simple," I whispered back. "He has to be careful around his family."

Trish looked at me like I was crazy. "Do you hear yourself right now? This is *insane*, Cait. I know I pushed you toward him last year, I know his family is secretive, but as soon as you showed up, weird shit started happening."

"Why do you think I'm going to the city for the summer?" I whispered back. "*To get away from them.*"

That part was actually more true than not.

Trish rubbed her forehead with her fingers, agitated. "All right, just tell me—if you know his family is nuts, why are you still with Adrian?"

I was so bad at thinking on my feet. What could I possibly tell Trish that she would not only believe, but that would put her suspicions to rest for good? She had to stop asking questions, *now*. If she got caught up in this, she would get hurt. Compulsion, memory wipes, who knows what else?

"Just put yourself in my shoes," I said finally. "You've just moved to Stony Creek. You start dating Ben. You find out his family is a little… intense. Would you dump him?"

"*Yes!*" Trish hissed at me. "Yes, for God's sake, yes, I would dump him! Caitlin, I love Ben, I do, but I put my own safety and well-being ahead of our relationship. I also put *his* safety and well-being ahead of our relationship. If I thought my family might hurt him, if I thought *I* might hurt him, I would let him go. Has Adrian done that for you? Has he thought about that at all?"

Actually yeah, I thought, *he has*. But I couldn't say that, because I couldn't explain it, not the details, not how Adrian had been an ass to me for months because he thought if he allowed himself to care about me the Council would find out and they would hurt us both.

"Trish," I said slowly, feeling my throat tighten with unexpected tears, "maybe you can't understand this because you still have your family. You have both your parents; you have all your brothers. But my parents are dead. I'm an only child. I've lost my family. And I can't lose anyone else. Not by choice."

Trish smiled bitterly. "That's the thing, though, Caitlin. You did choose. You chose Adrian even though he was a dick to you for months. You chose him even though he made you bawl in my truck after Winter Formal. You chose him even though it meant lying to your aunt and uncle. You chose him even when it meant making me lie on your behalf. I was there, Cait. Through all of it."

She held up her hands. "Look, I'm not gonna preach at you. But this I know for a fact: Adrian does not bring out the best in you. He makes you sad, he makes you lie, he ignores you and plays mind games and then suddenly loves you again. His family is fucked up in ways I don't even fully understand. And at the end of the day, you have to measure the guy you're dating not by who you want him to be, but by who he is *right now*, and how he treats you *right now*. I don't care how many Harleys that boy has—is he a good guy?"

Rachel walked into the kitchen then, stopping when she saw Trish. "Trish! Oh my goodness, hello! We're so happy you could make it!" She gave Trish a quick hug. Rachel was a hugger.

"I actually have to be going," Trish admitted when Rachel released her. "We have another graduation party to get to. It was nice to see you, Mrs. Master."

She turned to leave and I stopped her. "Look, I want to hear more," I started to say, then realized my aunt was listening, "about your uh… trip." I raise my eyebrows so she knew I meant more than her trip. "Can we talk when you get back?"

Trish searched my face for a long moment, then nodded. She grabbed Ben from where he was chatting with a few kids from the just-graduated-senior-class, passing Adrian who was walking back in the front door.

Adrian glanced at me, and I shot him a weak smile. It hadn't gone terribly, but it hadn't gone well, either.

What's worse—even though Trish didn't have the full picture, even though she didn't understand what was really happening, my gut couldn't ignore that she had a point. Adrian hadn't always brought out the best in me. His family was insane. His father was literally trying to kill me, or get me pregnant, or possibly both. If this were a normal, human world, Trish would be completely right. It would be better to leave. Safer, at least.

But it wasn't a normal, human world. And even if I wanted to, I didn't think the Council would let me walk away.

Besides, Lucian was still missing. As long as he was gone, and as long as that was partially my fault, I was in this. I was going to find him.

I was going to bring him home.

DATA

10

"Did anyone else notice this?" I asked, examining Adrian's frozen face.

Today my subconscious was dressed as Data from *Star Trek*. He was wearing a Sherlock Holmes hat, the kind with the funny ear flaps. Apparently when I was asleep I had a weird sense of humor.

"Look for yourself," Data replied evenly.

I glanced at Farrar, who, in this frozen slice of time, was looking at Other Me. I also glanced at Sabine, who was also staring down Other Me, waiting for a chance to strike. Julian was the only one staring directly at Adrian, since Vincent and Javan hadn't shown up to the cliff at this point. The only problem was, Julian had been blood-starved at the time, and half out of his mind. Even if he was looking right at Adrian, he probably didn't remember anything about it.

I stared at Adrian's eyes, entirely white. Not milky white, like he had cataracts, but almost crystalline; a vibrant, glowing white.

Where had I seen that before?

"Indeed," Data said. "Where *have* you seen that before?"

I turned to him and frowned. "If I were Captain Picard, I could order you to tell me."

"If I were actually Data, I would be obliged to obey."

My subconscious was a smart-ass.

But my mind caught on the word "obey," which made me think of compulsion, which made me think of Adrian compelling me to kiss him, which made me—

"Oh my god."

Instantly, the scene around us changed. We were standing in a different clearing during a different emergency: the fight with Tommie.

But this was pre-Adrian-temporarily-dying. Tommie had Adrian suspended mid-air, locked in a wind tunnel. Rather than being frozen or playing on a loop in real-time, like all the other dreamscapes I'd had, the memory played in extremely slow motion.

The unfortunate thing about how this whole dream-playback worked was that, if I hadn't directly observed something in the real world, I couldn't watch it in the dream. My mind would just fill in the shape of something based on…well, who knows what? Math, probably. When I'd first started having conversations with Tommie while asleep, my brain had conjured up a simplified version of the clearing, stripped of most details except Other Me and Adrian lying in the snow. The longer I'd been dreaming, the more detailed the dreams had become.

Still, if I hadn't actually seen something in real life, I couldn't see it here in the dream. Adrian had been standing right next to me when Julian tackled him over the cliff in the last dreamscape, and apparently I had been looking at his face well enough to see his eyes here, in my subconscious. He'd just gone over the edge so quickly in real life that I hadn't noticed his eyes flash white. I'd thought they were their normal size and color. Or well, his normal vampire color: silver, not white. Not *entirely* white.

Data stood politely next to Dream Tommie, arms held perfectly still at his sides, just like Data did in the show. I'd spent last summer watching all seven seasons of *The Next Generation* with my mom in her hospital room. We took jell-o shots every time Picard said "Mm-hmm" and every time Data became perplexed by figures of speech. And by jell-o shots, I literally just mean hospital jell-o, straight from the plastic cup. You come up with weird games when you're stuck in the same gray room for months on end. You also come up with weird games when your mom completely loses her appetite from chemo and you're desperate to get her to eat something.

I'd spent over a hundred hours over the course of seven seasons watching Data on *Star Trek*. He was as ingrained in my mind as a real person would be. And it was a hell of a lot less creepy talking to an android avatar than it was talking to subconscious versions of my friends and enemies.

I glanced over and saw Other Me lying flat in the snow, barely propped up on her elbows. Her lip was bleeding, a trickle of blood winding its way down her chin. Man, I didn't even remember that. She looked desperate, clutching at the snow, looking for something to throw or use as a weapon. Finding nothing, she looked back up at Tommie and Adrian.

That's when I'd realized Adrian had given me a clue about how to stop Tommie. Tommie couldn't absorb love, or any positive emotions; he couldn't use it as an energy source. But Adrian could. All I had to do was let go of my anger and rage and fear and latch onto positive emotions: love, hope, joy. I didn't even have to love Adrian in particular, I just had to remember anyone I'd ever loved; my mom, my dad, Trish, Rachel, Joe.

I watched closely as a shift took place, something I hadn't been able to observe closely at the time. Unfortunately, since I'd been back about thirty feet, walking closer to Adrian and Tommie in the dream produced limited results. They became blurry, out of focus, their edges indistinct. I could only see them as clearly as I'd seen them that night, which is to say, not very.

But there it was again: Adrian's eyes flickering from gray to silver to white.

What *was* that light?

The first time I'd met Adrian, during the storm, he'd compelled me to forget myself, then compelled me to forget that he'd been there. Eventually, he'd retrieved those memories for me. I remembered lying in the mud, the storm raging around us, and not being able to make out his face because his eyes were burning so brightly. But they'd been silver then, his normal vampire silver.

So what was different now?

I watched as the light spilling from Adrian's eyes became a flood. It was so bright it started to wash everything in the clearing of color.

Suddenly, I felt cold. Real me, not Other Me. My breath began to bloom in little clouds.

What the crap?

"Data!" I called over. "What just happened?"

"If you are referring to the temperature," he stated calmly, "I can only hypothesize that you are becoming better at this."

"At what?" I asked.

He spread out his arms to indicate the whole clearing. "At *this*."

Before I could ask anything else, a slow-motion pulse of light blasted from Adrian's eyes, becoming so bright that I couldn't see a thing. The whole world dissolved into a blank, white space. As before, when this all really happened, the only reason I knew I was still there in that moment was that I could feel the crunching snow beneath my feet.

Then it was dark, everything strobing. I'd been about to pass out at this point, and I literally couldn't see straight. Adrian fell to the ground while a vague figure—Tommie—ran past Other Me and disappeared into the trees.

For the first time since having one of these new, lucid dreams, I was scared.

Data appeared at my side.

"Do not be frightened, Caitlin. You are in no danger."

"How do I know that?" I asked him, starting to shake. "This place is becoming real, and I don't understand how or why. I don't understand what's happening."

Data smiled comfortingly. "But you will." He glanced over at Adrian's blood-drenched body. "And if you do not, you will die."

I looked up at him, a panicked question on the tip of my tongue, but he disappeared suddenly, along with the entire clearing.

I woke up in bed, drenched in sweat, breathing hard. My alarm was beeping irritably on my nightstand.

I took a few huge gulps of air and tried to calm myself down.

My subconscious thought I would die if I didn't figure all this out.

But how did it *know* that?

How did *I* know that?

What the hell was happening?

"Watch out!" Stephanie yelled, moments before Adrian caught a Frisbee that was headed straight for me.

I blinked a few times, my eyes trying and failing to focus on the neon-yellow disc six inches from my face. Adrian tossed the Frisbee back while Stephanie looked at me, horrified.

"I'm so sorry!" she called. "I'm really bad at this!"

"It's all right!" I called back. "I think I'm just going to go sit behind this bunch of trees, where it's safe."

I smiled at her to let her know I was joking, and she looked relieved and went back to join Tim, Jenny, Jack, and Mark in their game.

"Thanks for saving my face," I told Adrian as we sat down on our picnic blanket. "I would have looked super sexy with a broken nose."

Adrian snorted. "You would look super sexy no matter what."

I raised an eyebrow at him. "Oh, yeah? You think I'm sexy?"

"Have I not made myself clear on that point?" he asked, handing me a sandwich from the little picnic cooler Mariana had packed for us.

"No, I don't believe you have."

We were all hanging out in the park in the center of town, basking in the warm weather and the freedom of school being over. We were two days into summer vacation and Trish and her family (sans Mark, of course) had left that morning for the airport outside of Saratoga Springs on their way to England.

"Well," he said, biting into his own sandwich, "then let me lay your fears to rest once and for all: I find you adequately pleasing to the eye."

I snorted right back at him. "Such a poet, you are."

He grinned and I grinned and because he didn't grin very often, especially not the past few months, and because it was warm out and all our friends were having a good time and because it was summer and we were teenagers and I hadn't kissed him in days, I threw my sandwich back into the cooler and tackled him.

The kiss was melodramatic and silly but it almost immediately turned very serious and not at all silly.

Adrian broke away reluctantly. "They're probably here," he murmured. "Observing."

"Let them," I murmured right back. "Human folk are here. We

have an excuse."

"Cait—"

Before he could shut down and get all responsible, I yelled "Stephanie!" loudly over his shoulder. "Stephanie, watch me kiss Adrian! BECAUSE WE'RE IN LOVE!"

I grabbed his face in both hands and gave him an exaggerated smooch, then fell over, dragging him with me. I heard a few hoots and hollers and one honk from a passing car. I think I even heard Jenny laugh.

"There," I said, finally letting him breathe. "Now we have an excuse."

Adrian grinned, wrapping his arms around me. "I surrender. If an inquisition occurs, I'll just tell them how admirably you were dedicated to our cover story."

I smiled at him, but the smile faded. Not because I was upset, but because I wanted to kiss him. I mean *really* kiss him.

"What's that look on your face?" he asked.

"Nothing," I said, about to brush it off. Then I remembered that whole honesty agreement we had. "I mean, it's not nothing. I just…I would really, really like to drag you off into the woods and make out with you until we get into trouble."

His arms around me tightened and he buried his face in my neck, letting out a low groan of frustration. "You can't say stuff like that to me," he mumbled into my collarbone. "You think I have all this self-control, and I don't."

I ran my fingers through his hair lightly, staring up at the tree branches above us. "Yes, you do. You are the most self-disciplined person I know, next to maybe my uncle, or God."

"If you only knew," he muttered, "how hard it is to tell you no."

I wanted to tell him, *"So don't,"* but I couldn't. That wasn't fair.

"I'm sorry," I admitted a moment later. "I just don't think you understand how handsome you are. And wonderful. And just, good Lord, so hot."

He looked up at me, and I winked at him. He smiled ruefully, then rubbed his forehead against my neck, groaning.

"All right, all right, I'm done torturing you!" I promised. "You want to go play Frisbee?"

He let out a long breath. "Well, I would, but I'm not going to be able to stand up for a while."

I immediately blushed, glad he couldn't see my face. "Ah," I replied, intelligently.

"Yep," he said. "This happens. All the time."

"Well, since we're stuck here for a while and relatively alone, can I ask you something?"

He looked up at me, propping his chin on his hand. "Anything."

"How would you feel about trying to activate your super powers again?"

Adrian blinked. "My super powers?"

"You knocked Julian unconscious with a thought. You melted the skin off your father's body. We know that's not normal. We know it's dangerous to ask too many questions about it. So what if we tried to make it happen again, on purpose?"

"That might be dangerous," he said, hesitating.

"That's the thing, though," I countered, "I don't think it is. Both times it happened, what were you doing?"

Adrian frowned. "Fighting?"

"No," I said, glancing around to make sure no one was listening. "You were protecting *me*."

Adrian's frown deepened, the wheels turning in his head.

"Think about it," I continued. "Both times I was in danger. Both times you pulled some white knight juju out of your hat and saved our butts. Maybe you have some sort of protective power that only kicks in when someone you love is in danger. I mean, besides blood, your whole energy source is based on a sort of empathic conduit system, right? Maybe this is a side effect."

His eyes were unfocused, staring somewhere past my shoulder, which I knew meant he was thinking. Finally, he turned back to me. "If you're right, then the only way to test your theory is to put you in mortal danger."

I opened my mouth to argue, then closed it, realizing he was right. "I hadn't thought that far ahead."

I had full confidence in Adrian's ability to keep me safe, but there was a fine line between trusting him and tempting fate.

"But your theory is solid," he admitted.

"Has it happened before to anyone? Maybe it's a family trait. Something to do with your father. Julian ever had any of these powers?"

Adrian snorted. "Julian's never loved anyone more than he loves himself. According to your theory, these abilities would have never manifested for him."

"What about Mariana?"

"Not that I've heard of," he replied. "But I've never point-blank asked her. She's deeply loyal to the Council. I'm afraid to even bring it up."

"And—" I stopped myself, hesitating. "Lucian never…?"

Adrian's mouth pressed into a hard line. "No. He wasn't in this dimension long enough to learn to love anyone besides maybe me." He met my eyes. "Or you." He shook his head. "Either way, neither one of us was ever in danger in front of him. If he does have the same ability, we won't know unless—"

He stopped abruptly.

Unless we found him.

Unless we brought him home.

"What about other methods of research? Family trees and stuff?" A lightbulb went off in my head. "The *Matris Libri*. Doesn't that have a ton of information about vampire moms?"

"I hadn't thought of that," Adrian admitted. "I've researched my own mother extensively but not my siblings' mothers. There may be something there. Even something as simple as a pattern between why my father chose those women in particular. Perhaps a genetic predisposition?"

"You guys gonna make out all afternoon or you gonna come join us?" Ben called, walking toward us from the parking lot. He was carrying a spikeball bag and a cooler. Trish was gone, but it didn't look like he was going to let that stop him from hanging out with us, which I kind of appreciated.

"Talk more later?" Adrian nodded. I sighed dramatically. "Guess it's time to go be regular teenagers. How boring."

Adrian smiled and kissed me. "Don't you mean how *wonderful*?"

We played games all day, pausing only to pass around ice-cold sodas and chips and watermelon. When it was almost dark, we piled up into our trucks and wound our way up into the mountain, closer to Jack and Jenny's house. There was a lookout there, Stony Creek's version of Lover's Point. You couldn't see the town, but you could see for miles as the sun burned the forest and the mountains gold with light. We sat on the hoods of our trucks, watching the sun melt behind the horizon.

We stayed another few hours talking about school, about SATs and college, about moving away or staying put, about getting jobs and getting married. Jack was thinking of joining the military. Tim was thinking about moving to Chicago to join the Second City Comedy

Troupe to pursue stand-up, after Mark had put the idea in his head at Prom. Stephanie said Chicago was a little intimidating, but they had some good schools. Jenny had even admitted she was thinking of moving to Boston to go to college, though she wasn't sure what she wanted to study yet. Ben said if Trish ended up getting accepted at Oxford, he was going with her to "make sure none of them red coats get their hands on my girl." When Mark asked Adrian what he was going to do now that he had graduated, Adrian simply said, "Find my brother."

It got quiet after that.

But not uncomfortable. It was a companionable silence. We shifted our attention from the sunset to the rising stars as the last of the light faded into darkness. Mark pulled out his guitar from the backseat of his truck (or rather, his family's truck—it was the same one Trish used to get to and from school) and started strumming a sad little song. Jenny got out a blanket and curled up next to him. Stephanie and Tim held hands. Jack whistled a counter-melody to Mark's tune.

It was a beautiful night. Adrian was right. It really was these moments, more than anything, that I wanted to remember.

ENJOY THE HUG

11

"Why do you only show me vampire stuff?" I asked Data.

Of all my dream-avatars, he was quickly becoming my favorite.

"Why do you think?" he replied evenly.

"There's obviously something important you're trying to make me understand, or work out. But I'm not getting it."

"Not yet," Data admitted. "But you will. Or you will—"

"Die, yeah, I know."

I rubbed my eyes with my hands, frustrated. Next to us, Dream Adrian had Dream Me pinned in the mud, the storm raging around them. Or, well, it was frozen, so it wasn't raging, I guess. Adrian's eyes were burning silver, mid-compulsion. He was forcing me to forget myself.

"Look, can I have a night off?" I asked Data.

He stared at me, puzzled.

"I don't want to do this. It's exhausting. I'm irritated. If I have to be in charge of my own dreams, can I pick something happier?"

"Yes, but—"

Before he could finish, the scene shifted. I was back home, back in Mystic. My mom was at the sewing machine working on a receiving blanket. I was cutting out cotton squares and triangles for the quilt I was making. It was fall, and we were making a dozen blankets to donate to the hospital for newborns. It was one of our things.

"Caitlin, where's the seam ripper?" my mom asked.

"Uhhh," fourteen-year-old-me stalled, looking around. "I don't know."

My mom sighed. "It's your turn to buy a replacement. I got the last three."

"I don't know what happens to them!" younger-me protested. "They hate me. It's like I'm a magnet, and they're the opposite kind of magnet. I repel seam rippers."

My breath caught in my throat, watching the memory play out. It was a totally normal day, I hadn't even thought of a particular event. This was us, our life, before she got sick. It had been just the two of us for so many years.

God, I missed her.

"Caitlin," Data said, appearing at my side, looking stern. "This is a distraction you cannot afford. There is a purpose here, and this," he said, looking at my mom and my younger self, "is not it."

"Shut up, Data," I said, stepping closer to my mom. "Please, just leave me alone."

Instantly, Data disappeared.

I watched my mom and myself sew for hours, until my alarm went off and woke me up. And then I sat in my bed and cried softly.

Nothing made it easier. Nothing made her absence any more bearable; not Rachel or Joe or Adrian or school or even the prospect of an incredible design internship.

Below every other burden, she was the constant. The ache of missing her was the sadness upon which every other sadness rested. And as much as that weighed, as much as it hurt, it also kept me grounded. In the middle of all of the insanity, I could always rely on one fact:

I was my mother's daughter. And she had loved me, deeply.

"Caitlin, you got a letter," Rachel said, dumping a pile of mail on the kitchen table. "Oh," she said a moment later. Then, "Oh!"

I looked over at her from my place on the couch. I was working on the vampire law book, this time disguised with the dust jacket to *The Prisoner of Azkaban*. I'd just gotten back from Adrian's, where he'd tried to use his eye-light to melt a stick of butter. It hadn't worked. Julian had also volunteered to let Adrian try and knock him unconscious again. That also hadn't worked. It didn't disprove my empathic protection theory, but it also didn't prove it, either.

Rachel was frozen at the kitchen table, staring down at the envelope in her hand. I sat up, concerned. "What is it?"

"It's from Myriad."

I blinked, then scrambled off the couch, falling to the floor in my mad dash to the kitchen. I ripped open the envelope and scanned the letter.

"What does it say?" Rachel asked, looking as nervous as I felt.

I swallowed, then burst out laughing. "I got in." I looked up at her, stunned. "I got in."

"Aaaaah!" Rachel screamed, and crushed me in a hug. I hugged her back because *holy shit* I got in.

Joe walked in the front door, looking concerned. "Everything all right?"

"She got in!" Rachel shouted, dancing us over to him and adding him to the group hug.

"To the internship?" he asked.

"Yes!" I screamed.

Norah came in a moment later, looking equally concerned. "What's going on?"

"Caitlin was accepted to the design internship in New York," Joe explained.

Norah's face lit up. "Does that mean you're going to be gone for the whole summer?"

"Yep," I said, grinning.

Norah smiled. "Then congratulations!"

"*Norah*," Rachel admonished, but I waved her off and stuffed my cousin into the group hug.

"It's all right," I said, still grinning. "You guys can have the ranch to yourselves for the summer, and I'll be soaking up design knowledge. It'll be perfect."

"We're very proud of you," Joe said, lifting all three of us off the ground in a hug. Norah and I squawked in surprise.

"Oh my gosh I have to call Grandma!" I said.

"Tell her we said hello!" Rachel called after me as I ran up the stairs to find my phone.

My gram was hard of hearing, so it usually took her until the last ring to answer the phone.

"Hello?" she said warily after the line connected. She was a suspicious sort, and she loved to torment telemarketers.

"Grandma!"

"Oh! Hello, Sugar Plum."

"Hi, Granny Smith. Guess what?"

"You're pregnant?"

"What? No!"

"You're on the drugs?"

"No, Grandma!" It had been a while since I'd talked to her. I'd forgotten how feisty she could be. "I got accepted to that internship I was telling you about! The one in New York!"

"Bah. Useless city."

"Grandma."

"I mean congratulations, dear, that's wonderful."

I grinned. "Thanks, Grandma. I was thinking maybe I could visit you on my way there?"

"I'll have to check my schedule. There's a poker tournament in Buffalo in a few weeks that I'm competing in."

"The internship is for the whole month of July."

I could hear a rustling of papers. She still used a wall calendar and didn't own a computer. "Hmm, looks like I'll be gone, but maybe you can swing by after you're finished in hell. I mean New York."

I snorted. "Sounds good. Love you, Grams."

"Love you, too, Sugar Plum."

"Oh, and Rachel and Joe say hi."

There was silence on the phone. Then: "That's nice. I'll talk to you soon."

We hung up and I gathered my clothes to go take a shower before Adrian came over. My grandma was my dad's mom. She, like my mother, had a grudge against Aunt Rachel. I didn't know why. When the court had declined her guardianship over me, she'd been as angry as I was. She only spoke to Rachel and Joe if it was absolutely necessary. I'd grown to love them during my nine months here in Stony Creek, but she had not.

Rachel had promised to tell me the story of what had happened so many years ago that caused the rift in our family. I'd have to ask her about it again soon.

Adrian swung by after lunch. Rachel and Joe had lifted the ban on us being alone together, and I was allowed to come and go to his house as I pleased, although Rachel felt compelled to call over every single time to make sure Mariana was home to chaperone us.

As soon as he pulled up and got off the Harley, I jumped on him like a koala bear.

"Whoa," he said, hugging me back. "You're in a good mood."

"I got in," I told him, grinning. "To Myriad. I'm going to New York."

His face lit up. "That's fantastic!" He squeezed me and spun me around, laughing, then kissed me. "I'm so proud of you." The smile slipped off his face a little. "When do you leave?"

"Two weeks."

Oh.

Oh, crap.

On some level, I hadn't really thought I would be accepted. Which means I hadn't thought this far ahead. "I guess that means we'll be apart for the summer."

Adrian smiled lightly. "I'll come visit; don't worry."

"Yeah," I said, feeling suddenly emotional. "I guess it's only four weeks. That's not that long, right?"

"Hey," he said, bending lower to look me in the eye. "Don't be sad. This is great news; this is huge. You're going to kick ass."

"Yeah, and just forget for a month about everything that's going on? Forget about Lucian?"

"Of course not."

"I won't be any help there. I won't be able to look for him." I looked down abruptly at my shoes, eyes watering. I wasn't able to look for him here, either. I wasn't any help at all. If I stayed, if I left, it didn't matter.

At least, it wouldn't matter to Lucian.

"You'll be with Kalare and Julian," Adrian reminded me gently. "Maybe you can work on getting them to our side. Figuring things out with their help."

I thunked my forehead against his chest, letting out my own deep breath. "You're right," I mumbled. "I just…feel guilty. Leaving. The only reason I even knew about this internship was because of you. The only reason I had the supplies to make my application pieces was because of you."

"Caitlin—"

"No," I interrupted. "I just…wanted to say thank you. For believing in me."

He smile-frowned at me. "In my defense, you make it pretty easy. You're incredibly talented."

I must have made a face, because he turned serious.

"I mean it, Caitlin. I—" he looked away, searching for words. "I'm smart. I know that. Even for my kind, I'm intelligent. But…I don't know what I want to do. The truth is, I don't *have* to do anything. I don't have to get a job; I don't have to pursue a career, or a degree, or even a hobby. But you," he said, looking at me. "You know exactly who you are. You know exactly what you want. And you know how you're going to accomplish your goals. You have the skill and the talent and the determination to achieve what you want to achieve. And I think that's incredible."

I stared at him. Adrian thought *I* was incredible?

"I can't handle you being this nice to me," I muttered. "I don't even know how to process it. I feel like saying something sarcastic."

He smiled softly. "You're going to have to learn to handle it because I'm going to be right here watching you succeed, proud as hell."

Without warning, I burst into tears. Well, maybe not "burst." But

I sucked in a sharp breath, trembled for a second, then suddenly tears were pouring down my face.

"Oh god," I said, wiping at my cheeks. "I'm sorry. I don't know what's happening to me. Why am I crying?"

Adrian looked just as perplexed. "I don't know. Why *are* you crying?"

"I don't know!" I said, hiccuping. "I'm just happy. I literally feel like my stomach is going to explode, I'm so happy."

"Is that a good thing?"

I barked a laugh. "I think so? I don't know. I don't think I've felt this way before."

"I like it," Adrian said, smiling. "Not the crying part, but the happy part. I like you being happy."

I smiled, then grabbed his shirt and wiped my face off on it. Leaving mascara marks, I blushed, then smoothed the fabric down, patting his chest awkwardly. "Sorry."

"I don't mind."

I hugged him.

He hugged me.

Life was good.

Except for the parts that weren't. Like Lucian and Tommie and—

Stop, I told myself. *Enjoy the hug.*

So I did.

"Congratulations," Farrar stated evenly, neither frowning nor smiling. "Your acceptance is a great honor."

I nodded awkwardly, not knowing how to respond.

We were in the dining room, Adrian standing politely off to the side as I informed Farrar about the internship.

"There has been some concern about your leaving for such an extended period of time," he continued. "It creates…difficulties."

I frowned, honestly puzzled. "Why?"

"You are still under the protection of the Council until the demon has been properly eradicated."

"Oh. Well," I stalled, mind racing, "no offense, but unless there's something I don't know about, you guys don't seem to be any closer to finding him. My nightmares have stopped. Maybe he's lost interest in me?"

Farrar didn't respond, but he didn't object, either.

"Besides," I said, "you guys are the ones who told me to live my life as normally as possible. This is a huge opportunity for me. I know you all live forever, but I don't. I need this chance. I need the experience." I looked around the massive dining room, laughing a little at the absurdity of its scale and grandeur. "I mean for Pete's sake, I don't have a trust fund or an allowance or any of *this*," I said, gesturing around me at the mansion. "If you're telling me I can't go, then we have a problem."

That might have been too much, but A) it was true, and B) it played into the feisty-human-teenager character I put on around the Guard.

"Points I have already made to the Council," Farrar said evenly. "You are being allowed to attend."

I let out a breath in relief. "Thank you."

Maybe Farrar wasn't so bad after all.

"You should merely be aware that there may be some… inconveniences for you."

"Such as?"

"We would appreciate it if you didn't wander off into the city on your own. Keeping us informed of your plans would be very much appreciated."

That didn't sound too bad. "Done," I agreed.

He glanced behind me at Adrian, then back at me. "Will your family be accompanying you?"

"Rachel's driving me down and helping me get settled. I think she's going to stay a day or two, then head back to Stony Creek."

Farrar looked thoughtful. "Would she be open to the idea of Julian accompanying you?"

"I think she had kind of hoped we could make it into a girl's trip. Like, a bonding thing."

Farrar nodded. "Understandable. We'll have Julian, Kalare, and Sabine follow you to New York as your bodyguards."

"Oh," I said, glancing briefly at Adrian, who looked just as surprised as I did. "I—wait, what? What about Lucian?"

"Vincent and Javan are searching for him now, but you are of equal priority," Farrar assured me. "And our operations will not be disrupted, merely divided. I will remain here to continue portal research with Mariana and Dominic. Your program lasts a month?"

I nodded.

He nodded in return, as if everything was settled. "Very well. Congratulations again on your acceptance. It reflects well on both of you that you are able to achieve this kind of recognition in the middle of difficult circumstances. I have noted it in my report. I will be out with Mariana and Dominic taking readings at the site of the previous gateway. If you need anything before your departure, please address your concerns to Adrian."

I nodded awkwardly, barely stopping myself from doing the little half-bow I was tempted to give whenever Farrar dismissed me from a meeting. Instead, I hustled out, Adrian tailing me. We watched as Mariana and Dominic joined Farrar at the front door, apparently to hike through the forest to find the portal location Adrian's father had opened up last fall to get here from hell.

Everyone else seemed to be in their rooms or out on errands. "Do you still want to check out the *Matris Libri?*" Adrian asked. "Now would be a good time, since you won't be here much longer. I don't know when we'll get another chance."

I glanced around. It was dead quiet. "Can't hurt, right?"

He nodded and we escaped into the library, heading straight for the massive fireplace on the far wall. He scanned the nearest bookshelf, locating the *Matris Libri.*

We sat together on the couch, flipping to the last page. There, on the bottom left, was a photo of Adrian's mother, Lucita Abarca, and right next to it, a photo of Lucian's mother, Migle Ramanauskas.

"They don't look anything alike," I said. "Your mother was Spanish, living in Greece when your father got her pregnant. Twenty years old. Lucian's mother was Lithuanian, sixteen years old. They spoke different languages, had different interests, different education levels, lived in totally different places."

Adrian flipped back two pages and tapped a photo of a blonde woman with high cheekbones and brilliant blue eyes. "That's Julian's mother. Norwegian, twenty-three."

He flipped back again, this time about a dozen pages. We were back far enough in time that there were no photographs, only hand-drawn sketches. "Mariana's mother, Olyana Metsker. Immigrant from Russia, moved here when she was thirteen with her mother and eight siblings. Mariana was born right here in Stony Creek in 1857."

"Wait, hold on," I interrupted. "Mariana was *born* in Stony Creek?"

"Yes. I believe that was part of her reasoning in establishing a residence here. In fact, I believe the house she was born in used to reside on this very property."

I shivered. I couldn't tell if their building a mansion on the site where Mariana was born (and where, by default, her mother died) was creepy or nostalgic. Mariana didn't seem particularly nostalgic to me.

"So there's no connection," I said, feeling frustrated. "Nothing to tie them together."

"So it would seem."

We both stared at the book for a long moment. Of their own accord, my eyes wandered to the other side of the page where some other random vampire's human mother was displayed.

"What about the Guard?" I asked, getting an idea.

"What about them?"

"Well, that's just it," I said, "I don't know anything about them. Their moms would be in here, right?"

Adrian nodded. "It wouldn't tell us anything about the Council's agenda."

"But it would be something," I said a little too vehemently. I was getting frustrated with our complete lack of progress, and I was leaving in a matter of days. I needed to learn something to feel like I wasn't just running away from all this.

He nodded again and turned the pages, searching. "Ilsa Farrar, daughter of the German Duke of Farrar, spy for the Protestant Reformation. Arrested by her own father and put on trial for treason. She became pregnant in jail. Gave birth to Heinrich Farrar and died 7 November, 1518."

"Farrar's not his first name?" I asked, blinking. "And he's *German*?" He had a slightly odd cadence to his voice, but otherwise seemed to speak in a more-or-less British accent.

"Seems so. And his mother was some sort of spy. The Protestant Reformation sparked a war with the Holy Roman Empire that decimated Germany's population by almost half."

"Son of a female spy during a human religious war. That's quite a childhood."

"Not if he was taken immediately by the Council and brought up among his own kind."

I gave him a look.

"Well," he admitted, "*yes*, but not abnormal for a vampire."

We flipped the pages, tucking away the information about Farrar— or *Heinrich*—for later use.

Vincent was born in Scotland in the 16th century to a farmer's daughter. Javan was born in an unknown location somewhere in South America around the same time. Apparently the Council had been mostly European-based for most of its history and as limited as humans in their earth-bound traveling. It wasn't until the humans started building ocean-crossing ships that the Council consolidated itself as the premiere, global vampire power. Much of the vampires' history paralleled humans' because they relied on human technological advances. They'd spent much of their early centuries merely hiding and surviving. Now, though… Now they were powerful, global, tech-savvy, and immortal. It was an intimidating force to have as a potential enemy.

We flipped a few more pages. Sabine was, as Kalare had once told me, born in 1901 in Marseilles, France, to the wife of a surgeon. If the woman had lived, it would have been quite the scandal. As it was, she of course died giving birth to Sabine. Kalare, on the other hand, was born in Jersey in 1964. Abandoned at birth, she was discovered by a passing stranger and taken to the St. Gerolamo orphanage. She was diagnosed with a rare blood disorder and given transfusions until the Council finally retrieved her at the age of two. Mother unknown.

We flipped back through to Adrian's mother, and Lucian's, and Mariana's, eyes glazing over the information.

"Adrian," I said slowly, a sentence finally coming into focus that I hadn't noticed before. "Why does it say that Mariana is sister to a woman called Utuwe?"

"What?" he asked, distracted, reading through a different paragraph.

I pointed at the line I was reading. "Olyana Metsker gave birth to Mariana, younger sister to Utuwe."

Adrian blinked, then read the line I was pointing at several times. "I've never seen that before," he said finally. He looked at me. "I never looked at this page in the *Matris Libri*, only my mother's. What…"

He read the line again, then flipped hurriedly back through the book.

"Oh my god," Adrian said, staring at the much-older page.

There wasn't even a sketch this time, just a description.

Batani Utembe, princess of the Maneke tribe in central Africa, gave birth to Utuwe sometime in 782 A.D.

That was all it said. Where other vampires had multiple pages dedicated to information about their mothers, this woman had only a single line.

"I have a sister." Adrian's eyes were unfocused, staring blankly at the page. "I have another sister."

"Adrian," I said softly. "It says…it says she died."

He snapped back, leaning over the page, scanning the rest of the text. "Executed in 1472 by order of the Council for breach of law."

Next to me, Adrian was perfectly still. "I didn't know," he said after a long moment of silence. "I never even thought to look." He laid his fingers on the text in disbelief. "I was told I had a brother and a sister. I met Julian when I was eight. I met Mariana when I was twelve. I knew about Lucian, but he was taken by my father as soon as he was born. I never knew…"

He looked shell-shocked. I wanted to comfort him, but I had no idea what to say. *Sorry* didn't seem appropriate. How would I feel if I found out I had a 1200-year-old sister who'd been executed by my government over 500 years ago?

"Why didn't Mariana tell me?" he whispered.

"Maybe she didn't know," I said softly. "It says this woman died in 1472. That was hundreds of years before Mariana was born."

"It's right *here*," Adrian said, smacking the page. "It's right here. How could she not have known?"

"Known what?" a voice asked from behind us.

Adrian slammed the *Matris Libri* closed, but it was too late. Kalare was standing there, arms crossed, looking down at us.

We stared at each other for a long moment before her gaze traveled to the coffee table and the very conspicuous, very large leather-bound book Adrian was unsuccessfully trying to hide with his hands.

"Getting into some family history?" she asked, sitting down opposite us.

Neither Adrian or I answered.

"One of you," Kalare said calmly, "needs to tell me what's going on."

Next to me, I could feel Adrian gearing up for a lie. I'd had enough conversations with Kalare to know that would only piss her off. I put my hand on his arm, stopping him, then turned to the vampire sitting across from us.

"If I tell you," I said slowly, "what assurance do I have that you won't immediately run off to Farrar and report what we say?"

"None," she replied bluntly. "But I'm a reasonable person, so I'm willing to withhold judgment until I understand what game you think you're playing."

I glanced at Adrian. He shook his head, his eyes flaring softly into a light silver.

He was worried.

I had to play this carefully.

I opened the *Matris Libri* and turned to the page on Utuwe.

"Do you know who she is?"

Kalare glanced down, scanning the page. She shrugged. "Never heard of her."

"That's Adrian's sister," I said, watching her face closely. She looked mildly surprised. "A sister Adrian didn't know existed until about two minutes ago. A sister the Council executed half a millenia ago."

"Millennium," Adrian automatically corrected me.

I turned to him and frowned pointedly.

"Sorry," he muttered, blushing a little.

Kalare's eyes narrowed. "My condolences on your loss," she said, glancing at Adrian, "and your grammar. But I don't see your point."

"Doesn't this situation seem strange to you?" I asked, dancing slowly around the truth. "Mariana's vision about me, and the fact that no one seems to know what exactly that vision was? Tommie's behavior? Lucian's disappearance? An entire Praetorian Guard who seems to be in Stony Creek doing…nothing?"

Her eyes narrowed further, but she didn't speak.

Here was the real risk. Saying this part out loud. "Adrian can do things that he shouldn't be able to do. I have dreams that I shouldn't be able to have. Adrian's father…he said things. Things that don't make sense. Things we don't understand."

Her eyes flicked to Adrian, then back to me. "What sorts of things?"

I shook my head. "I can't tell you that. Not yet. All I can say is that we're trying to understand what's really going on." I tapped the page about Utuwe. "Can you honestly tell me that all of this adds up? That you're here for the reason you've been told? Can you tell me that the Praetorian Guard is doing *anything* to find Lucian? That the trip to hell went as planned? That Adrian and I aren't being watched far more carefully than the situation warrants? You yourself have been assigned to babysit me in New York. Why? Can you tell me that any of this is playing out the way it's supposed to?"

Kalare didn't speak, but she wasn't arguing with us, either.

"I'm human," I continued. "I have no context for any of this, other than what Adrian has told me and what the Council has chosen to share. But this is *my* life on the line. It's Lucian's life. Can you blame us for not trusting everything we've been told?"

Kalare let out a slow breath, then rubbed her forehead. "No," she muttered. "I don't blame you."

I glanced at Adrian. His jaw was tight, his eyes were still burning softly.

I grabbed his hand with mine, resting it on his knee. Kalare stared at it, then looked up at me.

"I trust him," I said quietly. "And I'm beginning to trust you." I held her gaze for a long moment. "*Should* I trust you?"

Kalare's mouth twitched. She held my gaze for an unbearably long ten seconds, then sat back, looking disgusted. Finally, she looked back at us.

"For God's sake, quit holding hands, you morons. We're in the house."

I glanced at Adrian, then slowly let go of his hand.

"All right," she said, leaning forward. "Say I believe you. Some of this doesn't add up. Truth be told, it's been bothering me, too, ever since I got here. Never been on a Praetorian Guard, though, so I convinced myself it was merely my own ignorance of protocol."

She looked away, chewing on her fingernail as she began tapping her foot restlessly. "Screw it," she said, looking back at us. "I believe you."

The knot of panic in my chest immediately loosened.

"But this is literally the last place we should be talking about this," she said, looking around. "Next time I'm on guard duty, we'll have a little chat. Capiche?"

Adrian and I nodded. She stood, letting out a frustrated breath. "Good. And seriously, enough with the PDA. It's disgusting."

I couldn't help but smile. She pointed at me, frowning deeply. "That is not the reaction you should be having. Stop smiling."

I did my best to wipe the smile off my face, but it was hard. She threw her hands in the air. "I give up. Dumb-ass teenagers."

She walked off, leaving us alone in the library.

"What…just happened?" Adrian asked finally.

"If I'm not mistaken," I replied, "I think we just gained a new ally."

BETWEEN WORLDS

12

o, *no*," my mother muttered impatiently, leaning over me. "You've got the thread all lumpy. What did you do, wind this by hand?"

Six-year-old-me shrank in her chair.

"I showed you how to load the bobbin," she continued, irritated. "Were you not paying attention?"

The truth was, the bobbin wound so fast, and made such a loud noise, that it scared me. Just like the vacuum cleaner.

"Unwind it," my mom ordered. "Start over, and do it right."

Fighting tears, the pint-sized dream-me sat huddled in the chair at the sewing machine un-spooling thread.

I watched from my vantage point sitting cross-legged on the cutting table.

I'd forgotten all about this.

My mom went over to the ironing board and began pressing a seam, slapping down the iron with far more force than was necessary.

With every whack of the iron, my younger self flinched.

My dad had died three months ago.

My mom was not handling it well.

"*Caitlin*," Data said, appearing across the cutting table from me. "I understand the appeal of reliving these sorts of memories. But there are things we must do."

"She was so mean," I said, ignoring him. "I forgot about that. She was mean to me after Dad died. For years."

"Caitlin," Data prompted gently.

I didn't want to see any more of this anyway. I didn't want to remember her like this.

The dreamscape shifted, dragging me into my bedroom at the ranch.

I blinked, confused. "Why are we here?"

I watched as me from just before Christmas sat up in bed, gasping. Adrian was sitting on a pile of pillows on the floor. He scrambled to his feet and sat next to me on my bed.

"What did we do differently?" Other Me asked. "Why didn't it work?"

Adrian opened his mouth, then closed it. "I don't know. Unless—" He paused, thinking. "The nightmares started right after you went to the mall, right?"

Other Me nodded.

"And that man—did he touch you?"

Other Me nodded again. "Briefly, just my wrist."

The memory jumped back a few seconds.

"And that man," Adrian asked again, "did he touch you?"

Other Me nodded. "Briefly, just my wrist."

The moment looped until I grew irritated and paused it with a thought.

"Adrian's father touched me at the mall last Christmas," I said, turning to Data, "and the nightmares started. We already know that."

Data waited patiently, saying nothing.

I paced, thinking. Suddenly, I stopped. "He touched me, and the nightmares started. The next time he touched me, the nightmares stopped." I looked at Data. "And in their place, you showed up."

Data nodded, looking pleased with my answer.

"What would happen," I asked slowly, "if he touched me again?"

"That," Data said, smiling slightly, "is the question."

Stony Creek—the actual creek, not the town itself—was dammed, creating a small swimming hole in the center of town. It was eighty-five degrees out and muggy, which meant it was currently crammed full of screaming kids and a few wayward tourists who'd probably been on their way to Saratoga Springs and taken a wrong turn. Across the dam, I saw some seniors from Adrian's class lounging on what passed for a beach. Or, well, I guess they weren't seniors anymore since they were graduated. What did I call them? Adults? They saw him and waved, and he waved back. We'd chosen the place because it was incredibly noisy, and the chance of being overhead by anyone from the Praetorian Guard was slim to none. And as far as Kalare knew, she was the only one on duty, which meant no one else was supposed to be near enough to eavesdrop in the first place.

We were all in our swimsuits, soaking up the sun. Kalare and Adrian had both taken double portions of blood that morning so they wouldn't burn in the heat. I often forgot that they had to do stuff like that. We were off in a slightly secluded section where we could talk without alarming any of the human townsfolk. Kalare did attract some attention with her purple-tipped hair, red lipstick, and black bikini, but she'd been seen enough around town that no one was alarmed by her presence. Also, she looked like a college student, and everyone knew she was "Adrian's cousin."

Still, we were all a little on-edge.

The one upside was that I had an excuse to look at Adrian shirtless. I would take my silver linings where I could get them.

"All right," Kalare said, pulling three sodas from the cooler and handing one to me and Adrian before popping open the third. "Start talking."

"Caitlin may trust you," Adrian said, "but I'm not convinced. Why don't you start by telling us what happened in hell?"

Kalare frowned at him. "I didn't go, remember?"

"But you're on the Praetorian Guard," Adrian said. "You know what they know."

"Not as much as you'd think," Kalare muttered. "Big brother's got a stick up his ass when it comes to secrets and protecting the Council's interests."

At first, I thought she was making a reference to the Council being Orwellian, like people referred to the government being Big Brother. Then I realized she'd said his "his" ass, not "their ass."

"Wait," I interrupted. "Big brother?"

Kalare glanced between me and Adrian. "You didn't know?"

Adrian and I shared a concerned look.

Kalare smiled wryly. "Farrar's my older brother. Why do you think I got assigned to the Guard?"

Vampires having very, very different mothers who lived in different centuries on different continents made family resemblances almost zilch between siblings. There's no way you would have known by just looking at the two of them that they were related. Plus, the *Matris Libri* had said Kalare's last name was Davis, not Farrar.

"How come your last name's different than his?"

"Use your head, dingus. Different centuries, different names."

"But the de la Maras share a name," I countered.

"They're the exception, not the rule. Julian had his name changed a few years back, at Mariana's request. He was born Julian Guerin. Didn't you know that?" she asked, looking at Adrian. He shook his head.

"My head is going to explode," I said, "if I find out about anymore surprise family connections. Sabine your sister, too? She lived with Farrar, didn't she?"

Kalare snorted. "No, thank God. I mean yes, she lived with them, but no, she's not my sister. Had a sister. Never knew her. The Council was really into corporal punishment in the Dark Ages."

I stared at her. "She was executed?"

She nodded like this was an everyday conversation topic. "Centuries before I was born. It was pretty common." She took a sip of soda, then set it down carefully, drawing nonsense designs in the condensation. "You want to know why I keep griping at you guys to be careful? Farrar's the one that turned her in. My brother is the reason my sister is dead, the reason I never knew her. So when I'm telling you guys not to fuck around, I mean it. He'll report you. One or both of you will die. He'll sleep just fine."

I could barely breathe. Farrar had seemed the most…normal, of them. Or at least the most even-keeled. If he'd done that…Kalare was right: he'd have no qualms about turning us in for punishment.

"Sometimes I think this is all a really bad dream," I muttered. "Because it's ridiculous. It's totally insane."

"Welcome to immortality, kids."

"Speaking of," Adrian prompted, "you were telling us about hell?"

Kalare leaned back, thinking. "Vincent, Javan, and Farrar have all been to hell before. They've served together on guards and small councils. Sabine and Julian haven't. I was, of course, left behind. From what's been said in meetings, and from what I've managed to pull out of Julian, they never actually got to hell."

Adrian and I shared a look. "Where were they, then?"

"Dunno. In the ether between worlds, maybe."

"Is that why they didn't signal that they were coming back?" I asked.

She nodded. "Apparently they have absolutely no recollection of that time. They remember going under, and they remember waking up. They have no memory of the three weeks they were gone, or where they were during that time. It's entirely possible they could have never come back."

"No wonder Julian didn't want to talk about it," Adrian muttered.

"What's more," Kalare continued, leaning forward, "is that there's a theory floating around about Lucian."

Adrian and I both looked up at her sharply.

"When he was brought back almost two years ago and questioned by the Council, he could not provide specifics about where he'd been or what he'd seen for the past ten years. Now that he has been once again taken by your father," she said, looking at Adrian, "some people are speculating that Lucian was never in hell to begin with."

I looked back and forth between them, confused. "What…what does that mean? If he wasn't in hell, where was he?"

"Stuck," she said slowly, "between worlds. A doorstopper your father used to suck in more energy than previously thought possible. His body was probably stuck here on earth while his soul was… elsewhere."

I stared at Kalare, trying to envision Lucian caught halfway between here and hell. If it was true, it was no wonder why he'd been so confused about having a body again and being around other people. He'd been alone for his entire life while his parasite of a father used him as an interdimensional wedge to siphon extra power.

"It's worse than that, though," she continued. "The trip to hell was just the latest in a string of concerning incidents. You were looking at the *Matris Libri.* Did you know it's out of date?"

I looked at Adrian. He shook his head. "I know they update them once a year, ship out additional pages, update the electronic version."

"They haven't updated the book since Lucian was born. Do you know why?"

We shook our heads. The amount of information I hadn't known was making me feel panicked.

"For the past millenia, our birth rate has been less than two hundred vampires a year." She paused, looking grim. "Since Lucian was born, that rate has increased exponentially. Since Christmas alone, there have been five *thousand* new vampires born around the world."

I dropped my soda.

Adrian blinked.

"I'm sorry," he said a long moment later, "could you say that again?"

"Five thousand vampires," Kalare repeated slowly, "born in the last seven months."

"That's insane," Adrian said, blankly. "That's not possible."

"You're right," Kalare replied. "It's not possible. And yet, there it is."

"How do you know that?" Adrian asked. "Surely the Council wouldn't let information like that become common knowledge."

"You're right," she agreed. "They wouldn't. Still got some old Petitioner contacts. They're far less tight-lipped than our dear Council."

She opened a bag of chips and held it out to Adrian, who shook his head. I took a handful but didn't eat any.

"I held up my end of the bargain," Kalare said, mouth full. "I'm officially guilty of treason. Your turn."

I glanced at Adrian. He still looked shocked, but he nodded. "Caitlin and I are in love," he said quietly, "so there's that."

He'd said it out loud before, but not in front of any vampires. Kalare didn't react much, just glanced between the two of us curiously.

"We're aware of the consequences. We're aware of the immortality problem. I spent months trying to distance myself from Caitlin, to convince myself I didn't have feelings for her, which led directly to my father finding an opportunity to…hurt her."

He didn't look at me. I didn't look at him. Again, Kalare didn't say anything, just glanced back and forth between the two of us.

Adrian cleared his throat. "Before we actually fought, my father made certain…claims. That the Council was lying to us, withholding important information. That Caitlin was different, significant some-how. That the Council wanted her dead. Or at least, that they would have found it convenient if he had killed her. He seemed to indicate that he did not want Caitlin dead, that he had some other purpose for her. He seemed surprised that I had not compelled Caitlin to love me. He…laughed."

Adrian's face twisted into a grimace. We didn't talk about that night very much.

"While my father did attempt to seduce Caitlin, as we were warned that he would do, it's never made much sense to me. We were told by the Council that he'd chosen her to be the next carrier of his child. But why?" He looked up at me, then Kalare. "Why, when he could have any woman? Why wait around when we knew he was here, when we knew he'd targeted her? It would be so much simpler to move on to someone else."

He shook his head. "Moreover, he had to have known that I was home. He set up that whole night. He set up the bait that led Mariana and Dominic to D.C. He knew that Julian was in New York. He knew that only Lucian and myself were at the house. He had to have known that I would have felt what was going on, that I would have come to intervene."

He looked up at us again. "My father is not stupid. If his goal was truly to impregnate Caitlin, why go to all that trouble knowing that I would interrupt him?" He stopped, staring down at the ground hard. "And yet, he did. He was on top of her when I arrived. It doesn't make sense."

Kalare looked at me, her face neutral. "I know what you told the Guard. But what did you experience when that happened?"

My face burned red in shame. "It started out normal. He asked if he could hug me, after he'd told me some sob story about how his family had died in a car crash. Hit me right where he knew it would hurt. So I hugged him. And then he kissed me. And then…it gets foggy. I was there, I was doing those things, making those choices, and yet…I wasn't. It felt like…well, like being drunk," I said, remembering the effects of last year's Halloween party. "But not. I don't know, I've never done drugs, but maybe more like that. Like I wasn't totally there. I remember…" I stopped, swallowing hard. "I remember thinking in the middle of it that he was Adrian. That I was safe, that I was with him and that everything was okay."

I shook my head. "I hadn't slept for weeks, though. For all I know I was hallucinating from pure exhaustion."

"What did you feel from her?" she asked Adrian.

He turned slowly red, fiddling with the tab on his soda can. "She was…interested, in what was happening."

"We're all adults," Kalare said evenly, "just say it."

Adrian swallowed hard. "I could tell she was…" he stopped and shook his head. "I can't say it. You know what I mean."

Kalare rolled her eyes. "Horny. She was horny. Like teenagers tend to be."

Adrian's blush turned a shade brighter. "Yes—but it was muddled."

"What do you mean?"

"I mean it was *muddled*. I don't—I mean, I've spent time with her. I know the shape of her emotions. They're specific." Kalare waved him on as if she knew what he meant. "The reason it took me so long to realize what was happening is that what she was experiencing wasn't clear. Not like…not like when she felt that around me. That's why it took me so long to get there. I didn't even realize it was her."

"That sounds like some grade-A rape compulsion to me," Kalare said bluntly. "Did he command you?" she asked me. "Give you any specific instructions?"

I shook my head, embarrassed. "No. And that's what doesn't make sense. I have no memory of him compelling me."

"Could he have compelled her to forget?" Adrian asked.

"Could—but she'd have blank spots. Do you have any gaps in your memory of that night?"

I shook my head slowly, thinking. "I don't think so."

Kalare let out a deep breath, looking thoughtful. "I can see why you didn't want to give the Council all the details."

"That's not even the part we left out," I muttered.

"Well get to the big secret," she said, waving us on. "What did you keep from the Council?"

Adrian took a deep breath, glancing around us. No one was taking any notice of us.

"We told the Council that I fought my father. That I injured him badly enough that he ran off. That's—" he paused, looking at me. I nodded. "That's not entirely true."

Kalare's eyes narrowed. "I was wondering how you took on a

demon singlehandedly. You're something of a legend now, for those in the know."

"I did injure him," Adrian said. "I did hurt him badly enough to run him off. I just didn't do it…naturally."

Kalare ate a handful of chips. "What, did you bore him to death with an incredibly long story?"

Adrian frowned. "I burned him. With my eyes. From twenty feet in the air."

She stopped chewing.

"I'm sorry, you *what?*"

"I burned him," Adrian repeated, "*with my eyes*. From twenty feet in the air."

Kalare glanced at me, then stared at Adrian. "What were you doing twenty feet in the air?"

"Getting my ass kicked," he muttered. "My father produced some sort of air vortex that lifted me off the ground. He was going to kill me. Well," he said, glancing at me, "he *did* kill me, temporarily. Caitlin saved my life."

Kalare looked at me. "*Her?* How? I mean, I heard about the pencil-in-the-neck thing—nice move, by the way—but after that he knocked her unconscious."

"I only blacked out for a second," I explained. In the version of the story we'd told the Council, I'd blacked out for the rest of the fight, only waking after Tommie had run off.

"My father had me pinned mid-air," Adrian continued. "I couldn't move. I could barely breathe. I was being punctured by debris; might as well have been bullets." He flinched, remembering. "I knew I was going to die. He was going to take Caitlin. She was going to die. I had nothing left. I couldn't fight. And then there was a power surge." He looked over at me. "She'd been afraid, and my father was feeding off that fear. And

173

then somehow, she did a one-eighty. It was the most powerful thing I've ever felt in my life."

He shook his head, then looked at Kalare. "You want to know why I'm willing to risk everything to be with her, it's because of that night. That moment. I'd been cruel to her for months. I'd given her no reason to think that I cared about her in any way. And when my life was on the line, she saved me. I felt calm. I felt so calm." His eyes unfocused, remembering. After a moment, he blinked. "I can't describe what I did. Suddenly, I was burning him. My eyes produced a light so intense it literally melted the skin off his body. It must have injured him severely enough that he couldn't maintain the air vortex. I fell to the ground and he ran off, leaving us behind. The next thing I remember was waking up to find Caitlin leaning over me, covered in blood. When we got back to the house, Lucian was gone. We were so exhausted we didn't discover his absence until the following morning."

He fell silent.

Kalare stared at him.

"I have a feeling there's more," she said, chewing on a mouthful of chips. "Though I don't know how that's possible."

I nodded, swallowing. "Before all this, I'd been having nightmares." The Council knew about that part. "After this, the nightmares stopped. But then I started having new dreams. Dreams I could control. Where I can, uh…" It sounded stupid saying it out loud. "Where I can sort of have conversations with my own subconscious."

Kalare stopped chewing. "You have conversations," she said, staring at me, "with your *subconscious?*"

"Um…yes. Yep. I can replay memories, anything I've experienced firsthand. I can freeze it, rewind it, play it in slow motion. And my spirit guide—er, my subconscious—I can make it look like anyone. It showed up as Tommie, at first—Adrian's dad, he called himself

Tommie—and now I can change its shape. Right now it's Data. From…
from *Star Trek*."

Both of them stared at me. I hadn't told Adrian about Data yet.

"Well," Kalare said after a pregnant silence. "That is…that's not good."

"Why not?" I asked, feeling my stomach tighten in dread.

"I can't believe I'm saying this, but it was wise of you not to tell the Council." She let out a slow whistle, leaning back. "Shit. This is really bad."

"We know that," Adrian said tightly. "What we don't know is *why*."

She let out a sharp laugh, like she couldn't believe she was saying this out loud. "Your girlfriend," Kalare said, looking at us with pity, "is an Unmaker."

WE'LL ALWAYS HAVE STONY CREEK

13

"Kalare wouldn't say more," I told Data, pacing. "She said it was too dangerous. And she wasn't a hundred percent certain I was this Unmaker thing. She needed to talk to some of her non-Covenant contacts—whatever that means—and see if she could confirm her theory without getting either herself or us killed."

I kicked at a pile of snow. "And we're just supposed to sit here and wait. I leave in a week. We have a *week* to figure this out before I'm going to be separated from Adrian all summer. I mean, Kalare's going with me, so at least I'll have an ally in New York, but this is nuts. It's *nuts*."

I looked up at Data, who waited patiently, his mustard yellow-and-black Starfleet uniform immaculate as ever. "Well? Anything? Any cryptic questions to make me have some sudden epiphany?"

Data just stood there, politely. We were in the clearing, as usual, but neither Dream-Tommie or Dream-Adrian or Dream-Me were there. Just me and Data.

"You gonna…do the thing?" I asked.

Data looked at me curiously.

"Y'know, the thing," I said, waving my hand. "The dream thing, where you show me things."

"I am showing you things," Date replied calmly

I stared at him, confused. "It's just us."

Data waited, as if expecting something to dawn on me.

"I'm slow tonight, Lieutenant. Help me out."

"You said 'us,' Caitlin. What do you think I am showing you?"

I stared at him, confused. I looked around and realized even the clearing had faded away. It was just me and Data against infinite white.

Us?

"You're showing me…you?" I guessed.

Data smiled.

"But you've been here the whole time."

"No, I have not," Data stated. "*You* have been here the whole time."

"You're hurting my brain," I muttered.

"Think, Caitlin," Data said, reasonably. "What do you believe I am?"

"My subconscious mind," I said, irritated. "We've already established that."

Data nodded. "And do you know of anyone else who has conversations with their subconscious?"

"Well, no, but…"

But what? So Tommie had made physical contact with me, so what? He didn't compel me to have conversations with my subconscious mind. How could he? That wasn't a thing that people could *do*. Vampires and demons could only compel humans to do things that were within their natural capacity.

"There is something wrong with me, isn't there?" I asked Data.

"*Wrong* is not the word I would use."

"But there's something different? About me?"

Data frowned at me sternly. "Caitlin—is that not obvious by now?"

I had four days before I left for New York. Stony Creek had recently decided to start doing more community events as a way to draw summer tourists, and tonight they were doing movies in the park on a giant inflatable screen. They were showing *Transformers*, which was, well, not my favorite, but as there wasn't much to do in Stony Creek (and because there wasn't a theater closer than a half hour away), I was taking what I could get, especially since I had so little time left to hang out with everyone.

We'd invited Ben, but he'd had to work. Apparently he'd gotten a summer job at one of the resorts at Lake George, and they had him working nights. He'd been surprisingly cool to me and Adrian, considering how much Trish was not cool with us.

Mark was leaning back against the cooler, and Jenny was leaning back against Mark. She had relaxed so much in the past few weeks, even more so now that Trish was gone. I think between Trish and me not getting along, and Mark being Trish's brother, and Jenny hanging out with me more than Trish, she'd felt super uncomfortable. Now that Trish was several thousand miles away, she'd chilled out.

"Why is Meghan giving you the stink-eye?" I whispered to Jenny.

Jenny glanced over at Laura and Meghan a few blankets over. I was surprised to see her expression turn angry. Jenny, not Meghan. Well, actually, both of them looked pretty pissed.

She glanced at Mark. He'd fallen asleep. Apparently he'd been up late the night before painting.

"Meghan's angry that Mark and I are hanging out."

"Why?" I asked. "I mean, she claimed dibs on him for the New Year's party, but that was a joke. Right?"

Jenny's face was set in a hard frown. "I think she's just mad that I got something she wanted. She's started spreading rumors about me."

"Wait, for serious? Like what?"

Jenny's frown deepened. "That I slept with Mark to steal him from her."

I blinked. "Are you shitting me?"

Jenny shook her head. "Stephanie told me that Meghan said it straight to her face. Asked her why she was hanging out with a slut."

I gaped at Jenny. "Are you…are you serious? She said that?"

Jenny nodded, her jaw tight. "It's not fair. I didn't do anything to her. I didn't even go after Mark; he's the one that started talking to me. She can't blame me for that." She shook her head. "I think part of her believes it. She literally doesn't think that he'd be interested in me. So I must have slept with him to get him to pay attention to me, instead of her."

She glanced down at Mark's sleeping face, looking pained.

"God, Jen, I'm so sorry. I had no idea that was going on. Did Stephanie say anything?"

Stephanie and Tim had been sitting next to us, but they'd snuck off about twenty minutes ago, probably to go make out in Tim's car. Adrian had disappeared about a half hour before to go grab us burgers from the food stand, but the line was crazy long.

"She said she didn't think that was true, and that maybe Meghan should talk to me directly if she was concerned."

Jenny let out a frustrated sigh, looking down at Mark's sleeping face. "I didn't think liking someone would involve so many other people."

I snorted, laughing. If she only knew.

Adrian came back then with food, and the smell of fresh burgers woke Mark from his nap. We ate, watched *Transformers*, and gave Stephanie and Tim a hard time when they wandered back to our blanket five minutes before the end of the movie.

I tried to ignore the fact that Farrar and Sabine had been sitting at the edge of the crowd watching us the whole time.

The next day, Adrian was over helping me pack for New York. We'd seen Kalare, briefly, but she'd simply shaken her head: she had no news. Until she did, she wasn't willing to talk to us. And believe me, I'd tried—she'd taken to hiding from me whenever I was at the mansion. Adrian had been searching the library when he could, looking for the term 'Unmaker,' but so far hadn't found a single mention, except in a book of children's vampire nursery rhymes.

Step light, speak soft, keep right—
Your fate waits in the white.
For every last lawbreaker
Must meet the grim Unmaker.

I truly doubted I was something that would show up in an old, slightly creepy poem. Also, it was totally novel to me that vampires had their own nursery rhymes. Made me wonder what their romance novels looked like.

Adrian promised to keep searching, but since it was my last few days in Stony Creek—and Kalare had promised to come to us when she knew more—we let ourselves have a short break to enjoy our last bit of time together.

And enjoy it I did.

With Rachel busy upstairs folding laundry and Norah out in the pastures with Joe and some customers for the next three hours, I pulled

Adrian into the laundry room and shut the door.

"What's—?"

I cut him off with a kiss.

"Wait," he whispered against my mouth, voice strained, "they can…over there, they can feel you."

"I don't care," I murmured and kissed his collarbone, then his neck.

"Caitlin," he choked, "do you have the blocks up at least?"

I slid my hands up his back, pressing close to him. "I think so," I mumbled, honestly not sure, and *really* not caring. I only had three days left with him. It was making me a little rash.

"Can you—God," he said, and picked me up, pressing his mouth to mine. I tangled my fingers in his hair and wrapped my legs around his waist.

A moment later, he broke away. "*No.* Stop it. I'm serious." His eyes were glowing brightly. He wasn't compelling me, he was just losing control.

"I miss you," I whispered fiercely.

"I miss you, too," he whispered back, kissing my jaw and the corner of my mouth. "But not enough to get you killed."

Damn it. He was right. Even Adrian kisses weren't worth dying for. He slowly set me down, and I stared forlornly at his chest. "Can we go to the cabin?"

He frowned, thinking. "Probably not. It's far enough away but they're watching us. They'll follow us if we go."

I was so frazzled. I had so much pent-up…*feelings* and no way to let them out.

I made a growling sound deep in my throat.

He rested his forehead on my hair, sighing. "It's not like this is easy for me, either. I want…*things*, too."

I let out my own sigh, gearing up to shut down the ol' hormone-factory, and looked up at him. His eyes were still burning, and he was looking at me in a way he rarely allowed himself to look at me.

I counted on Adrian to be the one with the self-control, because vampirism aside, that was sort of in his nature. I was the passionate, reckless one; he was the nerd who read Harry Potter and got accepted to Harvard and spent the majority of his life perfecting a look of polite indifference.

I forgot, sometimes, that he was eighteen. And a dude.

I plonked my forehead on his chest so that I could touch him, but kept every other part of my body away from his.

"I am going to explode," I mumbled. "If I can't kiss you regularly. Just poof, blood and guts everywhere. It'll be such a mess."

He carefully wrapped his arms around my shoulder and rested his chin on my head. "That's pretty gross."

I slid my arms around his waist and held on, listening as his heartbeat slowed to its regular pace.

"What if you compelled me?" I asked suddenly, looking up.

He frowned down at me. "Compelled you to make out with me?"

"No," I said, shaking my head, "compelled me to put up the blocks. You said yourself that mine are weak. I can't concentrate enough when I'm standing still to keep them up for long; trying to do it when I want to rip your clothes off is practically impossible. What if you compelled me to keep up the blocks?"

He looked stricken. "Cait, I don't think…I don't think that's a good idea."

"Why not?"

He grimaced. "Compulsion isn't natural. It's part of why we're so strict about using it only in emergencies. If I tell you to put up the blocks, it will by its nature interfere with how you're feeling. I don't…I don't want you to do anything with me because I've compelled you to.

That would kill me."

I opened my mouth to argue, then closed it.

"I understand," I said finally. "If it really would affect me, I wouldn't want that, either."

But that meant we were back at square one. No making out. Not even *thinking* about making out.

It was like asking the sun not to shine.

"I'll think of something," he promised, kissing my temple. "I am just as invested in finding a solution to this predicament as you are."

Adrian and I spent the next three days glued to each others' sides, mostly in town or at the ranch, in full view of my family or riders who'd come to check out the horses. Y'know, *humans*.

We took naps in the hammock Joe had set up on the front porch. We took naps on the couch. We took naps on the hill in the meadow overlooking the training rings where Norah taught younger kids how to command their ponies. Adrian would draw letters on my back with his finger while I sketched designs in my journal. For a full hour one day, he simply traced variations of the phrase, "I love you."

I really love you.

I love you a lot.

I loooooove you.

I love you. I love you. I love you.

Our whole group hopped in Stephanie's family's Suburban to go to Queensbury where we went bowling and then we found a convenience store that sold Pixie Stix. We got a little sugar-high and danced through the streets listening to music until a patrol car told us to go home.

We went to the Fields' house and admired Mark's paintings. He had a studio shed out back and had started on a massive eight-by-eight foot portrait of Jenny. It was still in the pencil phase, but I could see where he was going with it. Afterward, I found myself doodling little sketches of Lucian in various fantastical settings: as an Ewok, as a tiny Borg, as Frankenstein. I gave them to Adrian.

We helped my family do odd jobs around the ranch, grabbed ice-cream at the market in town, and did our best to pretend, for a few days at least, that our lives were normal. That everything would be okay.

My last day in Stony Creek, Kalare met us at the ranch.

"I have a meeting set up with a contact of mine, but it's not until we get to New York. Watch your backs. Be careful. Don't make out in stupid places."

After she left, Adrian and I discussed my trip.

"We can't text or call," I said, chewing on a pen cap, thinking. "If they can bug your truck, they can hack our phones."

"I know," Adrian replied. "I'm going to ask Julian to buy you a pre-paid burner phone, for emergencies. We won't be able to use it often; can't risk Sabine seeing it—or anyone else who might be watching."

"You'll keep me updated on everything?" I asked.

"Of course. But Cait—I want you to enjoy your trip. I'll do everything I can from here. But if you're not paying attention to your internship, there's no point in going at all. Promise me you'll have a good time, all right? There's going to be a day when all of this is over and things go back to normal. I want you to do everything you can to stay on track for the life you want."

I promised I would try. What I didn't tell him was that I had no idea how to shut off the side of my brain that was constantly worried, constantly paranoid. What I didn't tell him was that I wasn't sure things would ever go back to normal. Or that I would survive long enough to find out. But I would try.

That night, Adrian came over for a big barbecue. He helped Joe cook while Rachel and Norah and I made dessert. We set up the table outside on the porch and ate dinner under the light of the stars and a couple strands of those big round lights. We played card games, laughed, stayed up way too late. It was close to midnight before Joe and Rachel finally shooed Norah up to her room.

"Turn the lights off when you go to bed," Joe told me. He walked upstairs, closing his bedroom door behind him. Which meant he wasn't going to stay up and make sure that Adrian left.

Which meant he trusted us.

Adrian led me outside, closing the front door behind me. We stood under the soft glow of the lights, not saying anything.

Finally, he reached out and wrapped me up in his arms.

I closed my eyes, cheek pressed to his chest, listening to his heartbeat.

Despite Kalare's warning, Adrian reached down and kissed me, neither of us caring if it was smart or safe.

Even though I was only going to be gone for four weeks, some part of me felt like I was saying goodbye to him forever.

Without traffic, it was four hours from Stony Creek to New York, which meant it took Rachel and I five hours to get there and two hours to maneuver through city traffic. Myriad was in the fashion district, only a few blocks from where Rachel used to live twenty years ago.

"I barely recognize it," she said, looking up at the buildings. "It's crazy how much it's changed. It's like a whole different city."

We paid a ridiculous amount of money to park the truck in the garage of Enneman's School of Design. Myriad had set up a partnership with them to facilitate the internships. They had a college program and a high school program. We'd be living in the school's tiny dorms and commuting over to Myriad's offices five days a week. We were supposed to be two to a room, but Farrar had pulled some strings "for security purposes" to get me a single.

Julian's flat would be his, Sabine's, and Kalare's base of operations. One of them would be on-duty at all times as my bodyguard.

I felt a little bad about that, but only a little. Kalare already lived in Jersey, Julian already lived in the city, and I had no qualms about inconveniencing Sabine. I only wished there was an excuse for Adrian to be there.

Today, though, Rachel was determined to treat me. We hauled all my stuff up to my dorm and decorated it with the few things I'd brought. She put up the framed couture designs that Adrian had given me for my birthday last year, and she surprised me by pulling out a box that had a couple of my own designs in matching frames. By the time we were done, it looked like a real apartment, albeit a shoebox-sized one. I was just glad I had my own bathroom. Communal showers were not something I was ready for.

After registering with the floor's R.A., Rachel took me out to lunch at her favorite corner bistro a few blocks away, then showed me how to work the subway. I'd used it before, on my trips to the city with my mom, but the last time I'd come here I was twelve and hadn't really had to think too much about it because my mom knew where we were going.

It was actually fun to see this side of Rachel. She normally dressed in jeans and flannels, but she'd worn some of her trendier clothing for this trip and had done up her makeup more, even wearing lipstick. Seeing her face light up in the city, I could see how she had once wanted to be a model. She was beautiful.

We went to the Met and saw all the designer gowns on display, fashion from the past century. The architecture, the design, was as inspiring as it was intimidating. I was surprised by how much Rachel knew about it all, too. She rattled off trivia about the designers that even I didn't know. I realized she liked all this stuff. It made sense, I guess; she was my mother's sister. But while my mom had been an incredible seamstress, she had virtually no interest in clothing or design. She spent most of her time making quilts and curtains and embroidered wall hangings. I'd been the one constantly trying to figure out how to construct clothing. Rachel, by her own admission, wasn't much of a seamstress, but she understood the design aspect of fashion. She even admitted, walking past the Chanel display, that she'd once toyed with the idea of becoming a designer, after a career in modeling. That had all changed, of course, once she met Joe in Stony Creek, and never come back to the city.

Late in the afternoon, Rachel had another surprise for me, whisking me back to the dorm room without telling me why.

"I was going to save this for your birthday, but when I heard you got accepted to the internship, I couldn't wait."

She handed me a package and I opened it to find a brand-new set of make up brushes, foundation, eyeshadow, blushes, mascara, and some stuff I didn't even have a name for.

"Holy crap, Aunt Rachel," I said, knowing this must have cost a ton.

"It's sort of an early birthday present. Probably your Christmas present, too," she explained, so I wouldn't protest.

She spent the next hour and a half teaching me what each brush was used for, what order things went on, and how to achieve several different looks. I ended up with a semi-successful wingtip and was even feeling bold enough to throw on some red lipstick. Rachel and I changed into fancy dresses and then went out to a restaurant there was no way Rachel could afford. She told me to order anything, and even gave me a sip of her wine.

We were midway through dinner when Rachel set down her fork and put on her serious face.

"Caitlin," she said, hesitating. "I know coming to live with us wasn't your choice. And I know it's been a really hard year for you. But I just wanted you to know how much we love you. How proud we are of you."

I slowly stopped chewing, realizing how flustered she was becoming. She let out a deep breath, staring down at the table. "A while ago, you asked me to tell you the story of what happened between me and your mom. I was looking for the right time. I don't know if this is it, I don't know if there could ever *be* a right time. But I thought you deserved to know."

Her knuckles were white as she clasped her hands together on the table.

"Your mom was older than me by almost a decade. I was the surprise baby. When she and your dad got engaged, I was in middle school. I'd just started high school when they got married. They stayed in Mystic, but as soon as I graduated, I came here to go to college." She paused, letting out a short, sharp laugh. "Or, rather, to flunk out of college. Mystic was such a quiet place and New York was so vibrant and I…I got into a lifestyle that wasn't particularly healthy. I made poor choices.

"I was home in Connecticut for Christmas my freshman year. Your mom and dad had been trying to have a baby for a long time and couldn't get pregnant. They sat me down and asked me if I would be willing to be a surrogate for them."

My heart skipped a beat. Surrogate?

"They would pay me," Rachel continued, not looking at me. "They knew I was desperate for money, but they didn't know what I was really doing with my life in New York. I didn't really want to be pregnant, but the amount they were going to give me was…well, it was a lot at the time."

Rachel's hands started shaking, and she hid them under the table. I stared at her, my dinner completely forgotten.

"So I did it. And it worked on the first try. The procedure wasn't very common back then, but I got pregnant. They wanted me to stay in Connecticut with them, so they could go with me to doctors' appointments, but I told them I needed to be in New York to stay on top of my schoolwork. They had no reason to think I was lying to them. So I stayed here, and they visited me every month or so, and they paid me, thinking they were helping me stay in school."

What was she saying?

What in the actual hell was she saying?

She shook her head, eyes unfocused. "Liz was so happy. She'd wanted to be a mom for so long. I still remember the look on her face…"

Rachel realized she was crying, and wiped the tears off her cheek absently. "I had a boyfriend at the time, Rick," Rachel said, glancing up briefly to meet my gaze. "When I got pregnant, I stopped drinking, stopped…all the things I'd been doing. I did that much, at least. But I didn't give him up. I thought I was in love."

Rachel lifted a trembling hand and pushed a strand of hair behind her ears.

"He was a bad man, but I thought he just needed a girl like me to straighten him out. I thought if I just loved him enough, I could fix him. I could make him better." Rachel pressed her hand to her lips, too overwhelmed to continue for a full minute. Eventually, she cleared her throat, ignoring the tears coursing down her cheeks. "I was young. At least I had that excuse. He was drunk one night, wanted to take me to a party even though I was almost nine months pregnant. He was taking all the money your parents were giving me. He was cheating on me, too, not that that matters anymore. I knew he was drunk, but I was too uncomfortable to drive, to say something. So I got in the passenger seat. It was an old car, didn't have airbags. He hit another car head-on. Killed the driver. He walked away. Literally left me there in the car and walked away." A bitter smile briefly twisted her face.

"They did a C-section. I was in a coma for three weeks. Your parents were there when I woke up. They were holding you. You were a little premature, but you were just fine."

All I could do was stare at her, the words tumbling around my mind like leaves in a gale, frantic and violent.

She glanced up at me, but then looked down, as if my face was too painful to look at. "The police questioned me when I woke up. Your parents were there for that, too. Once they realized that it was Rick's fault, that I'd known he was drunk, that I'd put myself and you in danger, they were furious. Your dad forgave me. But your mom didn't. They paid my medical bill and left me in the hospital. I tried calling them, calling your grandma, trying to apologize. They wouldn't speak to me. Rick was arrested. He got life for vehicular manslaughter. I went back to school, but everything seemed so…so stupid. I was failing my classes. I dropped out of college, tried to make it a while longer as a waitress, but I couldn't pay my bills. My friend—one of my few friends that I'd actually met in classes and not through Rick—invited me to spend the summer with her and her family at Lake George. She didn't know what had happened to me, only that it was something bad. She felt sorry for me. Your parents had bought me a car, so I could get back and forth from Connecticut more easily. I sold everything else that I had and drove upstate. I got lost on the way there and my car broke down in Stony Creek. I met Joe."

The waiter came by, looking as though she was about to ask us if we needed anything, but she saw the tears on Rachel's face and backed away slowly.

"Your parents didn't come to my wedding. And they wouldn't let me come see you. I was shocked when your mom sent me a christening gown for Norah. By the time you came to live with us, I hadn't seen her in over fifteen years. When she was dying, I called your grandma. I asked her if I could come visit. And she said no. I was not allowed to say goodbye to my sister. I was not allowed to be there for you. And because of the things that I did, because of the choices I made when I was twenty years old, I had to live with those consequences. I had to let my sister die, still hating me for almost costing her you."

She looked up, finally. "I had to let *you* hate me. That's my burden. That's my secret." She looked down for a moment, then forced herself to meet my eyes. "You're allowed to hate me, still. If you did, I would understand. I just wanted you to know the truth. I wanted you to know that I'm s-sorry—" She bowed her head, trying to hold back fresh tears. She got control of herself, barely, and looked at me once more. "And I want you to know that Joe and Norah and I will always be here for you. We will always love you."

She hesitated, as if thinking about saying more, but she didn't. She just sat there, tears streaming down her face silently, waiting for me. Waiting for my judgment, my verdict.

And I couldn't.

I couldn't breathe.

I stood up and stumbled to the bathroom.

I locked myself in a stall, unable to control the full-body trembling that had overtaken me.

I couldn't think. I had no thoughts, no reaction, no emotions. I just stood there shaking.

I was wrong, all these years thinking I'd never met my aunt before moving to Stony Creek. All this time, everyone but me had known that she'd carried me around for nine months. She'd *given birth* to me.

It shouldn't have mattered, my mom was still my mom, my dad was still my dad, but somehow it did matter. Of course it mattered. It changed—what?

What did it change?

Ten minutes later, I walked back out. Rachel was turned to the window, her shoulders heaving quietly, crying. The check was on the table, already paid. She finally noticed me standing there and stood up. But I wasn't there. I wasn't really there. I was somewhere else, someplace far away. She stood when she realized I wasn't going to say anything. We walked outside, waited in silence for an Uber, and went back to the dorms at Enneman's. Several times she looked at me as though she were about to say something, then changed her mind, and remained silent.

I wasn't angry at her. I wasn't mad.

I wasn't anything. Not yet.

She walked me up to my dorm and saw me safely inside.

"I'm staying just a few blocks away," she said finally. "In case you need anything. Do you want to grab breakfast in the morning?"

I twitched, not quite meeting her gaze. "There's an orientation breakfast at Myriad. They have food there. It's early. You should leave before there's traffic."

Rachel looked hurt, but she just nodded. "Okay. Okay." She looked past me, into my dorm room, as if checking to make sure I had everything. "Call us if you need anything. Call us even if you don't need anything."

I nodded, mute.

She smiled, a painful, sharp, trembling smile. I don't know if I smiled.

She didn't hug me. She didn't touch me at all. She just patted the door frame once, then walked away.

"Rachel," I called.

She stopped.

"Does Joe know? About you and me?"

She nodded tightly. "Yes, he does."

"And Norah?"

Rachel pressed her mouth into a thin line, then shook her head. "She doesn't know."

14

I opened my eyes in the infinite white dreamscape. Data was waiting a polite distance off.

And so was Adrian. He was wearing pajama shorts and a loose t-shirt.

"Which memory is this?" I asked Data, standing. There was no scene, no room or landscape to clue me into which memory I was viewing.

"Caitlin?" Adrian asked, eyes wide. "What's going on?"

I glanced at Data, frowning. I didn't remember him ever saying that.

He took a step toward me. "Am I awake?"

I peered at him closer. He seemed to be making actual eye-contact with me. Me-me, not some dream-version of me.

"Adrian?" I asked, then reached out to touch his arm.

I jumped. "Holy shit, you're real."

He blinked at me. "So are you. What's going on?"

"How?" I asked, poking him in the ribs. He flinched. He was very ticklish.

"Are you back home?" he asked.

"No," I replied. "I'm asleep at my dorm in New York. At least I think I am. Where are you?"

"At the mansion. Are you okay?"

Immediately, my mind went back to the conversation Rachel and I had just had back at the restaurant a few hours before. "Yeah," I hedged. "I'm okay. Data, what's going on?"

Data just stood there politely, not saying a word.

"Stubborn android," I muttered.

"Is that…is that him? Or, I mean, you?" Adrian asked, looking at Data.

"Yep. That's subconscious me."

"Wow. He's very…detailed." Adrian walked over to examine Data. Data watched him, but didn't move. "I can see the texture in the wool of his uniform. I can see the scratches in his communicator. This is…" he looked up at me, intrigued. "This is incredible."

"Of course my boyfriend thinks the sci-fi uniform is incredible, not the fact that we're talking *while asleep* over two hundred miles apart."

He walked back to me, looking up and around at the infinite white dreamscape. "That part is definitely incredible, too. Do you have any idea how this happened?"

I shook my head. "I mean, this is what I dream every night. Data shows me some memory, we talk a little. But no one's ever shown up in my dream before—nobody real, I mean. It's always been memories from the past."

Adrian gently touched my arm, as if testing once more whether I was actually there. "However this is happening, do you realize what it means?" I shook my head. He smiled at me. "We have a way to communicate that the Council can't monitor." The smiled turned to a grin. "We have a huge advantage."

Before I could respond, the world turned upside down. I opened my eyes and found myself back in my dorm room, the alarm on my phone buzzing loudly.

I grabbed it, growling in frustration, and turned the alarm off. I started texting Adrian to ask if it *had* all been a dream—but then I remembered we couldn't freaking talk over the phone. I'd have to ask Julian when I saw him next. But Farrar hadn't filled me in on their rotation so I didn't know when that would be.

Frustrated but not knowing what else I could do, I showered, dressed, grabbed my orientation packet, and drifted into the hallway, melting in with the other students who were making their way to Myriad.

When vampire problems are temporarily unsolvable, revert to default settings:

Human.

"Good morning, ladies and—" the woman looked up from the paper in her hand and scanned the room until she found the sole boy among us, "—gentleman. My name is Olivia Renault and I am a designer here at Myriad. I am also in charge of both the high school and college internship programs."

Her hair was up in a complicated bun, she was wearing large glasses I wasn't sure she actually needed, and she had on a loose, boxy dress in a soft grey fabric. I was sitting too far back to determine the material, but it looked like it might be chiffon.

"Think of your summer here as Fashion 101, a precursor to what you will be studying at your design school. You will be assigned mentors and rotated throughout various departments. You will learn everything from marketing to illustration to pattern-making, manufacturing, and sales. You may be here because you think you would like to be a designer. Let me tell you this right now: half of you will leave this internship before it's finished. Of the half of you that stay, another half will quit during college. If you are here to prove something to me, or to Myriad, don't. If you have something to prove, prove it only to yourself. If you feel the need to compete with someone, compete against yourself. That is the only way you will succeed in this program."

She looked at us, her face a stern mask. "You hundred have been chosen out of thousands of applicants. You have potential. Your creativity is apparent. But do not mistake potential and talent with entitlement. You must work harder than you've ever worked before, you must be smarter than you ever thought you could be, you must be self-disciplined, and above all, you must be kind."

I could feel a rustling around the room as people muttered to themselves about that last one. "Don't believe me?" she asked, and the room fell silent. "This industry, in particular, has a vicious reputation. It chews young idealists up and spits them out. Who can tell me what Myriad's motto is?"

Dozens of hands shot up, including mine, but a girl in the front burst out, "Modern, ethical design."

Olivia nodded. "Let's please raise our hands from now on, yes?"

I couldn't see the girl's face, but she seemed to shrink in her seat.

"Ethical design does not," Olivia continued, "refer only to our manufacturing process, though that is important."

She stopped, pointing at the gold-carved Myriad logo displayed on the far wall.

"We are called Myriad because of you. Because of me. Because no one individual is the company. No one individual makes the clothing. And no one individual gets the credit. We depend on each other. We are a family. And you must earn the right to become a part of this family through hard work, intelligence, and yes, kindness. Those are our expectations for you. And that is why we are the premier fashion label in the U.S., outflanking companies that have been here for more than a hundred years."

She glanced at her papers again, then turned back to us. "We do not expect you to work twelve-hour days. In fact, we will kick you out every night at seven even if you're in the middle of a project. We expect you to find a healthy work-life balance. But we also want you to be proactive. We will assign you an enormous amount of work, and it is up to you to find creative ways to finish your duties in the time allotted. If you have finished a task, do not wait around to be assigned another. I don't care if you'd rather steal five minutes to play a game on your phone or catch up on how your friends are wasting their summers back home. If you are here, you are here to work."

Olivia paused, looking down at a girl who was bent over her phone. "And for the love of God," Olivia said, stopping right in front of the girl, "if I see you on your phones doing anything but taking a call, I will kick you out of this program faster than you can say *Twitter.*"

The girl looked up, swallowing thickly.

"I was taking notes," she said, holding up the phone. I was too far away to see if she was telling the truth or not, but Olivia nodded.

"I find social media vile. That is my *personal* opinion. Unfortunately for you, I am in charge of this program. If you want to stay in this program, do not give me a reason to send you home."

She raised her eyebrows at the girl and walked back to the front of the room.

"At the end of the summer, for those of you that remain, you will have an opportunity to present me with your final project. *If* I am impressed, I will choose five of you to go before the head designer here at Myriad, Peter Newport. You will have five minutes to present your project. If he is impressed—and there is no guarantee he will be—you will have a chance at a full-ride scholarship to Enneman's, as well as a guaranteed college internship here at Myriad."

We all stirred. That hadn't been mentioned on the company website or the application. Olivia smiled. "Are you ready? Because your first task is right now."

She turned, suddenly, and left. We scrambled up from our seats to follow her.

She pushed through the double glass doors of the conference room we'd been stuffed into and walked down the hall, greeting assistants, college-level interns (who had started over a month ago) and executives all by name. I couldn't tell if she genuinely cared about these people, if her speech about kindness was true, but she was putting on a great show if it wasn't.

Around me, the high school interns were buzzing. My mind was on fire. Olivia Renault may not have been a household name, but I knew her, or at least, knew *of* her. And meeting her in person was not at all what I had expected.

I was giddy.

While the other interns chatted excitedly amongst themselves, I looked up at the walls, the glass ceiling, the furniture and art, the assistants and editors. People fast-walked here. No one strolled. But people *smiled*. Everyone seemed busy, but…happy.

She led us down several more hallways into a long, skinny room lined with perfectly spaced work tables. The long walls had industrial sewing machines lined up every four feet. The back windows looked out over an alley.

We clumped around the door, afraid to venture too far into the room.

"You will find a sticker on the back of your keycards," she said, holding up her own keycard. "Somewhere in this room, another person has a matching sticker. Go find them. Introduce yourself to others. You have ten minutes. Go."

We scrambled like a disrupted hive of bees. I flipped my keycard and found a pumpkin sticker. "Pumpkin?" I called out, holding up the sticker. "Anyone got a pumpkin?"

"Fish!" a girl near me called out.

"Bus!" someone else shouted.

It was chaos.

I glanced at the corner of the room and saw that Olivia was standing there with her phone. When she said we had ten minutes, I bet she meant we had exactly ten minutes. Several other important-looking people entered the room and joined her, watching us, leaning close to talk to her quietly.

It gave me an idea.

"Hey," I said, gently laying my hand on the shoulder of a girl next to me. She whirled, looking frantic. I smiled and stuck my hand out. "I'm Caitlin Holte."

She blinked, then returned the smile, shaking my hand. "Stacee Rey."

"I've got a pumpkin," I said, showing her my keycard. "You match?"

She shook her head apologetically. "Banana," she replied, holding up her own sticker.

"Well it was nice to meet you, Stacee."

She returned the greeting and I tapped the next person on the shoulder. "Hi," I began when they faced me, "I'm—"

"Fire truck?" the girl interrupted.

"Uh, no, but—"

She immediately turned away, shouting the name of her sticker.

"All righty," I muttered under my breath.

I spent the next ten minutes introducing myself to my fellow interns. I met a few people, though I didn't dare exchange contact info after Olivia's warning about social media. She might think I was wasting—

"Time's up," Olivia called. "If you have found your match, please come up to the front."

About half the students surged toward her.

"Well done," she said, looking over them. She turned to the girl nearest her, glancing at the name on her keycard. "Now, Ms. Park, how many people did you introduce yourself to?"

That was the girl who'd interrupted me, the one with the fire truck sticker.

She blushed. "Well, I thought…I mean, I *talked* to a lot of people. I thought matching the stickers was more important?"

"Ducklings," Olivia called to us, "does anyone remember my instructions?"

"Match the stickers," someone called out tentatively, "and introduce yourself to others."

"Correct," Olivia said. "Now, in this program, you *will* have to prioritize. You will put some tasks ahead of others for the sake of time management. Tell me, Ms. Park, why did you think that matching your stickers was more important than introducing yourself?"

Her blush deepened. "Well, you said back in the conference room that our first task was about to begin. I…well, I thought that the stickers were our first task, or were leading to our first task. I thought introducing ourselves was just…extra?"

Olivia nodded, not seeming upset. "A reasonable assumption. However—this task was designed to show you, once again, that the *people* here are just as important as the work. You will be counting on each other this summer. You will depend on one another. That means you must trust them. That means you must *know* them. Which means introducing yourself, in this case, was as important as finding your partner."

The girl nodded furiously, embarrassed. Olivia tapped at her phone, then looked at all of us.

"You have ten more minutes. My instructions are the same. Go."

We burst back into action. The ten minutes felt even shorter this round, but by the time she called for our attention again, everyone had found their sticker doppleganger, and everyone seemed far more relaxed, since we were actually beginning to recognize a few people by name. I'd bumped into Stacee of the banana sticker again and we'd both gone for a high-five at the same time.

"Did everyone find their partner?" Olivia called when the timer went off.

A few people hadn't, and she helped them pair up.

"Throughout the day," Olivia said, voice carrying over us all, "I expect you to continue to get to know one another while you are about your tasks without losing momentum on your projects. To that end, here is your first real assignment: teach your partner how to do something that they do not already know. Pick a workstation. There you will find all the basic supplies you need. You have twenty minutes each. Go."

People literally began running to claim tables.

Olivia waved her hands, blowing a whistle. Everyone stopped.

"Back, back, come back, all of you."

My partner was a short, bubbly girl named Violet. The program didn't allow kids under sixteen, but she looked like a middle schooler. We'd found each other just before the timer went off so I hadn't had a chance to find out her last name or anything more about her. We hadn't gotten far, so we pivoted to face Olivia.

Olivia sighed. "I realize you are inundated with media that tries to convince you that everything is a life-or-death race. And while there is an aspect of competition to this program, it is designed to be a learning experience. This is not *Escape from Jurassic Park*. This is not *The Hunger Games*. Every table is exactly the same as the others. Please choose one in an orderly fashion. Thank you."

Violet and I picked a station at the far end of the room, near the windows. Underneath the work table—actually, it was two work tables stuck back-to-back so that we could work at the same time while facing each other—were labeled canvas bins. We had scissors, measuring tape, pins, pattern paper, and a huge role of cheap muslin. You could simply pull out as much as you wanted and cut it off. We also had two adjustable, rolling mannequins. They looked used, and I think mine had a coffee stain on it, but otherwise it worked perfectly well. It was actually a very efficient system, and managed to fit a huge number of us into a small space without feeling cramped. I also noticed there were pull-down ironing boards about every two tables. The irons were the same brand as the one I'd bought Rachel for Christmas. Good, sturdy machines. Rachel had thanked me—

No. Not thinking about her.

Not yet.

Over the next twenty minutes, my new partner—whose last name was Kessler, I eventually found out—showed me how to work the industrial sewing machines, since I'd only ever used domestic models. I showed her my illustration technique, since she'd never learned how to draw. We flipped through a few of my journals, stopping on the designs I'd done for Winter Formal and Prom.

"Those are super gorgeous," Violet said. "You *made* those?"

I pulled out my phone and showed her the pictures from the two dances. She gasped at the finished products.

"Who's that?" she asked, pointing at a slice of the back of Adrian's head in one of the photos.

"Oh," I said, blushing, "uh, that's my boyfriend."

She peered closer. "Is that…is that suit Armani?"

I was surprised she could tell just from the photo. "Um…yep. His family's pretty well off. It's a bit of a Cinderella match."

It felt like this was getting into dangerous territory. I hadn't meant to bring up Adrian to anyone here. Or Julian or Lucian or Tommie or any of it. Adrian was right: I needed to focus on being here if I was going to take the time do this at all. Otherwise it wasn't worth it.

"Well, the dress is just lovely," Violet said, seeming to sense my discomfort. "You did a lovely, lovely job."

I smiled, relieved she wasn't pursuing the topic of Adrian further, and dove back into giving her pointers on sketching. By the end of the twenty minutes, she'd made notes on the correct proportions for mapping out the head, body, torso, hips, and legs. Olivia and the mystery Myriad people had gone around the room quietly observing us as we instructed one another.

"Time's up," she called from the center of the room. "And well done. You will often be called on to assist each other in your duties, so be prepared to get to know everyone in this room. Learn each other's strengths and specialties. Offer each other help. For now, however," she said, looking at her wristwatch, "it is lunch."

We followed her to Myriad's cafeteria where Olivia abandoned us and a college intern explained how to use our keycards to get meals. The college students had dorms with floor kitchens, and they were free to use the meal plan or not use the meal plan. Our floors had no kitchens, and we were told to stay on-premises during the day, which meant we had to eat here for breakfast, lunch, and dinner. This was actually one of the more expensive parts of the internship, along with housing and a materials fee.

I had gotten a scholarship. I'd gotten one of the better scholarships, actually, but not their full-ride. Joe and Rachel were paying for my housing while Grandma was paying for my meal plan. I had insisted on paying the materials fee out of the pathetic amount of money I had left from my inheritance. I would be flat broke by the time I made it back to Stony Creek.

But I could already tell it was worth it.

Violet and I stuck together and bumped into Stacee, the girl with the banana sticker, and her partner, Truitt Brown, the only boy in our whole group. After grabbing our trays and filling up at the buffet-style serving bars, we grabbed a table by the windows.

"So where are you?" Stacee asked Truitt, apparently continuing a conversation from earlier.

"Couple floors up. I guess it's co-ed for the college program but they're not legally allowed to mix genders for the high school program. It is nice to have my own room, though."

He winked at us. I couldn't tell if he was winking about getting his own room, or about the idea of him being a threat to us girls. He was wearing fitted slacks, loafers, and a short-sleeved button-up with a yellow pocket square. The chances of him being gay were high, especially in a fashion internship, but after being seriously mistaken about Adrian's sexual orientation, I didn't trust my own instincts and didn't want to make an ass of myself by assuming one way or the other.

Also, it was really none of my business.

But still, as the sole male in our program, it was hard not to be curious.

We chatted about where everyone was from (I was the only person from in-state; Violet had come all the way from Idaho), how they'd gotten into sewing (let's just say I was not the only *Project Runway* fan, and almost everyone had a parent or family member that knew how to sew), and what everyone wanted to be (designers, all). I found out Stacee was on the floor above me at Enneman's and Violet on the floor below. Truitt was actually on my floor, just on the other side of the building. We all agreed to meet up that night to watch *The Devil Wears Prada* as an initiation celebration. Stacee offered to steal snacks from the cafeteria and Truitt said he would bring drinks. I wasn't sure if he just meant soda or if he was going to try and sneak in alcohol.

Olivia was busy the rest of the day, so a few of the college interns split us into bite-sized groups of ten and spent the rest of the day taking us on a tour of the building. It was twenty stories tall, so it ate up the whole rest of the day.

We saw the editorial offices (though only from the lobby, since they didn't like high schoolers wandering around disrupting them), the college workroom (an exact replica of ours, except with slightly newer equipment), and the photography studios. My favorite parts, however, were the mini-runway, where executives and designers got to test out lines before showing them to the public, and the fashion closet.

Oh sweet gods of sewing, I could live in that fashion closet.

It ate up an entire floor. Racks and rows and shelves and hooks full of Myriad clothing, shoes, and accessories, everything neatly labeled and categorized. The room itself was fancier than most of the others, with crown molding and wall art and mirrors every dozen feet.

"If you touch anything you are not assigned to touch," the college intern leading our group warned us, "you will be sent home. I am not exaggerating," she said sternly, looking at a girl in our group who was reaching out to touch the cuff of a nearby coat. She looked ashamed and withdrew her hand quickly.

We were led through the maze efficiently, which disappointed me because I wanted to stay there for hours and analyze all their current designs. Violet, Stacee, and Truitt looked like they felt the same way.

The place was packed, though, dozens of interns and designers running around in a frenzy. Twice, I almost got separated from our group because I had to stop abruptly when an assistant rushed past me wheeling a rack of dresses. And then I stared after the dresses because they were beautiful and forgot to catch up with the group.

We also checked out the photography studio, a large, partitioned room where a dozen shoots could be happening at the same time. Since there were several currently in progress, we could only look longingly into the room from our space huddled around the door before we were shooed back out by our college intern tour guide.

We headed back to the workroom after that and had a brisk lecture on workroom procedure (no running, no hogging machines, no open flames, no taking equipment out of the workroom, *ever*, no posting photos from inside the Myriad building especially of in-progress Myriad designs—that one was actually punishable by law, something about breach-of-contract). After that, we were shuttled back to the cafeteria for dinner, then kicked out of the building precisely at seven.

Rather than taking the subway, Truitt, Violet, Stacee, and I decided to walk the mile and a half back to the dorms, taking in the city. I was the only one who'd ever been to New York before, and that apparently made me the expert on directions. Luckily, it was a straight shot and we arrived about an hour later, after stopping every five feet so Violet could take pictures to send back to her sister in Idaho. I may have made everyone pose a few times, too. We couldn't take pictures inside the building, but they'd said nothing about posting pictures of the city itself.

We got back to the dorms and took over the small lounge area on my floor. Stacee spilled Rice Krispies bars from her pockets and Truitt came back from his room carrying four sparkling waters. We watched *The Devil Wears Prada*, slowly attracting another dozen girls from my floor until the room was packed to the rafters. We all agreed that we were glad Olivia Renault was nothing like Miranda Priestley. We all agreed they both dressed fabulously.

By eleven, I could barely keep my eyes open. I bid everyone good-night and practically sleep-walked back to my room, unlocking the door with my Myriad keycard.

I was so tired I didn't even flip on the light, just went straight to my bed and flopped down face-first.

"Long day?"

I sat bolt upright. I was the only intern assigned to my room, but they'd still left the other twin bed in place. Julian was stretched out on it, looking amused.

"Holy crap, dude," I said, putting a hand to my racing heart. "What are you doing here?"

"I'm on duty."

"Farrar didn't exactly fill me in on your schedule," I muttered, pressing the heels of my hands to my eyes. I looked up at him slowly. "Are you going to be here all night?"

"Believe me," Julian said dryly, "I'm not any happier about it than you are."

"But!" I protested, sputtering, "this is my room! Gross."

Julian raised an eyebrow. "I didn't hear you complaining when Adrian was assigned to your room last winter."

I blushed, glad it was dark so he couldn't see. "That was different."

"It shouldn't be," Julian said evenly. He turned on the lamp between the two beds. "We perform the same function. Keeping you safe from the monsters in the closet."

Julian knew Adrian and I were in love. But he was dancing around the fact.

"I have a…*rapport* with Adrian." I said, stealing a word I'd heard Adrian say before and hoping I was using it correctly. "He's familiar. You're not."

Was someone listening in? Was my room bugged? Was I being watched?

"Good, but not good enough." Julian scooted to the edge of his bed, leaning his elbows on his knees as he stared at me. "You need to have better answers. Answers they'll believe, answers so ingrained that they come automatically. You have to assume that someone is listening at all times."

"*Is* someone listening?"

He shook his head. "They haven't bugged the room—yet."

I kicked my shoes off, relieved. "Speaking of—I need you to get a message to Adrian for me."

He looked at me oddly. "Funny, he said the same thing. He said to ask you 'if it was real.' Does that mean anything to you?"

I failed at keeping a grin off my face. I hadn't just dreamed it all up—which meant we really had a way to communicate. "It does," I told Julian. "Can you tell him that yes, it was real?"

Julian frowned. "I can. But I won't unless you tell me what the hell it means."

"At this point, I honestly don't know."

He rolled his eyes and leaned back against the stack of pillows.

"Julian," I said, not sure this was a safe question. "Please don't take this the wrong way, but why are you helping me?"

He snorted. "I'm not helping you. I'm helping my brother."

"But you don't like Adrian," I said before I could stop myself.

Julian looked at me strangely. "I may not be affectionate, but he's my brother. I know the punishments for the kind of treason he continues to commit by..." he looked me over distastefully, "...being *involved* with you. I'm doing my best to keep him alive. I'm doing my best to keep *you* alive. You don't have to like it."

I blinked a few times, then hunched my knees up and rested my chin on them. "Is that why you did it? Is that why you convinced him to be mean to me?"

Julian shrugged. "It was the smartest course of action. But I severely underestimated your flair for the dramatic. You caused an uproar when you broke up with him."

I blinked, surprised. "Did I? I never heard a thing about it."

"Adrian had quite the inquisition. Had to explain how he'd failed at keeping you on-board with the plan."

I paled. "Did they hurt him?"

Julian shook his head. "The hearing was still in progress when my father returned and attacked you. It has since been dropped. Mariana convinced the Council that they placed too much strain on Adrian too soon. He's technically of age, but it's rare someone that young gets put on a protection detail. She argued that it was their lack of judgment that led to your...dismissal of Adrian, not his failure."

I let out a long breath, leaning my head back against the wall. "Is that why the Praetorian Guard came back to Stony Creek? Not because of Lucian, but because they didn't think Adrian was up to protecting me?"

"Partly," he replied. "But the moment the Council learned our father came back, there were at least two people watching you at all times. While the Guard was off searching for Lucian, Mariana and Dominic were doing almost nothing *but* keeping an eye on you, even when Adrian was on-duty. They got a break when Farrar and the others returned to Stony Creek."

"Makes sense why Mariana is always so cranky toward me. I wouldn't want to watch me all the time, either," I said, letting that sink in. "I guess it also means I really do have a reason to be paranoid. At least you're my new bodyguard. No offense, but your aunt—I mean sister, sorry—scares me way more than you do."

He smiled wryly. "I don't blame you."

I scooted back on the bed, resting my head against the cool, painted cinder blocks. "So Kalare seems decent for a vampire but Sabine doesn't like me very much," I threw out, watching his face for reaction.

"Sabine doesn't like anyone very much," he muttered, which was actually more of an explanation than I'd been expecting.

I stared at him for a moment, and he stared at me.

"So you're really just supposed to sit there all night?" I said finally. "Watching me sleep?"

He raised an eyebrow. "Not ideal for either one of us, rest assured. Rooms to either side of you were already booked, and the Council didn't decree this enough of an emergency to compel them away."

"Well," I said, sighing, "at least I know you, sort of. And Kalare's nice. But I will literally have nightmares if Sabine is in here watching me sleep. I'm pretty sure she wants to kill me."

"She would not disobey direct orders," Julian said almost absently, looking at his phone as if he'd already forgotten I was there.

Direct orders not to kill me? Or direct orders not to kill me *yet*?

"Great," I said, but he missed the sarcasm. "I'm gonna go to bed."

I grabbed my pajamas from the dresser and carried them into the bathroom. I brushed my teeth, washed my face, got dressed, and walked back out, crawling into bed. Julian was on the opposite bed still, leaned back against a stack of pillows playing some game on his phone.

"I'll see about adjusting the night guard arrangements," he said, unexpectedly. "This is weirding me out."

I snorted. "That makes two of us. Thanks, Julian."

He glanced over at me, then returned to his game.

I almost wanted to say more, but I also didn't want to ruin it. This was the most civil he'd ever been to me.

I turned over, burrowed into my pillows, and was surprised to find that I fell immediately asleep.

15

“Hey.”

Adrian was once more in my dreamscape, along with Data.

I rushed over to him and wrapped him in a hug. Adrian, not Data. Hugging Data would be weird.

“Did Julian get my message to you?”

“Yeah, texted me right before I fell asleep. So you’re real. And I’m real. And this is real.”

“Yes.”

He smiled down at me, brushing the hair back from my face. “How was your first day?”

“Good. Have a nice partner, excited about the projects. I think it’s going to be a great program.”

He kissed my forehead. “I’m so happy to hear that. I know it’s only been two days but I miss you like crazy.”

“I miss you, too,” I murmured, rubbing my nose into his chest. He felt mostly real. There was some unnameable quality to all this that made me aware it wasn't *real*-real, but for the most part he looked and smelled and felt like he did in the real world.

"Have you heard from Kalare?" he asked a moment later. "Has she met with her contact?"

I shook my head, breathing in his scent. "Not yet. Julian was on guard tonight, not Kalare. Hoping I hear something tomorrow."

"I've been digging in the library for the term 'Unmaker.' Haven't found anything yet, but I'll keep looking."

"I wish she'd given us more information to go on. We just have the one word."

His mouth twitched in a smile. "It would seem to imply that you un-make things."

I looked up and rolled my eyes at him. "Very *un*-helpful." I leaned back. "In all seriousness, though, I'm a *maker*, not an un-maker," I mumbled. "I make things. I sew things. I don't really *unmake* them. Unless I rip out a seam or disassemble something to upcycle it. But that's clothing. I don't think my secret power is really great sewing skills."

"Wouldn't that be cool, though?" he asked, looking genuinely thoughtful. "I bet you'd have an awesome cape."

"Best-dressed superhero of all time," I confirmed with a grin. Then I turned serious. "I wish we could just google stuff like normal people. Even if there is information out there, I have to assume the Council is monitoring my search history."

Luckily, it was mostly cat videos and sewing tutorials. If they were monitoring it, they were in for a very boring ride.

"I hate this," I muttered, frustrated. "I'm getting so paranoid. They can watch me on every level: they can listen in on my conversations, they can tap my phone, they can hack my e-mails, they can literally feel what I'm feeling. The only place they can't see what I'm doing is in here."

From behind us, Data cleared his throat emphatically.

A full three seconds later, my head snapped up to look at Adrian.

"Oh my god. They can't listen to me in here. And you magically appeared when I needed someone to talk to about all this, to work through it where they couldn't spy on me. What if I'm not an Unmaker, what if I just *snapped?* Like, I'm going schizophrenic or something?"

Adrian frowned. "Wouldn't that mean that I snapped, too? We confirmed in the real world that this has become a shared experience."

I opened my mouth, then closed it. "Right. Well, I'm all out of ideas. Data, do you have anything to show me?"

Data nodded, then looked off into the distance. "Computer, run Tommie Attack Simulation concurrently with Julian Attack Simulation."

I frowned at him, puzzled.

"It is a dream state," Data explained. "Am I not allowed to have fun with the avatar you have assigned me? Besides, the brain is a sort of computer."

As if to prove his point, two different memories materialized around us, almost like the holodeck from *Star Trek*. To my left, Julian was attacking Adrian in slow motion on the cliff edge. To my right, Adrian was blasting Tommie with white-hot light in the snowy clearing. They played simultaneously, both close enough in my field of vision for me to be able to track them at the same time.

"Whoa," Adrian breathed. "*This* is how you experience your memories?"

I nodded.

On the left, Julian tackled Adrian over the cliff. Because I hadn't been able to look over the cliff in real life, they simply disappeared from view here in the dream. On the right, in the other memory, Tommie's skin began to melt. I wish I'd been closer when this actually happened, so I could make out more details. Well, on second thought, I was pretty happy I didn't have a front row seat to the skin-melting. The stench had been bad enough.

Dream Julian's body landed back on the cliff ledge, unconscious. Dream Adrian crawled after him a moment later.

"Is he alive?" Dream Farrar asked.

Dream Adrian nodded, his eyes swirling silver. "He is not conscious."

Indeed, Julian simply looked asleep. He had no injuries, Adrian had simply been able to knock him out somehow, even though vampires could not compel one another, feel each other's emotions, or read each other's thoughts. They were voids.

And yet somehow, Adrian had done this to his brother. He'd managed to neutralize Julian without harming him.

"It's weird seeing it from your perspective," Adrian murmured. "Honestly, most of this is a blur. I don't remember this part."

On the right memory, Tommie seemed to let go of whatever magic was holding Adrian mid-air in the snowy clearing. The wind tunnel disappeared and Adrian fell in a heap to the ground, while Tommie ran off, trailing a frighteningly bacon-y smell. Cooked flesh. Unlike Julian, Adrian certainly hadn't neutralized *him* harmlessly.

The scenes looped back to the beginning and played again. I watched them several more times before it hit me.

"You didn't hurt Julian," I said slowly. "But you hurt your father. You managed to stop both attacks. But you stopped Julian without hurting him."

I scrunched my face, willing myself to see more. But that's all I had.

If my earlier theory was correct, that Adrian's powers were a result of his protective instincts kicking into gear, then this side-by-side comparison supported that theory. Adrian, though he might not willingly admit it, cared about his brother. He didn't want to hurt him. But he hated his father. And his father had been seriously injured.

I didn't know exactly what that meant, yet, but it could be important.

I felt heavy, suddenly, and tired. Which was weird, because I was technically already asleep.

"Adrian," I said, turning to him. "I think I'm about to wake up. I feel—"

The world upended.

"Humwha?"

I blinked, confused about where I was, what day it was, and what the hell that noise was. It took a long few seconds for me to realize the sound was my alarm, I was in my dorm at Enneman's, and I had to take a shower to get ready for the day.

"Did you know you snore?" Julian asked from the opposite twin.

I jumped, bumping my head back against the wall. "Ow," I complained, rubbing my skull.

I'd forgotten Julian was on duty.

"What are you still doing here?" I grumbled, really, really not ready to be awake yet. "Adrian was always gone by the time I woke up."

"That's because Adrian had to disappear before your family woke up. I don't."

"Oh," I said, yawning. "Well…good morning?"

He was still playing some game on his phone. "'Morning."

A tinkle of sound came from the game, and he glared at the screen. I think he'd just died.

"I do not snore, by the way," I said, sitting up and wrapping the blankets around me in a nest. "Adrian would have told me."

"Adrian worships the ground you walk on," Julian reminded me.

"A—not true. B—well, I don't have a B. I need coffee in order to have a second point."

"Fine," Julian admitted, "you don't snore. You do sleep-talk."

I paled. Adrian had mentioned once that I'd mumbled in my sleep about sexy pirate men, after the Halloween costume party. I hadn't thought it was a regular thing, though.

"What did I say?"

"'Data, where are you?' And then you went dead quiet."

Oh god. If I was talking out loud about my dreamscapes, that was really, really not good.

"Actually, it was odd," he continued before I could reply. "Usually when humans sleep, they still give off some emotional energy. Especially when they dream. But when you were dreaming, you shut off completely. Couldn't feel a thing from you. If I didn't see you lying there all night, I wouldn't have known you were in the room."

I blinked. "Really?"

He nodded.

Huh. Maybe my dreamscape really *was* secure.

I needed to get ready for the day, but I couldn't pass up an opportunity to take advantage of a chatty Julian.

"I was actually dreaming about you," I admitted, keeping my face carefully neutral.

He quirked an eyebrow at me. "Ready to toss aside Adrian so quickly?"

I rolled my eyes. "Not *that* kind of dream. I was dreaming about the day you guys came back from hell. I saw you tackle Adrian. I saw you guys go over the cliff. I thought you might both be dead. But then Adrian tossed you back, right at my feet. You were out. I still don't understand what happened. Did he…did he *hurt* you?"

I thought I knew the answer, but I wanted to hear his version. Adrian might trust Julian, but I didn't. I wasn't going to tell him about my dreamscape just yet. Or that I could talk to Adrian through it.

Julian's face grew blank. "Not that I'm aware of."

He glanced at his phone. "You're supposed to be at Myriad in thirty minutes."

"Crap," I muttered, scrambling out of bed. I grabbed a random assortment of clothes from the dresser and ran into the bathroom, locking the door behind me. By the time I came back out, Julian was gone, and I had to run to catch up with Violet and Stacee and Truitt in the lobby. I wondered which of my bodyguards was on-duty during the day, when I was at Myriad. And how did they watch me? Were they inside the building? Did they wait across the street for eight to ten hours while I was at my internship? Who knew that being a vampire could be as boring as babysitting a teenage girl at her summer internship?

As soon as the smell of breakfast hit me in the Myriad cafeteria, however, I forgot my questions and automatically transitioned into work mode. I downed three cups of the artisan coffee, less because I needed the caffeine and more because the mugs were tiny and the coffee was really, really good. Why my uncle insisted on buying the 30oz Folgers tubs, I'll never know.

We gathered in the workroom, automatically pairing up with our partners from the day before. Stacee and Truitt moved tables to be closer to us near the window.

We chatted until the clock struck nine, and Olivia Renault entered the room.

"Good morning," she called to us, looking amazing in black cigarette slacks, a white button-up, and a chunky, gold collar necklace. "I know you're all excited to begin work on your own projects, but today, you earn your spot on the food chain. You have all been assigned to one of our college interns. For the rest of the day, you will shadow them as they work on *their* projects. Listen to them, learn from them, and try to keep up."

She called us up in groups by last name. Truitt was in the first group, and I was in the second group along with Violet.

"Caitlin Holte," Olivia called, "you will be placed with Sabine Rousseau."

I nodded, starting to write down the name in my journal so I wouldn't forget it. Then my brain finally processed which name she'd said.

I looked up, horrified.

No way.

No, no, no, no, no.

Aaaaand, yep. There she was.

Sabine stood next to Olivia looking like the super model she was. Her long, platinum-blonde hair was in a bun and she was wearing hipster glasses and pale pink lipstick. It was almost unreal how trendy and attractive she was.

I was about to turn to Olivia, tempted to ask for a different mentor, but I closed my mouth. The Council had most certainly arranged this. How they'd gotten her into the college intern program so quickly, and without suspicion, was entirely beyond me.

Sabine didn't even reach out to shake my hand, just said, "Let's go."

I followed her out of the room, already angry.

This was *my* internship. My life. My *real* life. I'd come here to learn. And the Council had stuck me with a vampire bodyguard who hated me.

I followed Sabine, silent, through corridors and down halls until we made our way to a row of empty cubicles. There didn't seem to be anyone else around.

She sat down in the roll-y chair and promptly ignored me, pulling out her phone.

I stood there, not sure if she expected me to do something. After nearly half a minute, I cleared my throat.

"Are you…really an intern here?" I asked, not knowing how to speak to her.

"There is a paper trail indicating such," she said, not bothering to look at me.

"And…are you here simply to—" I almost said 'guard me' but I switched last-moment to, "—keep me safe? Or do you have a fashion-related task for me?"

Sabine glanced at me, looking me up and down. "I would be afraid to give you a task related to fashion."

I flushed red. True, my current outfit was not my best. I'd literally grabbed a random tank top with a random pair of boyfriend jeans and had put on the wrong pair of boots. But I didn't look like some backwoods hick, either.

"If you're not going to give me anything to do," I said, trying to keep my voice level, "then I'm going to find something to do."

I turned, about to walk off, when I felt her hand on my arm, vise-like.

"You're going to sit here," she said, pulling me back into the cubicle. "Like the obedient little girl you are. You are going to be quiet. You are not going to disturb me."

She forced me to sit on a little footstool in the corner. She smoothed her dress, then sat at the desk, her manicured nails tapping against the screen of her phone.

"Sabine," I said, struggling to keep the rage out of my voice. "I am not going to sit here all day. If you don't want to help me, that's fine. Just let me go work on my own."

Her eyes flicked to me, but otherwise, she didn't move an inch. "You seem to have this strange idea that you're the one in charge of all of this," she murmured softly, as if truly puzzled. Her French accent was lyrical and soothing, which made me hate it all the more. "Mariana has been far too accommodating. You have become spoiled by her generosity."

Mariana—*generous?*

I pulled out my phone, about to call Julian, but Sabine took it straight out of my hands.

"Uh-uh," she warned. "Sit. Be good."

She slid my phone into her purse. I felt suddenly vulnerable, naked without my link to the others.

"Sabine," I tried one more time. "I'm not. Going. To sit. Here."

I stood, walking toward the hall, but she grabbed me by the chin, blocking me.

"Apparently I haven't been clear," she said, holding me frozen in place with minimal effort. "This is not a debate. Sit, or I will compel you to sit."

Shit.

She couldn't compel me—but I didn't want her to know that. More importantly, I didn't want the *Council* to know that.

Glaring at her, I sat back down.

She went back to her phone.

And we sat there.

For three hours.

"What were your mentors like?" Violet asked our table at lunch. She was like a little bunny, all jumpy energy and smiles.

I was so angry I couldn't even touch my food.

"Mine was great," Stacee said, slurping up some tomato bisque. "She's a senior at Enneman's and she's in their marketing department. We got to play with a bunch of sample pieces and she showed me how they were putting together the marketing materials for the whole line. She was so smart but didn't make me feel stupid at all. I mean, I still *felt* stupid, but she was very encouraging."

"That's super awesome!" Violet chirped. "What about you, Truitt?"

"I helped my mentor in the Fashion Closet," he said, looking pleased. "We re-organized the entire men's shoe rack to accommodate the upcoming fall merchandise. She made me carry everything like a packhorse, but I learned about their coding system and how to check items in and out so I guess it was all right. What about you?"

Violet blushed. "I got assigned to a girl in Accessories. We were mostly organizing supplies, but she let me try on a few earrings and bracelets. I felt so pretty!" She leaned close and whispered, "But don't tell anyone, my mentor and I could get in trouble because we're not supposed to try stuff on."

She blushed, both embarrassed and proud of her own rule-breaking.

"What about you, Caitlin?" Stacee asked. "What did you do?"

I was tempted to tell them the truth. But that would be stupid. "We mostly just talked," I said. That was…more or less true.

"Well, I'm sure it'll be more exciting tomorrow," Violet reassured me. "Apparently they'll be our mentors for the whole summer!"

I very carefully kept my face blank.

A whole summer with Sabine as my "mentor."

A whole summer sitting on a footstool in an empty cubicle, doing nothing.

No.

Hell no.

Luckily, we were only stuck with our mentors for the mornings. In the afternoons, Olivia told us, we were to begin work on our personal projects.

"This includes," she announced, speaking from the center of the workroom, "independent study, a project proposal, written schedule, and artist's statement. You have this week only to develop your proposal. On Friday, you will present that proposal to your mentor. If they approve it, you will present it to me. If *I* approve it, you will spend your remaining time working on your project, in addition to your regular duties. Do not bite off more than you can chew. That being said, do not do something you have already done a million times. Push yourself, but be realistic. Your mentors will help you. You have the rest of the day to brainstorm ideas with your fellow interns. Go."

Violet, Truitt, Stacee, and I clumped together at my table. They started chatting excitedly about ideas, but I was still so mad about Sabine that it was hard for me to concentrate. Eventually, though, I wrangled my anger to the back of my mind and joined the conversation. Sabine might be stronger than me, she might be able to waste my time in the morning, but this was *my* time, here. I wouldn't let her ruin this internship.

By the end of the day, we each had several pages of ideas, and even a few sketches. Olivia had passed around handouts of guidelines. We were allowed to make up to three outfits, a dozen accessories, or four pairs of shoes, depending on our area of interest. I could hear some students from the table next to us vow that they were going to pull off an entire collection. Apparently they hadn't taken Olivia's warning seriously about having realistic goals for this particular project.

As we were walking home after dinner, I suddenly missed Adrian. His absence hit me out of the blue, and I felt myself trying not to cry as

Violet and Truitt and Stacee chatted about their projects.

My survival mechanism at the moment was to play dumb. To be meek. Agreeable.

The only problem was, I wasn't meek, I wasn't dumb, and I was only occasionally agreeable.

When we reached the dorms at Enneman's everyone wanted to have another movie night, but I begged off, saying I hadn't slept well the night before and I was tired. Stacee booed and threw kernels of popcorn at me as I made my way down the hall back to my room. She actually reminded me of Trish a lot, which only made it harder trying not to cry as I escaped to my room, closing the door behind me.

"Rough day?"

I jerked, looking up. It wasn't Julian this time, or Sabine.

It was Kalare.

As relieved as I was to see her, part of me just really wanted to be alone. Stress issues aside, we were literally surrounded by thousands of people all day at Myriad. I could use a few hours to myself.

I stuffed the almost-tears back down my throat. Kalare was sitting on the twin bed Julian had occupied the night before, smoking.

"Yes," I admitted. "But nothing I can't handle. Do you have… news?"

"I think we should go for a walk. It's a nice night. You haven't seen much of the city yet, have you?"

I searched her face, and it was blank. Eventually she quirked an eyebrow at me.

"Yeah," I said finally. "I'd love a tour."

"I came in a different way so the other design babies wouldn't see me. Meet out front."

She went to the door, listened for a moment, then left. I followed a moment later, but she was nowhere in sight. Since I'd told everyone

I was going to bed, I didn't want them to think I was lying by walking out right in front of them, so I took the emergency stairs down to the lobby instead of the main elevator.

When I got outside, Kalare was waiting for me.

We started walking.

And kept walking.

I glanced at her a few times, but she didn't look like she was planning on saying anything. I finally opened my mouth but before I could speak, she pointed at a subway sign. "Our line's just ahead."

We walked down, Kalare paying for us both, and hopped on the first train that pulled in. I wasn't sure if Kalare knew where we were going, or if she was picking a train at random.

It was crazy crowded this time of night but Kalare found us seats in the last car.

"You seem comfortable here," I said finally. It was a neutral enough statement.

She nodded. "Should be. I live right over the river."

Ah yes, she was from Jersey.

"Tell me about your internship," Kalare said after a long moment, leaning back against the seat and the wall. It was almost a hundred degrees out, but she was wearing a leather vest that went down to her knees.

"Uh…it's good."

She waved her hand in a rotating motion to indicate I should be more specific.

I told her about it, not sure where this was going. I talked about Olivia and Violet and Truitt and Stacee, about the workroom and the fashion closet and the cafeteria and our projects. Every time I paused, she asked me another question. I debated whether or not to tell her about Sabine, but I didn't, for two reasons.

One, Sabine had been so obviously mean to me that part of me was convinced she wanted me to tell on her to Kalare or Julian. I wasn't sure what her end-game there was, but she'd never dared treat me that way when I was in Stony Creek.

Second, I wanted to beat her on my own terms. Telling Kalare might make Sabine back off. It might even get me assigned to an actual mentor. But I could still accomplish what I wanted to accomplish with Sabine putting me in a cubicle prison three hours a day. I was convincing myself it was just a really peculiar *Project Runway* challenge: how to create something with office supplies in a five-by-five foot box.

Slowly, the train car began to clear out until it was only us and a half-dozen people on the other side of the car. Kalare was putting out a sort of "don't sit near us" vibe.

When it was mostly empty, and I'd completely run out of both interesting and non-interesting details about the internship, and my butt was starting to get sore from sitting on those uncomfortable metal seats for two hours, Kalare finally looked at me.

"All right, I got some good news and some bad news."

I glanced over my shoulder at the other occupants of the car. There was no way they could hear us.

"Good news first," I said.

"Dessert before dinner; my kind of gal." Kalare smiled, but it was brief and half-hearted. "All right, well, my source seems to think, based on my description—which I claimed was from a passage in a book I'd read, not on real-world circumstances—that you *are* an Unmaker."

"That's the good news?"

She nodded grimly. "The bad news is that I think I may have just kicked a hornet's nest. The fact that I'm on a Praetorian Guard is not common knowledge. We were told to maintain complete radio silence about our location, our objective, and you. As far as I'm aware, no one but the Council knows where we are or why we're there, and no one on the Praetorian Guard has snitched."

"I'm not sure I see what the bad news is."

"That's because I haven't gotten to it yet, you little turd. Be patient."

Kalare got out a cigarette and lit it, puffing irritably. I looked pointedly at the no-smoking sign.

"Sue me," she said, looking tense. "I'm still smoking this crap herbal shit. No secondhand smoke, you're fine."

She puffed on the cigarette another few moments, grimacing at the taste.

"The bad news," she continued, eying me over the cigarette, "is that now people know I've been asking questions about Unmakers. They also know I've been off-grid for a few months. People are already putting two-and-two together. They don't know who you are, but it's only a matter of time."

"But—I don't understand why they care. What *is* an Unmaker?"

Kalare blew streams of smoke from her nostrils. "Our bogeyman. When I told you and Adrian what I thought you were, I was half-joking. Or, maybe hoping it was a joke. An Unmaker is to us what vampires are to humans: a fun, ridiculous myth. In both our cases, there's more truth to the story than most people realize."

She took a huge drag and let out a long breath. "The bad news is, Caitlin, that if Unmakers were ever real, they died out thousands of years ago. Or rather, they were hunted down and exterminated, according to my friend; their entire line erased." She turned, looking me in the eye. "By the Council. I don't mean they ordered it done; I mean the Council fucking members did it themselves."

"But that doesn't make sense," I whispered. "The Council has been protecting me. I mean, you're my *bodyguard* for Pete's sake."

"Yeah, well, that may not be the case for very long. If you are an

Unmaker and they find out about it, you're moving to the top of their Convenient Accidents list."

"But," I protested, "I still don't know what an Unmaker *is*, or, or—*does*. Why on earth would they want to kill me?"

"Because they're afraid of you."

I looked at her, nonplussed.

"I know," she said, stubbing out the cigarette on the floor, "you're about as intimidating as a litter of puppies. But apparently Unmakers can kill vampires." She ground the cigarette with her boot then turned back to me. "Apparently, they can kill *demons*."

I stared at her, not really computing what she'd just said. "I'm sorry, what?"

"My contact wouldn't say more than that. Got real paranoid. Just said that if the Unmakers were real and they were exterminated by the Council, there was a good reason for it."

"If I could kill demons," I hissed, trying to keep my voice down, "don't you think I would have killed Adrian's father when he was trying to *impregnate* me?"

Kalare put up her hands. "I'm just telling you what he said. I look at you, and I see a regular-ass human girl. I don't get any Unmaker vibes. You're just…you. But I can't ignore what you guys told me about what happened. Between the nightmares, your new lucid dreams, what happened with Adrian's father, and what Adrian did to Julian, something is going on. Something really, really doesn't make sense. And I'm afraid that if I keep asking questions, even discreetly, things are going to end up badly for me *and* for you. Probably for Adrian, too. We're dealing with shit way beyond my experience." She pulled out a new cigarette and lit it.

"What the hell am I supposed to do?" I whispered at her. "Just wait for the Council to change their minds and send me neatly to my grave?"

"If I were smart, I'd let exactly that happen. You're not my problem," Kalare muttered a little too frankly for my taste. "But like I said, you've grown on me. I'd hate to see you end up floating in the bay."

She sighed, leaning her head against the wall, cigarette dangling over the edge of the seat.

"I've got some plans in motion. An extreme worst-case back-up just in case shit hits the fan. For your own sake, I can't tell you about it yet. But just know, you're not dying on my watch. All right?"

I nodded, feeling a little better. Kalare was tough. If she said she'd protect me, I believed her. If she had a plan to keep me safe, I trusted that she knew what she was doing. I hated not knowing, but I also understood the logic of not telling me details. I may not be compellable, but I could still be tortured or leveraged.

Wow, how did I switch so easily from eating pizza with Truitt and Stacee and Violet to thinking about ways to avoid interrogation?

"For now," Kalare said after a long silence, "you keep doing what you've been doing: living your life as if this is all just a minor inconvenience. Go to your internship. Call your friends back home. Watch movies with your buddies. I promise I'm doing everything I can on my end to figure this out."

I nodded, realizing that I was shaking slightly. I think it was unused adrenaline.

"Kalare," I said, having an idea. "What about Julian?"

Kalare snorted. "Your life is on the line and you're still trying to set me up with him?"

I blinked. "What? No. No—Julian might be on my side. Or rather, he might be on Adrian's side. He's protected us several times. He's kept secrets for us that he didn't have to, that we didn't even ask him to. Last night, when he was on-duty, he indicated that he…cared. About

Adrian, not me. But still. He might be willing to help. He doesn't seem to have any more love for the Council than you do."

Kalare looked thoughtful. "I'll think about it. But where you're concerned, I'd rather not take chances."

I nodded. "I have one more question. Have you ever heard of the Separation of Family law?"

She nodded. "Of course. What about it?"

I blinked, not expecting her answer. Julian had never heard of it. "Well—what is it?"

She frowned, as if the answer was obvious. "A law stating that no more than two vampire siblings can live in the same household at any given time."

I blinked again. "Isn't that kind of an odd rule?"

She shrugged. "Not really. Council's way of keeping everyone's loyalties to the Council, not to their family. It's pretty effective."

"Don't you think it's odd," I said slowly, "that everyone in the de la Mara clan lives together?"

It was Kalare's turn to blink. "Farrar never said anything about it. I assumed the Council gave permission. But..." she looked lost in thought. "That's recent, though. Julian only moved in with them a few years ago, but he's in New York half the time. Nothing for him to do in Stony Creek, but Mariana insists that he live with them at least half the year. Adrian moved in a few years before that. Lucian only got placed with them eighteen months ago."

"But why?" I asked. "Why would the Council agree to them breaking the law?"

Kalare shook her head. "I have no idea. Not sure it matters, though, Council has people experimenting and side-stepping laws for research purposes all the time."

I frowned. That didn't feel totally off-base, but it also didn't seem like a full answer. "Any ideas come to you, let me know. I feel like there's something there I'm missing." The train slowed, coming to a station. I stood. "Should we head back?"

"Yeah," she said, relaxing a fraction. "Sorry for keeping you out so late."

"It's all right," I said. "I don't do much in the mornings anyway."

BRIGHT PINK BITCH

16

That's insane."

"I know."

Adrian stood there blinking at me. "How…" he walked off then walked back to me. "*How?*"

"I don't know."

"But you would have killed my father—"

"I know. I know all the arguments. It doesn't make sense. And yet…" I looked around at the dreamscape, at Data, at Adrian. "…here we are. This isn't your dream, it's mine. Looks like I really might be this Unmaker thing."

He nodded, eyes lost in thought. "Setting aside the fact that we have no idea how your family line might have survived a Council-mandated genocide, this doesn't align with the fact that the Council has spent considerable resources protecting you. You have half a Praetorian Guard at your beck and call."

"Yeah, no," I protested, "I'm at *their* beck and call."

He raised an eyebrow. "Who's sleeping in who's room at night keeping watch?"

I blushed. He had a point.

"I forgot to tell you—Kalare knew the Separation of Family law. In fact, she reacted like it was common knowledge, which probably means Mariana and Dominic know what it is."

"What's it for?"

"Keeping vampire siblings apart. She says it's to guarantee loyalties are focused on the Council, rather than family, but that doesn't line up with your family in particular."

Adrian frowned. "You're right. In fact, it was odd that I got pulled from the Laroches in Paris at all, though I'd already been moved once before. They like to have us live in as many countries as possible to soak up languages as children. We're like humans in that way. Taking me from a world culture center to the backwoods of New York was an odd choice. And assigning Julian to live there, too, well after he'd come of age…"

I nodded, the rusty gears of my brain finally starting to move. "So there's a long-standing vampire law prohibiting something that your family has intentionally done the opposite of. You know what that means, right?"

Adrian quirked his head at me, puzzled.

"It means that Mariana probably knows why."

"Not necessarily."

"Think about it: Mariana's the one who chose to move back to Stony Creek because she's from there. Mariana's the one who's been in contact with the Council ever since I showed up in town. She's also the one who had the vision about me. And she doesn't like me. Or at least, she's not comfortable with me. She's had a direct line of communication with the Council from the beginning. I'm willing to bet she knows a hell of a lot more about what's going on than we thought."

Adrian let out a long breath. "The problem is, I can't ask her. She has a sense of duty where I'm concerned, but not a sense of affection. We're polite to each other, but I'm actually closer to Julian than I am to her."

"Maybe it's because of Utuwe."

"What do you mean?"

"Well, her older sister was executed. Maybe she's been afraid of getting close to any of you in case something like that happens again."

"Then why has us all live under one roof? Why bring us together?"

I shook my head. "I don't know."

As soon as breakfast was over, the college interns came to the cafeteria to pick us up for our morning assignments. Sabine came to our table and stared at me until I picked up my messenger bag and followed her. We wound through the hallways and corridors until we came to the same abandoned stretch of cubicles. She waited at the entrance, as if expecting me to protest. Instead, I smiled politely at her and stepped inside, immediately sitting on the footstool. Out of the corner of my eye, I could see her glaring at me, as though wondering why I wasn't making a fuss.

I pulled out my sketchbook and started making notes and brainstorming ideas for my project. I'd only jotted down a few thoughts when I felt the sketchbook being snatched out of my hands.

Sabine glanced through the pages, then calmly ripped out the designs and notes and ran them through the paper shredder, destroying them. She did it without saying a word.

I stared at her, shocked. It hadn't been one of my old journals, thank God, but it still represented hours of work and planning.

She looked at me for a long moment, as if to drive home the point that she could do whatever she wanted and there was nothing I could do to stop her, then pulled out her phone, sat at the chair, and ignored me for the next three hours.

"This," Olivia said, walking us into a large, dark room, "is the remnant room."

She flipped on the lights and a collective "ooh" went around the group.

It was a long, skinny room filled with shelves all the way up to the ceiling. The shelves were filled with rolls of scrap fabric, bins of mismatched buttons and zippers, and even leftover pieces of leather, buckles, and decorative chain.

"This is where scraps go to die," Olivia explained. "While you will have access to fabric and supplies, you are allowed to use whatever you want from this room to complete your personal projects. Each season, the room is cleared and the leftover scraps dumped. Enneman students are allowed to come and pick through the room at the end of every semester. We throw away anything they do not take. You, however," she said, turning to us, "have free reign of this room for the duration of your stay. The door is unlocked, so come and go as you please."

The remnant room was only a short hallway down from our workroom. I had a feeling we would soon look like a trail of worker ants, carrying bits of leftovers back and forth.

Truitt and Stacee joined Violet and I at our table. Everyone had plopped open their sketchbooks to group-brainstorm more ideas.

"*Caitlin,*" Violet gasped, "what happened to your sketches?"

"Coffee," I explained, showing them the stained cover and edge of the sketchbook. "Ruined the first third of the pages."

They were all properly horrified on my behalf. I'd gone to the trouble of staining the cover during lunch in preparation for this very question. I'd also decided that I would keep two notebooks from now on: one that I kept here in the workroom, and one that I took to my "mentor" sessions with Sabine.

We only had three days left to finalize our plans and present them to our mentors for approval. I had no idea how I was going to get Sabine to sign off on anything I did. I also couldn't go to Olivia and ask for a new mentor. Best case, it would piss Sabine off, or get the Council more involved than they already were. Worst case, Sabine would compel Olivia to do whatever she wanted to keep her cover. I didn't want to put Olivia through that.

Besides—better the devil I knew then the devil I didn't. To some extent, literally.

Sabine was a bully, but she was an obvious bully. And I knew that she was watching me at Myriad. If she was replaced, they might not tell me who she was being replaced by.

I didn't have a plan to work around Sabine, yet, but I'd think of something.

I had to.

"It's freaking gorgeous."

"You think?"

I was standing on the roof of Enneman's on their little patio. Technically we weren't supposed to be up here, even though there was a little patio with a table and chairs, but Kalare had picked the lock and let me up. She was off in the corner reading a book, drinking a beer, and smoking, her feet propped up on the ledge of the roof.

"Absolutely," I told Jenny, leaning against the railing, looking out over the city. It was hot as hell, but less stuffy out here than in my room. Air conditioning units were on the fritz and the repair guys weren't coming until tomorrow. I was pacing the roof while on the phone, trying to conjure up a breeze.

Jenny had texted me a photo of Mark's painting-in-progress. It was a modernist interpretation of Jenny looking straight at the viewer with her pale, otherworldly blue eyes. It was stunning. I'd had no idea Mark was *that* talented.

"He say what he's going to do with it when he's done?"

"Well, he's going to Paris in September, so he has to leave it at his parents'. He said I could keep it for him until he gets back, but it's huge. I don't even think it would fit in my room."

"How are you two doing, by the way?"

I could almost hear her blush through the phone. "Good, actually. Really good. I'm…happy." She laughed a little. "I don't know how I'm going to handle him going to France for a semester, though. I don't know how you and Adrian are doing it."

A sudden lump rose in my throat and I swallowed it back down. "It's not easy," I admitted. "But he understands why I'm here. Have you seen him lately?"

"No," Jenny said. "Actually, I haven't seen him at all since you left for New York."

"Could you maybe ask him out?" I immediately realized that sounded weird. "I mean, you and Mark and everyone? I think he's a little shy about inviting himself to things."

"Of course," Jenny said. "We're going to Saratoga Springs in a couple days; I'll see if he wants to come."

"Thanks, Jen," I said, feeling relieved. I knew Adrian could take care of himself, but I also knew if left to his own devices, he would just stay at the mansion all day, worrying about Lucian.

"How's the situation with Meghan?"

Jenny let out a slow breath. "Not better. She's got Laura on her side. Between the two of them, I'm...I'm struggling. They spray-painted "bitch" on the hood of our car. It's not even my car; it's my mom's car. She had to go to work like that. My dad sanded it off, but we can't afford a new paint job, so now our car is just...well, it looks bad."

I couldn't speak for a moment, I was so shocked.

"I can't believe she did that," I said, finally, struggling for words. "Are you sure it was her?"

"Pretty sure," she said. "She tweeted later that 'sluts get what they deserve. #bitch'"

"What did Trish say?"

"Trish doesn't know," Jenny replied, sounding uncomfortable. "I didn't want to ruin her vacation. Mark was angry. He wanted to go talk to her parents but I told him not to."

"Why?" I asked in disbelief. "Her behavior is totally unacceptable."

"Well—I don't know for sure, but I heard from Stephanie that her parents are getting divorced. And it's not going well. The divorce, I mean. It's not pretty. And her dad got that DUI. So...so if she needs to write 'bitch' on my family's car, then maybe that's what I need to let her do."

My mind went a million miles an hour. From across the roof, Kalare glanced up at me, then looked back at her book.

"Jenny," I said slowly, "I get how hard parent crap can be. Believe me. But it's not your job to manage Meghan's life. She *vandalized* your mom's car. That's illegal. I mean, I think it's great that you understand what she's going through, but allowing her to behave like that isn't helping her. It's just letting her get away with shitty behavior."

"I don't know what to do," Jenny said, sounding as stressed out as I'd ever heard her. "I mean, her parents obviously don't care. What else is there to do? Go to the police? How is that helping her?"

She had a point.

"Well, I know she won't talk to me," I said. "But maybe Stephanie or Trish could talk to her. This sounds like it's worth interrupting Trish's vacation. She's Meghan's friend. She'd want to know about this."

"Yeah," Jenny sighed, "maybe you're right. Thanks for talking to me, Cait, I didn't know what to do. I haven't even told my parents that I know who did it. I just feel trapped."

"Anytime," I told her. "For real. I'm just sorry we didn't talk more when I was in town."

"Well, I'll definitely be grateful when you're back."

"Me, too," I said, meaning it.

How strange. I really did mean it. I missed Stony Creek. I even missed Joe and Norah and—

Damn it. I even missed Rachel.

Jenny and I talked a few more minutes, and she promised me again that she'd invite Adrian on their trip to Saratoga Springs. I hung up and stared out over the city for a few minutes, lost in thought. Eventually, Kalare made her way over to me, leaning against the railing, cigarette dangling from her fingertips.

"You're a good kid," she said after a long moment.

I glanced at her. She met my gaze.

"I just wanted you to know that."

She patted my shoulder and went back to her chair and her book and her beer.

I stared back out over the city, watching the dying sun playing off a million windows in shards of golden light. Once again, I felt as though I were on the edge of something, waiting.

Kalare guarded me that night, reading by the light of a book-clip lamp while I slept. Having her and Julian there was weird, but it was also, in a way, comforting. And the one good thing about Sabine being my Myriad mentor was that she didn't guard me at night. That had been Julian's solution to my "please don't let Sabine into my room because she might kill me in my sleep" request. I had him to blame for her being my mentor, but I had him to thank for her not staring creepily at me while I slept.

With only three days left until our project proposals were due, I silently followed Sabine to my cubicle prison. I sat on the footstool, as usual, and pulled out my sketchbook. I'd barely started sketching when she took the book from my hands and started ripping out the page.

She stopped, suddenly, when she caught sight of what was on it.

I'd come prepared with a sketch. It was an illustration of Sabine herself, looking beautiful, fashionable, elegant—except she had a giant pig snout in place of a nose.

I hadn't drawn it to be petty (well, let's be real, it was a little petty), but rather to see how she would react. How far she'd go to punish me for insulting her.

She stared at the sketch for a long moment, then slowly ripped it out and shredded it. She turned back to me, glaring icily.

"Did that amuse you?" she asked quietly, a vein beating in her temple.

"Did you not like the sketch?" I asked innocently, doing my best to look puzzled. "I drew it just for you."

Her whole body tensed, her knuckles white as they gripped the arms of the chair.

"I tried to draw your Patronus," I explained, pushing her. I was being mean, but it had a purpose. "Did you not see the resemblance?"

She grabbed the stapler off the desk and slammed it against the cubicle wall, right next to my face. It shattered, sending sharp bits of plastic flying at my cheek.

She leaned over me. "Little girl," she said, almost murmuring, "you do not want to test me."

I looked up at her curiously, willing my heart to slow the crap down. "I think I do, actually. I'd like to see how far you're willing to go to keep me from doing what I'm here to do. Will you slap me? Chain me to the desk? What do you think the Council will do if they find out about this?"

Before she could respond, someone cleared their throat. We both looked up.

"Uh," a college-age girl said, looking down at us. "What are you guys doing here? This hall is closed for repairs."

Well, that would explain the massive water stains on the walls and floor.

Sabine stood, grabbed the girl by the shoulders, and said, "Go back to wherever you just were. Forget we were here. Do not come back to this hallway."

The girl blinked, once, then walked away.

Shit.

Sabine had just compelled her. In a very non-emergency situation.

That wasn't good.

As soon as the girl was out of sight, Sabine crouched down next to me. Her ice-blue eyes were still swirling, emitting a pale light. She was still in compulsion mode.

"You will forget what you just saw. You will obey me from here on out, no matter what I tell you to do."

Of course, the compulsion didn't work.

But it made me afraid. Sabine was not supposed to issue commands like that. Moreover, Kalare had warned me not to pretend to follow compulsory commands anymore. Besides, I couldn't obey Sabine's orders. What if she told me to do something dangerous?

It was time to let the cat out of the bag. I'd been hoping to avoid this longer, but it didn't look like I had a choice.

I stared at Sabine, then smiled. "No."

She blinked, as though not comprehending what I'd just said.

She grabbed my face in her hand, vise-like, and held my gaze. "You will *forget*," she said more vehemently, "what you just saw. You will obey me from here on out, no matter what I tell you to do."

I frowned at her. "I don't think you heard me," I said, prying her hand off my jaw. "I told you *no*. I know you don't hear that very often, but you're just gonna have to live with it. M'kay?"

I patted her shoulder sympathetically, then stood, grabbed my sketchbook and messenger bag, and left.

I'd either just made a really smart move, or really, really dumb move.

I'd find out one way or the other soon enough.

I sent off a quick text to Kalare and Julian, just in case it was the latter: *S just tried to compel me. Also compelled college intern.*

I was almost to the cafeteria when I got a text back from Kalare: *Stay in a public place. On my way.*

Julian texted me a moment later, saying, simply: *Shit.*

I grabbed a table in the cafeteria, thinking furiously, heart racing. The place was mostly empty, as it was only 9:30, too late for breakfast and too early for lunch. Not sure what to do, I stood in line at the espresso stand and ordered a latte. Caffeine was probably not what I needed right now, but I wanted to look like I had an excuse to be there.

I sat back down, distracted. I literally jumped when someone stopped at my table.

It was Olivia, and one of her assistants. She was looking down at me with a displeased expression.

"You'll have to excuse me," she said, searching my face. "I normally have everyone's names down, but we've doubled the program size this year."

"Oh," I said, startled. "I'm Caitlin."

"Caitlin," she repeated, as if cementing it in her mind. "May I ask what you're doing here?"

Shit.

"Um," I said, stalling. "My mentor didn't have anything for me to do today. I thought I'd grab a coffee before heading back to the work-room."

She turned to her assistant, who consulted a piece of paper at the back of her overburdened clipboard. "Sabine Rousseau."

"Why don't we check with your mentor and see if there's been some sort of mistake."

"No!" I said, panicking. They both looked at me strangely. "I mean, she seemed really busy."

Double-shit, I was honest-to-God terrible at lying.

"Caitlin—" Olivia began to say, but she was interrupted by her phone ringing. She looked at me apologetically, and answered. "Olivia Renault," she said, then listened. "Mm-hmm. I see. Thank you."

She hung up, and turned to me, looking concerned. "It seems your mentor has had to drop out of the program. Something about a family member dying unexpectedly. She's returning home for the summer."

"Oh," I said, slightly terrified that the Council had acted so quickly.

It had been less than ten minutes since I'd seen Sabine. "That's awful. Maybe that's why she was so upset this morning."

It was a lie. There was no death in the family. The Council was much, much better at this than I was.

"We'll see about assigning you a new mentor. For today, why don't you pair up with another intern? Leigh, who's available?" she asked her assistant.

"If it's all right with you," I said, interrupting. "I've made friends with Stacee Rey, Truitt Brown, and Violet Kessler. I wouldn't mind pairing up with one of them."

Olivia frowned at me reproachfully. At least it seemed that way. I don't think she was used to being interrupted. I shrank under her gaze.

"Very well," she said finally. "Ms. Rey and her mentor are working in the fashion closet this morning. Leigh, can you show her the way?"

Her assistant nodded. I smiled gratefully at Olivia, but she was already walking away. I followed her assistant from the cafeteria to the elevators, still not entirely convinced that Sabine wasn't going to jump out from somewhere and beat me to death.

My phone buzzed and I looked at it, careful not to let Leigh see my screen. It was a text from Kalare: *I'm at Myriad, nearby. J's dealing with fall-out. Act normal.*

I let out a long breath, relieved. If Kalare was here, I wasn't in danger. Or, at least not as much.

Stacee was surprised to see me, and I could tell her mentor was confused, but they both accepted me without too many questions. I tried to enjoy being in the fashion closet, but I was too distracted. I worked on auto-pilot, helping them return shoes to their proper places; scrubbing out dirt from the heels with Q-tips and leather-safe cleaning solvent.

Our usual group ate lunch, then worked together on our projects in the afternoon. I even made it through a round of telephone pictionary with them in the lounge at Enneman's before saying I needed to call my boyfriend.

When I got to my room, both Julian and Kalare were there. They led me silently up to the roof.

The three of us sat at the lone table and looked at each other.

"So," Kalare said, breaking the ice. "What the hell happened?"

I told them an abbreviated version of events. Julian's face turned stony.

"Damn it," he muttered when I finished. "I thought she'd be more professional than this."

"Did I mess everything up?" I asked, panicking again at his reaction.

"You did the best you could," Kalare reassured me. "Council's gonna freak when they realize you can't be compelled, but they're gonna be more pissed at Sabine. I still don't understand why she was elected to be a Praetorian. She's been volatile from day one."

"Farrar's got a soft-spot for giving people second chances," Julian muttered. "You know that."

She threw an irritated look at him and lit a cigarette, looking tired and frazzled as she turned to Julian. "Why'd you even tell Adrian about the paired compulsion?" Kalare asked him. "You know better."

Julian threw Kalare an irritated look right back. "You've seen him around her. He's a fucking puppy. If they weren't going to be able to control themselves, at least this would help protect them from self-incrimination. With our father's attack, Adrian had a legitimate excuse to use that method to protect Caitlin. It seemed like a good idea at the time."

Kalare rubbed her forehead. Julian stole one of her cigarettes and lit it, leaning his head back against his chair and letting out a stream of smoke through his nostrils. He looked down at the cigarette in disgust.

"What the hell is this?"

"Non-carcinogenic cigarette alternative. We hang out with a human every day; I'm making sacrifices."

"It's God-awful," he muttered, but took another drag.

If they were both this stressed out, it wasn't a good sign.

"What happens now?" I asked. "What do we do?"

"Wait," Kalare grunted, "as usual. I'm sure Sabine has told the Council her version of events. We told them ours, based on the information you gave us. The fact that they removed her so quickly as your mentor makes me believe that they're sticking to the current plan."

"Is there any other news?" I asked, looking at Kalare significantly.

Kalare shook her head. "I can't risk asking more questions. The back-up plan is in place, though. Shit goes down, we've got some options."

I suddenly felt tired, defeated. There was too much going on. "Should I just go home? Back to Stony Creek?"

Kalare shook her head. "No—you did well today, acting like you were irritated with Sabine. Acting like a teenager angry that someone was bossing you around. Makes it look like you don't know any better, like you aren't aware of anything else that's going on. Going home now would look suspicious."

"I am *not* good at this," I told her. "I'm not good at lying. I've never done this without Adrian here. I feel like it's just a matter of time before I slip up."

The door to the roof suddenly rattled. Julian had stuck a metal rod through the handle after we'd come up so no one could open it. We all tensed, watching it. We could hear some muddled conversation, then footsteps heading back down. Just curious high schoolers, trying to find their way onto the roof. We relaxed, marginally.

Kalare's phone buzzed. She answered it without replying, and listened for half a minute before saying, "Understood." She hung up and looked at us. "They're sending Farrar out."

"Is that a good thing or a bad thing?"

She looked at me evenly. "I have no idea."

My phone buzzed. It was Joe.

"Shit, I have to take this." I stood, answering the call.

We talked for a few minutes awkwardly. He wanted to know how my internship was going. I told him it was fine, very exciting. I asked how the ranch was doing. He said fine, very busy. He told me he and Norah and Rachel missed me. I said I missed them. He asked me if I would be okay if Rachel called me soon, to see how I was doing. He said he knew that she and I had talked in New York. I didn't answer for a long time. Finally, I told him that yes, she could call me. He told me he loved me. I told him I loved him, too. He said goodnight. I said goodbye.

The pressure of all the things I hadn't really dealt with was starting to build. I needed to resolve some of them. And that meant trusting a few people.

I turned back to Kalare. "I think it's time to loop Julian in."

She glanced at me, then at Adrian's brother. "You sure?"

Julian frowned. "Loop me in on what?"

"I'm sure," I told her. "He's already involved. I trust him."

Julian looked surprised at that. Kalare set down her cigarette and rubbed her eyes. "All right, kid." She looked at Julian, face blank. "J, we think Girl Wonder over there is an Unmaker."

Julian laughed.

Then he realized we were both dead quiet.

He glanced at us both. "You're shitting me."

She took a sip from her beer. "I shit you not."

Julian looked at me as if seeing me for the first time. "Well," he said finally. "That would explain a lot."

DREAM GHOST COAST TO COAST

17

I wandered around the dreamscape, waiting. Adrian hadn't shown up yet.

"Data, you got any thoughts on how I pull Adrian into my dreams?"

Data thought for a moment, then seemed to make up his mind. To our left, a memory began to play.

It was the day the Praetorian Guard came back to Stony Creek.

Adrian and I were sitting on the guardrail on the side of the road, debating whether or not he and I should pair.

"This is the best way for us to protect each other," Dream Adrian said. "And it's not all bad. Julian says they call it 'the sacred bond.' Although that may just be him bullshitting me. Of course it can be abused, but from what he says, most vampires who have done it have expressed a deep connection to the human they're paired with. It becomes more about synchronicity than mere compulsion. I affect you, but you also affect me."

The memory jumped back to the beginning and played again.

"All right," I told Data. "So it has something to do with our bond. Why didn't he show up before? When I was still in Stony Creek?"

"What'd I miss?" a voice called out from behind me.

I whirled, and found real the Adrian standing there. I smiled and hugged him. "I think Data is indicating that the reason I can pull you into my dreams is because we're paired."

"How come you couldn't back when you were in Stony Creek?" he asked.

"My subconscious is silent on that point," I said, throwing a stern look at Data. He didn't even have the decency to look bashful. I shrugged. "Maybe he doesn't know."

He nodded. "I don't know how things are playing out on your end, but Farrar's pretty angry about what happened with Sabine."

"At me, or at her?"

Adrian shook his head. "Both. Sabine for breaking the law, and you and I for being paired. I gave him my excuse, about doing it during the attack. They bought it, but they're not happy. Farrar's been locked in his office talking with the Council all day. They're planning something, but I don't know what. They took away my phone and computer."

I paled. "Why?"

"I imagine so that I can't communicate with anyone until they figure out what to do with me. They also instructed me not to leave the house. I'm under quarantine."

"I'm so sorry," I breathed. "Have they hurt you?"

"No, not at all," he said, smiling lightly. "They're just being cautious. It'll be okay, I promise."

I let out a breath. "Okay. Keep me updated next time you're asleep. I'll let Julian and Kalare know you're out of commission, phone-wise."

"Kalare come up with any new information?"

"No," I replied. "But I have to tell you something. Two somethings, actually."

He tucked a strand of hair behind my ear, fingers lingering on my jaw. "Okay."

I turned my face into his palm, wanting suddenly to ditch this whole conversation and just snuggle the crap out of him. But we didn't have enough time, not now. The dreamscape seemed to move at a different rate of speed than the real world. It never lasted as long as I thought it should.

I blinked, and looked back up at him. "First, Julian's now fully looped in. He knows Kalare's theory that I'm an Unmaker. He knows she's reached out to her contacts about getting more information. In short, he knows everything we do."

"Oh," Adrian said, sounding surprised.

"I'm sorry I didn't tell you. I know that should have been something we voted on, but with everything that happened with Sabine yesterday, I was afraid of waiting too long. Are you mad?"

He shook his head. "No. I think it was a good move. We have to start trusting someone. He's my brother. Underneath it all, I think he wants to help us."

I nodded. "That's the conclusion I came to as well."

"What's the other thing you need to tell me?"

I let out a deep breath, looking at the floor. "It's…it's not vampire-related. In a way, it's not even important. But it is."

Adrian frowned at me, not because he was mad, but because he was trying to understand. "Are you okay?"

"Yeah," I replied, "I mean, it's weird, but yeah, I'm okay. Rachel… Rachel told me about why she and my mom stopped talking."

He looked down at me, waiting patiently. I felt twitchy, nervous, and I wasn't sure why.

"Apparently my mom and dad couldn't get pregnant. And they

asked Rachel to be their surrogate. And she said yes. So…so my aunt is actually the one that gave birth to me, even though genetically I'm my parents' daughter."

Adrian's eyes widened. "Oh. Wow. That's…that's a lot to take in."

"Yeah. And that's not the weird part. Her boyfriend at the time got in a car accident, almost killed her and me. He did kill the driver of another car. Rachel knew he was drunk, but she let him drive. That's why my mom cut her out of our lives. She didn't trust her. And I don't know how to feel about that yet." I looked up at him, feeling lost and confused. "I mean, you've met my aunt. She's super responsible, just an über-mom type, y'know? It's weird to think of her like that. It's weird to know that she freaking *gave birth* to me. But she's not my mom. But she is, kind of, now. And I…"

I shrugged helplessly. Adrian held out his arms, hesitating, not sure if I wanted comfort or not. I glued myself to his chest, and he hugged me tightly.

"Does this change anything?" he asked gently. "About how you feel?"

"I don't know," I whispered. "I can't remember any of it. I wish my mom had told me. I had a right to know. But I don't want to be angry at my mom, because she's gone, she can't fix it now, so there's no point being angry. There's no point being angry at Rachel, either. She's a different person now. And yet I am. I'm angry."

"So what are you going to do?"

I hid my eyes in his shirt. "She's going to call me. Joe said she was going to call to check in on me. Should I talk about it?"

Adrian rested his chin on the top of my head. "I may be wrong, but it seems like you want to."

I blinked. He was right. I did want to talk about it.

"What do I say? I don't even know what to ask."

"I don't know, Cait. Maybe you don't ask anything. Maybe you just tell her you love her."

My heart clenched in my chest. I gritted my teeth to keep from crying. I did love her. Against my will, but I did. "Why do you always have to say the right thing?"

I felt Adrian's arms tighten instinctively around me. "Cait."

His tone had shifted completely. I looked up at him, but he was looking behind me. I turned.

I blinked.

I blinked again.

A woman was standing there, observing us. It wasn't Data wearing a new avatar skin, because I could see Data off to the side, glancing between us and the woman. Besides, Data couldn't have transformed into her, because I'd never seen her before.

She was black, tall, with sharp cheekbones and short hair. She was wearing sweatpants, bunny slippers, and a tank-top.

"Data," I asked slowly, "are you seeing what I'm seeing?"

"Yes," he replied. "A woman has appeared. She does not belong here."

"Did you bring her?" I asked him.

"No," he said simply.

The woman looked back and forth between us, as if curious.

"Hi," I said, calling out to her. She was standing about ten feet off. It was hard to tell distance in the dreamscape, but that's about how far it felt. "Don't mean to be rude, but…who are you?"

She looked at me, then at Adrian, a strange expression passing over her face that I couldn't read. Her gaze flicked to Data.

Then she disappeared.

No one spoke for a long time.

"What," I said finally, turning to Adrian, "was *that?*"

"I have no idea," he replied, looking deeply troubled. "But it might disprove your theory."

I looked at him. "Which one?"

"That I'm here because we're paired."

I was assigned a new mentor, a girl even shorter than me. Her high school intern had dropped out so she was free to take me on. I went with her to several meetings with junior designers but she didn't say a word the whole time, so neither did I. When the meeting broke up, we headed to her cubicle, a box she shared with two other interns.

"After the meetings, it's my job to type up the notes and put them on the task-assignment portal. This way the designers know exactly what's due, when it's due, and who it's due to."

Her fingers flew over the keyboard inputting information faster than I could follow.

"You been to the mail room yet?" she asked. I shook my head. "I need to mail a sample set for Edmond; I'll show you how to use the system."

By "show" she just meant "do" and expected me to follow. I took notes best I could but I didn't understand their system, had no idea who Edmond was, and didn't have the keycodes that would authorize me to ship things in the first place. She was nice enough, but operated at a speed I couldn't comprehend. Constantly sipping from her travel mug of coffee, she reminded me of the hummingbird that slurped up sugar water from the feeder on the porch back at the ranch.

When it was time for lunch, she wished me a cheery but distracted good day and left me at the cafeteria. If I was going to learn anything from her, I'd have to pay close attention, or I'd miss it. At least she was better than Sabine, and I had a shot at getting her to approve my project.

I met the others for lunch, then we all headed back to the workroom. Truitt had settled on his shoe designs, Violet was fluctuating between two different approaches to her accessories, and Stacee was just deciding which fabric she wanted to use for her three outfits.

I had nothing.

Oh, I'd drawn things. Dozens of sketches. The ones Sabine hadn't destroyed, I had. I was so distracted by vampire crap that I hadn't been able to focus on my project. Everything was turning out wrong.

"You're putting too much pressure on yourself," Stacee said as I hunched over the work table, head in my hands.

"I have two days left to finalize my project proposal," I grumbled at her. "And I have zero ideas. I think I'm putting the appropriate amount of pressure on myself."

"Have you tried taking a walk?" Violet asked. "The city is very inspiring. I designed a whole set of bracelets just looking at the stoplights."

"Yeah, maybe," I said, knowing it wouldn't help. New York was stunning, but it wasn't my city. I had no personal connection to it. I knew they were just trying to help, though, so I stood up and smiled. "I'm gonna go poke around the remnant room. See if anything jumps at me. If I'm not back in an hour, you'll find me crying next to the button bins."

Truitt snorted. When I was down the hall and out of view, I let myself slip back into my tired slouch. I was totally out of inspiration and motivation. I hated it when I was like this.

I opened the door to the remnant room and saw a few people milling around. I grabbed one of the tote bags they kept by the door and started down the aisles, glancing at the materials. Unlike the fashion closet and the stock room, this place had zero organization. Scraps were literally hauled in by the cartful every evening and dumped on whatever surface was available. It was OCD hell. I didn't have OCD, but still, even I felt dizzy in the chaos. The nice thing, though, was that there was new stuff in there every day. It was never the same, and it came directly from the designers' cutting tables, which meant you might just stumble upon a scrap of $150-a-yard fabric.

The problem wasn't the designs, really. The problem was with my brand. Our packets from Olivia had said to create either several distinctly separate items from different lines and seasons to display our versatility, or to design items that would belong in the same collection, to show cohesion. Truitt had gone for shoe designs that fit each season, and belonged to four different types of customers. Violet was doing summer accessories for high school students because "Might as well stick with what I know." Stacee wanted to do fall looks for dudes because "For the sake of America, there has to be a middle ground between hipsters and bros."

Which left me.

What was my aesthetic? What kind of customer was I designing for? Why was I even here, at this internship?

I was here because Adrian got me the internship. At the biggest fashion label in the country. I was here because of him, not because of me.

That wasn't fair—I'd worked my ass off on that application. Adrian had nothing to do with that. As far as I knew, his family had not interfered with whether or not I was accepted.

Or—had they?

I buried my face in the nearest pile of eye-height fabric, groaning.

I missed him.

And also felt a simultaneous low-grade resentment that he'd found this internship for me. Or maybe it was a low-grade self-resentment that I hadn't found it for myself. He'd been thinking ahead for me while I'd been stuck in my own world. He'd set up my studio. He bought the supplies.

Gah! What did it matter? I was here. And I was wasting time.

I took a deep breath, held it, then let it out, turning to face the room. I started walking slowly, eyes dancing from object to object, waiting for something to grab my attention.

Who was my customer?

Not me. I'd designed for myself before, worn my own clothes, but it felt weird and narcissistic. I didn't want to design for executives or business women because I didn't know anything about them. I didn't want to do menswear, or children. Didn't know a thing about making shoes or accessories. So, girls, or young women. Maybe?

After an hour of searching, I left with nothing.

At seven we all left Myriad, intent on seeing a movie at the nearby second-run theater. As soon as we got outside, though, my phone buzzed. It was a text from Kalare: *Farrar wants to talk. Meet at subway.*

"Hey guys," I told the group, "I'll catch up with you, okay? Gotta call home."

They waved goodbye and continued on while I headed toward the subway entrance. Before I could head down the steps, an Escalade pulled up, stopping next to me on the street. The door opened and Kalare got out. "Come on, loser, we're going shopping."

I grinned. Anyone who quoted *Mean Girls* was friend-for-life material.

I hopped in as Kalare went around and got in the front seat. Julian was driving and Farrar took up more than his fair share of the back seat.

"Hello, Caitlin," he said calmly, his voice and face a perfect neutral, neither menacing nor inviting. "Thank you for meeting with me."

"No problem," I said, trying not to let my heart rate rise. "I told the others I'd catch up with them at the movie — should I cancel?"

"This won't take long."

Julian merged into traffic.

"Please tell me in your own words what occurred at Myriad with Sabine."

I resisted looking at Kalare for guidance—barely.

"I was surprised when I found out she was going to be my mentor," I told him frankly. "Nobody gave me a heads up that she was going to be a part of the program. She refused to teach me anything or even let me do my own work. She kept me in a cubicle, grabbed me by the arm and face whenever I tried to leave, and shredded my designs. When an actual intern came by to question why we were in that section of the building, she compelled the intern to forget we were there. Then, she told me to obey everything she commanded. I told her no, then reported to Julian and Kalare because she was freaking me out."

Farrar nodded, as if my story concurred with what he'd already been told. "Sabine has been removed from your protection detail." He looked disappointed as he said it, not at me, it seemed, but at her. "We have assigned a new bodyguard to be on-premises at Myriad during the day, should you need anything. They will not interfere with your activities."

I nodded, truly grateful.

"From what I have been told, Sabine did not merely tell you to obey her. She attempted to compel you."

I blinked, struggling to keep my face neutral and my heart from racing. "Well, her eyes went all crazy," I said, playing dumb. "I don't know what she expected to happen, but I wasn't going to sit there and let her order me around for no good reason."

Farrar considered me for a long moment. "Based on your description, and her own admission, she attempted compulsion, and it didn't work. Do you know why?"

This was where having Kalare as an ally was saving my life.

"Well, probably because of Adrian, right?" I said, acting innocent. "With the thing he did, when his dad attacked me? The paired thing?"

I said it as if it was common knowledge. Farrar glanced at Julian, but Julian kept his eyes on the road.

"What 'paired thing?'" Farrar prompted.

"The paired compulsion thing. So his dad couldn't compel me anymore?"

I looked at him as though confused he didn't know this. I was getting better at lying. Not much, but perhaps enough to make it out of this conversation alive.

Farrar looked at me a long moment. My heart began to race again, even though I was begging it to calm the crap down.

"Do I frighten you?" he asked, unexpectedly.

I laughed—I couldn't help it. "Next to Adrian's dad, you are probably the scariest person I've ever met. No offense, but you look like a James Bond villain."

Farrar smiled, just a bit, then nodded. "Thank you for your time, Caitlin. Should we drop you at the theater?"

"That'd be great."

Julian pulled around the block and stopped at the curb. Kalare and I got out. I waved dorkily at the Escalade as it pulled away. When it was out of sight, I let out a huge breath, sinking to the curb.

"You okay?" Kalare asked.

"I thought I was going to pass out," I told her, watching as my hands trembled in front of me.

"I think you did well," Kalare said. "He's loyal to the Council, but he's fair. I think he wants to believe you. He only does shit like report people if he has irrefutable evidence. You gonna puke?"

I seriously considered the question before shaking my head. "Not yet."

"Movie's about to start; get in there. I'll be nearby."

I stood shakily. "You on duty tonight, or Julian?"

"Julian."

I nodded. "See you on the flipside."

She smiled, shaking her head while I disappeared into the movie theater and found my friends just as the film began to play. We spent the movie whispering excitedly to each other about what was going on and handing popcorn and peanut butter M&Ms back and forth. It was almost ten by the time the film was done, and I was beat, so I almost didn't notice the woman from my dream staring at me from across the street.

I stopped dead in the middle of the sidewalk, making Violet bump into me.

"Ow," she complained.

"Sorry," I said, not taking my eyes off the figure. It was dark, and hard to see. A truck trundled by, and by the time it was gone, so was the woman.

Holy bananas, was I going crazy?

Had I imagined her? I *was* tired. And no stranger to exhaustion-induced semi-hallucinations. The dreamscapes might happen when I was asleep, but they took up energy as if I was awake. I was getting more and more exhausted by the day, especially since the dreamscape had kicked up into high gear with full sensory input and telecommunications with Adrian. Most days I woke up feeling like I hadn't slept at all.

"What's up, Caitlin?" Truitt asked. "You see a ghost or something? Because I do *not* do ghosts. Grandma's house was haunted and nobody believed me."

I shook my head, laughing. "No. Sorry. Thought I did. Sorry, Violet."

"No problem," she said, and we continued back to the dorms. We split ways to our rooms back at Enneman's. Julian was already chilling on the second bed, playing a game on his phone as usual.

"Yo," I called at him, then collapsed onto my bed. He grunted a greeting in return.

"How awful was I today?" I asked him, voice muffled by the pillow.

"What was that?"

I sat up, hugging the pillow to my stomach as I leaned against the wall. "How awful was I?"

He shrugged, eyes on his phone. "You did well. Farrar is making camp at my apartment. He's not happy, but it doesn't seem to be directed at you."

I nodded, relieved. "Also, in case you didn't know, Adrian's on lockdown. Took away his phone and computer."

Julian grunted. "That would explain why he's not answering my texts."

I sat on the edge of my bed, leaning forward. "Also—and you can pass this along to Kalare—I had another visitor in my dreamscape last night."

Julian frowned. "What do you mean? Did your avatar change?"

I shook my head. "No—a woman just showed up out of the blue. Never saw her before in my life. Didn't say a word. Disappeared again after about a minute. Then tonight on my way home, I thought I saw her on the street. That could've been my mind playing tricks on me, though."

Julian sat up, setting his phone down. "That ever happen before?"

"Nope. Besides Adrian, of course."

He thought a moment. "I'll talk it over with Kalare."

"Thanks. Any other news?"

"Not yet."

I nodded and pulled out my laptop from under my bed and answered a few messages, deleted some junk stuff, and was about to close it down when a new message popped into my inbox.

It was from Trish.

Hey Cait, it began. *I hope you're doing well in New York. Jenny told me some of what's going on back home. My family and I will be landing at La Guardia in a couple days, I was wondering if I could stop by and talk to you before I headed back to Stony Creek. Let me know if you're available. — Trish.*

I read it again, then a third time, then replied and said I'd love to see her and of course she could stop by.

I waited a few minutes to see if she'd answer, but she didn't, and I couldn't keep my eyes open. I stowed my laptop under my bed and reached to turn off the light. But of course, that was the moment Rachel called me.

I stared at my phone until it almost went to voicemail, then reluctantly answered it.

"Caitlin?"

"Hi, Aunt Rachel."

"Hey, sweetie. How are you doing?"

I glanced at Julian. He was back on his phone. "I'm fine. Tired, but fine."

"You getting enough sleep? Are they feeding you?"

"Yes."

There was a long moment of silence. "I know it's been a while since we've talked," Rachel said finally. "Now that some time has passed, do you have any questions for me? Or for Joe? He's here, if you want to talk to him. Norah's out at a friend's."

I held the phone away from my face and let out a deep breath. How did I even begin this conversation?

"Uncle Joe never even met my parents, did he?"

I could almost hear Rachel shake her head. "No, he never did. I know he wishes he could have."

"And they *are* my parents, right? Genetically, I'm theirs?"

"Yes," she confirmed. "I only carried you."

My mind went off in a million directions. Across from me, Julian glanced up.

"Is Rick still alive?" I asked. "Your old boyfriend?"

There was a pause on the other end of the line. "To be honest, honey, I don't know. I never went looking for him after his trial."

If he was still alive, he was in a prison here in New York. If he was alive, I could go find him. The man who'd almost killed me.

Did I want to do that? He was the reason my family had fallen apart. He was the reason I'd never known Rachel.

"When you started dating Joe," I said after another long silence, "did you tell him?"

I could feel Rachel hesitate. "Not right away. But within a few months I did."

"And he still wanted to date you?"

I winced. That came out way blunter than I'd intended.

"Why don't you ask him that?" Rachel said. Before I could protest, I could hear the phone being passed.

"Hi, Caitlin," I heard my uncle say, coming on the line. "Rachel says you have a question for me?"

"Hi, Uncle Joe," I mumbled, feeling embarrassed. I hadn't meant to get him involved in this conversation. "I was just, uh, wondering how you took it when Rachel told you what…happened."

Joe was quiet for a long time, but it didn't seem strained, just contemplative. "It was a lot to take in, at first," he admitted. "But whoever your aunt had been in New York, whatever decisions she'd made before she came to Stony Creek, I didn't see that. I only saw the person Rachel wanted to be. That was all I needed to know about her."

A knot of tears was forming in my throat. "Thanks, Uncle Joe."

I could hear the phone being passed back.

"Do you have anymore questions?" Rachel asked after a moment.

I turned toward the wall, away from Julian, so he couldn't see the tears spilling down my cheeks. "Did you love her?" I whispered, voice breaking. "Did you love my mom?"

"Oh honey, of *course* I did," Rachel breathed. "She was everything to me. That's why I chose to do what she asked me to do. That's why I stayed away."

I pulled my knees up to my chest and pressed my face into them for a long moment, tears soaking into my jeans. Finally, I turned back to the phone. "For what it's worth, Rachel, I think she was wrong. I'm sorry that she never forgave you. And I'm sorry you didn't get to say goodbye. And I'm sorry I never got to know you before now, and that I was a brat when I moved in. You didn't deserve that. I'm…I'm sorry."

I could hear Rachel crying on the other end of the line. She cleared her throat. "Thank you, Caitlin. You don't know what that means to me."

"I love you, Aunt Rachel."

"I love you, too, Caitlin. So much."

CAITLIN HOLTE DESIGNS
18

What are these?" Data asked, looking at the three mannequins I'd lined up.

"Three-dimensional dream-depictions of the designs I'm submitting today?" I told him, pins stuck between my teeth as I made changes to the first look.

"Two observations," Data said, his eyebrow quirked in that look of perpetually serious puzzlement. "One—why use pins? If you want to change the look of your garment, you only need imagine it to be so."

I stared at him, then at the mannequin, then at the magnetic pin-cushion in my hand. I spat the pins onto the cushion and then imagined it away. I stared at the mannequin and thought about the changes I wanted.

Of course he was right—instantly, the garment changed. Ah, blast, the pockets looked like crap. I flipped through a few designs, the outfit changing instantly to align with my thoughts.

"Second," Data continued while I had fun putting ridiculous things on the mannequin, "why go to the trouble of working on those garments here? The real designs will not change once you awaken. In fact, the real designs have not yet been constructed. They are only illustrations in your project proposal."

"Yes," I agreed, "but as you so kindly pointed out, I can try things in here in an instant that would take me hours, if not days, in the real world. I can determine whether I like the look of something before I commit to the real-world labor."

"Intriguing," Data commented. "Do you not agree?"

Now I was making the mannequins dance the Macarena. The bodiless sleeves were animated and disco lights popped out of nowhere.

Before I could respond, something appeared behind Data. Or rather, someone.

It was the woman. The same woman as before.

She looked at me, then at Data, then at the dancing, disco-lit mannequins, looking perplexed.

"Hey," I called to her sternly. "I saw you earlier, out there, on the street. Who are you and how did you get here?"

She seemed to be distracted by the dancing mannequins, so I waved an arm (even though that wasn't strictly necessary) and banished them back into nothingness. She turned to me, a somber expression on her face that I didn't understand. Did she find dancing mannequins sad?

"Who are you?" I repeated.

She blinked, and turned, but I held out my hand again, freezing her in place.

Holy shit, I could do that?

She looked just as surprised.

Off to the side, Adrian appeared. He was wearing boxers and nothing else, which was highly distracting. Apparently he showed up in the dream wearing whatever he'd fallen asleep in. He blinked down at himself, blushing a little, then joined me as I walked up to the woman. Her eyes followed me as I looked at her clothing for clues. The woman was dressed in what looked like pajamas again: fashion sweats, bare feet, a light-weight shirt because it was hot as balls here in the summer.

Did that mean she was here, in New York, for real? *Had* I actually seen her on the street?

"Why are you here?" I asked. "*How* are you here?"

Once again, she looked surprised by my questions. She glanced at Data. "You're the one, aren't you?" she asked him. Data said nothing. She smirked, then turned back to me. "Pay attention, Caitlin Holte. You may survive this yet."

And with that, she disappeared.

"Did you let her go?" Adrian asked.

"No," I said, shaken. "I didn't."

Tensions were high in the Myriad cafeteria. Today was the day everyone submitted their project proposals to their mentors. Already, fifteen kids had left the program. Some were simply homesick and not ready for this kind of internship, while some had been sent home either because of breaking some rule or other or because they hadn't been able to keep up with the work.

"More accurately," Olivia had addressed us all in the workroom, "they had no sense of time management."

At breakfast Truitt looked calm except for the face that he was methodically tearing his toast into crumbs. "I'm confident in what I designed," he mumbled, "but I'm the only guy, and I'm one of only three interns doing shoes, and the only one doing men's shoes. I don't

271

know if that's going to be a good thing or a bad thing."

"Why on earth would it be a bad thing?" Stacee asked, opening her second yogurt.

He rolled his eyes at her as if it was obvious. "It could set me apart. If there's no competition, there's nothing to compare it against, which might mean I slide through easy. But on the other hand, if there's nothing to compare it against, maybe they'll be harder on it. They judge men more harshly than women."

"Okay," Stacee said, setting down her yogurt forcefully. "Do you really want me to school you on why that last statement was wrong, or do you want to figure it out for yourself?"

Violet sighed at them, looking dreamy. "I wish I had a boyfriend to fight with."

Both of them stopped and looked at her, then turned away, uncomfortable.

"It's not like we can do much about it at this point," Stacee said after a long, awkward silence. "Either they accept the proposal, or they don't. Olivia said some designs would get approved with recommendations for changes. Even if it's flat-out rejected, we have another three days to come up with a new proposal."

"*But*," Truitt said, crumbling the last of the toast into toast dust, "that's three days you aren't working on your project. I mean, I've never *made* shoes. They paired me with my mentor because she's got experience with that, but she's never done men's shoes before. I've never even *tried* it because I didn't have the right tools or materials back home. What if I find out I'm really bad at making shoes? What if I totally blow it?"

"Well we can't change anything now," I said around a mouthful of Cheerios. I was tired of listening to them talk themselves in circles, and I was, well, regular tired.

Truitt loosened his bow tie irritably. "Says the girl who pulled a miracle proposal out of her butt in *one night*. You'll do fine, Holte."

"This isn't life or death," I protested. And I should know. "This is the *high school* intern program. We're here to learn, not to win."

Truitt snorted. "Maybe your rich boyfriend's daddy can bank-roll your college fund, but if I don't get that full-ride, I'm not going to Enneman's."

Violet must have told him about Adrian, and the Armani suit, and the whole his-family-was-a-lot-richer-than-mine thing. She was chatty.

"I just graduated high school," he continued, rushing on before I could respond. "My family could barely afford to send me to this internship. My little sister couldn't get braces this year because they spent the money on me." He looked a little grey just thinking about it. "This is my only chance."

I had a lot of things I wanted to say in response to that, starting with *I'm sorry, but Adrian's family is not paying for me to go to college* along with *I didn't realize you had graduated high school* and *Oh yeah, I forgot we're competing for the same scholarship.*

"Well, panicking isn't going to help anyone," Stacee said cheerfully. "And low-blow, man. Does Caitlin look like the type of girl who's going to let her boyfriend do something like that?"

Was I the kind of girl who'd let my boyfriend pay for college? I mean, it's not like I could afford to go to Enneman's, either. Rachel and Joe barely made ends meet. Grandma was thrifty, but poor (and had a gambling problem), and my mom's hospital bills left me penniless.

If Adrian offered to pay for college, would I really say no?

"—I just think maybe it's too young!" Violet squeaked, gripping her chair with both hands, looking tiny and afraid. "I mean, I was trying to stick with what I know, but maybe it's too juvenile? What if they laugh at me? What if they think I'm childish?"

"Vi, your mentor looked at your preliminary designs, right? Did she say they were childish?"

Violet shook her head, but still looked like a frightened bunny.

"Then chill. Seriously, everyone just chill. The only thing we can do is be prepared, calm, and confident."

"Prepared, calm, confident," Violet repeated, whispering. "Prepared, calm, confident."

She relaxed marginally. Only a moment later, though, a group of girls walked by our table. I hadn't been paying that close attention, lost in thoughts about Adrian and money and college, but the girl at the front of the group was wearing super tall, trendy wedges. When someone at the table next to ours backed up suddenly, she tripped, startled, and spilled her entire breakfast tray on Violet.

The whole cafeteria stopped for a moment, in shock.

"I'm so sorry," the girl whispered, looking horrified. "I'll go get you some napkins!"

She hobbled off, leaving Violet covered in oatmeal, orange juice, granola, and chunks of syrupy pineapple.

Violet started to tremble, frozen in place.

"It's okay, Vi," Stacee said, jumping up. "We'll get you cleaned up."

"Presentations are in fifteen minutes," Violet said, her face turning a weird, mottled red-white. "I'll never make it to Enneman's and back in time."

"We'll figure something out," Stacee reassured her.

An idea came to me. "Violet, your hair looks fine, it's just your dress that got stained. Truitt, can you clean this up while we help Vi?"

He nodded, rolling up the sleeves of his white button-up so they wouldn't get dirty. A goopy brown trail of oatmeal and orange juice was headed straight for him on the table. He grimaced, but started mopping up the mess.

Stacee and Violet followed me into the bathroom. "Stacee, clean her up best you can. I'll be right back."

I ran to the workroom and grabbed my fabric tape, scissors, and safety pins, then ran to the remnant room. I grabbed the largest scraps I could find, along with a couple worn leather belts that hadn't made it past approval upstairs, and ran back to the bathroom.

"Just what are you doing, exactly?" Stacee asked, seeing the pile of supplies in my hand.

"Just help me already," I said, throwing fabric at her. "We've got five minutes to *Project Runway* the shit out of this."

Stacee caught on, a gleam in her eyes. We layered fabric on Violet, using her as a living mannequin, pinning and taping and topping it all off with an adorable little waist belt from the stack I'd brought, the only one that had been small enough to fit her.

When we were done, we stepped back. Observing our handiwork, Stacee gave me a high-five. "Tim Gunn would be so proud."

Were it any other day, the dress would look a little ridiculous. As it was, everyone was dressed up, since we were presenting to both our mentors and, if everything went well, to Olivia Renault herself.

We'd fashioned what could reasonably pass as a dress out of scraps of striped chiffon and lightweight black cotton. It wasn't particularly well-constructed, but it should last long enough for Violet to get through her first presentation. She could go back to the dorms during lunch and change into something that had less chance of falling apart.

"Crap, we gotta go," Stacee said, checking her watch. "Good luck!"

"Thank you guys so much!" Violet said, trying not to cry. We both hugged her and ran off in separate directions.

Patricia, my mentor, was at her cubicle. Not the most inspiring place for a presentation that could make or break my future career, but hey, I'd work with what I had.

I slowed down, checking to make sure my outfit and hair were in place, and that nothing had slipped out of my project packet, before walking in.

She was on the phone. I waited patiently, not sure she'd even noticed I was there. She finally put down the phone, which immediately rang again. She answered it, reaching into her drawer to grab a catalog, before she spotted me, jumping a bit in surprise.

"Yes," she said, using her Happy Phone Voice. "Yes, certainly. Of course. Absolutely. Immediately. Th—no, thank *you!*"

She hung up, sent a quick, apologetic smile my way, then rained a fire of e-mails on her keyboard.

Just as she was done, her two cubicle-mates' interns showed up. They had stations on the opposite side of the high school workroom from me, so I hadn't learned their names. We all smiled uneasily at each other while the college interns looked at each other, realizing we couldn't all use the cubicle to give our presentations.

"Kathryn, why don't we go, um…well, let's find a spot, yeah?"

I thought about correcting Patricia on my name, but I doubt she'd remember it anyway. At least it was sort of close.

I followed her as she darted down the hall, then darted back, grabbing her phone, a notepad, and a pen. We wandered, passing conference rooms already taken by other interns presenting their projects. Twenty minutes went by before Patricia threw up her hands and went into the women's restroom.

"Anyone here?" she called out. "Hullo?"

No one answered.

"Perfect!" she said, and turned to me. "All right, begin whenever you're ready."

I looked around, not sure if she was serious. But she had her pen and paper out and looked attentively at me for the first time since I'd met her. Her phone buzzed, and she tucked it into her pocket without answering.

I shook it off, smiled, and began my presentation.

Like Tim Gunn said, sometimes you just had to make it work.

"McGrumpy doesn't look as worried as before," Stacee observed to me as Truitt sat down at our lunch table.

He threw an irritated glance her way, cracked his knuckles in what looked like a nervous habit, and hunched in his chair. "Lyndsey said she was very impressed. She asked me questions; I answered them. She nodded. I don't think I could have done any better than I did. Now we wait."

Violet came running up to our table.

"Whoa, Vi, nice dress," Truitt said, sounding genuinely complimentary.

She blushed, then kissed me and Stacee on the heads. "You guys are angels, my mentor *loved* the dress, I told her all about how you guys rescued me. Honestly I like it so much I'd wear it all day but it's literally starting to fall apart so I'm going to run back to Enneman's. See you guys later! And good luck!"

She rushed off, almost bumping into someone and starting a whole other cafeteria accident on her way out.

"How'd you do, Stacee?" I asked, after we were all sure that Violet had made it safely out of the room.

"Good as I could," she said simply. "Marg is super hard to read. Barely said a word. She did tell me, though, that we're not the only ones getting graded on this thing. If they okay a project proposal that

Olivia thinks is trash, it has consequences for them, too. Part of their program is structured around leadership. Apparently they're all as nervous about this as we are."

"They just get a catered lunch out of it," Truitt grumbled, poking at his salad. I didn't know what he was complaining about. I would eat buffet-style every day if I could.

"You're cranky when you're nervous," Stacee said, flinging a crouton at him.

He tensed, jabbing even harder at his salad. "I am the only one who seems to be aware of the *stakes* here." He gave up on the salad and stood. "I'm going for a walk, I'm too nervous to sit still. See you guys in the workroom."

Stacee and I watched him walk off. She sighed. "He's just mad 'cuz we made out last night and he's all flustered now."

I stared at Stacee. "He's—I mean you—but he's—"

"Straight?" she asked. I nodded. She shrugged. "Straight enough to make out with me and get all silly about it."

"You like him?"

She shrugged, but smiled, watching him leave. "He's fun. Little tightly wound, but maybe that's why I like him. It's fun to push his buttons."

She laughed and dug into her pizza.

While I should have been more interested that two of my three friends here in New York were now sort of an item, my mind immediately wandered instead to Adrian.

Making out sounded like a really, really solid idea. Would it be weird to make out in the dreamscape? Would that be creepy?

Violet rejoined us just before the lunch hour was up. When we got back to the workroom, Truitt was already there, scowling at a mannequin near his work station. The high school interns chatted nervously for twenty minutes before Olivia entered the room. We stopped talking immediately.

"If I call your name, you will come with me. If I do not call your name, you will stay here."

Truitt's name was the third she called. His last name was Brown, so I wondered if she was doing this alphabetically?

Ah, nope—a dozen names later, she called Stacee Rey, which was after me and Violet in the alphabet, surname-wise.

Although that could just mean we hadn't been chosen.

It was with great relief that she called my name, second-to-last. But then the last name was called—

And it wasn't Violet's.

Truitt, Stacee, and I looked at her, stricken. She was already starting to tear up, but she smiled at us. "Go on," she told us. "I'll be fine."

I couldn't stand seeing her so sad. I swooped her into a hug. Then Stacee joined, and Truitt. I could feel Violet's shoulders heaving; she was probably leaving mascara stains on my shirt, but I didn't care.

"*Now*, please," Olivia called from the doorway.

We let Violet go. She smiled, wiping at her eyes. "I've still got a chance to make changes to mine, it'll be okay. Go."

We nodded, and left Violet and about half the others in the work-room while we followed Olivia up several floors to the senior design offices.

Her assistant, Leigh, ushered us all into a long conference room. There were pastries and coffee, but only a few people touched them. We were afraid of spilling anything on our clothes before seeing Olivia.

Leigh called us in one-by-one. An hour went by, then two. A few more people began picking at the scones. A few girls even gave in and tried out the coffee. One poor girl had just bitten into a croissant when Leigh came back in, announcing her name. She froze, a deer in the headlights, flaky pastry crumbs sticking to her bright red lipstick.

Stacee handed her a napkin, and the girl quickly brushed at her face. I gave her a thumbs-up and the girl followed Leigh out of the room looking frazzled.

No one touched the food after that.

After another hour, Truitt was called in. Stacee slapped him on the butt on his way out. He tried to glare at her, but it dissolved helplessly into a rueful smile. He rolled his eyes instead, blew us both a kiss, and left.

Once people left for their interviews, they didn't come back. It was unnerving.

Another hour went by, and another. They weren't doing this alphabetically. I couldn't determine any sort of pattern. My stomach began to rumble for dinner, but after Violet's mishap this morning and the girl with the croissant lipstick, I didn't dare go for the stale and yet somehow still-delicious-looking pastries. Even if I didn't spill on myself, what if I got something stuck in my teeth?

The room emptied slowly until it was six o'clock, then six-thirty, then six-forty-five. It was down to me and one other girl who looked as tired and on-edge as I felt. At ten-to-seven, she was called in. I gave her an encouraging smile as she walked past me out of the room.

Knowing it was almost my turn, my nerves shot back up to ten. My phone buzzed. It was Stacee. *You gone in yet?* she texted.

No, I replied, hands shaking. *So nervous I'm about to throw up.*

You got this, she said. *Just breathe. We're waiting for you in the cafeteria.*

I glanced at the clock. It was five after seven. They kicked us out at seven.

The last girl just went in, I texted her. *You guys can go back to the dorms without me.*

Nope, Stacee texted back immediately. *We'll wait on the curb if they kick us out. Kick butt.*

I smiled, then put my phone away. My hands were trembling so bad that I stood and walked around the giant conference table, shaking them out.

There was no reason to be nervous, there was no reason to be nervous. I'd spoken to Olivia before. Olivia was nice. Olivia was calm. Olivia was not scary.

"Caitlin Holte?"

I whirled to the door. Leigh stood there, looking tired. "You're last. Hurry up, we're behind schedule."

I grabbed my bag and my presentation and followed her out of the room and down a short hall to a frosted glass door.

She opened it and led me inside. "Caitlin Holte, last of the day."

"Thank you, Leigh," Olivia said.

She sat behind a large, modern desk. It was a corner office, with massive windows looking out over the city. The view was magnificent.

"Have a seat, Caitlin," she said, gesturing to the chair opposite her.

I took a deep breath and walked toward her, sitting.

"My apologies for keeping you so late," she began, sliding her glasses off her face and rubbing the bridge of her nose. "Some of your peers were a bit long-winded."

I smiled, hoping I didn't look nervous and crazy. She was silent for a moment, and I wasn't sure if I was supposed to begin.

"Regardless," Olivia said, slipping the glasses back on, "you can be assured that you have my full attention. Proceed."

She looked at me attentively. Poor woman had been listening to nervous seventeen-year-olds for six straight hours. I pulled out my presentation and slid the first page to her on the desk, knowing that despite her assurances, her mind was probably already on dinner and home and taking off her amazing but painful-looking shoes.

"You asked us," I began slowly, feeling an overwhelming tendency to rush, "to think about our brand. To consider what customer we were designing for."

I paused, taking a breath. Patricia hadn't given me any indication whether I'd done well or poorly. The fact that I was sitting here in front of Olivia must be a good sign, but I was about to take a gamble saying all this to one of Myriad's founders.

"So," I continued, showing her the next page, "I considered the options. Was my customer a business woman, a stay-at-home mom, a student, a young girl? I didn't know. I couldn't decide."

Olivia raised an eyebrow at me as if to say, "This does not sound good for you."

I rushed on. "Then I remembered what you said about social media. That you didn't like it. And it got me thinking about how the world has changed so quickly in the past century. In the past few years, even. And so has fashion."

I stopped, taking a deep breath. "Myriad is relatively new, as far as this industry is concerned. But it became the powerhouse label that it is in part because it was willing to evolve as a company. Designs you put out last season are refreshingly different than designs you put out five years ago, or ten, or twenty. But there is still cohesion to your brand."

Olivia's eyebrow raised even further. She knew all this. It was twenty past seven.

"The same is true of people," I said, finally getting around to my point. "People change, they mature, they evolve, and yet they are still the same person that they started out as. My concept builds on that idea of cohesion and evolution."

I slid the next page to her. It had a picture of Jenny from Winter Formal, and a picture of her at Prom.

"This is my friend Jenny. She bought that dress at Nordstrom and wore it to a dance this past February. She couldn't afford to buy a dress for Prom, so I made her an overskirt to wear with the dress that she already had, making it look like a new outfit."

Olivia frowned. "You're showing me a garment another company made that you minimally altered months before coming to this program?" Like Farrar, she had perfected a neutral voice. She sounded neither angry nor sympathetic.

"Only to lay the groundwork," I explained, trying not to panic. Was I losing her interest? Was this the stupidest idea in the world? Before I could psych myself out, I shoved the next page across the desk. "That's Jenny again, along with my friends Trish and Stephanie. They're three very, very different girls, but they're all the same age, from the same town. If you're looking at fashion from a purely statistical point of view, you would market the same garment to all three girls."

I quickly laid out three new pages side by side. They each had a design of an everyday outfit. It was easy to tell that the illustrated models, rather than being faceless skeletons, were obvious interpretations of my friends.

"This," I said, pointing to the Jenny design, "is something I would make for Jenny. This is an outfit I would make for Steph. And this one I would make for Trish."

I pulled out three more designs and laid them underneath the three already on the desk. It was Jenny, Trish, and Steph again, but older. The designs were more mature, but still matched each of my friends' personalities. In fact, the fabric itself was the same.

Then, I pulled out another three sketches, and another three, laying them out in a grid that barely fit on Olivia's desk.

"My brand is their brand," I told Olivia. "My concept is that we change while staying the same. If I'm a customer, I don't want to shop at a store that catered to me when I was twenty, but I felt embarrassed to shop at when I was thirty, or forty. The goal of a fashion company is to create loyal and happy customers *for life*. But if we're not serving the needs of women as they grow and change and enter new stages, then we're not serving them at all. *That's* my concept. Offering a cohesive line of looks that would provide age and career-appropriate options no matter what stage of life a woman is at."

I looked at the clock. It was seven-forty-five.

"I apologize for taking up so much of your time," I said, blushing. "I…I hope I have been, uh…clear."

Now that I was winding down, I was totally losing my cool. I was exhausted, I was hungry, I'd kept Olivia Renault way, way late at work. I didn't even like my concept all that much, I'd just thrown it together last night so at least I'd have something to show.

Olivia shuffled slowly through the pages, landing on the one of Jenny wearing her Winter Formal-turned-Prom dress.

"I spoke with Violet Kessler's mentor earlier today. She told me what you did. Even showed me a picture. How long did it take you to pull that together?"

I blinked, unprepared for the question. "Stacee and I did it in about five minutes."

"Whose idea was it?"

"Uh…" my mind stuttered, not sure how to respond. "Well, well, someone spilled food all over Violet just before her presentation, and she didn't have time to go back to the dorms to change. So I thought of the remnant room, because you said we could use whatever we wanted there. I went and grabbed some things and then Stacee and I just sort of whipped up that dress."

Olivia looked at me for a moment, then leaned back in her chair. "You will not repeat this, but Violet's mentor reported that she was more impressed with that dress than she was with Violet's presentation. When she asked if Violet had made it, she admitted it was you."

"And Stacee," I said, automatically.

"And Stacee," Olivia confirmed. "Caitlin, do you know how many applications we receive every year for this program?"

I shook my head. "I'm not sure. I know it's quite a few."

She smiled. "It's close to ten thousand."

My eyes widened. I hadn't realized it was that many.

"Do you know how many people review each and every application?"

I shook my head again.

"Three. An intern, an assistant, and a junior designer. I review the top five hundred applications. Which means I reviewed yours."

She reached into her desk drawer and pulled out my application packet, the one I'd submitted at the beginning of the summer, and spread it out on the desk. "These dresses are impressive. Modern, yet classic, well-designed, well-executed, even well-photographed. They are far more impressive than the designs you have just shown me."

My heart jumped into my chest. I struggled to remain calm. "It's true that they're fancier," I said, scrambling to make my brain work. "But they were designed for special occasions. It would be great if we could dress like that every day, but the truth is, most people need something comfortable, washable, and wearable all but a handful of days out of the year. I love those dresses—I'm proud of those dresses—but I'm not planning on being a designer who only works for celebrities. A stay-at-home-mom should feel just as beautiful as a movie star, just as important, and just as comfortable. Everyday women deserve good clothes."

That was true, but I was also grasping at straws, anything to justify my half-assed concept. Honestly, what was I thinking? Every department store had lines for women of different ages. That's why it was a *department* store. Women's section, juniors' section, formal, office, workout… I'd just pitched a concept that was a hundred years old.

"That's hardly a revolutionary idea," Olivia said flatly, confirming my self-criticism.

"I don't think you asked us to be revolutionary," I replied, trying to keep the desperation out of my voice. "I think you asked us to be smart. My mother always told me that it was better to do something simple and well than it was to do something extravagantly bad."

That much was true.

Olivia waited, as if expecting me to say more. When I didn't, she looked disappointed. "Very well. Thank you, Ms. Holte. You may leave."

I stood, and barely kept myself from bowing—Olivia had the same effect on me as Farrar. I laid the rest of the pages on her desk. "Um, they're numbered," I said, pointing at the bottom margin. "In case… you need to look at them again."

She blinked at me. "Thank you."

I nodded, smiled, and backed out of the room, almost tripping on her sofa before making it to the door. Once outside, I leaned against the wall and dropped my face into my hands.

"Caitlin?"

I jumped, looking up. It was Leigh, Olivia's assistant.

"I'm here to escort you downstairs. It's almost eight."

"Oh!" I said, pushing off from the wall. "Of course, thank you."

I followed her downstairs. It was still light out, but getting dark, the shadows long and thick.

"Aaah!" Stacee said, whapping me on the back as soon as I met them outside. "Congratulations, girl!"

"For what?"

"For rocking that presentation!"

"Rocking it?"

"Dude, you were in there for almost an hour," Truitt said, looking like he was trying to be friendly except his hands were stuffed in his pockets and he was half-frowning. "Most of us got less than ten minutes."

"Oh," I said, letting that sink in. "Oh. I don't know. I don't think it went that well."

"False modesty does *not* look good on you," Truitt muttered, kicking at an empty soda can on the curb.

"Guys, seriously, I don't think she liked it. I think I totally blew it."

Stacee rolled her eyes. "Right, yeah, no. Come on, Truitt stole some pizza for you from the caf. We can heat it up at Enneman's and watch *Enchanted* and pretend that we're not mad at you for stealing the scholarship."

They dragged me along as I protested. "The scholarship isn't even based on that project!" I said. "It's a combination of mentor evaluations, performance records, even attenda—"

"Shut up and accept your victory," Truitt said, "while we still sort of like you. Just know that I'm not afraid to kiss all of the butt required to take your place."

"Also, don't mention it to Violet," Stacee warned me. "She's pretty beat up about this morning."

We got back to the dorm, heated up the pizza, commiserated with Violet, who told us that she was being given a chance to modify her designs, rather than being sent home, and watched *Enchanted*.

No matter how much I protested, they didn't believe that I'd completely blown my shot at impressing Olivia Renault. If I *had* blown it, then this summer had been a waste. Time I could have spent searching more aggressively for Lucian.

For the first time, I felt truly guilty. I'd let Lucian down. I'd let my mom down with my crappy presentation. She'd taught me better than that. I'd let Grandma and Joe and Rachel down; they were helping pay for all this. And I'd let myself down. I was better than this. I could do so much better.

But I couldn't. Not when I was distracted, not when I was *divided*; half my life at the mercy of the other. I should drop out, go home. I'd be more help there.

Besides, it's not like I was going to make it as a designer. I mean who really makes it as a designer? Olivia had told us the odds our first day. One in a hundred of us would succeed.

I felt a lump rising in my throat. It wasn't worth it. I was making a fool of myself. Lucian was more important than this stupid internship.

I'd tell Olivia on Monday.

I was quitting.

SECOND CHANCES

19

Caitlin."

I opened my eyes.

Data was standing over me, looking concerned.

"What?" I said, feeling groggy. It had taken me forever to fall asleep.

"We have a visitor," Data said, looking over my shoulder.

I sat up and looked around, expecting to see Adrian or the woman. Instead, I saw Julian.

He looked extremely confused.

"What the hell's happening?" he asked. He was shirtless, wearing only striped pajama pants.

"Uh," I replied, "you're in my dream. This is Data," I said, pointing at Data.

"Hello," Data said politely. "It is nice to meet you in person. So to speak."

"Are you really here?" I asked Julian, "or did I dream up a version of you?"

Just because Adrian and the strange woman had appeared here didn't mean this was actually the real Julian. I didn't trust that this place wasn't playing tricks on me.

"How the fuck do I know?" he asked, looking freaked out. Well, that certainly sounded like him. "One minute I was asleep, the next minute I woke up here. Or, didn't wake up here. Where *is* here?"

I looked at Data. "How can Julian be in my dream? He's not paired with me. He's not even on-duty tonight."

It was true. Kalare was currently in my room, awake, guarding me. Julian was halfway across the city in his apartment, sleeping.

Before Data could reply, a new figure suddenly appeared on teh floor behind Julian. Seeing the look of surprise on my face, he whirled to face the newcomer.

Except unlike Julian, she was asleep. Or at least, lying down with her eyes closed. She appeared to be wearing pajamas.

"What the hell is happening?" Julian asked.

I was going to respond, but Julian's naked chest was distracting. No sooner had I thought this than an ugly Christmas sweater magically appeared, covering his chest.

He stared down at his torso. "This is getting weird."

"Caitlin," Data said. "We have more guests."

Three more people had appeared. All asleep.

Then another ten.

Then twenty.

Dozens more kept appearing, then hundreds. Soon, I couldn't count the number of people surrounding us, all asleep in my dream.

Finally, Adrian himself appeared, awake, wearing boxer briefs and a t-shirt.

He blinked, looking around. "I missed something, didn't I?"

"They just appeared," I told him. "Along with Julian."

The two brothers stared at each other.

"You're real?" Adrian asked, walking over to Julian. He tapped on his older brother's shoulder, testing his solid-ness.

Julian slapped his hand away. "Yes, I'm real. And not here by choice."

"So you're *both* in my head right now?"

They looked at me, then at each other. "So it would seem."

"Well, who the hell are *they*?" I asked, pointing at the crowd of sleeping people surrounding us.

Julian walked slowly through them, then stopped suddenly.

"I know him," he murmured. "His name's John." He looked up at me and Adrian slowly. "He's a vampire."

He took a few more steps, then stopped again. "So is she." He looked around, seeming to recognize several more people. "They're all vampires. They live here, in the city."

A chill went through me. There were thousands. And they were all surrounding me.

Julian looked at me, his face pale. "What *are* you?"

I had no clue. All I knew was that I didn't want them here.

Instantly, the crowd disappeared. All except Julian, Adrian, and Data.

I let out a shaky breath. It was good to know that I could banish them like I could banish anything here.

"What happened?" Adrian asked. "Where'd they go?"

"I got rid of them. They were freaking me out."

Julian nodded. "Good call."

"How is he *here*?" I asked Data. "How are any of them here? Julian is miles away from me in the real world."

"Adrian is two hundred miles away from you in the real world," Data countered. "That distance is much further."

"But Adrian and I are paired. Julian and I aren't."

Data didn't respond.

"God," Julian said, looking at Data. "This is weird. Hearing you talk about talking to your subconscious is one thing. *Seeing* it is another."

Data suddenly transformed into an exact replica of me. "It's less creepy," my subconscious said in my voice, from my face, "than me talking to a literal version of me."

Oh, god, that *was* weird. Instantly, she transformed back into Data.

"This form is more...palatable," Data explained. "A fictional character is more acceptable to the mind than a doppelgänger."

Julian stared, then nodded slowly.

"Caitlin," Adrian said, turning to me. "Do you think you could bring them back?"

"Who, the vampires?"

He nodded.

"Why would I want to do that?"

"To see if you *can*."

I hesitated, but then tried to bring them back. Instantly, they began to reappear.

Julian whistled. "This is some weird shit, even for me."

I banished the sleeping vampires with a thought, leaving only me, Adrian, Julian, and Data.

"Julian," I said, having an idea. "I'm going to try something. And I need you to tell me, next time you see me, what you remember about this place."

"What are you going to—"

"Wake up," I told him.

Instantly, he disappeared.

"Why'd you do that?" Adrian asked.

"I wanted to see if I could do something here that would affect the real world. If I didn't merely banish him back to his own dream, if I was actually able to wake him up from half-way across the city, that's certainly got to have some interesting implications."

Data nodded. "Indeed."

"I wonder…" I trailed off, turning in a slow circle. "I wonder if that woman who visited us was asleep. What if she was nearby, in the city, and asleep, when she appeared here?"

"But why was she conscious when the others were asleep?" Adrian asked.

"Why have *you* been conscious?" I countered. "Or Julian? Maybe only vampires who know me in some way can arrive awake. She said my name. She seemed to have a pretty good idea of who I am. I wonder if I can find her."

"That might be dangerous," Adrian warned. "She may know us, but we don't know anything about her. She was able to leave on her own last time—which means she has at least some control here."

He was right. "What else are we supposed to do? Just wait? She didn't hurt me or you. She barely said a word."

Adrian hesitated, but nodded. Data said nothing.

It was my call.

I concentrated on the image of the woman.

Nothing happened.

I frowned.

"Maybe she's not asleep," Adrian mused. "Think of Kalare. She's on-duty, she should be awake."

I nodded and thought of Kalare. My mind automatically went back to the last time I'd seen her, sitting on the bed, reading a book.

The dreamscape shifted, showing me that moment. Kalare appeared, sitting on the bed, turning a page in the novel she was reading, just as I'd left her.

"Kalare?" I called out.

She didn't respond. She didn't appear to hear me.

"Damn," I said. I had only conjured up a memory.

"It's not a total loss," Adrian reassured me. "We now know that only sleeping vampires can be summoned into your dreamscape. The fact that you couldn't conjure the woman from before suggests that she's not asleep. Or perhaps too far away for you to reach."

"I still don't know how I'm *doing* this," I said, feeling a little panicked. "How am I supposed to control something I don't know the first thing about?"

Adrian frowned, thinking. "Like anyone does when faced with something new. Trial and error."

I let out an irritated breath. "I just wish the 'error' didn't lead to possible death."

"At least this gives us more options," Adrian replied. "If we're all asleep, we can have unmonitored conference calls."

I cocked my head, thinking. He had a point.

"Speaking of," I replied, "you still on electronic lockdown?"

Adrian nodded. "Farrar's still got my phone and computer. I've agreed not to use any of the terminals at the house."

"What about—"

The white world upended suddenly.

Damn it, someone was shaking me awake. I sat up in bed, trying to fend them off, still groggy from the abrupt end to my dream.

"Wake *up*, Caitlin," Julian demanded, grabbing me by the shoulders.

"Julian, what are you doing?" Kalare barked, pulling him off me.

"Do you remember?" he asked as Kalare held him back. "Or am I going fucking crazy?"

I huddled against the wall, heart racing, confused. For a few moments, I hadn't recognized where I was, or what day it was, or who he was. Then it all came rushing back.

"You were there," I whispered. Then I frowned. "*Were* you there?"

He nodded, breathing hard. "Woke up in my apartment and came straight here."

Kalare looked back and forth between us. "Would someone please tell me what the hell is going on?"

Julian pointed at me. "She pulled me into her nightmare."

"It wasn't a nightmare," I muttered. "Trust me, you'd know the difference."

Kalare looked between us. "Say again?"

I sighed, rubbing the sleep out of my eyes. "Julian showed up in my dreamscape, along with several thousand other vampires."

She went still. "*What?* Did they—"

"They were asleep," Julian interrupted. "I was the only one awake, along with Adrian. While I was asleep. Shit."

"Did it work?" I asked, looking at him. "Did you wake up?"

He nodded, looking grave. "Instantly."

"Hold on," Kalare said, standing between us. "How about we take this from the top?"

I told her a brief version of the night's dream, with Julian jumping in with his own color commentary.

"You didn't feel anything when I tried to pull you in?"

She shook her head. "I was awake all night, reading. Didn't feel a damn thing. In fact," she said, sitting down next to Julian on the opposite bed. "I didn't feel *anything* from you. Not a single emotion. It's been weakening over time, but so gradually I hardly noticed. This is the first night I've legitimately felt nothing from you." She peered at me, her eyes widening suddenly.

She turned to Julian. "Is it just me?"

He shook his head sharply. "No. I'm getting the same thing."

I looked at both of them. "What?"

"You're not there," Kalare said, peering at me. "Emotionally, at least. It's like you're not there. If I close my eyes and ignore the fact that I can hear your heart beating, I wouldn't know a human was sitting across from me."

"What the *shit* is going on with me?" I hissed at them, trying to keep my voice down. The walls weren't so thick that my neighbors couldn't hear me having a conversation, if they were listening hard enough. "Kalare, I know you said it was dangerous to ask more questions from your contact, but this has to justify reaching out again. How long before Farrar notices I'm not, like, emoting or whatever?"

Kalare looked at Julian. "I'm out of my depth here," she told him. "It might be worth the risk."

His jaw tightened, but he nodded. "Do it."

Kalare stood. Julian reached out and grabbed her arm, stopping her.

"Be careful," he told her.

She looked at him, searching his face, then nodded. "Always am."

As soon as she left, I wrapped my blanket around me. "Julian, I need to know—who's my bodyguard at Myriad? Farrar didn't tell me who replaced Sabine."

Julian shook his head. "I don't know. He didn't inform us, either."

"Can you find out?" I asked.

"I can try."

"Sorry about, y'know, accidentally abducting you into my dream," I said, standing.

He shrugged. "More interesting than the dream I was having anyway."

I shuffled over to my dresser and started rummaging around for clothes. I was halfway to the bathroom when he called to me.

"Remember when I accused you a few months ago of being a dull, common star in a bright, vast galaxy?"

I searched his face, not sure where he was going with this.

He met my gaze. "I was wrong."

On Monday, I joined the others in the lobby to walk over to Myriad, not saying much. I'd remembered on my way down that today was the day Trish was coming back from England. Which meant today was the day she was visiting *me*. I should have been more excited about that, part of me was, but between the insane dreamscape episode two nights before, and deciding to quit the internship, I was exhausted and depressed.

Violet was quiet, too. Not mopey, just quiet. Truitt looked like he might puke, and Stacee looked calm, though she was picking at a loose thread on her sweater so forcefully I thought she might unravel the whole thing.

We grabbed breakfast at Myriad and headed to the workroom, not certain how they were going to announce who had gotten approved. Violet looked at us apologetically and immediately started working on updating her designs.

A few minutes later, Leigh Drisdon fast-walked into the room and made a B-line for me.

"Olivia needs to speak to you," she said quietly, then walked out again. I glanced at Truitt and Stacee, who looked as terrified for me as I felt, and followed Leigh out the door.

Instead of turning right to head to the main area, Leigh led me straight into the remnant room.

Olivia stood there with a very panicked-looking junior designer, a young woman I'd seen before, but had never spoken to. She had coffee spilled all over her dress.

"Caitlin," Olivia said when she saw me, "good, come here. We have a meeting in twenty minutes to present ideas to—well, it doesn't matter to whom. Carol here has had a bit of an accident, and I need you to do for her what you did for Violet." She looked down at her watch. "Make that nineteen minutes."

She smiled at me briefly, then left, Leigh following on her heels.

"But—" I said, just as the door swung closed.

I turned to look at Carol. She looked as panicked as I felt.

"What are you waiting for?" she burst out. "Help me!"

Oh god. Oh god, oh god, oh god.

"Why are you just standing there?"

She looked truly panicked. Shit. I finally started moving.

"What kind of meeting is it?" I asked, kind of stupidly. "I mean, how fancy?"

"Look at what I'm wearing now," she said, as if it was obvious.

Shit, I didn't know the designer. Was it a Myriad look? Shit, shit, shit.

She was wearing a tailored, square-necked, cream-colored dress with contrast stitching. Was that neoprene? I couldn't make a dress look anything like that in fifteen minutes. What did Olivia expect me to do in *fifteen* minutes?

She expected me to pull a miracle out of my butt, like we had with Violet.

Because I'd done it once already.

Which meant I could do it again.

"Okay," I said, skipping down the aisles, my eyes searching the haphazardly-flung fabric scraps. "I can't make something exactly like what you've got. In fact, I can't make anything like what you've got. How do you feel about draping?"

"As long as I don't walk in there naked or covered in espresso," Carol muttered.

"Good," I said, "because the only thing I can pull off is—"

There! Black was always a good choice. Even if she spilled coffee again, it wouldn't show.

I ran back to her, braiding four scraps of some sort of non-fraying synthetic fabric. It was cheap stuff, but it wouldn't matter. I worked the fabric into a fishtail pattern and handed it to Carol.

"Stay right here," I said, "I'll be back."

I ran down the hall to the workroom, interrupting a college intern who was handing out packets to everyone. I ignored her, ran to my table, grabbed my work basket, and ran right back out.

As soon as I got back to the remnant room I knelt on the floor, threading a needle with shaking hands.

"Get a bunch of safety pins ready for me, would you?" I asked Carol distractedly.

I didn't stop long enough to see if she complied, I just started bunching the black fabric around the braided collar, sewing on pieces as fast as I could. It was messy, but I could hide the stitches under the thick collar so no one could tell just how sloppy my work was. Getting that much fabric attached ate nine whole minutes.

By the time I was done, Carol had a line of thirty safety pins opened and ready to go.

"Stand up," I ordered, not even aware of how rude I was being. She didn't complain though, just stood in place. I wrapped the braided collar around her neck, right over the dress she was already wearing, and pinned it closed, hiding the metal on the underside. The fabric draped down in surprisingly graceful waves.

"Okay, walk toward me."

She obeyed, managing not to trip over the mess in her three-inch heels.

Damn. The fabric strips weren't sewn to each other, which meant that when she moved, so did the fabric, revealing the coffee stains underneath.

I had one minute.

I used the rest of the safety pins to quickly join some of the fabric directly over the coffee stains and had her walk again.

It covered everything.

And actually, it didn't look half-bad.

"Come on!" Carol said. I grabbed my sewing basket and followed her. We ran through the cafeteria and to the elevators, getting off on the fifth floor. I hurried, following her through the hallways until we got to the conference room.

But the conference room was empty.

Carol slowed down, walking calmly into Olivia's office.

"Ah, you're here," Olivia said, setting down some papers. She glanced at her watch, looking impressed. "And right on time." She was sitting behind her desk, looking collected and not at all like she was about to walk into an important meeting.

I was out of breath, glancing back and forth between her and Carol, confused.

"How'd she do?" Olivia asked Carol.

"Bit deer-in-the-headlights at first, but she snapped out of it soon enough. You can see the results for yourself."

"I—don't you have to get to a meeting?" I asked, worried that they would be late.

Olivia smiled. "In about an hour. We've got plenty of time for Carol to change into something from the fashion closet. Do you really think

I'd send her into a meeting wearing something one of our high school interns made from scraps?"

I stared at her, nonplussed. What the hell had I just done all that for, then?

"Don't look so upset," Olivia said. "I just wanted to see what you'd come up with. And while it won't be winning any awards, I must say I'm impressed."

She had Carol spin in a slow circle while she observed my handiwork. My heart stopped racing as my brain finally realized there was no emergency.

"Good thinking, keeping the original dress underneath. They look like they were actually created to go together. Well done."

She examined the collar and the black panels. "What did you use here to hold it together?"

"Safety pins," I said.

"Fabric tape would have been faster."

"I didn't want the dress falling off halfway through her meeting."

Olivia smiled, but not at me. She was still examining the dress. "Goodness, you actually sewed the fabric on at the collar. Quick little devil, aren't you? You even found a polyweave so she wouldn't look raggedy. How thoughtful."

She examined the dress for another few minutes before stepping back. "Thank you, Carol, you may go. Oh, and please have Andre take a few photos of the dress before you take it off; I'd like to keep it for our records. Thank you."

Carol nodded, winked at me, and left.

I stood there, still not entirely certain what was happening. Olivia walked back to her desk and sat, motioning for me to do the same.

"I apologize if I frightened you, Caitlin," she said, taking a sip from her cup of tea. "I wanted to see what you would do in a higher-stakes situation, and without the help of your friend Stacee."

"So…she didn't really spill coffee on herself? There's no big meeting?"

"Actually, she did spill coffee on herself, and there is a big meeting. But we had plenty of time to get her a new outfit. When I saw her dress, an idea came to me and I took advantage of it. Just like you took advantage of the materials you had at your disposal to make both Carol and your friend Violet new outfits in an impressively short amount of time."

I clutched my sewing basket on my lap, not sure where this was going.

"I can do better," I told her, "if I have more time. I know the stitches were sloppy, but I thought she had to present—"

"Yes," Olivia interrupted, looking amused. "That's the lovely thing about you, you were genuinely concerned that Carol needed to look presentable for an important meeting, and you did everything in your power to make her so."

She sat back, pulled something out of her desk drawer, and set it on the table. It was my presentation from Friday, along with my application packet.

"Caitlin," she said, laying a hand on each folder. "I see two different designers in these two presentations. In one, a very detail-oriented, ambitious designer. In the other, a very confused, directionless designer."

She pulled out her phone and showed it to me.

It was my Instagram account. I paled.

"I'm so sorry," I said, panicking. "You said we couldn't post photos inside the building, and I didn't, I just posted a few of Truitt and Violet and Stacee out by our dorms, I'm so sor—"

"Caitlin, Caitlin," she interrupted me, "you're not in trouble. You have a bad habit of jumping to the worst-case scenario. Scroll down. What do you see?"

I scrolled down. "My…family? And friends? And—"

Oh.

"My designs."

I'd begun posting some of my older designs, stuff I was pretty sure I was never going to make because I couldn't afford the materials, even with the fabric Adrian had purchased for me. This was couture. This was hand-beaded. This was expensive. I'd actually started getting a decent following, even a few people from other countries. More as a joke than anything, I'd started tagging the posts with #CaitlinHolteDesigns, as if I was taking the whole thing seriously.

"You have a natural eye," Olivia said, looking at the photos. "Your application proved that you could execute those designs exquisitely, though shoddy work can be easily hidden with clever photography. But I have to say, your presentation Friday disappointed me greatly."

My heart crawled up into my throat. I clutched the sewing basket harder, feeling small and young and intimidated. I was tempted to interrupt her, to tell her I knew what she was going to say, and that it didn't matter, because I was quitting.

"You played it safe, Caitlin. The designs you presented weren't awful, but they *were* boring—which is in some ways worse. It was difficult for me to reconcile the designs I saw here," she said, pointing at my Instagram feed, "and here," she said, pointing at my application, "with *these*," she said, finally pointing at the presentation I'd given her. "I appreciate that you were inspired by your friends, I do. But there was nothing original or unique about what you came up with. In fact, I'd go so far as to say it was condescending to me and to this company. Because I had seen better work from you, and because I know you had something of an odd start with your first mentor, and she may have given you poor advice on how to approach this presentation, I wanted to give you a second chance. Hence the little test with Carol."

My heart was racing. I wasn't sure if I was about to pass out or cry or both.

I was humiliated. I was ashamed. I wanted to leave.

"A test," Olivia said finally, "that you *passed*."

I looked up at her, blinking. What?

"Now, I can't ignore that based on your presentation alone, I would have rejected you from our program," she continued. "Not because it was the worst design I've seen from your group, but because I expected more out of you in particular. However, I see that you're a hard worker. I see that you are more than capable of thinking on your feet, following your gut, and utilizing the materials at hand. More than that, you far exceed your peers at time management. Patricia has told me that you have completed every task she's assigned you without complaint and ahead of schedule. This speaks very well to your character."

She closed the cover of my presentation. "I'm going to keep this, as a reminder for you." She slid it into her desk drawer and closed it. "The others are downstairs right now, receiving my feedback on their presentations. Some of them are being sent home. Most of them have revisions to make. But you're here. And you have a choice."

She slid my application toward me. "Either you can continue to limit yourself, to play it safe, and to fit in with the others by dumbing yourself down. Or you can accept the fact that you are well beyond your peers. You can stop using your age as an excuse to not take yourself seriously. Which do you want?"

I blinked at her.

And I honestly considered her question.

Part of me did know I was further ahead than the others. But I liked Truitt and Violet and Stacee. It felt uncomfortable to think of myself as more advanced than them. Like if I thought that, it made me a bad person who didn't deserve to have them as my friends. Plus, I'd totally dropped the ball on my presentation. I'd let it overwhelm me, and I'd turned in something I wasn't proud of.

But if they were really my friends, they would support my being able to grow at my own pace. Even if that pace was faster than theirs.

Olivia waited while I thought. I cleared my throat.

"I would like very much to take myself seriously," I said, voice suddenly hoarse and froggy. "And to learn all I can from you and from Myriad."

Olivia smiled, as if my answer pleased her. "I am very glad to hear that. As of today, I'm pulling you from the program."

My face went white. "But—"

"And placing you in a program I've just created."

If Olivia kept switching things up on me, I was going to pass out.

"Patricia will no longer be your mentor. I'm assigning one of our junior designers to replace her. You will spend the mornings with this new mentor, and act as her assistant. You will spend a half hour a day with me, after lunch. You will spend an hour a day either with our development teams or our marketing teams, because I believe you have an eye for the business of fashion as well as an eye for design. Which means you have almost two less hours a day to work on your final project. I expect a new project proposal in three days. I expect you to complete your project on-time. I expect you to do the rest of your work on-time. Do you accept these new conditions?"

I stared at her, trying to process everything she'd just said. Finally, I nodded. "I accept."

She smiled, then stood. "Good. You begin today."

She stood, so I stood. We shook hands.

I turned to leave, but hesitated. "Ms. Renault…what do I tell the others? The other high school interns, I mean?"

She looked at me as if the answer was obvious. "Whatever you'd like, Caitlin. As long as it's the truth."

"What the heck happened to you?" Truitt asked as I stumbled back into the workroom clutching my sewing basket, looking dazed.

"What?" I asked, sitting down at my work table without really hearing him. I placed the sewing basket on my lap and wrapped my arms around it.

"Where did you go?" Truitt asked again. "Olivia's assistant pulled you out an hour ago and then you ran back in to get your sewing basket and ran back out. What happened?"

I blinked, coming back down to earth. "Oh. There was an emergency. Someone spilled coffee on themselves right before a meeting and Olivia asked me to make her a new outfit, like Stacee and I did last week for Vi."

"And they asked *you?*" Truitt asked in disbelief. "That's what they have college interns for. Heck, that's what they have *designers* for."

"Truey, honey," Stacee interrupted him, "that's what they have the *fashion closet* for."

He scowled at her, and I wasn't sure if it was because she had thought of a more obvious reason, or because she'd called him "Truey."

"Well, it was just a test," I reassured them. "Olivia was thinking of kicking me out of the program so she took advantage of a coffee spill and had me think it was a real emergency. She *really* didn't like my presentation proposal, so she's giving me three days to come up with a new idea."

"Why did she let you present at all if she didn't like it?" Violet asked, looking shocked. After all, she hadn't been able to present to Olivia, only to her mentor.

"I guess my mentor thought my presentation was okay, but Olivia didn't. She's also giving me a new mentor."

Violet said, "Your poor mentor!" while Stacee said, "Isn't that your third mentor this week?" while Truitt said, "Why does no one else get as freaked out by this internship as I do?"

"What happened while I was gone?" I asked, desperate to change the subject. I didn't want them asking too many questions. I didn't want them knowing that my new mentor wasn't another intern, it was an employee. A real designer. I didn't want them knowing that Olivia Renault thought my potential was so great she'd given me a second chance to prove myself even though she'd hated my presentation.

"They got notes back on their proposals," Violet answered. "I'm still working on the notes my mentor gave me."

"Can you tell what this says?" Stacee asked, holding up the fourth page of her presentation. "Vi and Tru can't make it out. It looks like Klingon."

I was pretty sure that was Olivia's writing. The letters were tall and spidery and written in cursive. Looked more like Elvish than Klingon, but I wasn't about to say that out loud.

Gosh darn it, Adrian's nerdiness was infecting me like a virus.

Also, who writes in cursive anymore?

"I think it says, 'Be more specific'? Or maybe 'Be mauve pacific.' Not sure."

"I'm gonna go with the first one, unless 'mauve pacific' is a Pantone color I'm not familiar with."

We had the rest of the day to work on our project proposals, no intern duties. We worked until lunch (well, I helped Violet until lunch—I was still too rattled to start on a new proposal) and then walked to the cafeteria. The three of them were chatting while I was staring blankly off into space, thinking.

I'd always loved detail. While I understood and even appreciated the almost stark aesthetic of much modern fashion, with its clean lines and neutral colors and bold simplicity, I was always drawn to things with detail. And not just in fashion. I loved how the bubbles in ginger ale made the glass look like a tiny cauldron of golden magic, I loved macro photography that showed you the tiniest little bits of flowers and bugs and drops of dew, I liked the thousand and one different streaks of grey that made up Adrian's eyes. I'd spent hours hand-beading the collar of my Winter Formal dress, not because I had the time, not because it was strictly necessary, but because I'd designed it that way, and I wanted it that way, and it was complete that way.

But I didn't want to just design couture gowns. I mean, I *did*, but that wasn't practical. I wanted to show Olivia my range. I wanted to show her that my aesthetic could be applied to practically any customer, because that part of my presentation had been true. Every woman should wear clothes that make her feel beautiful. Women of all ages, all sizes, and all budgets.

"Helloooo?" Stacee said, waving her hand in front of my face.

Apparently I'd stopped in the middle of the caf, holding my tray of food, completely lost in thought.

"You wanna join the land of the living?"

I smiled sheepishly. "Sorry," I told her, "just trying to brainstorm a new design."

After lunch, we were taken on a tour of the fabric room. It was organized by type, color, and pattern. Anything with a red mark on the bolt we were not allowed to use because it was expensive. Anything with a yellow or blue mark was fair game, up to fifteen total yards for our final projects. People like Truitt and Violet who were doing shoes or accessories were given a separate tour of the workshop where prototypes were made.

We walked around for an hour, feeling different fabrics, pulling them out to look at them while college interns chased after us telling us how to handle the bolts properly and not get them disorganized or lumpy when we rolled them back up. Apparently they were in charge of keeping this place organized, so they had a vested interest in teaching us how to follow their system.

I'd been wandering for the better part of forty-five minutes, making note of bolt numbers to come and check out again tomorrow, but nothing had really called out to me.

Well, nothing that was marked yellow or blue. I'd found plenty of red-marked fabric that sparked my imagination.

By the time we got back to Enneman's, I was exhausted from the roller coaster of a day and a little bit sugar-high from the four cups of coffee I'd drunk.

I'd also somehow managed to completely forget what day it was.

We walked up to the dorms, and there was Trish sitting on the curb.

I stopped dead in the middle of the sidewalk, my tired brain taking a few seconds to place where she was from and how I knew her. Then it clicked.

I flung my messenger bag at Truitt and ran up to my best friend, wrapping her in a bear hug just as she stood up. She gently returned my embrace.

"I'm so glad you're here," I said, pulling back, slightly embarrassed. "How was your flight? Wait, hold on, guys, this is Trish! She's from my hometown—well, my hometown is Mystic, but she's from where I live in Stony Creek!"

The others joined us, Truitt carrying my bag very politely.

"This is Violet, Truitt, and Stacee," I said, introducing them by turn. Everyone waved a bit awkwardly. "Have you eaten yet?" I asked her, suddenly worried that she might have waited on dinner for me, and I'd just eaten at Myriad.

"I grabbed something at the airport," she reassured me.

"Good, good," I said, babbling. "You want to see the dorms?"

The dorms were nothing special. They looked like dorms. But they were new dorms and they were *Enneman* dorms, so I was proud of them. We all hustled inside and I showed Trish the hallway with the little mailboxes, the vending machines in the lobby, the lounge on every floor with the old TVs and the smelly giant beanbag chairs. At that point, everyone else begged off, saying they wanted to get some work done, and left me alone with Trish.

I finally showed her my room. No one was in there, since I'd warned Kalare and Julian and Farrar that Trish would be visiting today.

"Nice place," she commented, and I couldn't tell if she was being serious or sarcastic. I *had* tried to decorate a bit, make it less gray-painted-concrete-cinder-block-y.

"Thanks," I said, and sat down, then stood, feeling awkward. "Are you tired, or do you want to go see some of the city?"

I wasn't exactly an expert on the subway system but I knew enough to get around.

"Yeah, let's go for a walk."

I didn't know why that made me nervous, but it did. Maybe because she'd kind of sounded like a parent when she said it. Trish was still half a head taller than I was, and all muscle. I still believed she could wrestle bears and win, if she was in the right mood.

We headed outside, the air thick and muggy, the sun hot even at seven-thirty.

"Y'know, it's funny," Trish said as soon as we were outside, "I took the subway and got here a bit early, and I could have sworn I saw Adrian's cousin come out of your dorm."

My heart skipped a beat, but I kept walking. "Kalare?" I asked, trying to sound casual.

"She the one that wears all that leather even though it's a billion degrees out?"

"Yep. She lives in Jersey. We kind of became friends while she was in Stony Creek, and she stops by to visit whenever she's in the city. Must've just missed her."

"Hmm."

"How was your flight?" I asked, changing the subject as we walked down into the subway.

"Smooth," she replied. "And they had free movies."

"Those are the best kind."

Trish smiled a little at that. When had we gotten so distant and off-balance? It felt like I was having to make friends with a stranger.

We boarded the westbound train and had to stand. It was still close enough to rush hour that the place was packed.

Trish made a funny face at something over my shoulder.

"What?" I asked, looking around.

"Nothing," she said, hesitating. "Just thought I saw someone."

"Who?"

She peered into the crowd, then shook her head. "Weird guy from a couple months ago. I actually meant to ask you about him, but I totally forgot. He stopped by our place to ask if he was on the right road to get to your house. I think he was a repair man or something."

All the blood drained out of my face.

"Thought I saw him for a sec back there. Weird."

"Yeah, weird," I said, feeling my whole body flood with adrenaline. I smiled sheepishly at Trish, pulling out my phone. "Sorry," I told her, "my aunt's texting me."

She wasn't. I quickly texted Kalare and Julian about what Trish had just told me. I didn't know which one of them was on-duty, but I was certain one of them was somewhere on this train, tailing me. They'd be able to check it out. Or at least come to my rescue if worst came to worst.

My mind was spinning as I put the phone back in my pocket. Trish had seen Tommie. I hadn't even thought to ask her. Why would I? I'd assumed he'd come straight to my house. Trish didn't even live near me. Why would he have gone to Trish's place first? Just to mess with me? Or had he done something to her, maybe even compelled her to do something? But—what?

We got off at the next stop and walked back up to the street, then surged with the pedestrians into Central Park. I'd only made it here once so far, but I freaking loved it. Once you got into the trees, it almost looked like Stony Creek.

I was nervous. Both to talk to Trish and because Tommie might be around. But the park was packed with people. He wouldn't possibly try something in such a public area. After a few minutes of not seeing him, I started to relax.

Trish and I chatted a bit about her trip. She and her family had gone all over England and had even popped over to Paris for two days to take a look at the college Mark would be studying at in September. She'd visited Stratford-Upon-Avon, Stonehenge, whatever city it was that the Beatles had come from, Bath, and about a dozen other places, including London, of course. She was still a little pissed that Mark hadn't come, but after reading Jenny's e-mail, she was glad Mark had stayed to be with Jenny.

"Have you talked to Meghan?" I asked.

She shook her head. "I sent her an e-mail, but she didn't respond.

But I've seen what she's been posting on Twitter and Facebook and I'm worried about her."

"Do you think she did it?"

Trish looked at me funny. "Did what?"

I blinked. "Jenny's mom's car. The spray paint?"

Trish stopped walking. "What about Jenny's mom's car?"

"Isn't—isn't that what Jenny e-mailed you about?"

Trish slowly shook her head. "She just told me that she thinks Meghan's having a hard time because her parents are getting divorced."

That was very like Jenny. "Well, that's half the story," I muttered. We kept walking. "Someone spray-painted 'bitch' in bright pink spray paint on the hood of her mom's car. Apparently Jenny has reason to believe it was Meghan, because Jenny's dating Mark, and Meghan seems to think she had a prior claim to your brother."

"Good God," Trish muttered. "I leave for a month and everything falls apart."

I would have laughed if it weren't so true.

"She also started rumors about Jenny. Said she slept with Mark to steal him from her. Apparently she asked Stephanie why she was hanging out with a slut."

Trish stopped again. "Are you serious?"

I nodded. "She didn't, though—sleep with Mark I mean." Then I realized I didn't actually know if that was true. "I mean, I don't think she did. Not that it's any of my business. It's all…messy. Things got real weird after you left."

Trish wandered slowly over to a large pile of rocks and climbed up on one to sit. I joined her.

"Her parents have been at each other for years," Trish explained after a moment. "It must be getting worse. Meghan's not usually cruel. Not like that. I'll talk to them both when I get home. See if I can't find out what's really going on." She shook her head sadly. "We can be real dicks to each other when we're hurt."

I wasn't sure if she was talking about Meghan, or about me, or about herself.

"How was Ben when you last saw him?" she asked after a long moment.

"He was great. Hung out with him a lot actually. Him and Steph and Tim and Adrian and Mark. I like Ben. He's a good guy."

Trish smiled, but it didn't reach her eyes. "Yeah. He is."

Why did she look so…not happy?

"Are you guys okay?"

She looked up. "Yeah. Yeah, we're good. I just…" she trailed off, looking out at the sun through the trees. "This trip made me think a lot. I saw so much more of the world than I'd seen before, and even that was just a tiny portion. I love Stony Creek. It's my home. But I realized how much I want to travel. I want to go places. I don't think Ben wants to do that."

She grew quiet. I was almost afraid to speak. "I think Ben would go with you. In fact, I know he would—he said so. He's so proud of you."

Her smile turned bitter. "I know. But the thing is, he wouldn't like it. He loves Stony Creek. He loves being outside, working. His farm has been in his family for five generations. He's a mountain boy born and bred. And I love that about him. And I think if I took him with me, I would either change him or make him unhappy. And I don't know what to do with that."

"I don't know," I said after a moment. "I think he might surprise you. Ben doesn't seem the type to make decisions he doesn't want to make. If he goes with you, it's because he wants to go."

She smiled at me, really smiled. "Thanks, Caitlin. I think I needed to hear that. How's…how's Adrian? Any news on his brother?"

I tried not to let my surprise show. She was voluntarily asking me about Adrian, that was either a really good sign or a really bad sign.

"He's well. No news on Lucian. We haven't had a chance to talk much since I've been in New York; the internship keeps me pretty busy. I asked Jenny and Steph to take him with them as much as possible. I think without me there, he'd think too much about his brother." I cleared my throat, emotional. It was impossible to think about Lucian and not get emotional. "I miss the little guy. He was a sweet kid. *Is* a sweet kid," I corrected myself.

"Do you think it's possible," Trish said slowly, "that his disappearance has something to do with his family?"

I went very still, hoping to God that Julian or Kalare had followed me, not Farrar.

"I hadn't thought of that," I said, stalling. "What makes you ask?"

Trish shrugged uncomfortably. "Just seems strange. I know Lucian could have just gotten lost, but if he did, he's probably dead by now. No way that kid survived on his own for the past five months. And who would abduct him in Stony Creek? It's not that kind of town. The only other option that makes sense is if someone from his own family took him. I mean, nine out of ten child abductions are done by a family member or family friend."

Trish would know that. Trish watched a lot of *Criminal Minds*.

Also, she was right—he *had* been taken by a family member. His own father.

But once again, I couldn't tell Trish that. I had to lie to her.

For a moment, though, I was tempted. Trish was reasonable. Trish could handle the truth. She could keep a secret.

But I didn't know who was watching us right now, who was listening to this conversation. And even if it was just Kalare, involving Trish when things were this uncertain might make me feel less alone, but it wouldn't help. What could Trish do that Kalare and Julian couldn't? Telling her would put her in danger.

"Anything is possible," I said finally. "But I think it's more likely that he just wandered off. Though part of me hopes you're right—if someone took him, maybe that means he's still alive."

"Do you know anything about their parents?"

Damn, she wasn't going to let this go.

I shrugged, stalling. "Not much. Mom died. Dad isn't in the picture. Mariana and Dominic took them in."

I didn't know how much to say because I'd never asked Adrian what story they'd told the townspeople about their parents.

"Last I heard, their dad wasn't even in the country. Adrian moved here from Paris."

I knew she knew that, at least.

"Yeah," she said, staring off into space. "Maybe he came back."

A chill went through me. Trish was too close to the truth.

"Yeah," I agreed quietly. "Maybe."

Luckily, she didn't press any further.

We sat for a long time, just staring out at the crowd. I almost opened my mouth half a dozen times, but the timing didn't seem right. Finally, I worked up the guts to say it out loud.

"Trish," I said quietly. "I'm sorry. I'm sorry that I made Adrian more important than you. I'm sorry that I made you lie on my behalf. And I'm sorry if I ever made you feel like you weren't important to me. You are. I've never had a best friend, not even back in Mystic, besides maybe my mom, but…"

But she was gone.

"I don't know if you can forgive me," I continued, "but I really want us to be friends. Adrian and I are still dating and I know that's a problem for you. But I really need a friend right now. I need *you*. And

I'm sorry."

She looked at the ground, frowning slightly, but she didn't seem upset, just like she was thinking.

"I have to admit," she said finally, "Adrian has been different the past couple months. He seems happier. Dressing up as Harry Potter? That was pretty epic." She smiled a little. "Maybe he is changing. I don't know. Family still creeps me out, but Adrian himself seems more… human. More comfortable. That's probably because of you." She looked at me. "So of course I forgive you. And of course we can be friends. Just…be honest with me, all right? Don't use me. That's all I'm asking."

I nodded. "I can do that."

I could try at least. I could dance around the omissions I had to make to keep her and everyone else safe.

She smiled, accepting my promise.

When the sun started to set, we stood and walked back to the subway. We parted ways on the platform, me back to Enneman's, her back to the airport to meet up with her family.

"Hey, tell Jimmy I said congratulations," I told Trish as her train pulled in.

She grinned. "I will. Still can't believe the bastard's getting married."

We laughed, then Trish pulled me into a hug. Surprised, I hugged her back.

"Stay safe," she said, walking backward toward her train. "I'll keep an eye on everyone for you while you're gone. Even Adrian."

"Thank you," I whispered, but she was already gone, lost in the crowd of people.

As soon as the doors closed and the train pulled away, before I even had a chance to draw in a deep breath and let it out, Kalare and Farrar were at my side.

"Did you know?" Farrar asked in his usual neutral tone.

I blinked. "About what?"

"About the demon's visit to Ms. Fields' home the night of the attack."

"No," I said, relieved. "I had no idea."

He nodded. "We will investigate this matter. Kalare, escort Ms. Holte home."

Kalare nodded and hustled me onto the train while Farrar headed up the stairs toward the street.

"Good job, kid," Kalare muttered at me as we grabbed seats in the compartment. "I gotta say, you're getting to be one hell of a double agent."

SLEEPING BEAUTIES
20

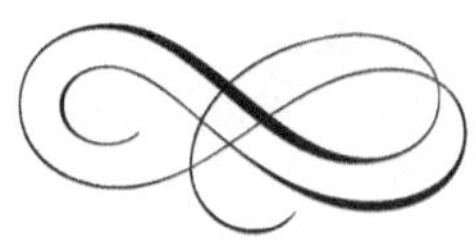

Adrian appeared first, then Kalare.

She blinked, looking around, then whistled. "Well, this is some surreal shit."

Julian was on guard, which meant Kalare was asleep back at his apartment across town. She had her own place in Jersey, but it was too far to commute every day. As soon as I'd come to the dreamscape, I'd thought of Adrian, then Kalare. They'd both appeared. It looked like I was capable of pulling in any vampire I wanted, if they were close enough. It also looked like I could bring them in either dream-awake or or dream-asleep as long as they were actually asleep in the real world.

All except the woman. I hadn't figured that one out yet. It was impossible to experiment, too, because she hadn't appeared the last several times I'd tried to bring her in.

"Farrar asleep?" I asked.

She nodded. "Best not to think too hard about him. Wouldn't want to bring him in accidentally."

I started sweating just thinking about it.

"Any news on the home front?" Kalare asked.

Adrian shook his head. "Using my time to search the library. Mariana and Dominic seem more irritable than usual, but I've heard nothing. Still on electronic lockdown."

Kalare nodded. "Ian's gone off-grid. Haven't been able to find him."

"Ian?" Adrian asked.

"My contact," she explained. "The one I asked about Unmakers. I've got other people I could go to for information, but none I trust to keep quiet."

"I don't have any news on the Unmaker front," I interjected. "But I have an idea on how to find Lucian."

They both turned to me curiously.

"I can search for sleeping vampires," I told them. "I can talk to Adrian over a distance of two hundred miles. Which means my search radius is pretty large. If Adrian's father still wants me, chances are he hasn't gone very far. Plus, Trish said she thought she saw him on the train."

Adrian took a step toward me. "*What?*"

"Keep your shirt on," Kalare muttered. "I was there the whole time along with Farrar. Your girlfriend's fine."

"What did he say?" Adrian demanded.

I shook my head. "Nothing. I didn't even see him, only Trish did. She also said she saw him the night of the fight, the night Lucian disappeared. He stopped at her house and asked for directions to mine."

Adrian's eyes narrowed. "That can't be all he did."

"Farrar questioned your friend on her way back to the airport," Kalare said, looking at me. "Compelled her to tell him about that night."

I paled. "Did he hurt her?"

"No. She told him exactly what she told you. If anything else happened, she was compelled to forget it long ago."

I felt sick to my stomach. "It makes my skin crawl that he talked to her. And who knows what else."

"You were saying something about the kid?" Kalare reminded me.

"Right. Like I said, there's a good chance Adrian's dad is nearby. Which means Lucian is probably nearby, too. I don't know if I can pull demons into the dreamscape—or even if I'd want to if I could—but I should be able to pull in Lucian."

Adrian and Kalare exchanged looks.

Kalare glanced at Data. "That sound about right?"

He nodded. "That is correct."

I raised my eyebrows, surprised he'd answered a question so directly.

"All right," I said. "Let's give this a shot."

Around us, sleeping forms began to appear. After what seemed like a few minutes, they stopped. "I guess that's as far as I can search," I said. "But without knowing who these vampires are, I can't tell you how far away they live in the real world."

Kalare scrunched her eyes, looking around. "If I had to take a stab in the dark based on the number alone, I'd say you're casting out about as far as the city, maybe some of Jersey."

"Can you narrow it down?" Adrian asked. "Focus on Lucian?"

I nodded, and concentrated.

The forms slowly began to disappear.

I turned in a slow circle. Something caught my eye, way off in the distance.

"There," I breathed.

We ran toward the sleeping figure. Distance was a tricky thing in the dreamscape. It was taking too long so I stopped and summoned the figure toward me. Adrian and Kalare came to an abrupt halt, confused. Then they realized what I'd done.

I sank to my knees, barely able to breathe.

It was Lucian.

The others crouched next to me.

He was asleep, lying flat on his back, eyes closed. There were dark purple bruises under his eyes. I realized this was the first time I'd ever seen him without his aviator goggles. He looked even younger without them, even though he was twelve years old now.

He was dressed in jeans, white socks, and a plain gray t-shirt. Not pajamas, but at least the clothing looked fairly new.

"Is it okay to touch him?" Adrian asked.

"I don't know," I replied. "I don't think it could hurt."

He leaned down and carefully brushed at Lucian's wavy hair. It had grown longer since I'd last seen him, and wilder.

Adrian's hand passed right through his brother's face.

He flinched, pulling back. Lucian remained asleep.

"Maybe if people aren't awake, then they're not totally here," I murmured.

Kalare looked at me. "Can you wake him up?"

I leaned over Lucian. "Hey, Lucian. Sweetheart, can you hear me?"

Lucian didn't stir. I tried reaching out to touch his shoulder, but like Adrian, my hand passed right through him.

I sat back, both relieved and frustrated.

"Well, we know he's in the city. That's something."

"So is our father," Adrian muttered darkly.

"Do we tell the Council? They have more resources, they might be able to find him."

"And how exactly do we explain that we know he's somewhere in the city?" Kalare asked dryly.

I opened my mouth, then closed it. Good point.

Adrian shook his head. "Lucian is wrapped up in this somehow. I don't know if I trust the Council getting their hands on him aga—"

The world tilted.

"Shit," I heard Julian say and then he mumbled something I couldn't hear.

I came back to the real world groggily, sitting up. Julian's phone was playing an annoyingly chipper soundtrack. He looked over at me looking at least sort of apologetic. "Sorry. Thought my sound was turned off. Did I interrupt anything more important than you and my brother snuggling?"

I rubbed the sleep out of my eyes and caught him up on finding Lucian.

"Oh," he said, looking impressed. "That's…actually good news."

"It's good news *if* we can find a way to wake him up," I muttered.

He raised an eyebrow at me.

"Sorry," I mumbled. "I'm cranky when I'm tired. What time is it?"

He glanced at his phone. "5:07. Sorry."

I waved a hand at him. "No worries. I'll just go in early."

I left a note on Stacee's door telling her I couldn't sleep and I was going to Myriad. I went inside and grabbed breakfast, glad that the kitchen staff got there at the crack of dawn, then headed to the work-room. They might kick us out at seven every night, but there'd been no explicit rules about what time we could come in.

Instead of working on my project proposal, I went on Instagram and scrolled through my feed. Ben had posted a photo of him sweeping Trish into a dramatic kiss. Jenny had posted a photo of Mark sitting next to a giant canvas, painting. Mark had then posted a photo of Jenny taking a photo of him. Norah had posted a photo of Pan, her horse. Her Instagram was literally nothing but pictures of the horses at the ranch. Adrian hadn't posted anything recently because his phone had been taken away.

I laid my head down on the work table for a moment and just breathed.

I missed him. I missed home.

I meant Stony Creek, but I also meant Mystic. It was so confusing to think of home and picture two different places. To think of family and picture two different groups of people. To think of friends and picture my childhood classmates in Connecticut, and everyone at Warren County, and even Kalare and Julian, and now Violet and Truitt and Stacee.

My whole world was expanding, stretching me thinner and thinner. And as grateful as I was to know more people, to do more things, a part of me missed the simplicity of my old life: sewing with my mom. Dinner with my grandma. School.

That was it. Simple.

That had been Olivia's complaint about my proposal. It was too simple. It was not the best that I could do. She believed I was capable of more than what I'd told her I was capable of.

Maybe she was right. Maybe I was afraid to be more.

I sat up, frustrated. I wasn't getting anything done in the workroom, so I grabbed my design book and headed back to the cafeteria. I grabbed another cup of coffee from the espresso stand and picked a deserted table. Still feeling uninspired, I leaned back in my chair, stretching, and stared up.

It was a beautiful ceiling. Stained glass, almost like a cathedral. Some abstract, but symmetrical design. The roof over this section of the building came to a pyramid point, letting in shards of red, gold, and white light with a few hints of blue and green. It was mesmerizing.

I must have been staring at it for a while because eventually someone cleared their throat, standing next to me.

"You're not the first person to be inspired by that glass," Olivia told me. "It was actually reclaimed from a church that used to stand here. They salvaged it when this building was built."

Flustered, I flopped my chair back down—I'd been leaning it back on two legs—and stood hastily.

"No, sit down," she said. "I didn't mean to interrupt you."

"I'm sorry, I didn't see you," I apologized, blushing. "I got a little lost in the light."

She smiled warmly, holding her to-go coffee. "An interesting way to put it." She looked down at the chair opposite me. "I have a few minutes before my first meeting. May I join you?"

"Oh—yes, of course," I stuttered. She sat, looking amused.

"How is your proposal coming along?" she asked.

I blushed harder. "I'm still developing a, uh…new approach," I replied, stalling.

She actually laughed at that. "Well said," she replied, holding her coffee up to me in salute before taking a sip. "Though I didn't expect you to have something new for me in less than twenty-four hours."

I took a sip of my own coffee, feeling silly. "May I ask you a question?" I said after a moment. She nodded. "How do you do it?"

She looked puzzled, and I realized that was a vague question.

"I mean, how do you do it *all?*" I added, gesturing at her outfit. "How do you look the way you look and do the things you do and act the way you act? How can you be successful and powerful and still be kind?"

She blinked, looking surprised. "And here I thought you were going to ask me a question about design." She set down her coffee carefully and looked at me, as if chewing on her answer. "I made a choice, many years ago, about the kind of person I wanted to be, and the kind of life I wanted to live," she said finally. "And every day I ask myself if that's the person I still wish to be. And every day, I say yes. Even when I'm tired. Even when things are going poorly. This is the life I want to live, and this is the way I want to live it. You'd be surprised, Caitlin, how much of life is less about circumstance or opportunity or advantage, and more about will."

She looked up at the ceiling. The sun was coming out from behind the neighboring skyscrapers and finally piercing the glass. The pattern played off her upturned face in gold and red light.

"The short answer," she said, looking back at me, "is that we choose who we are. You just have to decide who you want to be."

She glanced at her watch. "I have to go. I'll see you after lunch."

She smiled, stood, and grabbed her coffee, walking off.

After she'd disappeared into the elevators, I looked back up at the ceiling, getting lost once more in the colors.

Perhaps it was that simple.

The question was: who did I want to be?

Without even thinking about it, I found myself sketching the glass, not even looking down at the paper as I traced the curves and lines of the lead that held the pieces in place. I was so in the zone I didn't even notice how much time had passed until I heard a, "Whoa."

I looked up. Stacee, Violet, and Truitt were standing around me holding breakfast trays.

"Dude, Caitlin," Stacee said, looking at my sketchbook in awe. "That's…that's incredible."

I glanced down at my work. I'd pulled out my water color pencils and brought over a glass of water from the buffet table to paint in the colored light.

"Is that for your project?" Violet asked, looking at the design in awe.

Was it? I hadn't really been thinking about that, I'd just started drawing.

"Yeah," I said finally, "I think it is."

"How would you even make that?" Stacee asked, leaning in to more closely examine the design. "Custom print?

"I think I'd stain it by hand," I said, almost dreamily, thinking through the possibilities. "Like a painting."

"I thought you wanted to do daywear?" Truitt asked, looking confused and almost a little hurt. "That stuff's couture."

"I thought I did, too," I said simply. "But this keeps pouring out."

"Wait, what's that?" Truitt asked, pointing at the page beneath. He flipped it over. "Geez, how many of these did you *make?*"

We counted. I'd done seven designs.

Truitt threw his hands up. "That's it. I should just quit now."

Stacee poked him in the ribs. "Stop being a baby."

He frowned at her and rubbed his side. "If Caitlin can pull these off, no way anyone else in our program has a shot. That's just a fact."

"Well," Violet chirped, so high-pitched and nervous I could barely hear her. "Olivia *did* say that if we were to compete with anyone, it should be with ourselves. Not—not against each other. And Caitlin worked really hard on these."

Truitt slowly deflated. "You're right. I'm sorry. I've just wanted to come here for so long and I feel like next to you, I can't be seen as anything but mediocre."

"Truitt," I said, laying a hand on his arm, "we're not even in the same department. I don't think they can even compare our work, it's so different. You don't have anything to worry about."

"Yeah," Stacee chimed in. "Exactly what I said: stop being a baby." She grabbed the designs from Truitt's hand and shuffled through them. "Oh wow, this one is *gorgeous,*" she breathed, pulling out the one on bottom. "I love that seam running down the back," she said, pointing at the structured, floor-length half-cape I'd drawn. "What would you even make that out of?"

"Cashmere," I said automatically. "And silk for the lining."

"How are you going to make all those in less than three weeks?" Truitt asked.

"I won't," I said, spreading out the drawings. "I'm going to make these three."

I pointed at the drawing with the cape, the ball gown I'd been working on when they first arrived, and the coat.

"Forget how you're going to make it," Stacee said, "how are you going to *pay* for it? Those materials are way out of our budget for our projects."

She had a point, but at the moment it seemed trivial. "I don't know," I admitted, a slow smile spreading across my face, "but I'll find a way."

My new mentor was called out of the office unexpectedly, so I didn't get to meet her. I tagged along with Stacee and her mentor, instead. We all grabbed lunch together, but I was miles away, thinking about my designs. After lunch, I had my new, daily meeting with Olivia. Leigh had me wait outside her office a few minutes before letting me in.

"Caitlin, have a seat," Olivia said, gesturing at the chair across from her desk. "I—what have you got there?" she asked, noticing the pile of papers in my arms.

I laid the three designs I'd chosen that morning out on her desk.

"This is my new proposal," I said, feeling oddly calm.

Olivia stared at them. "When did you do these?"

"After you left," I replied.

She stared at me. "You did all of these since I saw you this *morning?*"

I pulled out the four other sketches and held them up. "And these. Those were my favorite," I explained, pointing at the ones on her desk.

Olivia frowned at me, then held up the sketches to her desk lamp, as if making sure they were real. "You didn't download these from somewhere," she asked, seriously.

I shook my head. Then I held up my hands. I still had paint and ink on them.

"Good Lord, Caitlin," she muttered, examining the designs. "These are exquisite."

"Thank you," I said, feeling pleased at her praise, but not embarrassed or uncomfortable. They *were* exquisite. They were some of the best designs I'd ever done.

She looked at me carefully. "You had two more days to come up with a new proposal."

I looked back at her. "I didn't need two more days."

The edge of her mouth quirked up, as if she was resisting a smile. "I take it you decided who you want to be?"

I shook my head. "No. But I know that's what I want to design. I figure that's a good place to start."

"This is…ambitious. How long did it take you to assemble the dresses from your application?"

"Three weeks for the green dress," I admitted. "But I was in school full-time, as well as sick. It took longer than it should have. The black top and red skirt took me several weeks as well, but less actual work hours. I learned a lot from constructing both of those garments. I'll be faster now."

Olivia raised a brow at me. "And what materials were you planning to use?"

"White silk," I said, pointing at the ball gown. "Here as well," I said, pointing at the underside of the cape in the second design as well as the slash of color down the back, and the interior of the coat in the third design. "And cashmere for the body of the cape. Wool for the coat."

Olivia looked at me a long moment, then leaned back in her chair. "I'll approve materials for one outfit. You have a week to construct it. If I like what I see, I'll approve materials for the other two."

I nodded. Somehow, I knew she was going to say something like that.

"I'm impressed, Caitlin," she said, holding my gaze. "But now you've raised the bar by an almost impossible amount. If you've done this just to make up for your last proposal—"

"I didn't," I said, interrupting her. "This is what I want to make. And I can do it."

Olivia smiled. "Then by all means, go make it."

I spent the next hour with the business development team. They'd been warned that I would be showing up at the meeting and mostly ignored me while I was there, though a few of them greeted me and introduced themselves. I sat at the end of the conference table, taking notes. They didn't ask me to contribute, and I didn't butt in with any unwarranted ideas. I was definitely out of my depth on this end of the industry. But being a fly on the wall was probably exactly what I needed to learn the business side of Myriad. Once I understood it better, I'd risk asking some questions.

After that, I headed back to the workroom. Violet, Stacee, and Truitt didn't believe me when I told them Olivia had approved my use of materials for one of the outfits.

"That's insane," Truitt said. "It's like you're magic." He rubbed my arm vigorously. "Give me some."

Stacee pulled him away. "I don't know whether to congratulate you or be mad at you," she said smiling, but also serious.

I grinned. "Wait until we see if this bombs completely. Then you can decide."

She grinned back. "Deal."

I took my materials acquisition form to the fabric room and handed it to the clerk. He glanced at it, then frowned at me. "Is this a joke?"

I shook my head.

Keeping his gaze on me, he grabbed his desk phone and punched in a few numbers. "Yeah, this is Harman down in fabrics. Got a high schooler here saying you approved ten yards of level-three fabrics."

He listened for a moment, a look of pure disbelief creeping over his face. "Yes, ma'am, I understand. Sorry to bother you."

He set down the phone and whistled. "Good luck, kid," he said, stamping my form. He personally escorted me down the aisles to pick out what I wanted. I asked him some questions about several different fabrics. He seemed surprised by my questions. Finally, he helped me narrow it down to a raw white silk that would take dye better than the other options. He also helped me choose between different weights of cashmere. I was making the cape option as my proof of concept and needed it for the outer shell.

"That's not an outerwear fabric," he protested.

"It's not an outwear cape," I countered. "It just needs to hold its shape."

"Well, you're gonna need facing," he said, pointing at the right angles I'd drawn for the shoulders. "And a lot of it."

He grumbled, but took me to find everything, then rolled all my fabric onto new tubes and handed them to me.

"I'm also going to need these dyes," I said, handing him my list. "Do I do that here, or is that another department?"

"What on earth you need that much dye for?" he asked, looking incredulous.

"An experiment," I told him. "Now is that here, or somewhere else?"

"It's here," he mumbled. "Give me a minute."

He rummaged around in the cabinet underneath the counter and came back with the six bottles I'd requested.

"Thank you," I said, putting them in a separate bag. "I was wondering if you could do me one more favor."

"What else could you possibly need?"

"The total." He looked at me blankly. "For the materials. I'd like to know how much this would have cost, normally."

He looked surprised, then pulled out his calculator, jotting down some numbers on a scrap of paper. When he was done, he ripped it off and handed it to me.

I swallowed.

It was over a thousand dollars.

"Thank you, Mr. Harman," I said, holding out my hand. He shook it, looking perplexed. "Thank you for helping me."

"You're welcome," he said. As I collected my bags and left, I could have sworn I heard him mumble, "Odd kid."

I got back to the workroom and hooked my fabric tubes on the bars underneath the table, out of sight, so no one could see the level-three materials I'd gotten special permission to use.

Instead, I pulled out the cheap muslin and a new sheet of pattern paper and my sketchbook, deconstructing my design down into its independent pieces.

I was so focused on my work Violet had to tap my arm to get me to go to dinner with them. I didn't want to leave, I was on a roll, but my stomach was grumbling and I knew I had to pace myself. Sometimes I got so in the zone on a project that I forgot to do things like eat or sleep.

As we were cleaning up, my phone buzzed. It was a text from Kalare: "Picking you up at Myriad. Meeting."

"I forgot I had plans tonight," I told everyone as we were leaving. "I'll see you at Enneman's later."

"Plans with who?" Stacee teased. "We're your only friends."

I rolled my eyes. "My boyfriend's cousin lives in Jersey. She wanted to take me out to dinner."

"Fine," Stacee sighed, "go eat two dinners, you pig."

I smiled and waved at them. As soon as they were out of sight down the street, a familiar black Escalade pulled up. Kalare rolled down the driver's side window.

"Get in."

I looked past her and saw that no one was in the passenger seat, so I walked around and hopped in.

"What's up?" I asked as she pulled into traffic. "Is there news?"

Kalare looked at me sharply, then shook her head. "Farrar called a meeting."

"About what?"

She shrugged. "Didn't say."

"You didn't ask?"

She looked over at me, brow cocked sternly. "Have you *met* Farrar?"

Point taken.

"Where are we going?" I asked, realizing we were heading into a part of the city I'd never been to before. That wasn't saying much, though—I hadn't been to much beyond the four or five blocks around Myriad.

"Julian's flat."

It took another thirty minutes through rush-hour traffic to make it to his building. She pulled into a private parking garage and led me to a private elevator, keying in a code that allowed her to select the fifteenth floor.

When we got out, I whistled.

"This place is swanky."

Kalare grunted. "Pretentious, if you ask me."

"Well, yeah," I said, spreading out my hands, "but swanky."

She rolled her eyes. "Come on."

We walked down the hall until we were at the corner of the building. She knocked on apartment 15F. A moment later, Julian answered the door. He glanced at her, looking tense, then at me. The expression on his face instantly made me nervous. He smoothed the look on his face back to neutral, then led us into the apartment.

Farrar was standing in the living room next to the point where the floor-to-ceiling windows met in the corner. Standing next to him was Adrian.

I stopped dead.

He allowed a brief smile to cross over his face when he saw me, then it was gone. He stood, hands in his pockets, looking blank, neutral, emotionless.

Kalare nudged me, and I continued walking toward them, hoping my face was as blank as Adrian's. I was in so much shock that I couldn't tell what it was doing. For all I knew, I was grimacing, or maybe had my tongue hanging out. I couldn't tell.

We stopped a few feet from them.

It was all I could do to keep from staring.

Adrian had cut his hair shorter than I'd ever seen it. The sides were almost shaved, the top a little longer, still dark and thick and wavy. He was wearing a t-shirt and jeans. Designer, but simple.

He looked amazing. He looked freaking perfect. He looked—

"Caitlin?"

Farrar peered at me expectantly, as if he'd just asked me a question. I blinked.

Kalare coughed. "Kid pulled a long shift at Myriad," she half-lied, covering for me. "She's a little tired."

"I'm sorry," I said, turning to Farrar, even though every fiber of my being told me to go run at Adrian and tackle him to the ground and kiss him until I passed out. "I haven't had a break all day."

"May I ask what's going on?" Kalare interrupted. "I wasn't informed that Adrian would be coming down to the city."

"Nor was I," Julian grumbled.

"The Council has decided to test the paired compulsion Adrian performed on Caitlin, to make sure the procedure was not done… improperly."

He looked coolly at Adrian. To Adrian's credit, he didn't flinch.

"What exactly does that mean?" Julian asked, frowning.

"Caitlin," Farrar said, ignoring Julian. "I promise this will not be unpleasant."

I looked at Kalare and Julian, alarmed. Adrian looked calm, but neutral. I couldn't read his face.

"Adrian, please compel Caitlin to tell you her name and the names of her parents."

"Hold on a minute," Kalare protested, "what about *operor non*—"

But Adrian's eyes had already flared into their luminous silver.

"Caitlin," he said gently, stepping forward. "Please tell us your name and the names of your parents."

I waited for my mind to get hijacked by his compulsion. But nothing happened.

Wait—what?

He wasn't compelling me. I mean, his eyes were all swirly, and he was making eye contact, but he wasn't compelling me.

"Caitlin Marie Holte," I said after just a moment's hesitation. I kept my voice neutral, my gaze locked on his. "My parents are James Edgar Holte and Elizabeth Norah Holte."

"Farrar," Kalare fumed, "this is against the law."

"The Council has sanctioned this test," Farrar said, glancing at her. "They are the law."

Kalare had no way of knowing that Adrian wasn't really compelling me. I kept my eyes locked on Adrian's face, not daring to glance over at her or Julian to reassure them.

"Adrian, please compel Caitlin to tell us if she knew that your father visited Trish Fields the night of the attack."

Adrian looked at Farrar, frowning, pretending this was news to him. "Caitlin," Adrian said, turning back to me. "Did you know that my father visited Trish Fields the night he attacked you?"

"No," I replied calmly. "I did not know."

"Ask Caitlin if she knows where Lucian is."

Adrian looked sharply at Farrar. After a moment, he turned back to me. "Caitlin, do you know where Lucian de la Mara is currently located?"

"No," I replied robotically. "I do not know where he is currently located."

How was Adrian doing this? How was he pretending to compel me? And could the others tell that he was only pretending?

Farrar was just barely in my right field of vision. He didn't appear to be surprised by my answer.

"Ask Caitlin if she is in love with you."

This time, Adrian only glanced at Farrar as though irritated before turning to me. "Caitlin, are you in love with me?"

Shit. They already knew how I felt about him. They could literally feel it. Time to hedge.

"I don't know," I replied in the same near-monotone. "I've never been in love before."

Kalare's eyebrow raised at that one. Farrar frowned very slightly.

"Ask Caitlin if Sabine compelled a human at Myriad."

He asked me.

"Yes," I replied. "Sabine compelled a college intern."

"Compel Caitlin to state that my shirt is blue," Farrar instructed. His shirt was black.

"Farrar's shirt is blue," I replied.

"Compel Caitlin to tell us," Farrar said finally, "if she is an Unmaker."

Adrian did a good job of looking bored. "Caitlin," he asked me dryly, "are you an Unmaker?"

I let a small frown crease my forehead. "I don't understand."

Kalare said that sometimes compulsion didn't take, because the human didn't understand the instructions. I figured if I was pretending to have never heard of Unmakers, this would be a good time to pull out the "I don't understand" card.

Adrian looked at Farrar for instructions.

"Ask her if she knows what an Unmaker is," he suggested.

"Caitlin, do you know what an Unmaker is?"

"No," I replied, blinking sleepily. "I do not know what an Unmaker is."

"Ask her if she has any unusual abilities," Farrar said.

"Caitlin, do you have any unusual abilities?"

I blinked. "I can sew," I stated simply. "I am very good at sewing."

Kalare snorted.

Farrar sighed, slightly. "Ask her," he said, looking at Adrian, "if she has any supernatural powers."

Adrian looked at Farrar as if he were crazy, then turned to me. "Caitlin, do you have any supernatural powers?"

"No," I replied. "I do not have any supernatural powers."

Farrar frowned at me, then looked at Adrian.

His eyes were still swirling, the silver irises mixing and melting in storms around his pupils.

"Thank you, Adrian," Farrar said. "Please compel Caitlin to forget this meeting. Kalare, when he is finished, please return Caitlin to her dorm."

"You will forget this meeting occurred," Adrian said, pretending to compel me. "You will remember that you were daydreaming on your way back to the dorm and lost track of time."

He looked to Farrar, as if to ask, "Is that good?"

Farrar nodded.

I blinked, my face remaining blank as Adrian's eyes slowed, melting back into their normal, human gray.

Kalare grabbed my arm and marched me to the door, closing it behind me.

I didn't know if they had cameras up in this place. I played mute as she led me into the elevator, through the garage, into the Escalade, and all the way back to Enneman's.

She dropped me off at my dorm, then drove away, saying nothing.

I blinked, as if coming awake, just in case someone was watching, then shook my head, found my keycard, and let myself into the building.

Five minutes after letting myself into my room, Kalare showed up at my door.

"Hey kid," she said, eyes tense. "It's a nice night out. I grabbed some snacks," she said, holding up a bag of chips and two sodas.

I followed her out of the room and up to the roof.

She let out a deep breath as soon as the door closed.

"We can talk," she said finally, seeing my questioning look. "Probably being overly paranoid. I'll check your room for bugs as soon as we get back."

I let out my own deep breath.

"I swear, I had no idea he was going to be there," she said, pacing. "Or that Farrar was going to make him do that. How in the hell did you resist his compulsion?"

"He didn't compel me," I said, sinking down into one of the three roof chairs.

"He—what?"

"He didn't compel me. Don't ask me how, but he didn't."

"His eyes were cascading," she said, looking almost angry, as if I was lying to her. "He was compelling you."

"No, he wasn't," I insisted, popping the top off the soda can. "I've been compelled by him before. I'm telling you, he was faking it somehow."

"That doesn't make any *sense*," she muttered. "Our eyes don't just cascade for shits and giggles; it's not a light switch."

"What do you mean? And what is cascading?"

"Julian told me you knew all this crap already."

"Yes, the thousands of years of vampire history, magic, and biology. I know it all," I replied dryly.

She threw me a dirty look. "Fine. We have photo receptors in our irises—similar to jellyfish or photoluminescent frogs and bugs and shit—that activate when we're compelling someone. The swirling colors, the light? It's not just for show; it's a hypnotic agent. The photo receptors are activated by our compulsive abilities. It's not just a gimmick; it's a biological response. We call it 'cascading.'"

"Oh," I said, surprised Adrian had never explained that to me before. Science was his nerd passion.

"That's why it doesn't make any sense for him to be compelling you, but for the compulsion to not work, *especially* if you guys are paired. It literally doesn't work that way. He can't be faking it," she muttered, almost to herself.

I'd only half heard her. The speech on photo receptors had made me think about Adrian's eyes, which had made me think about Adrian.

"It was so good to see him," I murmured to myself, leaning back in my chair. "I didn't realize how much I missed him."

"Right," Kalare said dryly, "let's focus on what's *really* important."

"Give me a break. I haven't seen him in weeks."

"Week and a half," she corrected me. "Such an eternity. I hate to break it to you, kid, but we've got bigger things at stake."

I glared at her. "I'm aware of that."

She cocked an eyebrow. "*Are* you?"

I set my soda can down with a sharp, metallic *clang*. "You don't get it, do you?" I asked, struggling to keep my voice calm. "This is my life. This crazy, stupid shit is my *life* now. I am trying to deal with it, to learn, to keep up. But I have to spin dozens of lies to keep I don't know how many secrets from the Council and my family and my friends, *while* pretending everything is completely normal. And so far, Adrian has been the only reason I've survived. Not the Council, not Mariana or Dominic or *you*—Adrian. Adrian literally died for me. I'm not just some dumb, horny teenager who's too stupid to keep her priorities straight. I love him, Kalare. And that's important. You can mock that if you want, if you're really that old and jaded and bitter. But you don't get to tell me how to feel. Stop calling our relationship gross and stop saying we're idiots. It's not, and we're not."

I sat back in my chair, fuming, my posture daring her to argue with me.

She opened her mouth, then closed it.

Then she stalked off to the other side of the roof. I leaned back, feeling a headache building behind my eyes. I slurped at the rest of my soda and ate the whole bag of chips, suddenly ravenous.

A few minutes later, Kalare walked back over and sat down.

"I'm sorry," she said finally. "I didn't mean to belittle your relationship. That shit just makes me uncomfortable. It's easier to make fun of you than to admit that you might actually be in love. Though at your age, I think it's absurd. Try some other flavors, kid, I guarantee you Adrian is not the hottest shit out there."

"I don't care if he's the hottest shit," I muttered, "he's *my* shit."

She snorted a half-laugh, then cracked a smile. "Well, far be it from me to get in the way of true shit."

I let the last of the anger drain out of me. "Thanks," I said. "Also, I ate all your chips."

"Our friendship is dead."

We both grinned, then turned serious. "How long will Adrian be here?"

Kalare shook her head. "No idea. I'll find out, though. For now, do what you've gotten eerily good at: pretending everything is normal."

21

"Caitlin."

"Nnn?"

"Caitlin, you don't have much time."

I sat up groggily. Data was standing over me along with Julian. "Was I asleep?" I asked, feeling stiff and tired. I hadn't fallen asleep in the real world until almost three. I couldn't stop thinking about Adrian.

"That is not clear," Data said. "Though you did have a vacant look in your eye and did not respond immediately to our queries."

"What's going on?" I asked. "Are you asleep, Julian?"

"Yeah," he said, helping me stand. "Look, we don't have much time. It's almost morning. Farrar's keeping Adrian in town for a few days; they're both staying at my place. Not sure if it's to interrogate you more, or if there's something else going on. You need to tell me to wake up, and then you need to pull Adrian here. And probably tell this one to take a hike," he said, nodding at Data.

"Why?" I asked, stupidly.

"Do you really want me to spell that out for you?"

I blinked, confused, then realized what he meant. "Oh."

Data frowned. "Caitlin, I am not sure—"

"Data," I said, cutting him off. "Let me have this." I turned to Julian. "He's asleep?"

Julian nodded.

"Thanks," I said, meaning it. "Wake up."

Instantly, Julian disappeared.

"Love ya, Data, but please go."

Data nodded politely and disappeared.

In the sudden quiet, I closed my eyes and thought of Adrian.

A moment later, there were hands on my arms, warm and familiar.

I opened my eyes.

Adrian smiled slowly, looking down at me. I smiled back, feeling the stress and tension melt away.

"You cut your hair," I said, reaching up to brush at it.

"I did," he confirmed. "Do you like it?"

I nodded, seriously. "I do. I really, really do."

"Good," he whispered. And then he kissed me.

I buried my fingers in his hair, grateful there was enough on top to grab onto.

After a long, long moment, he pulled back. "I'm so sorry, Cait. They have my phone, I couldn't warn you, I couldn't stop them—"

I crushed myself against his chest, squeezing him tight. "It's okay. I missed you so much."

"You don't even know," he said, squeezing me back. "I've been going crazy cooped up at the house, researching from dawn until dusk, waiting to fall asleep so I could talk to you."

"You're here now," I said, looking up at him, holding him tightly.

"And I—"

From one moment to the next, he was gone. I sat up straight in bed, heart racing, as my alarm beeped angrily at me. I slammed my hand down on the alarm clock.

"Bad dream?" Kalare asked from her bed. "Or good?"

I glared at her, though she couldn't see it because I'd buried my face in my pillow and was currently gathering my blankets into a cocoon of rage.

"I take it you didn't have long with Adrian?" Kalare asked.

"Only got one kiss," I muttered from my blanket nest. I sat up grumpily. "You know that really lovely speech I gave you last night about love?" Kalare nodded, warily. "Well, it was true. But you were also right. It's also hormones. I want to jump on him, Kalare. I want to smoosh my face against his face so hard."

"That sounds…pleasant," Kalare said, looking a little grossed out.

"Would you and Julian please make out already so you can understand my pain?" I asked, rolling onto the floor in a heap.

"No," Kalare said, throwing a pillow on top of me. "But thank you for admitting I was right."

"*Partially* right," I corrected, throwing the pillow back.

"You gonna be able to concentrate at Myriad today, Horny-Love-Pants?"

"Nope," I said. "Not at all. But I have to. But I won't. But I have to. So I will. Then I probably won't for a while. Then I will."

I looked up at Kalare from the floor. "Please tell me you'll find out how long he's staying. I need to see him in person."

Kalare gave me a mock salute. "I'll see what I can do."

"Come in, Caitlin," Olivia said, gesturing me over when she saw me hesitate by the door. I walked over and sat next to the woman. "Caitlin, this is Candace Mauk. She's your new mentor."

The woman, somewhere in her thirties, it looked, held out her hand. "Nice to meet you, Caitlin. Olivia speaks very highly of you."

I blushed instantly. "Thank you. It's nice to meet you as well."

"Candace is preparing to launch her first line here at Myriad. You're going to assist her in whatever way she deems necessary during your morning block. Candace, don't go easy on her. She's got what it takes."

Candace nodded, smiling. "Understood. I'll be grateful for the help."

"Good," Olivia said. "I'm off to a meeting, but I'll see you after lunch, Caitlin."

We stood and I thanked Olivia, following Candace out of the room. She was pretty, but not overly made up, wearing stylish but comfortable slacks, boots, and a loose top. Her hair was up in a messy bun, and she wore minimal make up. I liked her.

"Normally I'd take more time out to get to know you before throwing you to the wolves, but I'm in the middle of my launch, so you'll have to keep up best you can," Candace explained, leading me into another office down the hall. It was smaller than Olivia's by a decent amount, and she appeared to share it with another designer. "This is Mandy, my office-mate. Mandy, this is Caitlin, my new intern. She'll be helping on the launch."

Mandy waved, and started to say something, but her phone rang. She looked at me apologetically and answered it.

"Mandy is a junior designer, like me," Candace explained quietly, closing the door. "We were interns here together."

She gestured toward the one extra chair in the room while she sat at her desk. It had the look of someone who was normally meticulously organized, but had grown somewhat lenient in the wake of a crazy schedule.

"Now, Olivia said your first mentor had to leave unexpectedly. What did she cover?"

"Uh…" I stalled. I couldn't say "nothing," even if it was true. "Honestly, not much," I hedged. "I think she was distracted by some family matters. I tried to do as much on my own as I could."

Candace frowned. "Who was she again?"

"Sabine Rousseau."

"Sabine, Sabine…" A lightbulb seemed to go off in her mind. "Ah, yes. She wasn't here long, if I recall. Came a bit suddenly, left even more suddenly. Well, I'm sorry that you got stuck with her; it happens sometimes. Olivia was actually my mentor, back when I was an intern. College, not high school, the high school program didn't exist back then. Brilliant woman, I'm here because of her. If she says you've got what it takes, then I believe her."

Candace spoke quickly, organizing files on her desk while she spoke. "I'll do all I can to get you up to speed, but I'm afraid you'll have to figure some things out for yourself. Based on what Olivia's said, I don't think you'll have much of a problem. Come see what we've been working on."

She smiled warmly at me and led me out of the office and down the hall to a small workroom. Several college interns bustled around, draped in tape measures. They looked surprised to see me. "Everyone," she said, addressing the whole room, "this is Caitlin; she'll be helping us out. Be nice, teach her, don't bite, you know the drill." Everyone waved, looking curiously at me.

"All right, so this is the line," Candace said, taking me to the back of the room where a few finished pieces were hanging on mannequins. The recurring motif seemed to be a series of high-waisted pants in some sort of brushed cotton. "Going for a bit of an industrial look," Candace explained. "I love high-waisted garments but I hate wearing them. Cuts you off right across the stomach, makes you feel like you're going to puke if you bend over or eat so much as a salad. These actually hug you right across the ribs in more of an empire-cut. Breathable fabric, lightweight, easy to move in. Pair it with a fisherman sweater and you've got a lovely fall look."

She took me over to the rack of crop-top sweaters. "We've been having trouble choosing a weave we like. Do you knit?"

I nodded. "And crochet, and embroider."

She looked impressed. "Goodness, I see why Olivia likes you. Well, I need you to take these three samples down to our distributor accountant. He's going to tell you which weave will cost the most and which Myriad is willing to fund. Just get the quotes and bring them back to me."

She handed me the sweaters and was immediately surrounded by interns asking her questions.

I went to the door, then realized I didn't know the name of the man I was supposed to find, or even what floor he was on.

"Excuse me," I said, catching an intern as she walked by. "Do you know who the distributor accountant is and where I can find him?"

"Billy Wendal, sixth floor," she said, smiling briefly before dashing across the room.

I made my way to the elevators and got in, feeling self-conscious when a group of very well-dressed men and women got in with me. I hadn't had time to hit the button for the sixth floor, and I felt too embarrassed to ask one of them to push it for me, so I just stood quietly in the back corner and waited for them to get off at their three different levels before I finally hit the button for the sixth floor.

I also unsuccessfully tried to hide an enormous yawn. I was

exhausted.

When I got off, it took ten minutes of wandering before I finally found Billy Wendal's office. I'd thought about stopping to ask where he was located, but this floor was unnaturally quiet, and I felt like even whispering would disturb everyone. Plus, the people here were dressed more conservatively. This was not a floor of creatives; it was a floor of accountants. They kind of scared me since I knew nothing about them. I finally stumbled upon his office and knocked on the door, jumping when he barked, "Come in!"

I slipped inside and stood in front of his desk. It was a small office, but clean, stark white.

He looked up at me from behind his large, stylish glasses. Actually, I wasn't sure if they were stylish, or just really old. Either way, they fit his face. He kind of reminded me of a cranky old wizard for some reason.

"You are?" he said curtly, peering at me.

"Caitlin Holte," I said, not sure if I should stick out my hand or not. "Candace Mauk's new assistant?"

"Is that a question? Don't know if you're an assistant or not?" He waved his hand back and forth, cutting me off from a reply. "You were supposed to be here fifteen minutes ago. I have another appointment. Have Candace reschedule."

I opened my mouth, then closed it. He was already back to typing on his computer. I nodded, mortified, and left.

As I headed back to the elevator, I wondered if I should have stayed and demanded that he look at the garments and given me the quotes Candace needed. What if she needed them today? What if she couldn't wait? Shit.

I got back on the elevator, overwhelmed and not sure what to do. I didn't know enough about the structure here to know if Candace or

Billy ranked higher. Also, my wrist was starting to ache from carrying around the sweaters. There were only five of them, but they were bulky and heavy and the hangers were biting into my palm. Just before the doors closed, a college intern popped through the doors, breathing hard. She jammed the button for the ninth floor, then seemed to notice I was in the elevator.

"Hey," she said, "I'm Katie. Haven't seen you before. You look like you're about to cry."

I blinked, realizing she was right. "Sorry," I said, brushing at my eyes. "I'm Caitlin. High school intern. Just failed at my first assignment and not sure what to do."

"What's the task?" she asked.

"Take this to Billy Wendal and get a quote on the knits. I got lost and showed up late and he couldn't meet with me."

"Billy's good but he's got a stick up his keister," Katie reassured me. "Go back to the sixth floor and see if Maureen's available. She'll act grumpy but that's just her thing. Say it's for—who's it for?"

"Candace Mauk?"

"Say it's for Candace. Everyone likes her."

The doors opened on the ninth floor and Katie hopped out. "Nice to meet you, Caitlin!"

"You too!" I called as the doors closed. I hit the button for the sixth floor and got back out, wandering until I found a door labeled "Maureen Smith." I knocked.

"Who's there?" an older woman's voice called.

"My name is Caitlin," I called through the door. "Candace Mauk sent me."

There was a moment of silence, then, "All right, come in."

I opened the door and slid inside. Her office could not have been more different from Mr. Wendal's. It was painted a dark red, filled with fabric samples, swatches, and catalogs, with an antique silver tea set on a lacquered antique table in the corner.

She frowned at me from behind her desk. "Billy Wendal handles Candace's account. Why are you here?"

"I missed my appointment with Mr. Wendal and was told you might be able to help me. It's my first day with Candace, and I didn't want to go back to her empty-handed."

"Don't you college kids know the schedule by now?" she griped, taking a large slurp from her cup of tea.

"I'm a high school intern, actually. I'm…new."

Her eyebrows flew up comically. "Since when do they assign high schoolers to launches?"

"I—I don't know. Olivia placed me with her."

Her eyebrows flew even higher, in danger of disappearing behind her silver-gray bangs. "Well, then. All right, have a seat, I'll see what I can do. What's she need?"

"Quotes on the weaves for these sweaters?" I said, not entirely sure what that meant. My hands were bright red from switching the hangers back and forth; the metal hooks had made grooves in my skin.

She gestured for me to lay them on her desk as she put on a pair of thick glasses. "Uh-huh," she said, pouring over the pattern in the yarn. I sat down and massaged my hands out of sight, feeling the blood return painfully into my fingers. "Uh-huh," she repeated. She flipped the sweater over, inspecting the back-side, before examining the other two sweaters. "Mm-hmm," she muttered several more times, writing down a list of numbers on a form. "There you go. Candace'll know what all that means."

"Thank you," I breathed, surprised as how quickly it had gone. "I appreciate it very much."

"No problem, no problem," she said. "Just bring a rack next time;

you look ridiculous carrying those around. And make sure to be on time for Billy. He loves his schedule. Thinks he's a very important man."

"Is he?" I asked.

"Yes," she said frankly, "but it doesn't suit him to know it."

I smiled. I liked this woman. "Thank you again, Mrs. Smith."

"*Mrs.* Smith?" she asked, blinking widely behind her glasses. "Goodness, do I look married to you? I'm a spinster, and proud of it. But I like your style. Good manners. What's your name again?"

"Caitlin Holte," I said, holding out my hand.

She shook it. "Caitlin Holte. I like you Caitlin. Come visit me anytime. And bring cookies."

I smiled again. "I will."

I scooped up the sweaters and the form she'd signed, and left, thanking her once more as I went out the door.

Candace was busy when I got back to the workroom, so I hung up the sweaters on the rack and pinned the form to one of them, then asked one of the college interns if I could help. She looked relieved and immediately sent me off to the stock room to get replacement buttons.

By lunch, I'd learned most of the other launch assistants' names and had gotten a fairly good feel for their system. I was even able to grab Candace herself, briefly, to tell her the quote was pinned to the sweater. She smiled distractedly and thanked me. At noon, they all headed to the conference room for a take-out, lunch and I wished them a good afternoon and headed down to the cafeteria.

Stacee and Truitt peppered me with questions about my new mentor. Violet had decided to work through lunch to put the finishing touches on her second proposal. We ate quickly and headed to the workroom. I'd drawn up most of the pattern pieces yesterday, so I was able to quickly cut out muslin for the mock-up.

Violet stared at me, shaking her head. "I don't know how you work so fast," she muttered. It was the closest to a mean thing that I'd ever heard her say; more the tone than the words themselves.

"Just a lot of practice. My mom taught me to sew practically before she taught me to walk." I set down my scissors, seeing her slumped shoulders. "Do you need any help with anything?"

"No," Violet sighed. "I'm done with my presentation, just jealous of your skills."

"Well, hey, we're partners. You need anything, I'm happy to help."

Violet smiled at me genuinely. "Thanks, Caitlin." She looked at her watch. "I better go. Olivia's reviewing the proposals in twenty minutes. I'll see you guys at dinner."

I gave her a hug and wished her good luck. She rubbed my hair, like Truitt had started to do, to "get some of my magic." I rolled my eyes as she grinned and walked out the door. As soon as she was gone, I began to pin the last of the muslin, then took it over to the sewing machine. I was glad Violet had shown me how to use it; the thing was a beast. Since the fabric was so light, I was done in less than an hour. I fitted it on my mannequin and stepped back to observe.

"That the cape design?" Stacee asked, joining me at my work table.

"Yep," I said. "Just the mock-up."

"Shoulders look a little severe," she observed. "That intentional?"

"Yep," I said. "I'm using pretty thick facing to exaggerate the shape."

Stacee nodded, then shook her head, smiling. "Don't know how you do it."

"Ten thousand hours," I replied, pretending to bench press a roll of muslin. Stacee snorted at my dorkiness and I grinned. "Seriously, my mom was *intensely* crafty," I explained, putting the roll back on its hooks. "We literally sewed every day. Who knows if I have any real talent for this? Maybe my brain just got rewired because I've done it so often. I'm the Manchurian Designer."

Stacee laughed and snapped a salute at me. Truitt called for her, sounding stressed out as usual, and she smiled apologetically and went back to their shared table.

Everything I'd said was true (besides the Manchurian Designer part), but I was also out of polite excuses for why I was better than the others at this. I had more practice than most of them by a lot, especially at our age. That was honestly most of it, but I'd also spent more than half my life pouring over fashion magazines and anthologies of the history of design that I begged my mom for every Christmas. I'd started out making clothes for my dolls, then christening gowns for newborns, then my own clothing. In Mystic, I'd scour the neighbors' attics for old patterns and make stuff even if I didn't like the style, even if it was outdated by fifty years, and then give it away or sell it at craft fairs. I'd started drafting my own patterns in junior high. I'd even been commissioned to make the flower girl dress and ring bearer tux for my neighbor's wedding—when I was twelve. In short, I'd been practicing and studying constantly for over ten years. While I didn't, by any means, think that I knew everything, I *did* know a lot. The past year in Stony Creek—and the summer before, when my mom was in the hospital—was the least amount of sewing I'd done since I was five years old.

That's part of why I'd been so depressed when I got to Stony Creek. Because of my mom, of course, but also because I'd stopped making things. It was like voluntarily amputating my own limbs. Adrian had done more for me than he realized when he built the studio; when he gave me an opportunity to start creating again. But even as great as that was, I'd always sewn with my mom—with someone else at my side. And here at Myriad, I was surrounded by others of my kind. It felt, in a strange way, like being home.

Careful not to draw attention to myself or the mound of

ridiculously expensive fabric I had, I pulled out the silk and cut out the pieces for the lining, matching it with the wool interlining. I should have been nervous working with fabric that expensive, I usually was, but for some reason I felt totally calm. I knew what I was doing. I wasn't second-guessing myself.

I hid the silk back under the table and pulled out the cashmere. It was a beautiful, snowy white, startling in its softness. It made me think of Adrian, his sweaters. That wasn't why I'd chosen it, but I didn't exactly hate the reminder.

Adrian. Was he even still in the city, or had Farrar sent him back to Stony Creek?

Gah! Couldn't think about it. Concentrate. Do what you can. Compartmentalize. Here, there were no vampires or Unmakers or dreamscapes or hellmouths. Here, there was hard work and elbow grease and pure determination. I had to keep my brain in design mode or I'd lose my momentum and distract myself worrying about things I couldn't do anything about. I let myself have another ten seconds daydreaming about Adrian before I shoved him out of my brain. Work. I had so much to do and not much time to do it.

I laid out the patterns for the outer shell, carefully aligning the grain. You couldn't see the grain very well anyway, but this was one project I wasn't going to cut corners on.

By dinner, I had all the fabric cut out for the cape and the dress that went underneath. I toyed with the idea of starting to sew, but I was growing tired and sloppy, and it was almost time to leave the workroom. I folded up the pieces and stowed them under the work table, brushing the threads and scraps off the cutting board and onto the floor, then sweeping around my station and tidying the whole area. Some kids left their workstations messy overnight; they thrived creatively in the chaos. I preferred to clean up, partially because it made me feel better, and partially because I didn't want Olivia or even the college interns to wander by my station and find it messy.

At dinner, Violet ran up to us, waving her presentation. "She approved it! She approved it!" she screamed, hugging me and then Stacee and then Truitt. "Barely, but she approved it! That's good enough for me! I'm not going home!"

Truitt brought her over a slice of cake and we laughed and joked and celebrated until they kicked us out at seven. Just as we were leaving, I got a text from Julian: *pick u up on curb now.*

I glanced out the glass doors leading to the street. A black Escalade was pulled over.

I pretended to be giddy as we walked outside. "My boyfriend texted, he just got into town to surprise me! I'll see you guys later!"

"Bring him by the dorms; we want to say hi!" Stacee called out. "Also, Truitt wants to steal him from you so that he can afford to go to Enneman's." Truitt rolled his eyes. I laughed and promised them I would try and bring him by.

I waited until they were out of sight, then got into the passenger seat of the Escalade. Julian was driving.

I looked at him questioningly. He shook his head.

I sat in silence as he drove us over to his apartment. We parked and headed up to his loft. This time, Adrian was standing next to Farrar while Kalare sulked in a chair.

Also, Vincent and Javan were there, flanking Farrar.

That didn't seem good.

"Caitlin, thank you for coming," Farrar greeted me dispassionately. "We've asked Adrian to come up to New York to help answer a few questions."

Shit, I forgot I was supposed to be surprised to see him. According to Farrar's instructions, I shouldn't remember our meeting from yesterday at all.

I nodded at Adrian politely.

"How can I help?" I asked, trying to sound chipper and relaxed. "Is there news on Lucian?"

"Unfortunately, no. Adrian, if you will?"

Adrian took a few steps toward me until we were only a foot or two apart. His eyes began to change, cascading, as Kalare put it, from gray to silver. She was right, the effect was hypnotic, even if he was only faking. I hadn't had enough time in the dreamscape last night to ask how he was cascading without actually compelling me.

"Please ask Caitlin if she has been in contact with any vampires outside of the Praetorian Guard."

"Caitlin, have you been in contact with any vampires outside of the Praetorian Guard?" Adrian asked me gently.

"I have spoken to Mariana and Dominic," I said, not needing to lie. They weren't technically in the Praetorian Guard, just ancillary support.

"Ask Caitlin what Trish Fields believes about your family and about us."

Adrian asked.

"Trish believes you might be members of a religious cult," I said, blankly. "She thinks you guys are weird." It was hard to say that with a straight face. I could just barely see the corner of Adrian's mouth twitch, as if he was suppressing a smile.

"Does she suspect what we really are?" Farrar had Adrian ask.

"No," I replied. "She does not suspect what you really are."

"Have you been in contact with any demons, including but not limited to my father?" Farrar asked through Adrian.

"No," I replied. "I have not been in contact with any demons."

"Is there any point to this?" Kalare interjected. "She obviously doesn't know anything."

Farrar's gaze cut sharply to Kalare. I couldn't look at her because she was sitting slightly behind me, and I had to keep my eyes locked on Adrian's face.

"There is a point," Farrar said quietly, "that you will have to trust I understand."

He turned back to Adrian. "Adrian, compel Caitlin to turn in a circle."

Adrian frowned but compelled me to turn in a circle. I made one rotation, then stopped, my eyes going back to his face.

"Compel Caitlin to climb onto the back of the couch and jump to the floor."

In the corner of my eye, I could see Kalare stand abruptly, muttering something under her breath about "abuse of power."

"I have direct orders from the Council, Kalare," Farrar said to her. "Vincent and Javan can attest to this."

"It's a mockery of the law," she retorted. "And a waste of time."

"Nevertheless," Farrar said quietly. "Adrian?"

Adrian turned to me, his eyes tight with worry. "Caitlin, climb up on the back of the couch and jump to the floor."

I nodded, and immediately crawled onto the couch, inwardly horrified that I might be leaving boot prints on the pristine gray fabric. It took me a second to find my balance on the back of the couch, but luckily it wasn't very tall. I jumped down without incident, and stayed there, staring off into space. Adrian came around the couch to face me.

I heard a sound behind me and a rush of warm air.

"Compel Caitlin to climb onto the railing of the balcony and jump off," I heard Farrar say from somewhere behind me.

I was glad I was facing away from him, because I'm pretty sure the panic showed on my face.

"That's *enough*," Kalare said. I could hear her boots moving across the hardwood floor emphatically. "You're not putting that girl in danger. We are here to *protect* her."

"We are here," he said, "to carry out the instructions of the Council. Adrian. Compel her to jump off the balcony."

"She dies doing this, people are going to notice she jumped from *my* balcony," Julian said, sounding bored. "I'll have to move flats. I hate moving."

"Your sacrifice will be noted," Farrar replied dryly. "Adrian. *Now.*"

Adrian was facing me, so I could see his gaze glance in several different directions. I couldn't think of a way out of this. Surely Farrar wouldn't actually let me go through with it? If they were going to kill me, they'd find a far less public way to do it.

Adrian looked at me, finally. "Caitlin," he said, jaw tight. "Climb onto the rail of the balcony and jump off."

I nodded, lingering for half a moment longer than I should have, before turning to the open doors leading to the balcony.

In normal compulsion, the command was only as strong as the vampire's will and the human's lack thereof. Or rather, the human's actual willingness to do whatever the command was. Compulsion *could* be resisted given the right circumstances, and the right personality. But, as Julian had explained to Adrian and Adrian had explained to me, paired compulsion went far deeper than regular compulsion. It even outranked compulsion by demons. It was a complete melding of wills. Even though Adrian was only pretending to compel me, I still had to *act* like I was willing to do whatever he asked me to do. I couldn't think of a way out of this one.

Heart racing, I walked through the balcony doors, realizing just how high the fifteenth story really was. The view was spectacular; Julian lived in a nice part of town. I gripped the cold metal of the railing with my hands, then dug the toes of my boots into the lowest rung. I swung one leg over, then the other, feeling my stomach muscles contracting to keep me balanced on the edge as I sat with nothing but open space beneath me.

Shit.

I began to scoot forward. No one stopped me.

Double shit.

I leaned toward the street, heart racing. And still, no one stopped me.

I stood and released the railing with one hand, more of my body leaning over the street than not, when I was grabbed from behind.

I almost started crying I was so relieved, but I had to shove that way down deep, because I was still supposed to be in my zen compulsion bubble.

I realized, as whoever had grabbed me turned back toward the apartment, that I could see Adrian, Julian, Kalare, Vincent, and Javan. Which meant it was *Farrar* who'd prevented me from falling. He set me down on the balcony. My knees buckled and I collapsed into a heap.

"For the love of God, *enough*, Farrar," Kalare said, grabbing me by the arms and hauling me inside. "She's going to get compulsion sickness."

Farrar didn't respond, and since I was staring straight forward in drone-mode, I couldn't see his face, but I think he must have nodded. Kalare slung one of my arms around her shoulder and headed for the doorway.

"A moment, Kalare," Farrar called. "Adrian, please compel Caitlin to forget this meeting."

Adrian stalked over, radiating anger. A vein beat in his temple as he looked into my eyes. "Caitlin, you will forget that this meeting occurred. You will remember that you were daydreaming on your way home from Myriad. You lost track of time."

I nodded.

Adrian whirled back to Farrar, fuming. "We done?"

Farrar nodded.

Kalare carried me out instantly, half-dragging me to the elevator. I kept the blank look on my face all the way down the elevator, all the way in the car on the way back to the dorms, even all the way up to my room.

As soon as the door closed, I sank to the floor and started sobbing, shaking so badly I had to wrap my arms around myself.

A few minutes later, Kalare was back from parking the car and slipped into my room. She grabbed the blanket from my bed and draped it around my shoulders. Then she knelt down beside me and crushed me against her chest in a hug.

"I'm done," I choked, face pressed to her collarbone. "I'm done, I'm done, I'm—"

"Shh," Kalare said, holding me tighter. "It's okay."

I was shaking so bad I could barely breathe. "He was going to let me die," I mumbled, still in shock.

"We wouldn't have let that happen," she assured me quietly. "If Farrar hadn't moved the second that he did, I was going to grab you. So was Julian. So was Adrian. He was testing us as much as he was testing you."

I was on the verge of hyperventilating, there was so much adrenaline coursing through my system I couldn't handle it. "Kalare, I can't do this anymore. This is insane," I hiccuped. "He's insane. The Council wants me *d-dead.*"

Kalare grabbed me by the shoulders and sat me up. "Listen to me. The Council is not going to kill you. They don't want you dead. Not yet. And even if they do, I'm not going to let that happen. All right? You've made allies, you little turd. We're on your side. Got it?"

I nodded miserably.

"Now pull yourself together. You're not dead. You're not alone. And you've got work to do tomorrow at Myriad. Right?"

I nodded, feeling myself starting to come down from my panic.

"All right. Go take a hot shower, I'll make you a snack, and you should get some sleep. Okay?"

I nodded numbly and she helped me stand, even going so far as to get the hot water in the shower going for me. As soon as she left the bathroom, I locked the door and looked at myself in the mirror.

I was white as a sheet, tears carving rivers through my make up.

I crawled into the shower and huddled on the floor of the tub for a few minutes, unable to stop the tremors from shaking me. Eventually, the hot water woke me up enough to stand. I finished, got out and dressed, and felt almost normal again by the time I joined Kalare in my room. She had gotten me a chocolate muffin from somewhere and a cup of hot tea.

"Thanks," I said, my throat hoarse.

"No problem. You, uh…need anything else?"

I shook my head.

She nodded. There was a moment of silence. "Wanna watch a movie?"

I nodded. She pulled out my laptop and logged into her Netflix account. She picked something random, a comedy, and by the time I finished the muffin and the tea, I'd fallen asleep, exhausted.

Let's Talk About Sex, Baby

22

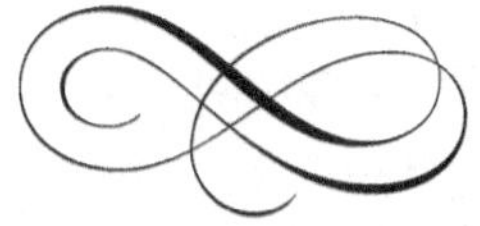

Why do I wake up more tired here than when I don't dream at all?"

Data blinked, his yellow android eyes eerie as ever. "The dreamscape supersedes your REM cycle. Rather than recharging, allowing you to drift unconsciously through random dream motifs, you are fully aware; fully in control."

"I don't *feel* in control," I muttered.

"This," he continued, ignoring me, "does not allow you to rest properly while asleep."

"Isn't that dangerous?"

He nodded. "Over time, yes. Unfortunately, circumstances being what they are, it is also rather important to continue these sessions."

I nodded, huddled in a giant bean bag I'd conjured up. I'd gone to sleep early, and apparently hit REM sleep sooner than usual because try as I might, I couldn't pull Adrian or Julian into the dream, which probably meant they were still awake.

"Do you have anything to show me tonight, Data?"

"I—"

He cut himself off, looking to the right. "I believe we have guests."

I sat up in the bean bag. Julian was standing there, along with Adrian.

I scrambled out of the bean bag chair, but it was so huge, I got tangled up and couldn't get out. Then I remembered I could just will it away, so I did. I fell with a soft *thud* to the white, formless floor, then ran at Adrian, vaulting myself into his arms.

"I'm so sorry, Cait," he whispered into my hair. "I didn't know he was going to do that. I didn't know what to do."

"It's okay," I mumbled into his neck.

I squeezed him for another minute, my arms latched around his neck, my legs wrapped around his waist, totally forgetting about Data and Julian.

Finally, Julian cleared his throat. "Not to break up this precious moment, but we have some important things to discuss."

Adrian slowly let me down, pressing his lips to my cheek softly. We separated, cleared our throats, and walked back over to Data and Julian.

"What happened after Kalare and I left?" I asked.

Julian and Adrian exchanged wary looks.

"I was questioned," Adrian admitted.

Julian barked a rough laugh. "That's putting it lightly."

"What did he ask?"

I realized we were all standing and imagined up some couches. Data sat immediately. Julian and Adrian blinked before sitting. They were still getting used to this place.

"Holy crap," I said suddenly.

"What?"

"Sorry, I just realized what this place reminded me of." I turned to Adrian. "It's like the Room of Requirement from Harry Potter. Except it's in my head. Or, well, my head is the room. And I'm Hogwarts?"

"Fascinating," Julian said dryly. "As I said, we have *important* things to discuss."

I blushed. I may have read Harry Potter twice through, now that Adrian and I were dating.

Adrian cleared his throat. "Farrar wanted to know about you. What I'd observed about you, if you'd said anything that might indicate you were more than what you appeared to be. Wanted to know more about our relationship, if I was in love with you."

"Got so personal even *I* wanted to punch him," Julian muttered. "Can't believe you kept your cool."

Adrian shrugged uncomfortably. "I had to."

"They finally stopped interrogating him around midnight. Adrian and I gorged on blood and came here as quickly as we could."

"Makes us sleepy," Adrian explained at my puzzled look.

Ah. Like turkey on Thanksgiving. Except it was blood. And human.

"Your friend, Trish—her comment about Tommie sparked a new investigation," Julian said, leaning forward. "The Council assumed he'd created a new body for himself, in order to impregnate you. He didn't. He's possessing a twenty-four-year-old named Tommie Reynolds. Lives a few counties over from Stony Creek. That story he told you, about his family, the car accident? That was true. Our father merely borrowed a real tragedy for his own agenda."

"Why didn't he just make a new body?" I honestly still wasn't sure how this worked.

Julian shook his head. "That's what doesn't make sense. Demons can only impregnate humans when they create bodies, *not* when they possess living hosts. As Tommie Reynolds, he could have gotten you pregnant, sure, but genetically it would have been a purely human baby."

"What does that mean, then, that he possessed a body instead of making his own?" I asked.

"It means he wasn't there to get you pregnant," Julian said frankly. "It means he was there for something else."

"But—why kiss me? Why…" I trailed off. I hated talking about this in front of Adrian.

"I don't know," Julian said. "But Farrar obviously has more information than we do. The fact that he brought up the Unmaker question in front of all of us means the Council *is* aware of the fact that you might be one. And it has them scared."

"But that doesn't make any sense," I sputtered. "I can't do anything!"

Julian looked around the formless white dreamscape. "I beg to differ."

I rolled my eyes. "So I can conjure up dream couches, big deal. That's not something the Council should want me dead over."

"Caitlin," Julian said slowly. "You can locate *unconscious* vampires. Over a twenty-mile radius. Two hundred, if you count when Adrian was in Stony Creek. You don't think that would concern the Council?"

I blinked. "Well, okay, sure, but didn't Kalare say Unmakers can kill demons? I know I can't do that, or I would have done it when Tommie attacked us."

"Maybe you couldn't then," Julian agreed. "But maybe you can now."

There was a moment of silence. A wave of goosebumps passed over me. My "powers," such as they were, *did* seem to be expanding, at least here in my mind.

"Okay, let's say, for a moment, that I can kill demons—so what?" I looked back and forth between the brothers. "You guys kill demons all the time. You banish them back to hell. You told me yourself," I said, looking at Adrian, "demons can't really *be* killed. Their bodies can be destroyed, but they just go back to hell, and then eventually come back here. Why does the Council care if I can destroy demons' bodies? Why does that *scare* them?"

"I don't know," Julian said. "And that's why Kalare's going to meet up with her contact as soon as possible."

"Isn't that dangerous with Farrar in town?" I asked. "Couldn't she just search the Council database instead? She's got the security clearance."

"She could, but they'd know the second she did. Which means we don't have much of a choice. Kalare and I may be on the Guard, but Farrar's obviously in league with Vincent and Javan and the Council. They're not sharing everything they know. If Farrar's willing to dangle you off balconies to prove a point, we're running out of time."

"What about you?" I asked, turning to Adrian. "Do you know how long he's keeping you in town?"

He shook his head. "I'm at his beck and call at the moment. I'm not supposed to leave Julian's flat unless ordered. My phone is still confiscated."

"How did you do it, by the way?" Julian asked, looking at his brother curiously. "How did you get her to lie under compulsion?"

Adrian shrugged. "I didn't."

Julian frowned at him. "That's not possible."

He sounded like Kalare.

"You know compulsion is a two-way conduit," Adrian replied. "You can't compel someone to do something that is completely beyond their nature. But you also can't compel someone to do something *you* don't want them to do. It's about willpower, on both sides. I didn't want Caitlin to answer those questions. But I did want her to stay safe. My desire to see her safe activated the cascade, but my desire for her to not answer my questions kept me from actually compelling her."

"You *partitioned?*" Julian asked, looking stunned. "That's something gatekeepers can't even do."

"I…I didn't know it was called anything," Adrian admitted. "I just knew I couldn't compel Caitlin. I promised her I wouldn't."

"Shit," Julian said, leaning back. "That's good. No way Farrar will believe you're capable of that."

"So we're safe, for now?" I asked. "Farrar believes that Adrian really asked me all those questions, and that I gave truthful answers?"

Julian rubbed his face, lost in thought. "Yeah," he said finally. "He must. You both may have just bought us some breathing room." He laughed, unexpectedly. "No wonder he was so bent out of shape tonight. Council's telling him you're an Unmaker, and he's got evidence right in front of him that says you're not."

"What did Farrar say about my Myriad guard?"

"Nothing. Said it wasn't my concern. He's playing all this close to the chest."

"So we continue to hold our breath," I muttered.

Adrian rested his hand on my back, since I was hunched forward. "Have you searched for Lucian tonight?"

"No," I admitted. "I was waiting for you guys."

I closed my eyes, thinking of Lucian.

He appeared right at our feet, asleep on his back as usual. He was wearing the same jeans but a different shirt; blue this time.

We all knelt around him. "Lucian," I murmured. "Can you hear me?"

He twitched.

I glanced at Adrian and Julian excitedly. "Sweetheart, can you hear me?"

His eyes pinched, but didn't open. I rested my hand on his shoulder—or at least tried to, my hand still went straight through him.

Adrian tried waking him up, and Julian. No luck.

"What if we—"

The world tilted, and I opened my eyes to the bright red blinking numbers on my alarm clock. I turned it off and sat, blinking.

"They there?" Kalare asked from her bed.

I nodded. "You should grab coffee with Julian if you can. Catch up."

She nodded. "Lucian still there?"

"Yes, he's still there."

Kalare grunted. "That's something at least."

"You look like crap," Stacee said, sitting across from me at breakfast.

"Not sleeping well," I replied. Not true, exactly. Sleeping fine, just not *resting*.

My phone buzzed, and I pulled it out of my pocket. It was a text from Trish: *Tried to invite your boyfriend out for a hike with me and Ben, but I can't seem to find him.*

I quickly typed back: *He surprised me with a visit to New York. He's staying with his brother a few days. I think he'll be back soon.*

Trish texted back a thumbs-up.

I hesitated, wanting to ask her how Jenny and Mark and Meghan were, but breakfast was almost over and I didn't have time to get into a long conversation.

It was almost nine. Truitt, Stacee, Vi, and I cleared our dishes before parting ways to meet up with our mentors. Candace had me label and categorize their master patterns and run a few errands around to different departments. I was slowly learning the layout of the building. She even got Olivia to up my keycard clearance so I wouldn't have to ask someone to open the door for me every time she sent me past level five.

After lunch, I met up with Olivia. She asked me how Candace was, and I told her she was great and kind and I was learning a lot from her and her other assistants. I even told her the story about going to Maureen for quotes, instead of Billy, and she laughed.

"She likes the sugar cookies," Olivia confided. "The cafeteria keeps them stocked just for her."

She asked me how my project was going, and I told her I had all the patterns complete for the look she'd approved and all the pieces cut out. I was ready to start staining the silk, and then it was on to sewing.

"You *are* fast," she muttered. "Just don't mistake speed for quality."

I promised her I was being meticulous, and she looked amused and excused me to go work.

I spent the rest of the afternoon constructing the dress. It was simple, a high boat neck gown with three-quarter sleeves, fitted to the hips and then pencil-width to the floor. It was extremely simple, but striking. With the cape, it would be stunning, riding the line between fantasy and modern couture.

I was about to call Trish as we were all walking out after dinner when I got a text from Kalare: "Curb. Escalade."

I stared out through the glass doors.

She had to be kidding me.

I plastered on a smile and turned to the others. "Adrian's taking me on a date. I'll be back later."

"Gross," Stacee said.

"We ever gonna get to meet him?" Truitt asked.

"Hope so!" I waved at them as they got to the street corner. Once again, I waited for them to walk out of sight before I climbed into the Escalade.

Kalare was silent, as usual. It wasn't safe to talk in the car.

We pulled into Julian's garage and walked up the stairs. I remembered to look surprised this time when I saw Adrian.

"What's he doing here?" I asked Farrar, nodding at Adrian.

"He's going to ask you some questions. It shouldn't take long."

I looked at him, puzzled, and sat on the couch.

Vincent and Javan were standing near the windows. Julian was nursing a whiskey in a wingback chair, looking his usual, bored self. It was only because we'd spent so much time together lately that I knew it was an act. Well, mostly an act.

Kalare sat in a chair next to my couch and kicked her boots up on Julian's coffee table. He frowned at her. She ignored him.

"Adrian, please ask Caitlin what she is."

Adrian glanced at Farrar. Farrar did not repeat the question.

Adrian turned to me, his eyes cascading into swirling silver. "Caitlin," he said with an irritated sigh, "what are you?"

I blinked, pretending to go blank. "I am a girl," I said automatically.

Adrian glanced at Farrar. "Ask her," Farrar said, "what two plus two is."

He did.

"Four," I replied.

"Ask her what the square root of seventy-three is."

Adrian asked me.

I thought about it for a long moment, keeping my expression neutral. Could an odd number even have a square root? Would it be a fraction? "I don't know," I said finally.

"She's…not great at math," Adrian explained.

"Ask her how she feels about demons," Farrar said.

From math to personal feelings? What was he getting at?

"Caitlin, tell me how you feel about demons," Adrian said.

I blinked again. "I don't like them," I said robotically. "I don't like what they do."

"What do they do?" Farrar had Adrian ask me.

"They kill women," I replied. "To make more of you."

That much was true. Farrar glanced at Vincent and Javan before turning back to Adrian.

"Ask her what she thinks about vampires."

"Caitlin," Adrian said slowly. "What do you think about vampires?"

Shit. What answer was he looking for? I decided to go with the most literal approach.

"They are immortal. They drink blood. They have pretty eyes."

Kalare managed to turn her snort into an almost-believable sneeze.

"Ask her," Farrar corrected himself, "how she *feels* about vampires." Adrian asked.

"They are interesting," I said as blandly as possible. "They are strange. They are mostly nice, except Sabine, and sometimes Mariana."

That was as much of the truth as I was willing to spit out.

"How do you feel about the Council?" Farrar had Adrian ask.

"I don't know the Council," I replied.

"How do you feel about the Council's actions concerning you?"

"I am grateful for their protection," I said monotonously. Was that too ass-kissy to be believed? "I am frustrated the Council makes me hide things from my family and friends."

I hoped that was good enough. Grateful but irritated, like a normal teenager.

"If you could harm the Council, would you?" Farrar made Adrian ask.

I blinked, a frown creasing my forehead. "I don't understand."

Farrar made Adrian repeat the question.

"No," I said simply. Sometimes it was better to be short with my answers.

Out of the corner of my eye, I saw something small and white fly and land on Julian's shirt. Was that a paper football? Farrar looked sternly at something just past my field of vision.

"What?" Kalare said, somewhere out of my line of sight. "You expect me to take this seriously? This girl is no more capable of harming us than I am of becoming the Queen of England. You know I'm against this interrogation, I've filed a formal complaint. You can make me sit here and watch this, but you can't make it worth my time."

I heard a rustling of clothing and her boots across the floor. "You got any more of that whiskey, J?" I heard her call from what I assumed was the kitchen.

"Top shelf, second cupboard," he called, sounding bored. "Bring the whole bottle."

Farrar looked displeased. But it was better for them to look bored than it was for them to look anxious. If they looked anxious, it might appear that they were worried about me. If they were worried about me, it meant they liked me. If they liked me, it might mean they were in league with me. And if I was an Unmaker, like they suspected, that made them the Council's enemy.

Yes, far better to appear insolent than mutinous.

Kalare returned with the bottle, slapping down a glass before filling it, and Julian's, to the brim.

"I do love your little meetings," Julian drawled, "but this *is* my apartment. Paid for by me. I've got a show on at eight, and I'd really love you all to be gone by then."

Farrar stiffened, but turned to Adrian. "One last question. Ask Caitlin the name of your father."

Adrian looked puzzled, but turned to me. "Caitlin, what is the name of my father?"

"He called himself Tommie," I said. "I don't know his real name."

Farrar sighed, looking as irritated as we all felt. "Stand up," he said, but he was talking to Adrian, not me.

Still cascading, Adrian stood, frowning. Farrar searched his eyes, even holding onto Adrian's face to look closer. After a long, long moment, Farrar released him.

"Enough," he said finally. "Adrian, wipe her memory of this meeting. Kalare, take her home."

Kalare stared longingly at her full glass of whiskey, then stood. Adrian did his usual spiel of "you lost track of time," and "you were daydreaming."

I blinked and stood when he was finished, following Kalare out of the room.

As usual, we said nothing on the drive home. With Farrar using Julian's apartment as a temporary base, Kalare had been my night-guard more often than not. I wasn't complaining.

She met me in my room after parking the car.

"At least he didn't throw me off a building this time," I said as soon as she shut the door.

She snorted. "I could tell he was frustrated. I think he's beginning to question the Council's evidence. Julian caught me up on Adrian's partitioning. That's a Hail Mary that's saving our asses big-time."

"He keeps it up, though, I'm going to forget one of these times to pretend that I haven't been through this before. I'm getting my lies mixed up."

"Just pray he doesn't ask you the same question twice."

I yawned, sinking onto my bed. "Do you—"

I was cut off by a knock at the door. Kalare quickly disappeared into my bathroom. I looked through the eye hole then opened the door.

"How'd your date go?" Stacee asked, grinning.

I grinned back. "None of your business."

"That well, huh?"

I laughed. "What's up?"

"We're watching a movie, wanna join?"

Honestly, that sounded kind of nice. But I didn't need to fake the yawn that escaped me. "I'd love to, but between my new mentor and my project, I'm exhausted. Maybe tomorrow?"

She nodded and wished me a good night. I closed the door and let Kalare out of the bathroom.

"I killed a spider for you," she said, tossing a wad of toilet paper into the trash. "You're welcome."

"My hero." But I was secretly grateful. I hated killing spiders. "I know it's like, eight-thirty, but I'm gonna go to bed."

Kalare snorted. "You're the worst teenager ever."

"Yeah, yeah."

I changed into some shorts and a tank top. The air conditioning unit was acting up again and the room was hot. I crawled into bed, turned off the light, and fell almost immediately to sleep. It only felt like five minutes later that someone gently nudged me awake.

"Cait?"

I blinked, opening my eyes. It was dark in the room still. I looked up at the figure next to me.

"Adrian?"

He smiled. "Hi."

"What are you doing here?" I murmured sleepily.

"I kind of missed you."

"Mmm," I purred, rubbing my face against his knee. "I missed you, too. How are you here, though? I—I—" I interrupted myself with a huge yawn. "I thought you were stuck at Julian's?"

"Julian threw a fit, said this whole operation was a sham and he was sick of it. Told Farrar he was going to take me out on the town and not come back until we were both, and I quote, 'shit-faced.'"

I laughed into his knee. "That's funny. Bet Farrar liked that."

"Cait."

"Mm?"

He softly brushed the hair off my face. "Julian gave us one night."

I blinked groggily, turning to face him. His eyes were already burning a low silver, but not—what was it Kalare had called it again? Cascading? They weren't cascading, just glowing. "What do you mean?" I asked, still really not awake.

"I made a deal with him and Kalare. We have one night to…to do whatever we want."

I blinked again, slowly. "How?"

"He and Kalare will keep guard in exchange for an unspecified favor of enormous proportions."

I felt like I could barely breathe. "Are we having sex?"

He froze. "No! I mean—we don't have to do anything. We don't have to do anything, Cait. I haven't seen you in weeks. I just wanted a few hours for us to be alone." His eyes slowly met mine. "But if you want to, we can."

My heart jumped in my chest, pounding.

"I haven't shaved," I whispered. "My legs are like cactuses."

His mouth twitched in a smile. "I like cactuses. Under-appreciated plant."

"Do you have a condom?" I asked, freaking out.

He blinked at me. "I'm sterile."

Ah, yes. "What about STDs?" I blurted. Because there's no sexier foreplay than talking about STDs.

He blinked again. "Cait…I've never done this before. And even if I had, we don't get diseases, and we don't pass them on."

I mentally smacked myself. I knew that already. "Right, yes, shit. I'm sorry. I'm ruining this. I just woke up and I'm very confused."

He smiled softly. "You're not ruining anything. And I was serious when I said we don't have to do anything. We can spoon all night if you want. Or write terrible poetry. Or play Obscure Hangman."

I laughed. And then my mind rewound and snagged on his earlier statement: he hadn't done this before.

Adrian was a virgin. I mean, I'd suspected, but he'd never really spelled it out before. I was his first girlfriend and there were strict rules about the whole no-coitus-with-humans thing, but for all I knew he'd lost his v-card a long time ago with some vampire girl.

"So," I said slowly, "I've also never done this before. So…and, well, we've never really talked about this. And…" I blushed hard, glad it was dark in my room. "Look, can we just…play it by ear?"

He smiled. "Yes. Just tell me to stop if I do anything you're uncomfortable with."

I nodded very seriously. "Same."

I pulled him close and kissed him, it suddenly clicking in my brain that he was really here, and we were really alone—really, truly alone—for the first time in months. But he gently pushed me back. "Cait," he said, eyes finding mine in the darkness. "I'm serious. I want you to know that no matter what happens tonight, I love you. I—" he ran a hand down his face, frustrated. "I can't explain. I speak five languages and I don't have the words." He frowned softly, thinking. "You make sense to me in a way nothing in the rest of my life makes sense. You are…" he shook his head, unable to speak. I'd never seen him this tongue-tied before. "I love you," he said finally. He cupped my face in his hand. "I love you," he repeated.

And then his mouth was on mine.

As the kiss deepened, I made some little noise that I hadn't necessarily intended to make and then his eyes were burning even brighter and he was on top of me, but frozen, arms locked around me like a vise, breathing hard. I could feel his heart beating through his chest.

"Are you okay?" I whispered.

He didn't respond for a moment. Finally, he relaxed just enough to hide his face in my neck. "Yes," he murmured. "I'm just fucking nervous."

"You know what's crazy?" I said, my heart beating furiously. "I kind of feel like crying."

He pulled back enough to look at me, horrified.

"No, I mean like, like, I'm happy, but scared." He didn't look reassured. I knew I was messing this up. "For some reason that's making me feel like I should burst into tears."

It was true. I could feel them clogging the back of my throat.

I put my hands on either side of his face and smiled even as a few rebellious tears slid down my cheeks. He looked absolutely horrified. "No, believe me, I'm h-happy." I started trembling, but I smiled up at him, feeling a billion things at once. "I'm *so* happy," I whispered. "I think I'm just scared about how happy I am."

Finally, he nodded, as if he understood. I tightened my grip, crushing him against my chest. "I'm going to just hold you for a second," I explained, every muscle in my body shaking uncontrollably, as if I were freezing cold, even though it was hot in the room. He nodded into my hair and squeezed me back.

I let the tears soak into the shoulder of his shirt. I literally couldn't explain why I was crying other than that I felt a completely overwhelming mixture of fear and gratitude and love. I think it was just too much for my brain to process all at once.

After a few minutes, I finally calmed down and loosened my death-grip on Adrian. He leaned back to look at me. I smiled, wiping away the last of the tears.

"I really don't want to break the spell, but I honestly would feel a billion times better if I could go shave my legs."

He barked a laugh and kissed me. "Of course. I'll be here."

I kissed him back and almost let myself get distracted by his enthusiastic response, but I finally tore away and stood on wobbly legs and hobbled into the bathroom, closing the door behind me.

Good Lord, I was a mess.

My reflection in the bathroom mirror was…not great. I'd fallen asleep with my hair in a messy bun and between tossing and turning in my sleep and tossing and turning with Adrian, it had gotten all gross and matted and yucky.

I also had sleep-lines across half my face from my pillow. Great.

I sniffed my arms. Yep. Definitely needed a shower.

I turned the water on hot and stood there for a long time in the spray, fighting off the occasional full-body tremble that I couldn't seem to shake.

Adrian was waiting in my bed.

We had the entire night to ourselves.

No one would know, except Julian and Kalare.

Shit, but Julian would know. That was weird. Kalare would just be amused.

Screw Julian.

No, shit, Julian was being nice. He was here to help. He was putting himself at risk so that we could be here and do…whatever.

Did I want to do whatever?

I slowly frothed shampoo through my mane of hair while I thought about that.

I was attracted to Adrian. Even when I'd initially thought he was gay, I was attracted to him. And after everything we'd been through, it went so far beyond that. I wanted him. I mean I *wanted* him.

But I loved him, too.

And I hadn't really had to think about it until now. With the Council breathing down our necks every second of the day, it hadn't even crossed my mind that we'd have an opportunity to have sex. I'd been daydreaming about the chance to steal plain old PG-kisses. Honestly, kissing was really all we'd done. Now we were here and we could do…more.

Rachel would be horrified. Joe would be disappointed. Norah would just think I was being gross.

Trish would finally be right about us. I would actually have slept with Adrian. I could see her shaking her head. It's not like she was a virgin. She and Ben had definitely had sex. Well—at least I think she had. She'd told Stephanie who'd told me, because she thought I already knew. And it wasn't like Trish would disapprove of me getting some action, but even after our Central Park heart-to-heart, she was still so anti-Adrian that I couldn't help but imagine her disgust.

What would my mom have thought?

We'd never really talked about sex. I mean, by the time I was in high school, she'd already started to get sick. There hadn't been the time or the emotional energy to talk about boys. I didn't notice them at all. I didn't have room for them when my mom was dying right in front of me.

But she was gone now, and I'd never asked her. I didn't even know if she and my dad had waited until they were married. Or if she'd had sex with anyone before my dad. Or if my dad had had sex with someone before my mom. They were all questions I hadn't thought to ask. Rachel might know—but Rachel would judge me if I brought up stuff like that. Or would she? She'd been surprisingly not-judge-y lately. She and I had spoken a few times on the phone since I'd last seen her. We were good now, we were okay. But I couldn't ask her about this. I couldn't ask anyone.

But shit—Adrian was out there *now*.

In my bed.

He'd been in my bed before. We'd slept next to each other dozens of times. And that had been amazing. I'd loved the simplicity of that, the lack of expectation. Just curled up against him, safe.

But he was here, and he was mine, and he was waiting.

What did *he* want? I hadn't exactly asked him point-blank.

Shit, this was confusing. Shit, double-shitting shitballs.

I didn't know what to do.

I shaved my legs carefully. Even if we just cuddled I didn't want to scratch him with my porcupine leg hair.

And if we did have sex, did he prefer a full Brazilian sort of situation down there, or did he care? Did *I* care? Shit.

There was a light knock on the door followed by a soft, "Cait?"

"I'll be out in a minute!" I called, dropping the razor. "Almost done!"

"Okay," he said, sounding amused. "No rush."

My brain went suddenly mute, like it couldn't possibly think any more coherent thoughts. I finished shaving in a daze and finally turned off the water. I peeked out from the edge of the curtain—good, he hadn't come in.

I toweled off my hair but didn't brush it—it was going to get tangled again anyway. Or was it?

Shit.

I wrapped myself back up in the towel, turned off the bathroom light, and opened the door.

He'd kept the lights off in the room, which was a relief. I padded over to the bed in my bare feet and stopped. He was sitting on the edge, still fully-clothed. Well, he had his shoes and socks off. But everything else was in place.

His gaze traveled the length of my body. He cleared his throat, tried to speak, and couldn't. He cleared his throat and tried again. "So, you're in a towel."

I nodded. "Yes. That is accurate."

We stared at each other for a long moment.

"Are you…are you just wearing the towel?"

I nodded again and did a weird little wand motion with my hand. "Ten points to Gryffindor."

If I was making Hogwarts jokes, this did not bode well for us.

His lip twitched in a smile. "Should I—take off my shirt?"

I blushed instantly, and the room felt suddenly warmer. I couldn't even come up with a witty response, so I just nodded stupidly.

His eyes flicked down to the edge of my towel, then back to my face. Without breaking my gaze, he reached for the neck of his shirt and pulled it over his head.

Sweet Jesus.

It had been a while since I'd seen him shirtless. It's not that I forgot, exactly, how beautiful his body was, it was more that in-between viewings, I convinced myself that I was exaggerating.

But it wasn't an exaggeration. He was mesmerizing.

And I felt like I was going to pass out. He saw the look on my face.

"Cait, we don't have to—"

"I know," I interrupted. "I know. Just…give me a second."

He sat there politely, shirtless on my bed.

How did I deserve this? What on earth had I done in my short and unremarkable life to deserve this moment?

Nothing. I'd done nothing interesting or brave or selfless or good or kind. And yet Adrian was still here. And I was here.

I took a deep breath.

"So, no one's ever seen me naked before," I admitted, trying to sound like I was talking about the weather, or sports, or other un-interesting things.

"Same," he murmured.

We were lit mostly by the faint orange glow coming through the windows. My room faced an alley, and the building across from me had no windows, just old brick, so I often slept with the blinds up because no one could see in. There was also no fire escape and I was on the fifth floor, so no one could *get* in, either.

I was gripping the towel so hard my knuckles were white.

I stood there so long Adrian finally said, "You don't have to—"

I dropped the towel.

Well, I dropped the towel to my waist. Baby steps.

Adrian's eyes flicked down, then back up to my face, then down again, as if he couldn't decide if he should look or not.

"Now we're even," I said, nodding at his bare chest.

"Yeah," he laughed, but it was strained. "I guess so."

"They're real, by the way," I said, feeling weirdly chatty.

He nodded slowly. "Yep," he confirmed, "they very much look real."

A long moment passed in silence with Adrian's gaze constantly flicking back and forth between my chest and my face. "Am I…this feels so weird. Can I…?"

I blushed. "I didn't drop my towel to test your ability *not* to look."

Slowly, he let his gaze travel downward, and it stayed there for a good long time.

"I don't think this is the proper way to do things," I said finally. "I'm pretty sure we're supposed to just jump into the whole 'having sex' thing and do a lot less of the 'awkward, half-naked conversation' thing."

"I'm pretty sure we get to make the rules," he said, looking me in the face. "And I like awkward, half-naked conversations. It might be my new favorite type of conversation."

I laughed because he was trying to lighten the mood, and it honestly was funny. The whole situation was actually really funny. But as composed as I finally looked on the outside, I was still freaking the hell out on the inside.

"So, do you want to…get…more naked?" I asked.

He nodded. "I do. I very much want to get more naked." But he hesitated. "Do *you* want to get more naked?"

I couldn't help but glance down at the waist of his jeans. "We could do it at the same time. Like ripping off a band-aid. Except the band-aid is our clothing."

He nodded as if that were a totally logical explanation. "Okay."

He stood slowly, his hands going to the button of his jeans. I watched, fascinated, as he worked the zipper and slid the jeans to the ground, kicking them to the side.

I stood in my towel; he stood in his boxer briefs.

"On three?" I suggested, feeling a little light-headed.

He hooked his fingers in the elastic of his underwear. "One."

I trembled. "Two."

At the same time, we said "Three," I dropped the towel, and he dropped his boxers.

"Holy shit."

"What?" he asked, covering himself up on reflex.

"No!" I said, blushing. "I'm so sorry, no, it's beautiful! I've just never seen one up close before."

"It's…beautiful?"

"No! I mean…yes? I don't know. It's…it's there. On you. Right there."

I pointed at his nether region.

He turned bright red but remained calm. "Yes, that is where such things tend to be."

"Shit, I'm so sorry, I'm babbling."

"No, I…thank you, for thinking it's beautiful. When you said 'holy shit,' I thought it was a negative 'holy shit.' Like, a critical 'holy shit.' Like, 'holy shit, that's a really underwhelming penis.' "

"No!" I breathed, mortified. "Not at all. I mean, I don't really have anything to compare it to except my anatomy books and HBO, but it looks wonderful."

He barked a laugh, burying his face in his hands, which left the view open for me to stare.

And stare I did. Finally, he looked back at me. "How about we just…appreciate the view for a moment?"

I nodded, blushing again, but already feeling a little less self-conscious.

I let my gaze wander where it wanted, knowing he was standing four feet away from me, doing the exact same thing.

After a good thirty seconds, I admitted, "Naked bodies are kind of weird."

He laughed again. "Yeah. But nice."

"Yeah," I agreed. "They *are* nice."

"So," he said, glancing at the bed. "You want to write some really bad poetry?"

Instead of answering, I stepped forward and stopped just shy of touching him. He looked down at me, his gaze firmly planted on my face, less because it seemed like he was trying to keep himself from looking anywhere else and more because it seemed as though my face was actually where he wanted to look.

I plonked my forehead on his chest.

He hesitated, but a moment later I felt his arms come around me, pressing me lightly against his torso. It was crazy how different it all felt when there were no clothes in the way. I could feel him suck in a sharp breath as our naked chests met. Slowly, I slid my arms around around his waist.

He slid his hands up my back and up into my hair, looking down at me.

"Caitlin," he said quietly, looking serious. "I am in no way disappointed by your naked body."

I tried to suppress a smile, but couldn't. "That is the most romantic thing I have ever heard."

He grinned. "Let me try again: you are so beautiful it causes me physical pain to look at you."

I cocked my head to the side, frowning. "I think that might have been a step backward, actually."

He laughed, then turned serious. "You are, in your entirety, what I want," he said finally. "You are so beautiful."

I stared up at him, at his burning silver eyes. "So are you."

I had the sudden urge to push him back onto the bed, less because I was in a rush to get things started and more because I thought it would be funny and the moment had gotten super serious. The nerves were starting to come back.

Instead of pushing him, I kissed him, reaching up to hold onto his shoulders.

He tightened his grip around my waist.

And then something touched my leg.

"*Holyshitwhatisthat?*" I asked, jumping back.

He sighed, looking down. "That would be my penis again, saying hello."

I leaned down and stared at it. "Whoa. I didn't know it could move that much."

"Yep," he confirmed. "It…does that."

"Aw, why is it going away?" I asked, disappointed.

He scrubbed both his hands across his face. "God, Cait, you are literally killing me."

I hopped back to him and wrapped my arms around his torso. "No! I'm sorry! I'm just curious! This is new! This is all *very* new."

He looked down at me sternly. "The next time something happens, can you just…look less like a small child examining an interesting new bug? It's kind of wreaking havoc on…things. For me."

I nodded vigorously. "I am very sorry. I apologize. I will be one-hundred-percent focused and sexy as hell from here on out."

He snorted. "This is going so well."

I wiped the grin off my face and turned serious. "Adrian, I…thank you. For making this possible. For being here."

I felt like I had so much more to say, but I couldn't find the words.

He kissed me lightly.

And then the kiss turned deeper.

I didn't flinch this time when I felt him move. My grip on his back tightened.

He turned, holding me, and swept back the sheets, lowering me to the bed.

He had that look in his eyes again, the one that he didn't let me see very often, the one that said he wasn't thinking about the Council or about rules or about anything or anyone other than me.

Me.

He slid into bed and pulled the sheet back over us. My hair was still damp against the pillow but it was hot inside the room and it felt cool against my neck.

Adrian propped himself up on one elbow and looked down at me. I could feel the panic returning, adrenaline coursing through me. My skin felt like it was buzzing. Were we really doing this? Would it hurt? What if I sucked at it? What if *he* sucked at it? What if it changed things?

"How far do you want to go?" he asked quietly, interrupting my thoughts. I'd been staring straight at his collarbone, avoiding his face.

I shook my head, feeling weird and almost helpless in my indecision. "I don't know."

He didn't say anything, just lay down next to me.

"I want to be sure," he said after almost a full minute of silence. "I want us both to be sure."

I started trembling. "I'm so sorry," I whispered, feeling the tears threatening again. "You went to all this trouble."

"No," he murmured, pushing my hair back so that he could see my face. "Don't be sorry. I didn't come here expecting anything. I just wanted to be with you for one night without worrying about anyone else. That's all."

I nodded, but I was crying and shaking. "I'm just so scared. I don't know why. I want to. I *love* you. But I…I—"

He interrupted me with a light kiss. It was so soft and so tender it made me cry even harder. I buried my face in his chest and he wrapped his arms around my shoulders.

"It's not the right time, that's all," he said, holding me. "And that's okay."

"Are you sure?" I mumbled, hiccuping. I felt guilty, for some reason. I knew that the feeling of guilt was wrong, but it was there, sitting in my chest like a lead weight.

Adrian tilted my face so that I was looking at him. "Caitlin Holte, it would kill me if you'd simply done this because you thought I wanted to. And I *do* want to—but not until it's right. And that's not tonight. And that is not only fine, it's *good*. It means we value what we have. It means that this is important. And it *is* important. At least, it is to me."

I smiled weakly and wiped at my eyes. "It is to me, too."

He smiled. "Then everything is exactly as it should be."

"How did I deserve you?" I whispered.

He frowned, but it was his thinking frown, not his upset frown. "I don't…I don't think we ever really deserve each other. I think we just have to be grateful that we have the time we have."

I nodded. It was just like Adrian to get super deep when we were both naked.

"I'm going to put my clothes back on," he said slowly. "I think I'll do something stupid if I keep touching you like this."

I nodded, but for some reason the idea of him putting his clothes back on made me unbearably sad. Like he was rejecting me.

"Wait," I said, putting my hand on his chest. "Can you…can we be…partly naked?"

That came out wrong. Or at least, it sounded stupid. "I mean, I understand what you're saying. But I want to be near you, even if we don't…do things. Does that make sense?" I asked, looking up at him, hoping desperately that he understood.

He nodded. "I would like that."

He kissed my forehead, then disentangled himself from me and stood, fishing around the floor for his boxer briefs. I slid slowly out of bed and got some underwear and a tank top from my drawer and slipped them on. When I turned around, he was already lying back in bed, waiting for me.

I slipped in next to him and glued myself to his side. He wrapped me up in his arms, and once again I felt like bursting into tears. Not because we weren't having sex—but because I didn't understand how I could possibly love someone as much as I loved Adrian.

And I didn't understand how he could possibly love me as much as he did.

SABOTAGE

23

I didn't dream that night. No regular dreams, and no formless, white dreamscape.

I did wake up several times to make out with Adrian. That was pretty nice.

Who am I kidding? It was the best ever in the history of people making out. His skin was just so soft. I found myself rubbing my cheek on his chest and running my hands up and down his back. He would snort-laugh then, because I was tickling him on accident, and then he would tickle me back, and then we'd get distracted with wrapping ourselves around each other and kissing and that would devolve into snuggling, which would devolve into sleeping, and then one of us would move inadvertently, which would wake the other one up, and we'd start the process all over again.

It's hard to describe that night adequately. It just sounds cheesy every time I try to put it into words. I loved the kissing and all of that but honestly my favorite moments were when he fell asleep just before

I did, and I could look at him, totally at peace, and feel like I was going to explode because I couldn't possibly be happier.

Around four-thirty, the alarm went off, waking us both. I knew he had to leave before everyone else in the dorms was awake—and before Farrar realized where he'd been—but it had been so long since we'd seen each other that I didn't want him to go.

"Please stay," I mumbled sleepily. "Just five more minutes."

He sighed, burying his face in my neck. "Remember that willpower you think I have?"

I nodded.

"It's gone. You stole it from me."

I smiled and wrapped my arms around his back, squeezing him close. "Good."

"Not good," he mumbled, kissing my neck slowly and methodically from my ear to my shoulder. "Not good at all."

I shivered. He pulled back, eyes burning a low, molten silver, and kissed me on the lips. I ran my fingers through his hair, pulling him closer, and he kissed me again, shifting until he was on top of me.

Whoops.

His kiss had just turned deep and insistent when there was a knock at the door. We both froze. After a moment, he relaxed.

"Just Julian," he muttered, collapsing on top of me. He was heavy, but I liked it. Like a giant, solid human blanket.

Sense was starting to return. Adrian had to go. He'd probably stayed too long as it was.

"When will I see you again?" I asked his shoulder, since his face was buried in my hair.

"As soon as humanly possible," he replied, voice muffled. He sat up, arms on either side of my face. "Also as soon as vampirically possible."

I smiled. "You're a dork."

He nodded, grinning. "Mm-hmm."

Another knock sounded again, this time more urgent.

Adrian frowned at the door, then kissed me lightly. "I love you," he said, resting his forehead against mine. "And as much as I'd like to do things right now, I think we made the right choice."

"Me, too," I murmured.

He kissed my cheek gently and sat up.

Even in the dim light from the alarm clock, his body was just—wow—goodness.

He caught me staring, smiled, and swung his legs over the bed. "Where are my pants?" he muttered.

"I think I burned them while you were sleeping," I murmured, yawning, "so you could never leave."

"Sneaky," he said, finding them on the floor. "I guess I'll have to wear yours."

I grinned, sitting up. He finished dressing and sat down again to put on on his shoes. I sat next to him and drew random designs down his back, leaning my head against his shoulder.

Finally, there was nothing more to do but say goodbye.

I walked him to the door, and we both stopped.

He smiled. I wrapped him in one last hug.

There was a third knock.

Adrian sighed. "I'll see you as soon as I can," he promised.

I nodded. He let me go and opened the door, smiling at me one last time before slipping out into the hallway.

I went back to my dresser and got out a pair of sweatpants, crawling back in bed. A few minutes later, another knock came. I looked through the eyehole in the door just to make sure it was Kalare, then let her in.

"You don't look properly disheveled," she said bluntly as I crawled back into bed.

"Please tell me you guys weren't listening."

"We were up on the roof. Why, was there something to listen to?'

"Besides awkward conversations about whether we were going to have sex or not? No, not much to listen to. I may have snored a bit."

Kalare paused, looking at me. "You guys didn't get gross and freaky?"

"Nope."

"Like, was Adrian having problems, or—"

"Ew, no!" I said, throwing a pillow at her. "He's…he's definitely fine in that department, trust me. We just decided not to."

Kalare sat on the opposite bed, looking genuinely surprised. "What in the hell did you guys do all night then?"

I wrapped the blanket around me. It still smelled like Adrian. "Cuddled, mostly. Slept. Made out a bit." I closed my eyes, smiling. "It was perfect."

Kalare snorted. "I cannot wait until Julian hears about this."

"Did you guys get any rooftop action?" I asked, teasing her.

Instead of rolling her eyes, like I expected, she grew suddenly uncomfortable. I sat up quickly. "Wait, *did* you?"

"No!" she spat, leaning back against the wall. "He just…he fell asleep for a few minutes. With his…head on my shoulder," she muttered.

I grinned, loving this. "Please let me be your flower girl."

"I'll be putting flowers on your *grave* if you ever mention this again."

"All right, all right. But when you guys make sweet, sweet love, I want details."

Kalare threw the pillow back at me. "No."

I floated through breakfast with Truitt and Stacee and Violet and did all my tasks for Candace with a dreamy smile, even when she sent me down to the cafeteria to get lattes for everyone.

I met with Olivia after lunch, updating her on my progress with the project as well as my duties with Candace. She said Candace told her I was picking things up quickly and had a good work ethic. I left feeling proud.

I'd been with the business development team the day before, which meant it was time to shadow the marketing team. Leigh took me to the correct conference room and introduced me, and I did my fly-on-the-wall bit and sat at the edge of the room taking notes. I was pretty amazed by the minutiae of what went into their advertising programs. Who knew that companies had branded hexadecimal colors? It wasn't just *red*, it was #8A1420.

I took notes, but found myself drifting back to Adrian, to the night before.

I'd seen him naked. He'd seen me naked.

That was pretty awesome.

I was wondering if Julian could manage to sneak him over to the dorms again that night when the meeting broke up. I blinked, realizing I'd missed the last five minutes of the conversation, and stood with everyone, leaving the conference room. I was usually very focused: vampire stuff before and after the internship, internship stuff during the day.

But memories of naked Adrian was a legitimate mental distraction. I mean, who knew that penises were so mobile? It's like they had a mind of their own. What was he doing right now? Was he at Julian's apartment? Was he thinking of me? Could we—

Gah! No. Focus.

But shirtless, pantsless, sockless Adri—

No.

Focus.

Battling some very tasty daydreams, I headed back to the workroom. I finished hiding the zipper to the dress in the back center seam under a floor-length panel of silk and decided it was done. The dress wasn't the focal point; the cape was. I couldn't decide if I wanted to construct the shell first before staining the silk strip that would go down the spine, or dye it first.

Ah, hell, I was too excited to keep sewing.

I cut out half a dozen small pieces of the silk to test my design on. I'd never done this before, and I had no idea how the colors would take on this material—but since it was a natural fiber, not synthetic, I had high hopes. After talking back and forth with Harman down in fabrics about his dyeing technique, I'd set my base the night before, mixing it with a sodium alginate thickener and leaving it to thicken overnight. Now that it was at the proper consistency, I added soda ash and the Procion dyes. Once mixed, it had a short shelf-life, so I combined the dyes with the bases in small amounts, not wanting to waste it if I screwed up.

I did a strip of each of my six dyes on individual squares to see how the fully-saturated colors would turn out. I wasn't totally sure yet if I wanted to go primary with the colors, or throw some tertiary mixes in there to mute the effect a bit.

After an hour of mixing colors and letting them set, the first batch seemed garish, stark against the white fabric. Tertiary it was, then.

I cut out a few longer pieces and pulled out my brushes from my bag. I knew what I had pictured in my mind, but I wasn't sure how to achieve the look I wanted. The first couple of attempts failed utterly. It didn't have the free-flowing watercolor effect I wanted. I tried dampening the cloth, which ended up looking incredible. I even experimented with dribbling water down the silk to make the dye run in places, then painting over it with a light wash to make the colors bleed further. It ended up looking like molten stained glass, all reds and yellows and oranges; the setting sun melting through a forest of fall leaves. Over the next few hours, I'd collected a bit of an audience.

"I've never seen anything like that before," Stacee muttered, watching me work. "Where'd you learn that?"

"I didn't," I admitted, taping down the protective plastic sheeting to the floor for the fifth time so I didn't stain the hardwood. "I'm making this up. With a little help from Google and Mr. Harman."

Stacee shook her head. "You're nuts, Holte. Totally nuts. And I like it."

Not everyone was as complimentary. It didn't take long for the other high school interns to realize that I'd somehow gotten my hands on fabric that they hadn't been allowed to even think about using. One girl point-blank asked me if I'd stolen it from the fabric room. Even though I'd assured her I had not, she said she was going to report me to her mentor. I'd just shrugged and told her she should do what she had to do.

I was halfway through painting the final strip—the one that would actually go on the cape, not the test pieces—when I got a text from Julian that said: *Meet me out front in 5.*

We weren't supposed to leave in the middle of the day, but they didn't exactly have security guards keeping us from going. I wasn't sure how long this would take, so I capped the dye bottles and threw a sheet of plastic over my work-in-progress, then headed out front.

Julian was waiting in the back seat of an Uber, not the Escalade. He motioned for me to get in.

"What's going on?" I asked when I was buckled in next to him.

"Everything all right?"

"Farrar's sending Adrian back to Stony Creek in an hour." He glanced at the driver. The guy was playing music, but we couldn't exactly have a private conversation.

The Uber went around the corner and down about five blocks, then pulled over. Julian and I got out, and he led me into a Starbucks.

Adrian was sitting at a table, a to-go cup sitting in front of him. He stood when he saw me, smiling.

"Hey," he murmured, wrapping me in his arms. "Julian took me out for coffee so I could say goodbye."

I looked up at him, worried. "Why is he sending you back? Are you in trouble?"

He shook his head, smiling. "The opposite, actually. I'm getting my phone back. Apparently Farrar is as frustrated with the Council as we are. Reported back to them this morning, told them he saw no evidence that you were a you-know-what, or that you and I were in league, or that I was in love with you. He's going with me, taking Vincent and Javan, too, to continue the search for Lucian."

"Kalare and I will stay here as a precaution," Julian muttered at us, trying to keep his voice as low as possible in the loud cafe. "Council orders. But it looks like you guys bought us a hell of a lot of breathing room. Now that the heat's off us, Kalare is meeting with her contact to get more information. After that, we can make a more definite plan."

He glanced at his watch. "We need to go. There's an Uber waiting outside for you," he told me.

I looked at Adrian. He smiled in that incredible, soft way of his. "I'll see you soon," he promised. "I owe you a real date."

I smiled back, trying to swallow the tears that were suddenly threatening. There were still two weeks left in my internship. It wasn't that long, but it was long enough.

"Hey," I said, suddenly remembering an e-mail exchange with Trish I'd had the day before, "I promised Trish you'd help out with her brother's wedding."

"I'll be the best ringbearer possible," he said solemnly. "Or am I the maid of honor?"

I shook my head, smiling. "I'll miss you."

He kissed me softly. "See you in your dreams."

I snort-laughed, hugged him one more time while Julian kept an eye out for trouble, looking extremely uncomfortable, then went outside and jumped in the waiting Uber. Traffic was already building up for rush hour, and it seemed to take forever to get back to Myriad. By the time the Uber pulled up, I'd been gone for almost forty-five minutes.

As we stopped, I saw Olivia Renault standing in the lobby talking to Leigh and a few others I didn't recognize.

Crap.

There was no way to get past her to go to the work rooms without her seeing me. I noticed that the Uber driver had a Starbucks cup up front.

"Hey," I asked him, "is that empty?"

He nodded when he saw what I was pointing at.

"Want me to toss it for you?"

"Sure," he said, looking surprised. "Thanks!"

I grabbed it and headed to the front doors, looking properly frightened when Olivia called me over.

"Caitlin," she said, looking stern. "High school interns are not permitted off-site during program hours."

"I'm sorry," I said, looking sheepish. "They don't do hazelnut lattes at the espresso bar here and I was having a craving. My app said Starbucks was just around the corner, but it ended up being a lot further than it said. I thought I could just pop out for a minute to get it, I'm so sorry." I carefully hid the fact that the cup said "Steve," not "Caitlin."

She glanced at the empty Starbucks cup in my hand and sighed. "Get back to work. This counts as a first strike. Don't leave this building again during hours, understood?"

I nodded vigorously.

"Go on," she said, turning back to Leigh. I scampered off.

I didn't like lying to Olivia. Hell, I didn't like lying to anyone, not Trish or Rachel or even the Council. Worse, I didn't like that I was getting better at it.

I tossed the cup in the trash and headed back to the workroom.

"Where were you?" Violet asked. "You were gone for almost an hour."

"Got a call," I lied. "Took longer than I thought."

She accepted the answer immediately. "Couple people tried to peek at your dress but I shooed them away and told them to mind their own business."

I laughed at the image of Violet swatting at people and gave her a quick hug, grateful. "Thanks, Vi. You're the best."

I went back to work, finishing the paint just before six. I was worried about getting dye on the stark-white dress, so I'd quickly sewn a mannequin cover out of muslin to keep the fabric safe. I laid the painted strip of silk on the work table and covered it with plastic, then joined the others for dinner in the caf.

Since Adrian was now gone—along with Farrar, Vincent, and Javan—I watched a movie with Truitt, Stacee, and Violet back at Enneman's. After that, Truitt taught us poker, and then he and Stacee went off to "find his phone," and never came back. Violet and I played a few more rounds, but neither of us knew what we were doing, so we eventually devolved into Go Fish, which made me think of Lucian, which made me sad. We said goodnight around ten thirty and headed to bed.

Julian and Kalare were both waiting for me in my room when I got back. We headed up to the roof to talk.

"Adrian make it back all right?" I asked as soon as the door was closed behind us.

Julian nodded, grabbing a seat at the rooftop table. "Safe and snug in Stony Creek. Got his phone back, texted me himself. Farrar's pissed, though. Thinks the Council sent him on a wild goose chase. Claims they're growing paranoid in their old age."

Kalare snorted, lighting up a cigarette. "The irony is probably lost on him."

"This is great news, isn't it?" I asked, feeling a faint flutter of hope.

"Yes," Kalare said firmly, daring Julian to contradict her.

"Sort of," Julian contradicted her. "We still need to be careful. Just because Farrar's off our backs doesn't meant the Council doesn't have redundant spies."

"But his report may have convinced them that they have bigger fish to fry," Kalare countered.

"What bigger fish?" I asked.

"Hellscape's gone berserk," Kalare said around her cigarette. "No one's been able to get in for months."

"So it wasn't just you guys?"

She shook her head. "Everyone's locked out."

"Not to mention the birth rate has gotten totally out of control. They're pulling special teams just to keep track of the number of new vampires. Collecting information on the mothers alone is taking up half their back force."

"The Proceres are starting to notice. They've snatched over a hundred infants before the Council could get there."

"I hadn't heard that," Julian muttered, frowning.

"Just found out today from Ian."

"Wait," I interrupted. "What is a Proceres? And who's Ian?"

"Segment of the Outcast," Kalare said, as if that explained everything. "The Proceres, not Ian."

"What are the Outcast?"

She looked at me, then at Julian. "She doesn't know about the Outcast?"

"I assumed Adrian would have told her," he said, shrugging. Then he frowned. "Although Mariana keeps him pretty damn isolated. Maybe he doesn't know."

Kalare sighed, settling further into her chair. "I hate working with newbs. All right, short version. Outcast are all non-Covenant vampires. Either they've been exiled from the Covenant, left voluntarily, or were never members to begin with. They make up about, I dunno, maybe half the total vampires in the world."

"They're divided up into various factions," Julian added. "Covenant vampires are the largest and most powerful group. That's why we're in control. There are downsides to membership..." He glanced at his gold-plated watch, admiring it. "But there are also perks."

"Wait, hold on," I interrupted. "What are Covenant vampires?" And why was this the first time I was hearing about the fact that there were whole huge chunks of the vampire community that weren't under the direct control of the Council?

Kalare pointed at herself, then Julian. "We are. Adrian. Mariana, Farrar, Vincent, Javan. The Council is the head of the Covenant faction. Name goes back to having a covenant of peace between humans and vampires, a non-interference worldview. If members of the Proceres found you and thought you were an Unmaker, you can be sure as shit they wouldn't be playing as nicely as the Council has been. You'd be locked up and bartered and kidnapped back and forth between gang leaders."

"Not to freak you out or anything," Julian said, looking at Kalare pointedly.

"No use hiding the truth from her at this point," she said around her cigarette. "My contact, Ian, he's one of the Petitioners," Kalare explained. "Non-Covenant. Bit of a rebel, but not militant. Old as dirt and still thinks he's hot shit."

"You liked him well enough," Julian said, glancing at her.

Her face grew dark. "That was a long time ago."

Julian stole a cigarette from the pack on the table and lit it. "Before I was born."

Kalare's glower deepened. I wasn't sure if they were about to start fighting or making out.

"Wait, so is a Petitioner the same as a Procera-whatever?" I asked.

Kalare shook her head. "Both are Outcast, different factions. Polar opposite belief systems."

"Petitioners are a bit like American Protestants. Used to be Covenant, but they split off from the main church, so to speak. They're mostly pacifists." Julian paused to take a drag from the cigarette. "Proceres, on the other hand, are violent narcissists who think vampires should be at the top of the food chain and humans should be their slaves. I quite like them." He winked at me and Kalare rolled her eyes.

"If you two disagree with the Council so much, why are you still a part of their faction thing? Why not join the Petitioners?"

They both glanced at each other, then away. "Family," Julian said finally. "Usually comes down to that. And resources."

Kalare nodded. "Like Julian said, membership has its perks. Council is strict, harsh, and occasionally cruel, but they're also the oldest and most powerful vampire faction. They keep order, they keep discipline, they provide very well for their members. It's not ideal, but given our longevity, it's less…chaotic, than living without rules."

"Even when they kill your siblings?" I blurted out.

Kalare smiled darkly. "The executions do tend to make you question your loyalties." She took a long drag from the cigarette, smoking it down to embers. "When I found out about my sister, about what Farrar had done, I left for a while. That's how I met Ian. Joined up with the Petitioners for a few years. But I'd grown accustomed to order, and they were disorganized. No head, no tail, no leader, no rules, no security. Wasn't cut out to be a rebel. I was accepted back under probation. Farrar was to be my keeper for the next decade, until I'd proven myself. Getting appointed to the Praetorian Guard was his way of showing he had faith in me. It was his way of trying to get me to get ahead, to advance." She shrugged, laughing bitterly. "I was never ambitious like him. No, ambitious is the wrong word…I was never a believer."

"A believer in what?"

She stubbed out her cigarette and lit a new one. "Some people have faith in God, some have faith in humanity, others in the Universe or crystals or whatever. Farrar had faith in the Council. Absolute faith." She glanced at me. "This is the first time I've ever seen him question it."

I found Lucian again in my dreamscape. Adrian, Kalare, and I tried to wake him but couldn't. He looked thinner, smaller; the circles under his eyes were darker. He looked sick, gaunt. None of us knew why or what was happening to him. The one thing that gave us hope was that he was still alive, and still near enough for me to locate in my dreams.

Adrian wanted to sneak back to New York to look for Lucian.

Kalare talked him out of it, saying that pissing off Farrar just when he'd vouched for us to the Council was only going to hurt Lucian. Cutting back on their sleep, Julian and Kalare started combing the city when they weren't guarding me, looking for Lucian. I wanted to come with them in the mornings and evenings, but they said it was too dangerous and refused to bring me along.

But the city was huge, and as vampires, they couldn't sense other vampires.

Even narrowed down to a twenty-mile radius, in a city of eight million people, it was still like looking for a needle in a haystack.

The next few days flew by. In no time, I'd become a functioning part of Candace's team, offering to do the menial tasks the other assistants were tired of doing, partly because I wanted them to like me, and partly because I wanted to practice doing the basics. The accountants on the sixth floor got used to seeing me. A few even began to remember my name. True to my word, I brought Maureen cookies. We ate them while she gossiped about her coworkers and showed me pictures of her Pomeranians. I soaked up every nugget of information Candace sent my way and was constantly asking the other assistants questions, usually about something they were already doing so that I wasn't distracting them from their task.

My meetings with the marketing and business development teams slowly began to make sense. Most of it had gone way over my head at first, in part because they used a lot of industry jargon I wasn't familiar with. And the acronyms! My god, the acronyms. I'd finally started writing down every word I was unfamiliar with and googling it when I got back to the dorms. If I still couldn't find it, I'd ask Olivia in our little post-lunch sessions.

Jimmy got married on a perfect, seventy-five degree day in Stony Creek. Trish, Jenny, Adrian, and Stephanie sent me dozens of pictures. Adrian got a fantastic shot of Trish catching the bouquet after the ceremony, with Ben cheering her on in the background. She looked extraordinarily uncomfortable. Stephanie got a great shot of Mark and Jenny dancing. Trish got a shot of Adrian helping Mark escort a drunken second-cousin off the dance floor.

Jenny called me, said she'd talked to Meghan briefly, just a tentative "hi" and "hello," nothing more. She said it was better than the awful silence they'd had for months and thought maybe they could really talk things over soon. Apparently Meghan was basically living at Trish's while her parents were finalizing their divorce. With the amount of family they had in for the wedding, I don't know where they were putting her, but Trish said her parents didn't mind. Having met them, I knew that they probably didn't mind at all. They were good people.

Only one weird thing happened. I'd texted Adrian a picture of my cape outfit because it was finally starting to come together. Apparently he'd shown it to Mariana and Dominic, after they'd asked how I was doing at the internship. As soon as Mariana saw the outfit, she dropped her glass, shattering it on the floor. Adrian said she went pale, started trembling. When he asked her what was wrong, she wouldn't say. I made a lame joke that she thought my fashion sense was so bad that it made her want to puke. He laughed a little, but something about her reaction—and her lack of explanation—had him on edge.

Besides that, everything was going smoothly. Farrar was gone, the Council was off my back, my friends were making up, we knew Lucian was alive and nearby, and my internship was going well. I had just completed the first outfit of my final project Thursday night when Truitt, Stacee, Violet, and I walked into the workroom Friday morning.

We were all about to head to our mentors, but we usually stopped at the workroom first to grab our small sewing kits, just in case we needed them upstairs. I was going to present the outfit to Olivia after lunch as a proof-of-concept so that she'd approve materials for the other two garments.

But halfway across the workroom, I slowed, then stopped.

The muslin cover I'd made for the mannequin was in a lumpy pile on the floor.

The mannequin itself was empty.

Stacee slowed, realizing I wasn't following them, then stopped and saw what I was looking at. She rushed over to my table and picked the cover up off the floor, then turned to me, horrified.

I walked over slowly, feeling a tight knot of panic building in my chest.

I sank to my knees, gathering the shredded fabric that had once been the dress and cape. It was in mutilated strips now, no piece bigger than a dollar bill. Someone had spent hours methodically slicing it into rags.

The room began to fill up, and it didn't take long for people to notice the four of us standing in a silent circle. Even the girl who'd said she would report me to Olivia for using unapproved fabric looked horrified when she came over and saw what had happened. Someone must have told a mentor because a few minutes later a group of college interns came into the room, along with Leigh and Olivia.

They stopped at my table, surveying the damage.

I looked up at Olivia, feeling numb. "I just finished last night," I mumbled. "It was fine when I left."

My phone buzzed in my pocket but I barely noticed.

Olivia looked out over the high school interns. "Does anyone have any knowledge of who did this?"

No one spoke. Olivia's face grew dark. "Mentors, take your students to their morning tasks."

The college mentors sprang into action, grabbing their interns and hustling them out of the room.

"Ms. Rey, Ms. Kessler, Mr. Truitt, you, too."

My friends looked at me helplessly. I nodded at them to let them know it was okay. Reluctantly, they left, following their mentors. I stood slowly, gathered the shredded fabric, and set it on the table.

Then I remembered my phone. I checked it, numbly.

It was a text from Sabine. I'd gotten her number in case of emergency as soon as we'd come to New York. I had to read it three times before the message clicked. All it said was: "Hope you liked my improvements."

The look on my face must have given me away.

Before I could hide my phone, Olivia glanced at the screen. She read the message and surely could see whom it was from. I had Sabine's name programmed as the contact.

Her face went blank. "Leigh, cancel my next appointment. Caitlin, come with me."

She left quickly, and I scrambled to keep up. As we walked, she got on her phone and began to talk to someone in French, her voice growing quieter and angrier. She hung up, then called someone else, this time speaking in what sounded like German.

Since when did Olivia speak German? Or French, for that matter?

We were at her office before I could ask. She closed the door behind me and indicated that I should sit. She took her place behind her desk and let out a deep breath, then looked at me.

"I do not like bullies, Ms. Holte. I am sorry about what happened to your project. Please rest assured that the party responsible is being dealt with."

I couldn't help but let out a sarcastic little laugh. Right. Olivia Renault was going to 'deal' with Sabine Rousseau.

Olivia raised her brow. "You don't believe me?"

"I'm sorry," I said, looking down. "I know you'll try."

"I've just spoken with Farrar," she continued. "He is stripping her completely of her status as a member of the Praetorian Guard and issuing additional, formal punishments."

I nodded. It took me several moments to realize she'd said Farrar. And Praetorian Guard.

Olivia Renault didn't know Farrar. Or the Guard.

I looked up at her slowly. She slid her glasses off and set them carefully on the desk. "When Mariana contacted me last year about the idea of your applying to this internship, I resisted. She said there were extenuating circumstances about your life that her younger brother felt responsible for. Mariana was apprenticed under me in Paris over a century ago. Her word has a certain degree of clout as far as I'm concerned, but I told her you still needed to apply, like any other student."

I stared at her, not comprehending.

"Unfortunately, Farrar convinced me of the necessity of placing Sabine at Myriad as a precaution. Sabine actually has some fashion experience, so I'd hoped she would take her role seriously and help you in your studies. I'd never met the girl before, so I didn't know her... personality."

She glanced down at the desk, then back at me. "I asked Farrar not to tell you what I was. I wanted you to have a normal experience here. To rise to the challenges I set before you on your own merit, not because you were afraid of me."

I blinked, the information finally catching up with me. "You're my watcher."

She nodded. "It was the lesser of two evils. Farrar wanted to place another bodyguard here. I refused. The only option, then, was for me to keep an eye on you."

"But," I said, my brain stalling with the new information, "you're *Olivia Renault*. I'd heard about you before I ever got involved with… with the de la Maras, or Farrar. You've been at Myriad for *twenty years*."

"Yes," she said, looking tired. "Luckily, my industry is obsessed with looking young. Between rumors of plastic surgery and the newest miracle supplements, I've got another few years before people start noticing that I haven't aged." She leaned forward, growing serious. "Caitlin, I'm telling you all this because I want you to believe that Sabine will be dealt with. I also want you to understand that you have not advanced in this program because of preferential treatment. If you hadn't surpassed my expectations with that little test with Carol, I would have kicked you out after your first presentation. You have earned your place here. And you will continue to earn your place here. Is that clear?"

I nodded, slowly, thinking *No, no, it's not clear, how are you involved, how are you not* human?

"Good," she said, uncapping her pen. "I'm going to clear you for materials for all three outfits. Harman is going to huff and complain, but he'll be fine. You'll have less than two weeks to do all three looks. Can you handle that?"

I blinked, the idea of recreating the cape overwhelming me for a moment. But I nodded. "Yes."

She nodded briskly, signed the form, and handed it to me. "I'll e-mail a copy to Harman as well, so he'll be prepared."

She stood, so I stood. "My apologies again for Sabine's behavior."

I nodded, and since she seemed to be finished, I headed toward the door.

"Caitlin," she said just as I began to open it. "I wouldn't have released the materials if I didn't think you could do it. Prove me right."

My mind was still reeling, not wanting to believe that she was involved with all this, not wanting my two separate worlds to touch, especially at such a vital intersection. I respected Olivia. I valued her advice, her attention, her belief in me. Knowing she was a vampire, that she'd known who I was this whole time, made me feel…

What?

I didn't know. Off-balance, at the very least. Confused. A little betrayed.

But vampire or not, she was still a world-renowned designer. I nodded at her from the doorway.

"I will," I promised.

MYSTIC
24

ata was currently modeling my coat. I'd been having trouble deciding on the hem length and was making him try on a dream version so I could imagine it at different lengths. Julian and Adrian were apparently not asleep yet. I was fiddling around with my designs, waiting for them so we could search for Lucian once more.

"Has Kalare been successful in contacting Ian?" Data asked, not seeming to mind in the least that I was using him as a human mannequin. Or, an android mannequin. Or, well, a dream avatar android mannequin.

"Nope," I muttered, lengthening the coat by a foot until it touched the tops of Data's shiny Federation-regulation shoes. "Kalare said he went dark. I've looked for him, too. Either he's not in New York, or he doesn't sleep at night."

I'd had no word from the Council since Farrar left, and no word from Farrar, for that matter. The only thing Julian and Kalare could glean was that things were tense all around. Word of the high birthrate, and the Proceres' infant kidnappings, was starting to get around, and everyone was on edge. Between that and Ian's disappearance, we were all getting fidgety.

"While I am pleased to help you with your project," Data said politely, "I do have something to show you. It is…urgent."

I glanced at him. He was being more direct than usual.

"Why urgent?"

He didn't reply.

I glanced one last time at the design, then willed it away. Data turned and brought up a memory.

It was Lucian. Last fall, in the library. I'd been strapped into the harness, working on chemistry homework. He'd been hiding under the coffee table, staring at me.

"Where were you before?" Dream Me asked Lucian.

He stared at me from behind his big goggles, his eyes too dark behind the tinted glass to see what color they were. He replied without blinking, without breathing, without moving a single muscle besides his lips.

"Where my father lives."

Dream Me shivered, creeped out by his answer. "Did you like it there? At home?"

He tilted his head slightly further to the side and held his hands up in front of his face as if they were alien objects. "I didn't…I don't remember…these…" His expression turned frustrated. "Everything gets in the way." He let his hands drop limply at his sides again.

The memory paused and I turned to Data. "Back in Stony Creek, Kalare said there was a theory that Lucian had never gone to hell. That his body was trapped on earth while his mind was…somewhere else. Do you think that's happened again?"

Data smiled, but didn't reply.

We'd all assumed that Lucian was nearby, but simply asleep every time we looked for him. If what Data was trying to show me was correct, he wasn't just asleep, he was *trapped*, like before.

"*Why*, though," I muttered to myself. "What does Tommie gain from that when he's already in this dimension?"

I didn't know enough about how the bloodlines worked, the connections between demon fathers and their vampire offspring. I understood their physiology, at least in part, because Adrian had explained it to me, but I didn't understand their magic. I just knew that it revolved around emotions.

I looked up at Data, a look of horror creeping over my face as an idea came to me. "Demons can't feed off positive emotions: love, hope, joy, gratitude. Only negative ones. Fear, anger, envy. When Tommie touched me at the mall last year, I immediately started having nightmares. Awful, terrible nightmares. They were never happy, never good. What if… what if he was feeding off that somehow?" I glanced over at the paused memory, the blank, emotionless look on Lucian's face. "What if he's been doing that to Lucian for years? Keeping him in a nightmare so he can feed of his son's negative emotions?"

Data didn't say anything. But he didn't contradict me, either.

I felt sick to my stomach.

If that were true, then Lucian's life had been far worse than I'd imagined.

Behind Data, Adrian appeared, followed a moment later by Julian.

Adrian was smiling, but it slipped off his face the moment he saw mine.

"What's wrong?" he asked, coming toward me.

I caught him and Julian up on my theory.

Adrian looked as sick as I felt.

Even Julian looked queasy.

"That's why your father took him after our fight. "He's been draining Lucian his whole life, probably brainwashed him to do it voluntarily. He was on the verge of death, at least his body was. But if he could put Lucian back into a nightmare state, conjuring up all those negative emotions…he'd have a constant power supply."

"But demons are like vampires," Adrian argued. "We can't sense them, they can't sense us. I know Kalare told us that theory back in Stony Creek, but the fact is, demons can't feed off the emotions of vampires, only humans."

"Are you sure about that?" I countered. "Because your father pinpointed you guys. He came straight through from hell into your backyard in Stony Creek. All of you were there: Mariana, Lucian, both of you. Maybe you can't sense him, but as your father, he can sense *you*. I don't know; it all just seems like too much of a coincidence."

Adrian and Julian exchanged glances. "If that's true, then why did the Council agree that we could break the Separation of Family law? If what Kalare says is true, that law's been in place for ages."

"They didn't just *agree* that we could break it," Julian muttered. "They demanded it. I wasn't given a choice: I had to spend at least half the year in Stony Creek, even though I'd never lived with Mariana or you before."

I paced, thinking. "Maybe the Council knows about demons being able to sense their kids. Maybe they did it on purpose, to draw him there, to…"

To what?

"To trap him," Adrian said quietly, looking up at me. "But you were there. We had to split up to find you, to protect you. And he got away."

Julian looked at me as well. "And then Mariana had her vision about you. *After* our father came through the portal."

"Do you know what it was?" I asked him. Adrian didn't, but we'd never asked Julian.

He shook his head. "Visions are closely guarded because they can be interpreted and acted upon in terrible ways. Only Mariana and the Council themselves know what it was. I doubt even Dominic has been told. I know Farrar hasn't."

I sighed, frustrated. "Okay, let's say for a moment this is all true. Lucian's back in some sort of nightmare hell, but his body's here. We haven't been able to wake him up. If your dad is feeding off him, he still has to keep Lucian's body alive. But I saw you guys when you came back from hell. Another few days and your organs were going to shut down from starvation. Lucian has to be somewhere that his body can be taken care of."

"And if he can compel people," Adrian said, "then a logical place would be a human hospital."

Julian blinked. "That's brilliant. Compel the staff to care for Lucian and not ask questions. Hide out in plain sight. He knows hospitals are hard for us to be around, temptation is too strong, too much blood and misery, we'd gorge ourselves and lose control. God, why didn't I think of this before?"

"There's a lot of hospitals in New York, but that still narrows it down considerably."

"Even if we find him," I interrupted, "can we risk moving him?"

"Kalare might know of a safe clinic we could place him in," Julian suggested. "Keep him hooked up if we can't wake him."

"So it's settled?" I asked. "We'll search the hospitals tomorrow?"

"I'm on-duty as soon as I wake up," Julian said. "But Kalare can search."

"Farrar's not in town anymore," I argued. "I still have Olivia to keep me safe."

"Olivia?" Adrian asked.

Oh. I hadn't told them that part yet. "Yeah. Freaking head of Myriad is my watcher. She replaced Sabine. Look, if our theory is true, Tommie has to stay by Lucian's side to keep gaining power. You almost killed him last time, Adrian—if he's really in a human body, that kind of damage isn't going to heal quickly, even with magic. That's probably why he hasn't come after met yet—he's still recovering from the fight. He'll be glued to Lucian's side; he's not going to be anywhere near me."

After a moment, they both nodded. "All right," Julian said. "We'll start at the edge of town and work our way in. I imagine he's been close enough to come and observe you from time to time, but far enough away that we wouldn't run into him on accident. I'll catch Kalare up to speed when we wake up. Anything else to discuss?"

"One more thing," I said. "I think I have an idea of how wake up Lucian, from inside the dreamscape."

They looked intrigued.

"It's like when Adrian fought his father. Even though I didn't want to, I was strengthening Tommie because I was afraid, and he was feeding off it. But as soon as I focused on positive emotions, he couldn't draw from me anymore. But Adrian *could*. That's how we beat him. Every time Lucian's shown up here, I've been afraid."

They started nodding, catching on to my idea.

"It's worth a shot," Julian said. Adrian agreed.

I thought about Lucian, and moments later he appeared at our feet, asleep.

I laid down on the floor next to him and imagined up a dream-copy of *Frankie the Boy*. I opened to the first page and held it above him, as if he could see it.

"Once upon a time," I said, "there was a boy named Frankie who loved to do strange things…"

I read the whole book slowly, methodically, willing myself to fall deeply into the memories that had inspired the book, memories about Lucian. The whole story was about him, taken from experiences we'd shared. I'd written and illustrated it for Christmas. He'd read the thing hundreds of times. It was a story about him, as I saw him. It was a story I'd written out of love.

"Caitlin," Adrian whispered after a moment. "It's working."

I glanced at Lucian next to me. Adrian had his hand on his brother's shoulder. Solidly—no ghosting through.

Lucian's eyes pinched. He stirred, sighing.

I brushed his hair back. "Lucian…can you hear me?"

Slowly, his eyes opened.

They were blue.

I'd never seen them before. He'd always been wearing his aviator goggles.

His eyes were glassy, unfocused, the circles under his eyes deep and purple.

Finally, he seemed to see us. He glanced from Adrian to Julian to me.

"Lady?"

Then he disappeared.

"Shit," Julian said, staring at the empty white space where he'd just been. "Where'd he go?"

"Maybe I accidentally woke him up in the real world," I said, panicking. "I'm so sorry, I didn't think that would happen!"

Adrian sat back heavily. "He woke up, though. That's a good thing. He recognized you."

Lady was one of Lucian's names for me, before he'd started calling me Caitlin.

"Chances are, our father simply puts him back to sleep. He has no reason to suspect we were involved. Nobody but us even knows this place exists."

"Except he's a demon," Adrian countered, looking at his brother. "And ancient. If Utuwe is as old as the *Matris Libri* says, and if she was his first child, it stands to reason that he was alive the last time Unmakers existed. He may know exactly what just happened—he may know exactly what Caitlin is."

"If he does, he should be scared," I said. "Supposedly, I can kill him."

"But he's not," Adrian replied, sounding frustrated. "He's been shadowing you since he got to this dimension. The fact that Lucian is somewhere in the city proves that. He still wants something from you."

"Even so," Julian countered. "What's his move? Abandon Lucian? Caitlin's protected twenty-four-seven; he can't get to her while we're around."

"Maybe. But I think only one of you should go tomorrow. Let's keep a closer eye on Caitlin, not relax. If he's been healing and getting stronger this whole time, that should make us nervous."

I was about to protest, but Adrian cupped my face in his hands. "Please," he whispered. "Please do this for me. I'm not there; I can't protect you. Let them do their jobs."

I glanced at Julian. He nodded. "Okay," I said. "Only one of them will search tomorrow."

Adrian looked relieved.

"Is there anything else?" Julian asked. "Because if not, I'm gonna get a move-on with the search."

Adrian shook his head. Data said nothing.

"Meet back here tomorrow night," I told them. "Wake up."

Instantly, they disappeared.

I looked around the dreamscape one last time, then willed myself awake.

Blinking, I sat up in bed. The disorientation of waking back up in the real world was lessening over time.

"Last day," Kalare said from the opposite bed. "You ready?"

I let out a long breath. "Yes."

I caught her up on the plan, and the fact that we'd been able to wake up Lucian. She blinked, nodded, and said she'd coordinate with Julian.

Truitt, Stacee, Violet, and I scarfed our breakfasts so we could get fifteen extra minutes in the workroom before heading out to our mentors. I spent that fifteen minutes pinning and re-pinning the hem on the snow-white coat, finally deciding to leave it at the tea length I'd originally designed it for. On the two mannequins next to it stood the cape dress and the ball gown. I'd been able to re-construct the cape outfit in two days, since I'd done it once already. The ball gown was a simple enough silhouette: sweetheart neckline, a billion layers of crinoline to poof up the skirt followed by a layer of lining, covered by the silk. Whereas the cape and the jacket were white cashmere and wool with a strip of painted silk each, the ball gown was all hand-painted silk. I'd spent three full days with ten yards of it laid across our whole work table, trying to get a seamless design done.

After my first design was destroyed, most of the other interns had forgiven me for getting fabric they weren't allowed to have. And after seeing what I was *doing* with the fabric, only a few had held their grudges. There were wild rumors flying around about who'd done it. Some people had even claimed I'd done it to my own garment, to get sympathy from Olivia. That one hadn't made a lot of sense, though, and it died away. I was so engrossed in getting the three looks done on time that I barely noticed. Violet was more bothered by it than I was.

Candace and her assistants surprised me when I showed up in the launch workroom. They couldn't make it to my final presentation later that day, so they'd gone to Starbucks to get me a hazelnut latte and some donuts, and we had a half-hour mini-party. They even made me take them down to the high school workroom to show them my designs. Candace was in awe. So were the assistants. I blushed a lot as they examined my garments.

"I can't believe you're still willing to do coffee runs," Candace said, hugging me. "You're gonna be running this place in no time."

Julian and Kalare sent me vague text messages throughout the day, just a simple "Nothing yet," which I assumed meant they'd finished searching at least one hospital.

It was early afternoon, and I'd just finished sewing the hem on the coat. There was still a couple hours of work to do on the ball gown before I presented the final look to Olivia, but I was in the home-stretch. My phone rang. It was Rachel, which was odd. We'd talked a few times over the phone, but I was so busy here, and she was so busy on the ranch, that we hadn't spoken in over a week.

I hesitated. It might be important. But it was my last day and I was on a roll and Olivia didn't like us to be on our phones. I ignored the call and put it back in my pocket, gathering the coat from the sewing machine to head back to my table.

Before I got halfway there, my phone rang again. I quickly draped the coat on the mannequin and stepped into the hall.

"Hello?" I said, dodging an intern who was running from the remnant room to the workroom.

"Caitlin? Hi, sweetie."

Her voice sounded strained, but I was distracted by the bustle in the hall.

"Hi, Rachel. What's up?"

"Um…" she trailed off and cleared her throat. "I have some bad news."

I froze. "What kind of bad news?"

"It's—honey, it's your grandma. She passed away last night."

It took a long moment for my brain to register what she was saying. I'd thought she was going to say something about Adrian or Lucian.

"What?"

"She caught a cold on her trip to Buffalo last month, and apparently it developed into pneumonia. She didn't tell us. She didn't tell anyone. Her bridge club went over to her house when she didn't show up for their game last night. I'm…I'm so sorry, Caitlin."

I stood there in the hall, not bothering to move this time when a few interns hurried past me to get to the remnant room.

"I don't understand," I said finally. "What do you mean?"

"Caitlin…your grandma died. In her sleep."

I put a hand to my head and turned in a short, helpless circle, then leaned against the wall. "What do you mean she's dead?" I asked again, starting to shake. "She's fine. I was going to visit her on my way home."

"I know, honey. I'm so sorry."

I slid down to the floor, "She's not that old," I said, as if I could convince Rachel of the absurdity of this situation.

"She was eighty-five," Rachel reminded me, gently.

"That's not that old!" I protested.

"I know this isn't…I know this is hard. But her funeral is tomorrow, in Mystic. Her will had all her funeral arrangements planned out. Her lawyer contacted me and said that her house will be put on the market as soon as…as soon as you've gone through it and claimed what you want. She said anything you didn't want would be sold."

What was she talking about? What was happening? I had a dress to finish. I had a presentation in two hours. The biggest presentation of my life.

"Caitlin?" Rachel asked after I'd been silent for a long time. "Do you want to go to the funeral? I can pick you up in the morning."

I buried my eyes in the heels of my hands, letting the phone drop away from my ear.

I could hear my aunt calling my name.

"Adrian's cousin lives here," I said, speaking back into the phone after a long moment. "I'll get a ride with her and meet you there."

"Are you sure?" she asked, hesitating. "I don't mind coming to get you."

"It's fine," I said shortly. "If you come all the way to the city that's an extra two-hour drive. What time is the funeral?"

"Two p.m. Do you want me to bring Joe or Adrian?"

"Joe's busy," I said, feeling myself slipping into automatic mode where I was speaking words but not really feeling anything. "But if Adrian has time, I'd like him there."

"Okay," she said. "I'll speak to Mariana."

"Thanks," I said automatically. "And…she's probably busy, but could you ask Trish? If she could come?"

"Of course," Rachel said. Then we both went silent for a long moment. "Caitlin, I love you," she said quietly. "And I'm so sorry."

I paused, not knowing what to say. "I love you, too."

I had two hours left to finish the dress. I wiped at my eyes, slid the phone back in my pocket, and went back into the workroom, operating on automatic until it was four.

I presented the looks to Olivia robotically, briefly explaining that I'd just gotten bad news, apologizing for my scattered presentation. She said she understood.

An hour later, Olivia took me to the top floor, several college interns wheeling my three outfits on mannequins.

We went into Peter Newport's office, the head of Myriad. His office was twice the size of Olivia's.

I was one of five students who'd made it, though I didn't know who the other candidates were. I hoped one of them was Stacee or Truitt. I knew Violet hadn't made it in, even though she'd worked hard on her new ideas.

Olivia whispered something to Peter, and he glanced at me, nodding.

"It's nice to meet you, Caitlin," he said, holding out his hand, which I shook. "I'm Peter Newport. Olivia speaks highly of you."

"It's nice to meet you," I managed, hoarsely. My voice wasn't working right.

I showed him my outfits, explained my brand. He asked me questions about my experience, what got me into fashion. I told him about my mom, her death. I hadn't meant to mention that part, but it kind of slipped out. He asked me about my technique, how I'd done the staining. He examined the stitches, the hand-painted dye. He told me he was impressed.

I tried to pay attention, to smile, to be engaged. This was the most important meeting of my life. But everything was foggy. I wasn't even thinking about my grandma, it was more like I was underwater, where everything was blurry, where the sounds were muted, where nothing made sense. It was just noise.

I remember shaking hands with him, with Olivia, and being dismissed. They'd make their decision by Monday. I'd know then.

I met everyone in the cafeteria for our last dinner together. I knew they'd all presented to Olivia, but I didn't feel like asking if any of them had spoken to Mr. Newport.

It should have been jovial, we should have been celebrating. But they could tell something was wrong. They just weren't brave enough to ask *what*. I didn't blame them. I knew I could be scary when I was like this. When I was in shut-down mode. I'd been like this when I first showed up at Stony Creek, fresh off my mom's funeral.

And now my grandma.

It wasn't processing. It wasn't sinking in. She'd always been healthy. Smoked every day of her life for as long as I could remember and still managed to be fit as a fiddle. Sassy and strong, she'd gone right along living her life after my grandfather died, well before I was born. My dad was her only son. I was her only grandchild. And I hadn't been there for the last year. I hadn't been there when she died, alone in her house. I'd been here, at this internship.

When we got back to Enneman's, I briefly explained to everyone that my grandma had died and that I'd be gone for the weekend for her funeral. I'd try to be back Monday for the announcement. Violet looked like she was about to try and hug me, but Stacee held her back.

I walked back to my room and closed the door. Kalare slipped in a moment after me.

She looked at me closely. "Everything all right?"

"My grandma died," I said, pulling off my shoes. "I need you to drive me to Mystic tomorrow to go to her funeral. My aunt is bringing Adrian. I assume Julian will need to come with us, though I don't know how I'd justify him to Rachel."

Kalare was silent for long moment. She sat down on the opposite bed. "Shit, kid, I'm sorry. You all right?"

I glanced at her. "No. But I will be eventually."

She nodded. "Sounds about right."

The funeral was at the Mystic senior center. My father had been a quietly religious man, but Grandma was an outspoken atheist. She wanted her funeral to be held where she'd spent most of her time: at bridge club.

Julian had come but was lying low. They hadn't found anything the day before but had only had time to search two hospitals—the places were huge.

I'd shown up at my grandma's house with Kalare, driving what I was surprised to discover was her actual car: a rust red station wagon from the '80s.

We'd beaten Adrian and Trish and my aunt there, but I still had a key. Even so, we just waited on the front porch until they arrived. I didn't want to go in yet. If I went in, she wouldn't be there.

As my grandma's only living relative, the funeral director had contacted me, asking if I wanted to give a speech. I'd said sure. I spent the car ride up trying to write something eloquent and thoughtful, but for the life of me could only think of really inappropriate stories, usually about my grandma's mild gambling problem or her Monday-night sherry habit. She'd been a hard woman, not particularly kind or loving, but she'd been mine. And she'd been there. Every day I was at the hospital with my mom, she'd been there. Packing my lunches, making sure I was keeping up with homework, bringing me blankets when I fell asleep in the chair next to my mom's bed. She was a complainer, always going on tirades about the government and the mail man and the shows on TV. But she never once complained about taking care of me when my mom was dying. Never once made it seem like I was an inconvenience, even though she was, as Rachel had reminded me, old.

I'd borrowed a black dress from Kalare; she'd gone back to her place in Jersey to get it. I hadn't brought anything funeral-appropriate with me to New York. I could have asked Rachel to grab something from my closet, but I hadn't thought of it in time.

Kalare drove. That made sense, I suppose; it was her car. She didn't say a word, just played music and drove, Julian silent in the back seat. She was a lot like Trish in some ways. She didn't feel the need to cover sadness with small talk. I'd apologized for delaying the search for Lucian, taking them away from New York just when we'd made a breakthrough. They told me to stop apologizing; Lucian would still be there when I got back.

Kalare had also heard something disturbing from Farrar. True to her word, Olivia had reported Sabine's sabotage of my dress to Farrar, who had reported it to the Council. She was supposed to appear at some sort of disciplinary committee, but hadn't shown up. She'd dropped completely off the radar; wasn't answering calls. They'd tracked her phone to a dumpster in Queens. She'd gone rogue; possibly defected to another faction. I knew I should be more worried about that considering how Sabine felt about me, but in all honesty I was just relieved that she was out of the picture.

When Rachel and Trish and Adrian pulled up to my grandma's house, I stood, smoothing out my dress. They approached me, looking like they didn't quite know what to do. I knew my aunt wanted to hug me, but I didn't really want to hug her. Not right now. Trish smiled at me and I think I smiled back, but I was in a fog still.

"Should we carpool?" I asked, instead. "The lot will probably be full."

For a snarky old woman, Grandma had been quite sociable. I was sure her funeral would be packed.

Rachel nodded, and we piled into Kalare's station wagon, since the truck was only a three-seater. Rachel sat up front with Kalare while Adrian, Trish, and I climbed in the middle. I was sandwiched between them, two of the most important people in my life, and I couldn't bring myself to look either of them in the eye. Adrian put his hand on his knee, palm up. After a moment, I reached for it. A moment after that, I leaned my head on his shoulder.

Julian was hanging back a safe distance, since my aunt and Trish didn't know he'd come with us, but he'd be near at hand. The funeral was a blur. Too loud, too jovial. The old people weren't as sad as I'd expected. Apparently Grandma's will had stated that she wished the service to be short and the gambling to be long. There were bottles of champagne and bridge games laid out on every table. A few of her friends got up and told bawdy stories about her. I stood at the podium, the linoleum edges cracked and peeling, and said something. A few people laughed so it must have been funny. I honestly don't remember.

Some of her friends came up to me afterward and hugged me. I knew most of them. Some of them lived on the same street; I'd grown up with them almost as second-grandmas. They said it was good to see me, and they were so happy I'd gotten such a big internship in New York. They said my grandma had been proud of me, too. Maybe she had been, but she was like my mom and didn't see much of a point in fashion. Sewing maternity ward blankets, sure, crocheting doilies, absolutely. Couture gowns? Waste of time. Still, maybe she'd been proud of me. I hadn't asked her. She hadn't said. Shirley McClair, one of Grandma's friends, asked me to design her funeral outfit when the time came. I think I just nodded, not knowing how to refuse that kind of request.

Adrian was my shadow, always standing by my side, or just behind my shoulder. Judy, who was losing her memory but not her spice, made a friendly reach for his behind, which he expertly dodged. Grandma's friends were as sassy as she was. Trish brought me a glass of water and some cheese and crackers, but she hung back with Rachel for most of the funeral. I was grateful. I should have been paying more attention to her since she'd come all the way out here, but I couldn't concentrate.

Finally, I forced myself to look at Grandma's casket, leaving Kalare and Rachel and Adrian and Trish at the back of the room. This, I wanted to do myself.

She'd requested an open viewing, "to give everyone one last chance to look at my beautiful face," according to the funeral director. They'd pumped her full of whatever chemicals they pump dead people with to make them look alive. Her friend Mabel had done her post-mortem make-up. She was wearing her favorite outfit: a black beaded dress with giant shoulder pads that she'd bought in Vegas in the 90s. I couldn't help but smile when I saw it.

"Hi, Grandma," I whispered, looking down at her. Her hands were folded over her chest. They'd even picked out her favorite rings. "It was a great funeral. Everyone's losing money." I stopped, feeling the feelings break through the ice, feeling it all come rushing up from the pit of my stomach. "I'm sorry," I said, tears spilling down my cheeks. "I'm sorry I wasn't here. You were always there for me, and I wasn't here for you. I'm sorry."

I held on to the casket to steady myself.

I laughed, still crying. "I know you'd hate to see me like this. You never cried. Not when Dad died, not when Mom died. Probably not when Grandpa died. But I miss you, so I'm going to cry. Just to make you mad."

I could just imagine her rolling her eyes and telling me to grab her box of Prince Alberts. She always smoked cigars when people got emotional. Said it fortified her constitution.

"Goodbye, Grandma," I whispered, touching her cheek. It was cold, and hard. I flinched, and pulled my hand back. "I love you. Please don't give the angels too much trouble, if there are any."

I looked down at her for a long moment, some part of me still not really believing that the body in front of me was *her*. I found Rachel at the back of the room and asked if we could go. Kalare had gotten involved in a bridge game, but she saw the look on my face and folded, excusing herself.

We said our goodbyes and headed back to the house. I unlocked the door and let everyone in, but I couldn't make myself go in, not yet.

"Rachel, do you mind if I show Adrian and Trish my house?"

"No, honey, I don't mind." She turned to Kalare. "I just realized I haven't eaten since breakfast. Do you want to go grab some dinner with me to bring back?"

Kalare hesitated, but I waved her on. Julian was around—between him and Adrian, I'd be fine. They got into Rachel's truck and left for a Chinese restaurant a couple miles away while Adrian took my hand. He and Trish flanked me, almost like guards, as we walked five houses down and stopped on the sidewalk.

And there it was.

My home.

It was Victorian, with a sharp, peaked roof that covered the oddly-shaped attic. It had been painted green when I lived here, a dark, deep green. Now it was blue with white trim. The maple in the front yard had been cut down, and they'd put up a fence. My dad had put a tire swing in the maple for me. After he died I'd never used it, but it had still been there when I moved. Now it—and the tree itself—was gone.

A little girl was playing in the front yard with her dog. She noticed us staring at her and ran inside.

"I guess someone else lives here now," I said. "That's weird."

The house had sold within a week of my mom's funeral. Two days after I'd moved to Stony Creek, a new family had moved in. I guess they had a child. And a dog.

"That was my mom's room," I said, pointing at the big window on the second story. "My room was on the back. The first floor was pretty much all sewing studio."

Adrian wrapped his arm around my shoulder. "It's a beautiful house."

"Swank neighborhood," Trish commented. "I can see I nicknamed you well."

"Yeah," I said, fighting another wave of tears. "It was a good house."

A moment later, a man came out the front door and turned on the porch light. It was getting dark. "Can I help you?" he called to us, looking stern.

"Used to live here," I called back. "Just passing by."

"Oh," the man said, peering at us closer. "Are you…are you the girl whose mother died?"

I smiled bitterly. Yep. The girl whose mother died. The girl whose father died. The girl whose grandma died.

"That's me," I said. "I didn't mean to disturb you; we'll be on our way."

I waved and headed back down the street before he could reply. Adrian and Trish caught up to me. After a moment Adrian he reached for my hand.

"I'm sorry," I whispered. "I'm trying to be okay and I'm struggling."

He squeezed my hand. "Don't worry about me. I just came for the wild bridge game."

I snort-laughed, despite myself. He put his arm around my waist and Trish wrapped her arm around my shoulder and I leaned into them both, grateful that they weren't fighting, grateful that they were here for me. They walked with me up the steps to my grandma's house. I stopped and put my hand on the door.

How many times had I come through this door? Thousands? Tens of thousands? This was my second home. I'd spent almost as much time here as I had at my house. And it was empty now. Because she was gone, and that made it just a house. Just like any other.

I pushed the door open and stepped inside.

The lights were off; Rachel hadn't been inside long enough to turn them on.

It smelled like her. Like cigar smoke and sherry and toffee and cinnamon.

"Oh my god."

Adrian squeezed my arm urgently. I turned to see where he was looking, my eyes taking longer than his to adjust to the dark. Then, I saw it.

Lucian was sitting on my grandma's couch.

All Hell Breaks Loose

25

"Holy shit," Trish said, blinking. "That's Lucian. That's, like, *Lucian* Lucian."

"Adrian," I said, the hair on the back of my neck rising. "Something's not right."

Footsteps sounded on the porch and then Julian was next to us, breathing heavily. "I felt a spike of fear, what's—"

"Oh, are you finally here?" a voice called from behind the TV.

Someone's head popped up from behind my grandma's ancient, wood-framed television, a pair of needle-nose pliers in his hand, wearing an old pair of my grandpa's slacks and one of his sweaters. It took me a moment to realize who it was.

"I was just trying to get this lovely old set to work while I was waiting," Tommie said, patting the television affectionately. His face was fine, not burnt, not melted. "They don't make them like they used to."

"Cait, what is the plumber doing here?" Trish asked, staring at Tommie. "That's the guy that stopped at my house when he was looking for yours." She glanced behind us at Adrian's brother. "And what is *Julian* doing here?"

Adrian snarled, his teeth sharpening, growing. Julian took a step forward and grabbed his arm, but Adrian's eyes were already a raging silver. Trish backed up a step, eyes wide.

"Julian," I whispered to him, nodding at Trish.

Julian's eyes melted into vibrant gold and dark, ocean blue. "Trish," he said calmly, "please wait outside."

She twitched, but didn't move. "I don't want to wait outside," she said, looking a bit foggy and confused.

"Oh, let her stay!" Tommie called, standing and dusting off his hands. "There's not much point in keeping secrets any longer. Besides, she's been very helpful; she deserves to watch the show."

"Caitlin," Trish hissed at me, looking more awake now that Julian's attempted compulsion hadn't taken hold. "*What the hell is going on?*"

"Trish, darling," Tommie called, "you can remember now."

Trish blinked.

Then the blood drained out of her face. She raised a trembling hand to her lips. "Oh my god." She looked at Tommie. "Oh my *god.*"

"What did you do to her?" I demanded.

"Not much," he said cheerfully. He looked at Trish like they were old friends. "Would you like to tell them, or should I?"

Trish looked like she was going to be sick. "He had me spy on you. I called him every day; told him what you were up to." She looked at me, horrified. "I told him about the internship. I told him about the *funeral.*"

"Very dutiful assistant," Tommie said, raising the pliers at her in salute. "My back-up plan in case things went wrong back in Stony Creek." He looked annoyed. "Which they did."

"How did you make me do that?" Trish demanded. "How did—"

"I completely understand that you have questions," Tommie said, cutting her off, "but I'm afraid we haven't got the time."

I wanted to reply, but I couldn't think, couldn't form words. And I couldn't take my eyes off Lucian. He was dead still on the couch. Tommie was between us. I could only tell Lucian was alive because his t-shirt rose and fell ever so slightly as he breathed in and out.

"You're looking well," Tommie remarked, eying Adrian. "Much better than when I last saw you."

"Give me Lucian," Adrian said quietly, "and I promise to kill you quickly."

Almost instantly, Adrian fell to his knees, clutching his chest. Tommie sauntered over to the couch to sit beside Lucian. "Funny little trick of biology the Council likes to keep secret. Did you know, my dear son, that as your beloved father I can borrow some of your life force?"

Adrian made a gasping sound, as if he couldn't breathe. Trish, Julian, and I grabbed him. She checked his pulse, fingers pressed to the artery in his neck, her mouth set in a grim line.

"Bit ironic, really," Tommie said casually. "I was using your own energy to kill you last time we met. Our lovely Caitlin intervened, as I hoped she might."

Trish and Julian glanced at me sharply, but I couldn't focus on them.

Lucian sat motionless, his eyes covered by his aviator goggles. He didn't look up as his older brother gasped for air.

"Stop it," I said, trying not to let the panic in my voice show as I let go of Adrian and stepped between him and his father. "Just tell me what you want."

"I want *you*," he said, seeming to magically release Adrian. "As I always have." Adrian fell forward gasping. Julian grabbed the arm Trish wasn't supporting and kept him from falling over.

"Don't call for back-up, Julian; it will ruin everything," Tommie said, sounding bored. Julian's hand began to tremble. A vein beat in his neck as he sucked in a strangled breath, his phone shaking in his hand.

Glaring, Julian stuck his phone back in his pocket.

"Much better," Tommie said, releasing Julian as well. Julian took in a deep breath, looking pissed, but saying nothing. For now, neither of them seemed to be permanently injured. "Isn't it interesting to feel weak?" he asked both his elder sons, ignoring both me and Trish. "That's what humans feel like all the time. Limited. Gasping for air."

"Lucian," I called gently, ignoring Tommie. "Are you okay?"

He looked at me—or at least, cocked his head robotically in my direction. I couldn't see his eyes through the goggles.

"Lucian's not exactly here at the moment," Tommie explained, patting Lucian on the head. "But don't worry. He will be soon."

Behind me, Julian and Trish tried to haul Adrian to his feet, but his legs wouldn't support him. I'd only seen him look this weak once, in the clearing after Tommie had nearly killed him.

"My aunt is coming back soon with dinner," I said slowly, some part of my brain still working even through my fog and fear. "Along with the rest of the Praetorian Guard."

Tommie rolled his eyes. "Farrar and the others are in Stony Creek, searching for Lucian like a needle in a haystack because *you* neglected to tell them that he was in New York. Yes, don't look surprised. As soon as you woke him up, I knew you were ready. As for your aunt, she is out with Kalare. They're getting Chinese food and someone misplaced their order. They won't be back anytime soon."

I narrowed my eyes. "Then what do you *want?* What, after all this time?"

He stood, and Lucian stood with him. "Like I said before: I want *you.*"

As if on cue, Lucian suddenly darted forward. He jumped on me, snarling rabidly.

I screamed, falling backward to the floor. Abandoning Adrian, Julian ran toward me, but crumpled to his knees. "Tut, tut," Tommie tsked, "don't interfere with play time."

I couldn't watch for more than a second because Lucian was on top of me, biting at my face with his fangs. He was half my size, but he was still a vampire, which meant he was stronger than me.

"Lucian!" I screamed again. "*It's me! It's Caitlin!*"

But he didn't hear me. Or if he did, he didn't care. I blocked his face with my arm and he sank his teeth into my wrist, biting down to the bone. I screamed in pain. Out of the corner of my eye, I saw Trish prop Adrian against the wall and crawl toward me.

"Trish, *stay back!*" I screamed at her. She stopped, looking torn.

"Come on, Caitlin," Tommie said, sitting on the arm of the couch to watch, "fight like a girl!"

Lucian reared back, dripping blood, and struck again, raking his teeth down my other arm as I blocked him just in time. "Lucian," I begged, crying. "Stop!"

But he wouldn't. He grabbed my wrist and pinned it to the floor. I had my hand around his throat, trying to simply keep him away from me.

But he was stronger. A twelve-year-old was stronger than me.

By a lot.

"He's not going to stop, Caitlin," Tommie said, goading me. "So what are you going to do about it?"

This time, Trish didn't listen to my warning. She ran for me, but Tommie stood, stepping between us, and simply looked into her eyes.

"I'm sorry, my dear, but I can't let you interfere. Stand in the corner like a good girl."

Trish froze, then walked over to the corner near the door and stood facing us, a slave to his compulsion.

Lucian hissed at me, spitting blood. My hand was slipping. He'd be on me in a second. Why was Tommie making him attack me? Why was he just sitting there, watching? What was he trying to get me to *do*?

Then it came to me. He was trying to get me to do what I'd done the last time we'd fought.

I pushed the fear aside, left it hovering in the back of my mind. I reminded myself who this was: it was Lucian. He was vulnerable. He needed me. And I loved him, fiercely.

"Lucian," I whispered, feeling oddly calm, just as he slipped out of my grip. "*Stop.*"

And to my great surprise, he stopped.

An inch from my face.

I could just make out his eyes behind the goggles, he was so close. "Caitlin?" he whispered, fangs retracting. "Where am I?"

"I need you to run, Lucian," I whispered. "Can you do that for me? Go run and hide. I'll come find you. Just like hide and seek."

He nodded, serious. "Okay."

He got up, scrambling toward the kitchen. But of course Tommie was standing right there. He reached out and grabbed Lucian by the throat.

"Impressive," Tommie said, glancing at his youngest son, then back to me. "I think you're ready."

He reached down and grabbed my arm, dragging me to my feet. Rather than pull me toward him, he simply stood there, holding me in place. I tried to wrench away, but even with a merely human body, Tommie was stronger than me. He'd chosen a tall, muscular adult male to possess. Even though Adrian had nearly *destroyed* this body back in February, it looked like it had been completely healed. I was no match.

But he wasn't trying to harm me. He wasn't trying to do anything but hold me still.

Then I remembered something Data had said.

I'd asked him what would happen if Tommie touched me again. The first time, at the mall, the nightmares had started. The second time, when we fought, the lucid dreams began.

Now, he was touching me again, holding my arm, skin on skin. Waiting.

A headache began to form behind my eyes. Within moments, it was blinding. I sank to my knees, and still Tommie held on.

"Caitlin," Adrian wheezed from behind me, struggling to his knees, his face pale and sweaty. "*You have to kill him.*"

"I don't know *how*," I gasped, barely able to see. My head felt like it was about to split open. My eyes felt like they were going to burst out of my skull. It was like Adrian's paired compulsion, but worse.

Julian, barely recovered from the last attack, made another attempt to reach me, but before he could even get to his knees he collapsed at my feet, writhing in pain.

Tommie's fingers were so tight around Lucian's neck his face was turning red, his lips blue. He scrabbled, choking, clawing at Tommie, but even in a human body, Tommie had two feet and a hundred pounds on his son.

Adrian looked at me, his eyes glowing brightly, cascading into molten, swirling silver. "I'm sorry," he whispered to me, trembling from across the room. "I don't have a choice."

"No!" I called desperately, "Adrian, *don't!* We don't know what will ha—"

I interrupted myself with a scream, clutching at my skull. The pain was unbearable.

Adrian looked torn, barely conscious, a vein beating hard in his neck. Finally, he nodded, but his eyes were still cascading. "Caitlin," he said, meeting my gaze, "*protect yourself.*"

The compulsion took hold instantly. How, I don't know—I didn't know how to protect myself, so the compulsion shouldn't work. And yet I found myself turning calmly to Tommie.

Quietly, the room disappeared, melting into infinite white. My headache disappeared with it.

We were in my dreamscape, everyone but Trish, who had disappeared. Data stood off to my left, looking as though he had been expecting me.

"Hello, Caitlin," he said calmly. "Are you prepared?"

"No," I whispered, staring at him, panicked. Why wasn't he panicking? *I* was panicking; didn't that mean he should be, too?

"Do not be afraid," Data said comfortingly. "It is only the beginning."

I looked at him like he was crazy. "The beginning of *what?*"

He ignored me. "Remember, when this is over, that there is a balance. For every advantage, a disadvantage. For every gain, a loss. Remember, and you will forgive yourself in time." He gaze turned sad. "Perhaps you will even forgive me."

I looked at him panicked, confused. Lucian was here in the dreamscape, along with Adrian, Julian, and Tommie. Tommie still had his hand wrapped around my arm, looking around.

"Incredible," he murmured, gazing at the expanse. "It's beautiful."

Tommie let Lucian go, tossing him to the white floor like a rag doll. Lucian crawled a few feet further, then collapsed, unconscious.

But he was alive. I suddenly knew that. Not by much, but his heart was still beating. I could feel it. Adrian was barely hanging on to consciousness. Julian was the least injured, the closest to me, right at my feet.

"I release the knowledge to you," Data said quietly, and then murmured something in the same language Adrian used when he compelled me, a language I couldn't understand; couldn't comprehend.

And then I could feel it, suddenly.

What I had to do. What was necessary to fulfill the compulsion.

I looked at Data, horrified. He simply smiled at me, a bit sadly.

"You bastard," I whispered, looking not at Tommie, but at Data.

Data just nodded, accepting my accusation.

I reached for Julian, laying my hand on his hair.

I couldn't even tell him I was sorry.

There was a bond between Tommie and his sons. Nothing I could see with my eyes, but it was there. A connection. We'd been right about that. I cradled Julian's face in my hand as he looked up at me, weak, listless. I put my other hand on Tommie's chest—or no.

No, no, his name wasn't Tommie.

It was Hedonin.

The answer came to me like a long-lost memory, like a thing I had always known, but forgotten.

Tommie—*Hedonin*—smiled at me, looking almost grateful. That seemed wrong—he should be afraid. He should be terrified.

But of course not—he didn't know what was coming.

Something inside me came rushing to the surface, an impulse, a sixth sense. Like being born blind and suddenly being able to see. I was more than I had been a moment ago.

And I was about to do something unforgivable.

Kalare had called Unmakers a myth, a bogeyman, the convenient monster vampires used to frighten their children into obedience. I understood why, now.

I had no energy of my own. I had no magic. But I was an Unmaker.

I could *take* magic.

I could move it and reshape it. I could make it do terrible things.

I'd done it before. It wasn't Adrian who had burned his father in the clearing; it was me. I'd hijacked Adrian's abilities and instinctively used them to hurt his father. It had been sloppy, ill-defined, but it had done the job. It had also almost cost Adrian his life.

It was also me in the forest, when Adrian knocked Julian unconscious. I hadn't wanted to hurt Julian, but I also didn't want Julian to hurt Adrian. I'd reached out, a wave of panic and love and fear, and twisted Adrian's magic again until it fit my will, my intention. I'd disarmed Julian harmlessly; caused him to fall asleep.

But it cost something both times. Adrian barely survived the first encounter. And his healing abilities had taken a hit the second time. That's why he'd passed out. That's why his wounds hadn't closed up. Because I didn't know what I was doing, and I'd taken too much.

Now, Julian was looking right at me, helpless, his face turning pale. His eyes—amber and dark blue—were cascading, but the light slowly changed, the colors fading until they were white.

Brilliant, crystalline white. Data had been trying to show me all along.

But he *hadn't* shown me; not really. He'd dodged and maneuvered and hidden the truth.

And now it was too late.

The light faded from Julian's eyes, traveling through me, crawling up my arm. His magic felt different than Adrian's. Like the sun, just as it turned from winter to spring.

The light pushed through the fingertips of my other hand, dissolving into Tommie. A moment later, he, too, fell to his knees, looking up at me in rapture.

That was still wrong. He shouldn't be happy. I wasn't going to do what he wanted me to do.

A fog started to form around him. Not the body, not the human shell he'd been inhabiting, but *him*, the entity, the consciousness. The body just fell to the ground. The fog wriggled and writhed, as if alive, surrounding the demon. It was all for show, my mind coming up with something I could see, something tangible I could wrap my brain around.

Slowly, I could feel Hedonin's elation turn to panic. I could feel him, even though he was no longer in the body he'd once possessed.

He tried to lash out at me, but this was *my* dreamscape. My domain.

I pushed down on him with my will, wrapping the fog around him until it crystallized; a floating sphere of white ice.

Julian slumped to the floor at my feet.

I looked at Data—everyone else was unconscious.

"You," I said, voice shaking with rage, "will have hell to pay for this."

Data stared at me, looking suddenly ancient; tired. "What you don't understand, Caitlin, is that I already have."

He waved his arm, and the dreamscape dissolved, taking the sphere with it.

In a moment, we were back in my grandma's house. Paintings had trembled off their hooks, lamps had shattered, picture frames had cracked.

My ears were ringing. I don't know how long I stood there. I had no concept of time. But slowly, the world came back into focus.

Kalare was standing at the front door with Rachel, looking horrified. Trish was still in the corner, silent, looking angry, frustrated, terrified. What had she seen? How long had they been there? My aunt was screaming, trying to run to me, but Kalare was holding her back. Adrian was unconscious, in a heap by the door.

I looked at Julian.

He was there, at my feet.

I looked away. I couldn't hear them. I couldn't hear anything but my own heartbeat. I saw Kalare's eyes flare into a soft golden light. She spoke to Rachel, both her hands on my aunt's shoulders, looking her straight in the eye. Rachel suddenly grew calm.

Tommie Reynolds was on the couch. The real Tommie. The body. Adrian's father was gone from it. Was the body dead? Or just sleeping? I didn't know if I'd killed the host. It was just some college kid, caught up in all this.

Kalare was on the phone. I could see Lucian. Lucian was breathing. Lucian opened his eyes.

Julian's eyes were open, too.

I'd seen that much.

Kalare was cursing at whoever was on the other end of the call when she finally saw Julian. She dropped the phone right on the hardwood floor. The screen cracked, shattering into a spiderweb of glass. She rushed to his side. She was talking, talking so fast, saying words I couldn't hear, couldn't understand. Julian's face was in her hands; she was whispering to him. His eyes were open. She laid her ear against his chest, she checked his pulse. She did CPR.

Interesting. I didn't know you could do CPR on vampires.

Julian's eyes were open. They'd been open for a long time.

Sound slowly returned.

"J, *please*," Kalare whispered, pumping his sternum rhythmically with her hands, tears streaming down her face.

"Caitlin," a voice called from the door.

I looked up. It was the woman, with the dark skin and the short hair. The one from my dreams. She wasn't wearing pajamas this time—which meant she was actually here. Right?

"Caitlin," she repeated calmly, "we need to go."

"I need to clean up," I whispered.

"The Council is on the way," she said, more urgently. "Not just the Guard. Caedin, Inauj, Loris—"

"We need to bring his body," I said, voice a dull monotone.

"Okay," the woman agreed. "But we need to leave. They felt what you did all the way in New York. This place is going to be crawling with a lot of people you really don't want to meet in just a few minutes. You don't want to be here when that happens."

I nodded. I didn't want to be here when that happened.

I didn't want to be here at all.

Both Rachel and Trish watched the woman, their eyes darting back and forth between her, me, the bodies…

The woman stepped carefully through the rubble, picking her way over to us. "Kalare," she said carefully. "I'm a friend of Ian's. I'm here to get you all out."

Kalare ignored her, pumping at Julian's chest. He was gone, though. She didn't know that yet, but I did.

Ian appeared at the door. I knew it was Ian because Kalare had shown me pictures of him so I could look for him in the dreamscape. He was tall, gangly, wore an old denim jacket and an unfashionable hat.

"Got company," he called to the woman.

"Kalare," she said. "You can keep giving him CPR in the van. Grab him and let's go."

Kalare slowed, then stopped. She wiped her face off on her sleeve and nodded. She stood slowly, scooping up Julian's body effortlessly. I wanted to close his eyes. Maybe he'd be more comfortable with his eyes closed.

"Keep him cold," I said, not sure who I was speaking to.

The woman scooped Lucian into her arms and nodded, heading

out the door. Adrian was on the floor. He was alive, but unconscious.

I couldn't lift Adrian, he was too heavy. Couldn't drag him, either. Ian was standing next to Rachel and Trish, saying something to them, his eyes awash in green cascading light. I walked past him, outside, feeling as though I were floating a few feet outside my body, feeling as though it was someone else walking heedlessly over the painting my grandfather had made for my grandmother on their first wedding anniversary. It was someone else who saw a van pull up and squeal to a halt, the doors flung wide open. It was someone else who watched Kalare haul Julian's body into the back of that van. It was someone else who watched the woman lay Lucian down on the floor. Rachel and Trish obediently climbed into the cargo space, sitting calmly on a stack of blankets. The woman and Ian were about to head back to the house, about to grab Adrian, and the human body Tommie had possessed.

But an SUV turned the corner suddenly, speeding down the street.

And a car.

Two more. A truck. Another van.

Three motorcycles.

They skidded to a halt, cutting off the southbound end of the street.

Vampires poured out of the vehicles. Vampires I'd never seen. Fangs out, eyes cascading in every conceivable color. So beautiful.

Lucian was in the van. Kalare was in there, too, holding Julian's body. I had one hand on the door, looking back toward the house. Why was Ian running back toward me? Why weren't they getting Adrian?

Ian ducked, the sound of a bullet pinging off the neighbor's Mercedes. More pings soon followed. Guess Kalare wasn't the only vampire who didn't find it convenient to chew people to death.

The woman jumped into the passenger seat. Ian dove for the van and knocked me onto the floor, slamming the door closed.

Our driver slammed on the gas and the van sped away, leaving

Adrian behind.

"He's there," I said, slowly, pointing back toward the house. "He's back there. You left him."

"I'm sorry, kid," Ian said, bleeding from a shoulder wound. "You're more important."

"He's my family," I murmured, still feeling disconnected. "We're not leaving him behind."

I could hurt Ian, if I wanted to. If I had to.

"I'm sorry," Ian said as I reached for him. "But we can't do that."

I'd gotten so used to the idea of vampire powers, of compulsion, that I never saw the taser coming. I blacked out as the electricity hit my nerves, falling to the floor of the van as Ian caught me. The last thing I saw was Trish and Rachel looking at me as if they were afraid.

Not afraid *for* me.

Afraid *of* me.

"Caitlin?"

I opened my eyes. Data was crouching over me.

"Data?" I sat up slowly. "What happened?"

"You are unconscious," he replied. "And I am afraid to let you wake up."

"Why?"

"Because then you might remember."

I blinked at him. "Do I not want to remember?"

He hesitated. "No. I do not think you do."

I nodded. That sounded about right.

EPILOGUE

$\mathcal{I}$ opened my eyes.

A ceiling fan whirred lazily above me against a stucco ceiling.

My throat was dry. My head was pounding.

"*Mm,*" I tried to speak, and found I couldn't. "*Hhh—*"

The woman—the one from my dreams—stood over me. "Take it easy, Caitlin. You've been out for a while."

She propped me up a bit with her arm and gave me a sip of water. Light was coming from somewhere, so bright that it hurt my eyes. I gagged on the water at first, then finally got the hang of it, my aching muscles loosening up enough to swallow.

She set the cup on something nearby and propped me up with a few pillows.

I looked around. We were in a house, it seemed. There were Native American tapestries on the wall, a brown tile floor, woven shades over the windows. There was a bandage wrapped around my arm where Lucian had bitten down to the bone.

"Where are we?" I asked, throat hoarse. "What happened?"

"Someplace safe," she assured me. "Kalare and Lucian are in the other room along with Ian and the others."

I looked at her. "Julian?"

"We kept him cold, like you asked."

Had I asked that? Why had I asked that?

Then it came back.

I pinched my eyes shut, everything hurting. "Rachel?"

"Your aunt and Trish are here, resting. They're safe."

I covered my face with my hands, trying to find some darkness—the damn light was so bright. It was too much.

"Caitlin," the woman said gently. "They have Adrian. He's been detained."

Detained. Detained didn't sound so bad. Detained sounded better than executed.

"Caitlin," she tried again when I didn't respond. "He was a priority. We meant to leave with him because they know he's paired with you. But there was no time. We were severely outnumbered. They would have taken you, if we'd stayed to get him. But that means now they're going to try to use him to control you."

I blinked rapidly, trying to keep my brain from understanding what that meant.

"You're the last member of your family," she explained, as if I didn't know. "You're the last Unmaker. Getting you out alive, before the other factions could claim you, was our main objective."

I didn't reply, didn't so much as twitch.

She frowned at me. "Do you even understand what you just *did?*"

I slowly looked up at her. "Yes," I said darkly. "I know what I did." My gaze narrowed. "You knew what I was all along. You could have told me. Prepared me. But you didn't."

"I wasn't certain I was right," she explained, face a neutral mask. "I had to wait and see."

I smiled bitterly. "And that turned out so well."

The woman cocked an eyebrow. "You're alive, aren't you?"

I shoved the blanket aside. "I need to see him. Now."

She gave me a look that said she clearly didn't like being ordered around, but after a moment she scooped me up easily and set me down in a nearby wheelchair. My body ached, protesting every movement. I was so weak I could barely hold up my head. She wheeled me into another room. We weren't in a house, after all; it was some sort of clinic.

Julian was lying in a hospital bed, Kalare curled up at his side, asleep. She was wearing the same clothes I'd last seen her in, which meant it couldn't have been too long that I'd been out. Julian was hooked up to several machines, things that made whirring sounds, a soft *hshhhh* of air.

"I admit, I've never seen a vampire need one of these, but we did what you asked. We kept his body cold. We kept his heart pumping."

It was. I could see the monitor. It *blipped* every ten seconds or so.

"He has no brain activity," she said casually. "He's a vegetable."

"It was necessary," I muttered, but my heart ached. I'd done this to him.

I'd done it to protect myself.

She crossed her arms and leaned against the doorway. "I'm not the one you need to convince."

She glanced at Kalare.

How was I going to explain this to her? After everything she'd done for me.

I looked down in shame. I'd figure that out later. When I could think, when I could *breathe*.

"We're not in New York, are we?" I asked.

"New Mexico." She eyed the southwest decor. "You've been out about two days. Kalare hasn't left his side. Lucian hasn't left yours. I had to sedate him. He kept attacking anyone that came near you. He's asleep in the other room."

I closed my eyes, grateful that he was safe, that I had him back. At least one good thing had come of this.

I glanced at the woman. "I need to see Trish and Rachel."

She hesitated, but the look on my face must have convinced her. She wheeled me out and down the hall, stopping at the open door to some sort of waiting room. Trish had her feet kicked up on a table reading a dated version of *Southwest Life*. Rachel was pacing. They both stopped dead when they saw me.

"Caitlin!" Rachel breathed, running toward me. But I wasn't actually in the room, just in the hallway outside it. She came to a sudden halt at the door, looking angry.

"Let me see her," Rachel demanded, looking at the woman. "Is she all right?"

"She needs to rest," the woman explained. "I just wanted to show her that you two were safe."

Trish had scrambled up from her chair and darted over, stopping abruptly just like Rachel at the doorway. "Goddamn it, Caitlin, you scared the shit out of me," Trish fumed. "What's going on? They're not telling us anything."

"You compelled them?" I asked the woman, guessing.

She nodded. "We've asked them not to leave this room, for their own safety."

"*Asked*," Trish snorted bitterly. "More like brainwashed us into keeping ourselves locked in."

"Caitlin," Rachel said, kneeling, trying to reach out to me, but not letting her hand cross the threshold of the door. "Are you okay?"

I shook my head, eyes blurring. "I don't know," I admitted.

"Cait," Trish said, kneeling to look me in the eyes. "I remember things now. About that guy, about calling him, spying on you. I don't know what's going on, but I'm—" she paused, blinking back confused tears. "I'm *so* sorry."

I blinked, trying to come up with a response. My brain didn't seem to want to work.

"Ian will bring you lunch soon," the woman told them before I could respond. "I need to speak to Caitlin privately."

"You keep your hands off her," my aunt warned. "You touch one hair on her head and you will have *me* to deal with."

To her credit, the woman didn't smirk. She merely nodded and said, "Noted."

"I'll come back," I promised Trish as the woman started to wheel me away. My head hurt. It hurt so badly.

"And tell that henchman of yours that I'm sick of pizza!" Trish called after us as we disappeared down the hall.

"You won't compel them anymore," I told the woman when we were out of earshot.

"We will compel them as necessary."

"Not if you want my cooperation."

She came to a stop outside Julian's room and came around the wheelchair to look at me. "We're on the same side, Caitlin. We're not hurting them. In fact, I argued that they should be brought along. That you would need support. So don't go barking at me."

I glared at her, but said nothing. I didn't understand enough, not yet.

"So," she said, clearly thinking the matter settled. "You want to tell me why we're keeping Julian's body alive when he's clearly dead?"

"He's not dead," I muttered. "He's the dam."

She looked at me strangely. "Beg your pardon?"

I shook my head, not sure how to put it into words. "Back in Mystic, after Adrian compelled me, I could suddenly feel it. I just *knew*." I knew because Data had finally allowed me to know. But I wasn't going to tell this woman about Data, not yet. "Maybe because I'm an Unmaker," I continued, "maybe because I'm paired with Adrian, and Adrian is, in a way, paired with his father. Demons and their children are connected, we were right about that. Hedonin wanted me to—" I cut myself off abruptly.

I didn't know this woman. I didn't know if it was safe for her to know what Hedonin wanted. But it was hard to focus; hard to keep things clear.

I shrugged. "I don't know. Something bad. So I tricked him." I smiled bitterly. "The funny thing is, he gave me the idea. He trapped Lucian's mind in the hellscape. So I trapped him in my dreamscape. Julian is his son. Julian is connected to him. And Julian is the only thing keeping him from breaking free. So you have to keep his heart pumping. You have to keep him alive. Or Hedonin goes free." I rubbed my gritty eyes and muttered, "It's a temporary solution."

I glanced up at her. "The only thing I don't know is who you are and how you're involved."

She looked surprised. "Forgot I hadn't introduced myself." She stuck out her hand. "My name is Utuwe. That kid you put in a magical coma is my brother. So is Lucian. So is Adrian. Mariana is my little sister." When I didn't reach out to shake her hand, she leaned down until she was eye level with me. "And you, my dear, had better be worth the sacrifice they're all making for you."

She straightened, smiling in a way that sent a shiver down my spine. "So. You ready to change the world?"

Book 3 of the Velvet Trilogy coming soon

www.bytemplewest.com

ACKNOWLEDGEMENTS

Many, many people made this book happen, but I owe a special debt to the following:

Joel Heumann and Brianna Bartelt for once again bringing Adrian de la Mara and Caitlin Holte to life, both on the cover of this book, and in the marketing materials and book trailers. You both have been a dream to work with, and this series would not be the same without you.

Matthew Simmons and Emily McGonigle for the insanely gorgeous *Cashmere* photoshoot, and Jenny Garner for stepping in last minute to do hair and make up. You guys are the reason everything looks so damn sexy.

Blake Guidry (Director of Photography), Zachary Layman (Gaffer), Seth Tovey (Sound), Chelsea Smith (Hair and Make Up), Max Hsu (Stunt Driver), and Aaron Smith (original score) for shooting the incredible *Cashmere* book trailer. Sorry for making you guys run uphill all day with camera gear in 100 degree heat and 90% humidity. That was my bad.

John Bucher for guiding me through the setup, layout, and printing of this book. John, thank you for not defriending my after the 56th e-mail with the thousandth screenshot.

Bryan Gough for his design advice and Adobe Creative Suite troubleshooting. Also for his magnificent beard.

Stacee at *Adventures of a Book Junkie* for answering all of my book blogger community questions and for being my constant sounding board for literally everything that went into this book.

My beautiful, bodacious beta readers: Alexis Loughead, Ashley Oczkewicz, Audrey Ney, Dan Marchant, Debbie Montzingo, Julie Mayfield, Kimberly Tumambing, Kristen Rea, Laura Smith, Lauren Scobell, Samuel Tucker Young, Shelby Etcheson, Stacee Evans, and Rachel Womelsduff Gough.

MAKING CASHMERE

Cashmere is a novel eight years in the making. I wrote the first book in the series, *Velvet*, in under six months during my freshman year of college. I also wrote the first couple chapters to its then-untitled sequel. After unsuccessfully attempting to get *Velvet* published, I shelved the whole series, busy with college and work.

When I was twenty-five, however, *Velvet* got a second chance at life. After publishing it in 2015, I sat down and pulled out the old chapters I'd started writing for the sequel. And I kept sitting.

I had a massive case of writer's block. I'd never written a sequel before, and I had no idea that it would be a completely different beast than a one-off. I got overwhelmed, moved across the country, and started panicking more and more as the days trickled away.

Growing up, my mom had a motto: "Find a way, not an excuse." In September-ish of 2016, my friend and fellow author Kate Evangelista posted on Twitter a variation on that phrase: "If it's important to you, you'll find a way. If it's not, you'll find an excuse." And somehow that slight change in perspective was the kick in the pants I needed. I decided *Cashmere* was important to me. I was going to finish what I started.

I wrote the first 10,000 words of *Cashmere* when I was 19. I wrote another 15,000 words in the year and a half after *Velvet* was published. After listening to what Kate Evangelista wrote on Twitter, I sat down and wrote the next 90,000 words of *Cashmere*...

...in 17 days.

Cashmere is now 126,000 words, by far the longest and most complex story I've ever written. I'm exhausted and proud and have learned a great deal about writing, publishing, design, business, and self-discipline. I very much hope you enjoyed *Cashmere*, and I promise you this: I'm hard at work on the third and final book.

REVIEWS

Reviews are the lifeblood of books. If you enjoyed *Cashmere*, a review / rating on Amazon, Goodreads, Barnes & Noble, or your blog would be deeply appreciated. Thank you!

TEMPLE WEST

Temple spent four months in Oxford holed up at the Radcliffe Camera amongst the hush of ancient books and the rich musk of academia. Returning to the U.S., she acquired degrees in English and film, mostly as an excuse to write essays about *The Princess Bride* and *Hook*. She can sew (poorly), drive stick (please fasten your seatbelt), and mostly lift her feet off the ground while stuttering into first gear on a very small motorcycle. You will often find her hunting through thrift stores for unique treasures or at home in her sweatpants in a nest of blankets, writing. She currently lives in Seattle, WA.

www.bytemplewest.com